MW00620368

PHOENIX

by

A.J. SCUDIERE

GRIFFYN INK

Phoenix
Copyright © 2012 A.J. Scudiere
Published by Griffyn Ink

All rights reserved. No part of this book may be reproduced (except for inclusion in reviews), disseminated or utilized in any form or by any means, electronic or mechanical, including photocopying, recording, or any information storage and retrieval system, or the Internet/World Wide Web without written permission from the author or publisher.

This book is a work of fiction. Names, characters, businesses, organizations, places, events and incidents are used fictitiously, and any resemblance to actual persons, living or dead, business establishments, events, or locales is entirely coincidental.

For further information, please contact:
Griffyn Ink
www.griffynink.com
Mail@GriffynInk.com

For ordering information or special discounts for bulk purchases or book clubs, please contact Griffyn Ink at Mail@GriffynInk.com.

Phoenix
A.J. Scudiere
1. Title 2. Aughot 3. Fiction
All rights reserved.

ISBN: 978-1-937996-06-2

"Great fast-paced mystery with enough twists and turns in the plot to keep the most avid reader hooked!"
                    -Ellen C., Blogger

"It's not a book you read and forget; this is a book you read and think about, again and again . . . everything that has happened in this book could be true. That's why it sticks in your mind and keeps coming back for rethought."
                    -Jo Ann Hakola, The Book Faerie

"Absent of any obvious clichés, exaggerated drama or highly improbable actions, this felt refreshingly real. This is what a novel of contemporary fiction grounded in logic should read like."
                    -Alex Sheldon Savva,
                    Book Reviewer, Goodreads

There are really just 2 types of readers—those who are fans of AJ Scudiere, and those who will be.
                    -Bill Salina, Reviewer, Amazon

Dedication

When I started writing, I had two students in my seventh grade math and science classes who thought the fact that their teacher was writing a book was just so cool. They said one day I could dedicate a book to them. Little did they know, I had over ten stories in my head waiting to be written, and all that time ago I decided this one was for them.

For Kevin and Nick.
Kevin – you will be missed by all for far longer than you were here.
Nick – this was always a story about lost brothers, I'm sorry that Kevin isn't here to see it.

This book is also for all the first responders out there.
You may not see them, you may not like the ticket you get or being told you can't light your campfire, but someone you love is alive today because of them. Tell them thank you.

Acknowledgements

Though writers spend countless hours submerged in created worlds, writing is not a solitary endeavor. I will never be able to repay the people who helped with this novel.
As always, thanks go out to Eli, who makes things happen, to all the ladies at JKS and to my family, who are always behind me.

Special thank yous go out to the following people:

Susan Benesh, who said "You need to do a ride-along with a fire station? I know people." Susan, you are a fantastic friend, thank you so much. Susan introduced me to . . .

Fire Chief Wyatt Coleman, who said "Of course you can ride-along. When would you like to come?" He and his crew could not have been nicer to me. They answered all my questions, never made me feel stupid for asking, and gave me what I needed to make Jason and the Southfield Fire Department come alive.

Thank you to every member of the West Columbia Fire Department in South Carolina and to those who went the extra step and granted me interviews:
Matthew Rowlette
Phillip Reddick
George Norris
Nate Harper Jr.
Sean "O B" O'Brien
Kellen West
Ryan Harris
Thomas Sharpe
Jeff Padgett Jr.
Tommy Anderson
Michael Jordan

Daniel Roberts
Thomas Carson
Garner Wilkins

My local volunteer station – Number One Fire Department of Hendersonville, TN – also graciously granted interviews and showed me all their trucks and gear!
Eddie Durham
Chris Edgerton
Ian Durham
James Boyd
"Jay"

And one last thank you to *Mike Bunch*, a firefighter and first responder in the Middle Tennessee area who helped with editing and technical issues.

These people all voluntarily and happily helped me out with this project expecting nothing in return. Any mistakes are mine and all the wonderful insights and quirks of the fire fighting life are theirs. Thank you all for sharing your world with me.

Southfield Fire Station #2

Shift	A	
	O'Casey	Captain
Engine 5	Standard	Engineer
	Mondy	FF2 / P1
	Grimsby	FF1
Rescue 1	Wanstall	FF3
	West	FF2
	Merriman	FF1

Intro

The bell rings.
Your once-warm bed is already cold
because you've thrown back the blanket
and sat up before you were even awake.
The bell does that to you.

A.J. SCUDIERE

For a moment your uniform feels funny,
it still carries the warmth of the bed.
But this, too, is normal for you.

PHOENIX

In less than thirty seconds,
you've talked to the Captain who has told you all
that both trucks are needed, everyone is going.
Then, with no memory of how
you made it from the hall to here,
you are standing in front of your gear.

Your pants are tucked into your boots
and though they look like they were simply abandoned
the last time you came in, the opposite is true—
they wait, at the ready.

You step into the set up, boots on feet,
and pull up the suspenders that hold
the thick padded pants in place.
You grab the rest of your gear
with one sweep of your hands;
it, too, hung ready for you to grasp
in a single economy of motion.

In the glare of the lights in the truck bay
you don't register much of anything.
The fire engines still gleam from their cleaning
earlier in the day, each one carefully polished
and every piece of gear checked.
Though it's not necessary now
that the trucks be spit-shined,
the care in each piece of equipment is vital.
But you are always ready and don't think about it
as you grab the rail and haul yourself into the front
passenger seat. No matter how tall you are,
it's a climb to get into the truck.

The blast of the horn would wake the
neighborhood residents if they weren't so used to it.
The truck gives an epic bounce as you move
from ramp to street and take a hard left
into the cool dark of night.

PHOENIX

As you ride, you adjust the straps on your air tank.
Embedded in the back of the truck seat,
it was waiting for just this kind of thing,
all you have to do is buckle it on.

The world around you pulses red from the lights on the
truck, and everyone has eyes on the side roads, looking for
unsuspecting drivers and idiots who aren't paying attention.
At one intersection you blast the siren to warn the two cars
already there to wait and let you pass.

At what feels like a snail's pace,
you finally make it through.
Though you speed,
though you wonder what waits ahead,
you don't rush.

Besides, it might be nothing.

Two turns later you are parking,
taking up the whole street in a small neighborhood—
and it's not nothing.

A single-story home is pouring smoke from the windows
and roof vents, flames are visible at one end and you have
already put your hood over your head, your mask in place.
You are connecting your air tank and shrugging into your
jacket while you settle your helmet onto your head and
absently check the GPS tag you wear at the back of your
gear. Though the house is fully involved,
it could still be simple.

Then you feel something at your arm.

Turning your whole head to see through your mask,
you find a woman there.
Frantically, she tugs at your sleeve
and yells at youthrough your heavy gear.

"My husband and two little boys are trapped inside."

Chapter 1

Jason

The sound of the phone ringing pulled him from the fire.

With a grunt, Jason rolled off the mattress, his feet hitting the floor with too much force and bringing him further awake. He hadn't expected the floor to be so high. Or maybe it was that the mattress was unusually low.

His eyelids tried to remain stuck together as he fumbled his way into the living room, bashing his toe on the coffee table, now situated smack in the middle of the floor. He cursed fluently and grabbed the phone without looking.

"Uh-lo." His mouth couldn't even form the full word, and whoever was on the line had better have a good reason for calling him now. If it was Kelly he would either kill her or hang up. He hadn't decided.

"Hello. This is Clark Jernigan with the *Birmingham News*."

The straightforward tone and Standard English told him what he didn't want to hear.

"Hmm." It was really more of a grunt, just a sound to stop the guy from talking.

Jason hung up.

Why he still had a home phone was beyond him. He didn't have much of anything else. The coffee table had to be a joke. The mattress was the only decency in a mire of meanness. The phone had appeared to be a decency, too, until this. But there was no way Kelly could have predicted this onslaught of phone calls.

The phone rang again.

Half-asleep and whole-stupid he had automatically answered the phone, not even looking at the number on the screen. He sighed the greeting, "Heh-lo."

"I'm sorry, Mr. Mondy. I'm afraid we were cut off." The man began speaking before Jason could insert a "hm" or a "no thanks" and hang up. "I'd like to do an interview with you regarding the Thurlow house fire and the rescue."

This time Jason managed actual English words. "No thank you." And he hit the off button again.

Then he pulled the cord from the back of the phone and left it hanging over the counter to remind him it was unplugged. That was funny. Like he needed a reminder—there were only about fifteen things left in his whole house, if he counted the two blankets as separate items.

Jason stumbled back to bed, once more stubbing his toe on the stupid Ikea coffee table, then fell forward onto the mattress on the floor and dreamed again of the fires he had seen.

∧ ∧ ∧ ∧ ∧

He didn't wake up until the early hours of Thursday morning.

At four a.m. his problems seemed amplified. No one could have predicted Tuesday.

But even with the lights blazing inside, the darkness beyond the windows formed a blanket around his empty cocoon. He stood in his apartment living area and surveyed the damage in the quiet of the near dawn.

The dining table was pushed into the far corner of the eat-in space in the kitchen. Made from an old butcher block, it was a sturdy, quality piece of furniture—the only one he had left. The four chairs that sat around it until Tuesday morning had vacated the premises sometime that day—along with the majority of his other household items.

The bed frame had disappeared, only the mattress had been left on the floor. Which was interesting, because it had been stripped bare and there wasn't a single sheet in the place.

The dresser—something he had picked up at Goodwill years ago—still stood. The empty drawers on the right had been left slightly open, for effect he guessed. The end tables had gone with the bed frame and he now had his wallet and two books on the floor by the blanket-strewn mattress. When he'd left the other morning there had been a mix of close to a dozen paperbacks and hardbacks stacked there. That most of them were gone really pissed him off.

His desk and computer were all that remained in the second bedroom/office—in a rude gesture, his chair was missing. The main room had been entirely cleared around the lone coffee table. Of course the TV was gone: it was a nice fifty-five-inch Sony. Now the only thing left was the cable hanging from the wall. The DVDs were missing, too—except for three of them. Though he had no way to watch them, he was glad to still have *Grindhouse* and the director's cut of *HellBoy*. But *Backdraft* was a small "fuck you" propped against the wall.

Tired of looking at the pillaged space around him and starving after his eighteen-hour nap, Jason hit the fridge to find that it, too, had been nearly cleaned out. He had hot sauce, mustard, three hard-boiled eggs and a lone wine cooler. Again, the wine cooler was a little 'screw you' left just for him. A clear note that all the beer had been taken.

Damn Kelly.

He found a single take-out pepper pack and two tiny salts and pulled one of the remaining two chipped plates from the cabinet. The eggs yielded their shells quite easily and he dumped the trash into the bag he'd set out when he discovered the trash bin gone yesterday. He'd paid for that stupid, seventy-dollar, step-lid trash can she had insisted they needed. He should sue the hell out of her. If he could find her.

With his plate of two eggs rolling in the salt and pepper mix, he went to sit at the table. But there were no chairs, not even a couch. The Bitch had taken that too. So, with only his boxers to keep him from bare-assing it, he jumped up on the counter and ate there.

He wouldn't sit on his butcher-block table. He liked it. And if Kelly had known that, the table probably wouldn't still be here. Three minutes later and still hungry, he rinsed the plate and left it in the sink. Then he took a moment to be grateful the sink was bolted down.

Jason checked out the bathroom before he showered. Had to be sure he had soap and a clean towel before he climbed in. He would have to get out of here and eat some actual food and make a rational decision about Kelly while he wasn't looking directly at evidence of her evil side . . . and his stupid one.

When he'd gotten home Tuesday morning he'd come in the front door with the trash from his Joe's breakfast biscuit firmly in hand. His brain simply hadn't registered that the apartment was cleaned out.

Automatically assuming he'd been robbed, he'd left the door open and immediately run through the small unit calling out for Kelly. He'd been afraid for her, afraid the thief might still be inside. But she hadn't been there.

By then certain they'd been robbed, he pulled out his cell and called Rob Castor before reality hit and he understood that he didn't need his friend in the police department to find Kelly or dust for prints.

Jason had sworn a blue streak, right there in his combination living room/dining room/kitchen space, his hallway door still wide open.

Kelly must have come with a moving truck and paid movers. She couldn't lift the couch, and lord knew she and her friends would never break a nail to do it. She didn't have any male friends loyal enough to lift furniture for her—unless she was already sleeping with someone else. It wasn't like Kelly to go it alone, he thought.

Jason stepped out of the shower onto the used towel he'd set out in place of the missing bath mat. Grabbing the clean towel off the press-on hook that Kelly had complained about, he rubbed his head with it for a moment, then wrapped it around his hips.

She'd known what she was doing. If she had touched his computer, or taken the desk out from under it, if she had taken his shirts that she liked to wear, he would have come after her. Would have found her and made her miserable, would have sued her ass into the ground. He might still. He needed to eat before he decided.

They recognized him when he walked into Joe's. That was becoming a problem he likely wouldn't remedy any time soon now that he had no one at home to help fix meals. Though he loved that about Southfield—the small town feel—it was clear he had been to Joe's too many times recently.

After plowing through his ham biscuit, he headed to Publix to stock his fridge. He had to get home and get to sleep tonight. He was on shift again starting at eight tomorrow morning.

The grocery store was a maze. He hadn't been in one with any regularity for nearly a year, Kelly always got their groceries and he'd grown complacent with that.

He'd thought they had a good arrangement, but clearly he'd been wrong. So wrong, in fact, that he had not even seen this coming. So wrong that he had run through the apartment worried for her safety. What an idiot he was.

At the checkout, his total came to well over a hundred dollars, something he had not expected. And as he loaded the mass of stuffed plastic bags into his car, it hit him that rent was due in two weeks . . . and he now owed the whole of it.

Jason squeezed his eyes shut. Fuck her.

Actually, fuck him. She'd sure done it royally.

She'd talked him into the gated building, the riverbank-facing unit, the two-bedroom layout. All of which cost more than he could afford. But *they* could afford it, she'd said. And *they* could. But *he* couldn't.

Kelly out earned him. Something he hadn't had a problem with . . . until today. Until his eighteen-hour reprieve from his new reality had come to an end.

He had four more months on this stupid lease. For an apartment that was higher end than he wanted, bigger than he needed and in an area of town where his friends didn't live. And he'd just earned himself a full share of the power bill, the cable, the water . . .

His brain turned that thought all the way over as he drove his car back to the building that he'd never really liked. After parking in the underground garage, he looped all the grocery bags up his arms and hit the stairs. The sixth floor was nothing, even loaded down as he was. If he couldn't do that, then he didn't deserve the one good thing he seemed to have going in his life.

With a great deal of clumsiness, he got it all into the apartment and the groceries put away. And with nothing else to do, he went to turn on the TV.

Crap.

No TV, no couch.

He mentally started a list of what he needed. And maybe what he thought he could get back from Kelly. If and when he found her. And then he plugged in the phone.

Big mistake.

11

It was an older model with a flashing red number and buttons that played back messages. Looking more closely at the flashing red numbers now he saw that he had seventy-three new messages. Holy shit.

No good deed goes unpunished, he thought.

Almost nine months ago, he'd let go of his stubborn streak and moved here on Kelly's whim. That had earned him strike one. Just over thirty-six hours ago, he'd done another good deed . . . and this shit-storm had busted loose. Strike two. He was so close to out.

The first message was from the Birmingham local ABC TV affiliate. They wanted to talk to him. CBS had called approximately fifteen minutes later. According to the electronic voice—which still had not learned that he didn't give a crap what the caller's number, digit by painstaking digit, was—both calls had come in before he'd even gotten home from his shift.

Had he been interested in any of it, he would have started over, grabbed a pen and paper and listened with a little more care. But he didn't. And since his system was old, he didn't have options to delete the message before it finished. So he put the handset on speaker and made a sandwich while a perky voice who claimed to be with Fox News Alabama suggested he call back to schedule something with her. He deleted messages as he went, getting more and more upset.

At one point, Castor's gravelly voice came on. "Dude. I was just calling to check on you. Why does the machine say 'you have only reached Jason Mondy'? In Kelly's voice? Did something go down, bro? What, she doesn't want to be nailing the reigning town he—"

Castor's message was cut off. But it had pointed out that as soon as Jason finished wading through this crap, he had to fix his outgoing message. Hell, he should check his cell; she could have jacked that message, too.

After the sandwich was gone, but the messages weren't, Jason pulled out his cell and called his friend back.

"Hey, bro." Rob Castor answered with his usual unprofessional, non-authoritative sound. "What's going on with you? Hey, who's that in the background?"

"Some message from a chick from Channel 4."

"So what's up with your message?"

"That's what I was calling you about." He scrubbed a hand over his face. This was not going to be easy to man up to, but he was going to have to do it. "Kelly walked out while I was on shift Tuesday."

"Wow. I knew she was cold, but she couldn't pick a better day?"

"She must have been gone before the shit rained down. Look, she took everything. Cleaned the place out. I don't have a chair to sit in. TV's gone, couch too. No bed, just a mattress . . ."

"Holy crap! You report that? She take your computer?"

"No, but she got the X-box and the PlayStation."

Rob's voice turned sour. "Oh, report it. That bitch is going down."

"I don't even know where she is."

But he could hear Rob scribbling on something. Probably one of the many small notepads he kept scattered around his place, for just such occasions. "She take more than a grand?"

"Oh yeah. I mean, not in cash, but in stuff, yeah, easy."

"That's grand larceny, we'll nail her."

"Really?" It paid to be friends with a cop.

"She walked without dividing it with you or coming to an equitable agreement, my friend. Welcome to larceny, baby."

"I don't even know where she is. But I want my TV and couch back." He sighed.

"I'm on shift at three. Give me her cell number. I'll triangulate her if I have to. I never liked that bitch."

"I know. I was counting on that." Jason smiled for the first time since the bell had rung at 3 a.m. Tuesday night/Wednesday early morning. Tuesday had been a pisser.

He gave Rob all the info he had on Kelly. He finished deleting all the messages. Called back two guys on C-Shift and told them he was fine. He ate another sandwich, his appetite finally fading after Tuesday's twenty-hour grind and the full-day nap that had followed. Then he went back into the bedroom where the blinds leaked like sieves without his blackout curtains. What the fuck had he done to her to deserve this? He started a mental list of the things he would need to demand back from her.

Not quite tired yet, he arranged his two remaining blankets from where he'd tossed and turned in them. Then he propped the three worst pillows they had owned against the wall and looked at the two books he'd been left. One of them he'd already read. So discourse on the state of the European economy was it.

Soon the European economy put him to sleep. And in his dreams, the fire came again.

∧   ∧   ∧   ∧   ∧

Though the fire station was a beautiful old brown brick on the outside—the classic, can't-burn-it-down firehouse—the inside was merely painted cinderblock. Another nearly-impossible-to-burn substance. Which was important, because Grimsby left the oven turned on almost daily.

In the kitchen with its two tables shoved end to end, Jason sat down by himself to eat his breakfast biscuit. It briefly crossed his mind that he'd had far too much eggs and cheese in the past two days, but he shoved the thought aside and flipped open the newspaper that had been left on the table and scanned the front page for anything of interest.

Well crap.

The "anything of interest" was a huge color picture of him— not that you could tell one of them from another decked out in PPE gear—with a soot-blackened kid tucked under each arm. Wanstall was in frame right beside him, just a shorter version of the same, only Wanstall had an axe in each hand. But there was no department headshot of his partner next to his. A full three by five inches, his face smiled out from the blue background, the same picture on his ID, from last year when he'd had slightly longer hair.

He scanned the article, which was quite extensive considering he hadn't granted any interviews. It was even yesterday's paper, probably left for him because he was nothing if not predictable in his morning ritual.

Five minutes before roll call he cleared his spot, the only thing different when he left was that the paper was placed with his photo face down.

As he found himself a spot in the chairs set out in the bay, he watched as C-Shift wound down. They reported a relatively uneventful shift. LOL with an MI. Or as the little old lady had reported it "she thought she was going to have a myocardial infarction, she could feel it coming on" and could they just give her a lift to the hospital as soon as she packed up her cigarettes?

Engine 2 had crawled through a house that "smelled faintly of smoke" and prevented a full-blown house fire. No, C-Shift had not had to weather the shit-storm that had been Tuesday.

While he waited, Wanstall came out of the back. She'd probably been in the sleeping area arranging her stuff like Jason she was always just a touch early. Grimsby wandered in exactly at eight, and behind him came West and Standard. O'Casey came out of the training office with the Chief and it was time for lineup.

C-Shift took over the chairs while A stood, which was about as formal as they got. Giving each of them a cursory look up and down, Chief counted off, "O'Casey, Wanstall, Mondy, Grimsby, West, Standard" then he sighed.

Merriman was missing.

And they were all glad. It was another mark in the growing column of ticks against him. Captain was trying to get him released, and since no one liked or felt safe with Merriman, they had all become tattle-tales. Good times.

With another sigh, Chief Adler turned to C-Shift in their chairs, "Anyone willing to hang for a bit or even cover shift if Merriman doesn't show?"

Weingarten looked left and right and raised his hand.

With a wave, Chief Adler put him into the lineup. Unfortunately, they all knew Weingarten wouldn't be there more than fifteen to thirty minutes. Merriman always eventually came in. Always with some bullshit about why he was late. Which was a pisser. Jason would take Weingarten over Merriman any day.

With a slight smile, Chief pulled Merriman's tag from the magnet board and put Weingarten back up on Engine 2 with Jason and Kellan West.

Shit. That meant he and West had to ride herd on the Great Grape when he rolled in. Kellan looked over at him and shook his head.

Weingarten shrugged. "Hey, maybe I'll stay."

"Dream on." Kellan shook his head and the line broke up.

At least the name change on the board made things official. Merriman would get docked. He'd been formally warned and still failed to show on time. Jason just hoped they didn't catch anything big with the Great Grape at his back.

The rest of C-Shift headed off for home while A started on shining the engines and inspecting all the equipment.

Jason had done a full visual inspection of all the tanks on Engine 2 and was starting on checking pressures when Weingarten came by, "Chief wants you."

"Fuckmonkeys." He knew what this was about.

But moments later he was sticking his head around the open doorway and into the Chief's office. The older man opened the conversation with, "Heard the news stations contacted you."

Nope. No reprieve here. "Yes, sir."

"And?"

"I didn't talk to any of them."

"I'm aware. They've been calling here, too." Chief showed off a stack of yellow paper slips. "You need to return these calls."

With incredible reluctance, Jason took the papers. "I'd prefer not to do interviews. I was only doing my job."

"Too bad. We could use some shine on our image." Chief leaned back.

"Our image is like chrome, sir. The Thurlow save boosted us way up."

"Yes, and your gracious interviews will help."

Jason tried another tack. "Wanstall was there. She should do them. 'Female firefighter' and all that."

The gray-haired head shook slowly back and forth. "No one called Wanstall." His hand shot up, palm out. "And, yes, I specifically asked her that this morning. You need to do this."

Inside his head, Jason cursed. Several times.

"I just don't get what I can do to improve our image. It's good right now. Opening my fat mouth probably won't help." But the facts wouldn't change and he should quit whining like a baby.

"Our image is going to need every boost it can get."

"Why? Is there some shit-storm about to rain down upon us that none of us knows about?"

Adler held his tongue—just sat in his big leather Chief's chair and tried to keep his expression neutral.

"Crap, what's happening, Chief? Is this about Merriman? Is he suing or something?" He was leaning forward, concerned, brows pulled tight, hands worrying together between his knees.

"It's not Merriman. And that's all you're getting."

Jason nodded. *Holy hell.* As he stood, yellow phone slips in hand, Adler gave him one more task, "Give every interview you can, and by God make us shine like gold."

PHOENIX

∧　∧　∧　∧　∧

When he arrived home on Saturday morning, his things were back in place.

The living room was nearly all there. A quick check with the remote revealed the TV was plugged into the TiVo and the TiVo was connected to the cable. He had chairs around his kitchen table, four of them. Though the frothy, feminine side chair remained absent from the corner of the living room along with the tall reading light, Jason didn't miss it.

Rob Castor must have put the fear of God, or at least prosecution, into Kelly's cold heart, because a hell of a lot more than half the things had been returned. When he searched the bedroom he found that the bed was back in place—assembled and everything.

It didn't take long to check things as the apartment wasn't that big to begin with. But he searched the place top to bottom, concerned that she could have put sharp things in bad places or rigged booby traps he wouldn't find until weeks later. She could have simply rearranged the kitchen and screwed him good.

But she hadn't.

In the end, all he found was an envelope with her key. The writing had not said "Jason" on it, but merely "asshole". Perhaps she thought that sufficed for his name. When he woke up, he'd call the super to get re-keyed. And he owed both Rob and Bart English, the Southfield ADA, a beer for making this happen. Maybe several beers.

At last he relaxed on the couch and watched the TV shows he'd missed the night before. Sometime partway through *Jeopardy*, which was really taxing his brain today, he fell asleep on the couch.

When he awoke, he was stiff and sore. His mouth tasted of old coffee and had the thickness of fear. He had sweated there on the couch. Jason told himself it was because he hadn't removed his jacket and his uniform. He wanted to believe it was because he was on the couch—not the best place to rest. But he knew that wasn't the real reason.

He hadn't slept because of the fire.

It chased him. In slow, stupid waves it followed him through his sleep. Heat made his skin crack and peel in black sheets. And

17

though he was petrified, dream-Jason hadn't the sense to get away from it. He watched people he knew burn. He saw the Thurlow boys as twisted and blackened corpses. And told their parents—burned to a crisp, but walking and talking just the same—that he hadn't been able to get the children out. No one else was there, just him and the shiny red truck.

In the dreams, his GPS tag was always missing. No one could find him and no one was coming.

It wasn't that the dreams were scary; they were idiotic really. Station House #2 had *saved* the Thurlow boys. The parents weren't burned to a blackened charcoal-like state. And fire just didn't do that, damnit.

It was that the dreams stole his sleep.

Though he had slept some last night at the house, he hadn't slept all that well apparently. Or he wouldn't have crashed on his own couch with Alec Trebec talking to him like he was an idiot for not knowing exactly which monarch presided over the annexing of India.

Peeling himself from the couch, Jason climbed into his re-assembled bed and prayed that being in it would help him find real rest.

It wasn't to be.

Southfield Fire Station #2

Shift	A	
	O'Casey	Captain
Engine 2	Standard	Engineer
	West	FF2
	Grimsby	FF1
Rescue 3	Wanstall	FF3
	Mondy	FF2 / EMT
	Merriman	FF1

Chapter 2

The fire station bustled with activity as A-Shift started the day. The brick building had a feel of its own, different from the homes of any of the firefighters, different even from when they were all together elsewhere.

They each underwent a personality change at eight a.m. every third day as they came through the back bay doors. For some it was subtle, for others drastic. To a certain extent, they became children—the Chief was in charge, no questions asked. With sharp belief, the firefighters all did as they were told, when they were told. Though they were expected to think for themselves, place themselves in danger and handle anything that came at them— which it often did, and sometimes did so while on fire—their demeanor and manners were military obedient once they entered the station house.

Though the back room was full of creative and fluent swearing, anyone who called on the phone or came through the front door was "sir" or "ma'am". "Thank you" and "please" flowed alongside a genuine politeness that was as deeply bred into them as the skills of the job. And though there was a lot of lamenting about the "stupidity of people" in general, a person would have to be a real ass to get any label other than "idiot" or "just drunk". And never to their face.

At eight-fifteen, A-Shift had finished lineup. With Merriman missing again, they had begun their start-of-day cleaning and inspection like a well-oiled machine.

In his office, too high in the ranks to be part of the clean-up crew, Chief Adler settled back into his desk chair and called

Station House 1 about the shit that was about to hit the fan and his hopes that Mondy could start them off with a nice shiny buff.

None of them ever hoped for house fires, never wished for trapped kids. But since it had already happened and everyone was all right, Chief Adler had to be willing to milk it for all it was worth. He looked at his watch. It was nearing ten a.m. If Mondy wasn't on the phone by eleven begging reporters to come ask him questions, Adler was going to go out and threaten to write him up for disobeying a direct order. Not that he wanted to do that.

When the phone rang, he sighed. He knew what the call meant and he answered it while waiting for the bell to ring.

In the main room, Jack Standard heard the phone in the Chief's office and stood up from his planted position in the recliner. He checked both his shoes by tamping his heel down into the floor. Left, then right. He tugged at the cuffs of his long-sleeved shirt, left then right. After adjusting his belt, he was ready.

As Standard finished, Mondy, West and O'Casey were already at the front office waiting for word from the Chief. Adler looked at them all and nodded, then held up two fingers. Both trucks were going. Wanstall came into the group, apple in hand and saw the two fingers. Nodding in response, she tossed her half-eaten fruit in the trash as she went by to gear up.

While he waited for the men to gear up, Adler printed the information and climbed into the pickup. Just then, something caught his eye . . . and the air all went out of him.

A red-faced Merriman jogged up to O'Casey who waited in the office to turn the traffic light to red. The Captain brushed the slacker off pointing him toward the Chief's truck.

Adler scrolled the passenger window down. "We're on a run, Merriman. You've been replaced. If you want to keep your job you'll go inside and wait, and then you'll see me in my office when I get back."

Later, after they returned, he made a point of singling out Mondy and with the side of his fist he tapped the kid on the shoulder. "You got any interviews lined up for this afternoon?"

"This afternoon?" Mondy looked surprised. "I figured I was on duty now."

"Nah. Set them up as soon as you can. I'll take you out of rotation 'til they're done." He turned to Alex. "You're on overtime. You willing to take over for Mondy now 'til his interviews finish?"

Alex raised his eyebrows. "Mayhaps."

"What does that mean?"

Though Alex enjoyed the chuckle from his hard-as-nails Chief, he kept his mouth grim. "A word?"

A brief nod sufficed for so much around the house, and he followed the older man into the big office where he shut the door but didn't have a seat. "I realize that if I sub out, I'm just a part of the crew and I go where I'm told. But I really don't want to be in charge of Merriman after thirty straight hours on shift. Honestly, that's what's keeping me from saying yes."

The Chief's voice was full of regret. "Oh god. Fact of the matter is that no one wants Merriman at their back. But since you have the most hours logged in a row, I'll grant you that wish." Chief gave the one short nod before he said, "Thanks for staying."

Adler watched Alex leave, a damn fine firefighter, that one. Then he sucked in his breath and did what he had to. "Merriman, get your ass in here!"

"Yes, sir." The kid hauled his butt out of the waiting chair at reception and rounded the corner. Then he plopped it down. "I was just about to go across the street and get one of those free coffees they're offering us."

Red flashed in front of the Chief's eyes, and then he told himself to take three seriously deep breaths before speaking. He found he needed a fourth and a fifth, before he finally gave up and yelled. "That's for real firefighters!"

Merriman blinked up at him. Then looked down at his own uniform, then up, entirely befuddled.

It hit the Chief like a slap. The kid had no clue whatsoever.

As a house they had two options: help Merriman learn, the way they did with all newbies, or fire him. Problem was, Merriman had been here long enough that he should be well out of 'newbie' status. He was less than a year younger than Grimsby, but Grimsby had his shit together. Stephen Grimsby was only at the rank of firefighter one, and not a top choice to partner with, but he got shit done and had your back. No one even wanted Merriman around.

Merriman was lethal.

But HR demanded that the proper channels be taken to fire him. Three suspensions. Chief hopped on that right away. "You're suspended."

"What? How long? I told you my alarm didn't go off." Merriman clutched something in his hands, and for the first time the Chief recognized the McDonald's bag he was holding. He took two more deep breaths.

"Today plus another shift."

They would be a man shy of a full load for the rest of the shift with Mondy giving interviews. But they could yank him onto a truck if they had to. That would be some real excitement for a reporter, right?

Adler just prayed that he could get Merriman up to the required three suspensions for firing. And that it didn't cost the lives of any of his other men or any civilians while they waited for that to happen.

He needed a beer. What he got was not a beer but an iced coffee. Standard came in loaded with the coffees and handed him the first one off the tray. In here, Mondy was not the reigning hero and Adler was highest in command. With his usual by-the-book pattern, Standard reported that the coffee-shop girl had tried to give Mondy his coffee for free. But he and West had paid for it—at the usual fifty percent off.

The two men then continued through the station house, and it was Standard who looked at each cup and handed it to the right person with unfailing accuracy and that slight nod.

They passed Mondy as he headed up to the Chief's office.

Adler looked up as the hometown hero reported in. "I have two newspapers lined up for this afternoon. *Southfield Press* will be here ASAP, *Birmingham News* at four. And Channel 6 wants to know if they can film a short segment live from the house at about six fifteen."

"In front of the house. Front door, by the flag."

Mondy started to pick up his cell phone, but the Chief stopped him. "Tell Grimsby to mow and Wanstall to rake up after him."

"Yes, sir."

With a sigh deep enough to show how the interviews pained him, Jason returned the call to Channel 6 and waited for the *Southfield Press* to show up.

The interviewer was young and green. She seemed nervous about being in the firehouse though they all did their best to simply be polite and ignore her. Only Mondy had to step up and try to make her more at ease.

Jason watched as she fumbled to get her laptop open and turned on. The poor girl nearly dropped it when the bell went off, she was so startled by the noise. As Wanstall and Weingarten went by to grab gear and head into the bay, Wanstall gave him a look of sympathy. Weingarten didn't even glance to the side.

"Is it always that loud?" The reporter tried to smile. It didn't quite work.

Jason folded his hands on the table and wondered if that was her first interview question. "Yes, ma'am, it is."

Dear God, he had three of these today.

She asked stupid questions, and he gave the appropriate stupid answers.

Chief Adler stood in the doorway and watched as the interview progressed at a snail's pace. Apparently the reporter didn't have a recording device with her, so she typed out what Mondy said, word for painstaking word.

He told her he had just been doing his job. Pointed out that Standard had rescued the family's kitten and that it was Wanstall who had heard the noises of the children trying to hide from the fire. Chief was glad that Mondy didn't add that the children were likely hiding from the firefighters, too.

A fireman in full gear was a monster as he came out of the smoke and flames. Children usually ran the wrong way and crawled under the bed, screaming when someone tried to pick them up and save them.

But Mondy said none of those things. He was a smart guy – they all really were in some way or other. But Mondy could be counted on to think before he spoke. He explained how it was really Wanstall who found the kids. How he had carried the children because Missy was known to be a hound dog with a nose for clean air when inside a burning building.

With his shoulder propped against the doorway, and out of view of the already nervous reporter, Chief Adler listened to the story. How Missy had found the back window and axed it open. How she had gone down first, and how—thanks to GPS tags that all the firefighters wore—the others were waiting outside where and when they emerged.

Jason made it sound as though he only lifted the children and handed them out the window.

The reporter nodded, then stayed silent for a few moments while she typed. Jason stared out the window, a dull expression on his face. But the Chief knew that they needed what they were buying with this.

The girl's pert voice grabbed their attention again as she asked her last question. "Are you excited about being a hero?"

She really hadn't paid attention to anything, had she? At least it would make a good story.

Jason tilted his head to the side. "I'm not a hero. Everyone worked together. But it was a good day: everyone made it out alive. Even the kitten."

The Chief turned away then. Mondy was right—it had been a good day. But as he walked away, he thought of other fires, other times when everyone hadn't made it out.

He left Jason alone to wait for the second reporter, who came several hours later and clearly knew what he was doing. As before, the Chief posted himself at the door and silently monitored the proceedings.

The first clue that Clark Jernigan was a professional was the handshake and clear introduction. The second was the microrecorder that was set on the table between them and the simple way Jernigan leaned forward and started speaking with ease.

"It's nice to meet you Mr. Mondy. Can I take a moment and confirm your credentials and those of the other firefighters at the Thurlow house fire?"

"Of course, sir." Mondy sat with his back straight, his feet planted square, the military-like precision in sharp contrast to the reporter's more relaxed form.

Jernigan smiled. "Please don't call me 'sir'. I think we're of an age."

"All right then." Though Mondy nodded and smiled, he didn't relax much more than that.

"Okay—you are a level 2 firefighter, right?"

"Yessir—Yes. That means I passed an upper level test and can handle bigger blazes, more difficult situations."

"You're also listed as Paramedic rank 1. That's in addition to, and almost separate from your fire fighting skills."

Mondy nodded. This was a time when the Chief wished Mondy was the loquacious sort. But it was what it was, and Clark Jernigan seemed to be able to work with it.

"Missy Wanstall, your partner at that fire, has the rank above you. According to my information, she's a year or so younger than you."

Jason smiled. "Yes, she is. Missy's one of the best. Graduated from training while she was finishing her bachelor's in building engineering, and went straight for the promotions."

Chief's heart grinned. No one was going to get a scratch of sexism off Mondy. The kid had it in spades at a bar or out in his life, but in this house all of them knew that Wanstall was one of them, and she had your back better than most.

"You know Ben and Henry Thurlow said they thought you had come to kill them. But now they know you're the hero who saved them."

"You talked to them?" Jason looked startled.

Still listening quietly, the Chief realized that he wasn't needed here. Jernigan had done more than his share of research and Mondy could hold his own. There was paperwork to be done.

"I interviewed the Thurlow boys yesterday." Clark found Mondy's question interesting.

"How are they doing?" The fireman seemed genuinely interested in the answer, leaning forward, his eyes focusing in a way they hadn't before.

"They're fine. Both have a bit of a cough. Ben, the younger one is still on oxygen and his mother is hovering. But the neighbors and the community have come out to help them rebuild."

It wasn't always that way. Not everyone inspired the community to gather and he knew the whole story was uncommon. "So, live saves are relatively rare. How many do you all get in a year?"

"That depends on your definition of 'you all.'"

Clark was starting to like Mondy and he hadn't expected to. He had expected an egotistical, swaggering alpha-male, instead he found a seemingly modest man, which just made the whole thing that much more interesting. "Let's say that means your whole station house."

"If you're talking about all three shifts, then maybe one to three." Jason shrugged, as though it wasn't a big deal and it wasn't anywhere near as glorifying as the movies made it out to be.

"Can you tell me, in your own words, why that is?"

And that was *it*: the point that made this man talk. Clark knew he could find it, that button that all people had, something they wanted to tell you about. This man knew fire. So—even though it was all being recorded—he leaned forward and listened intently.

"Burning in a fire isn't something people should worry about. It's the smoke that kills. So once a fire gets big enough to draw attention and someone alerts the station the smoke is already everywhere. What usually kills people is one of three things: they don't wake up in time and they get trapped, or they panic and get trapped, or they're too drunk or stoned to know they need to get out and get trapped. By the time we get there, there usually aren't any live people to save."

Though this seemed to genuinely bother him, it didn't affect him too horribly either. So Clark pulled at another thread. "What was different about the Thurlow fire?"

"Everything. It all worked together to get that family out. The fire started on the end of the house opposite where they slept. And they had a dog who alerted them. Also the long design of the house kept the whole thing from going up in flames all at once. The kids' bedroom was on the lower floor, so they got less smoke."

"But you pulled them out of the upstairs room."

"Yeah. They got scared and tried to find their own way out. Wound up in the mother's office. Standard and Grimsby checked the kids' rooms and found the kitten. We thought Wanstall and I were just doing a regular search."

"The parents and the dog were out by then."

"Right. The dad tried to find them, but we stopped him. It was Missy who heard the noises and found the kids. I carried them both, so she could point us to clean air, since the far end of the house had already hit flashover and everything was on fire."

"This makes you quite the hero."

There, if that didn't get Mondy strutting, then he might be the real deal. Interesting.

"No sir. I'm not a hero. I like my job. I like that I have skills that make things better. Usually we save property, not people. But that's a good thing, too. I like the adrenaline, and I like the schedule. In a fire, we're a machine: we each do what we have to and watch each other's backs so everyone makes it out alive. And we usually do, if we do things right. Once in a while, the machinery does something great and the Thurlows are all fine. Even the kitten. Although I haven't heard about the dog yet."

"Actually, they found the dog this morning."

"Good. That's good." Jason nodded, his short, dark hair matching the eyebrows that pulled together only the slightest amount.

Jernigan stayed a while longer. Asked more questions about being a firefighter, about the luck of the Thurlow house, about being a paramedic within the firehouse and, lastly, about being a minor celebrity.

After the reporter gathered his recorder and his jacket, Jason walked him to the door and thanked him for coming. Only one more to go, but it would be on camera. Jernigan had stayed for an hour and a half, he had less than forty-five minutes before Channel 6 showed up for the taping.

In the restroom, Jason brushed his teeth and ran a comb through his short hair. He checked out his face, his shirt, his pants and shoes, and figured he looked about as good as he was going to get.

The bell went off again and with a pang in his heart, he watched Standard load up his team and saw Engine 3 roll out. He could have gone. But instead he would be here with the vapid blonde reporter, smiling for a camera.

After a few seconds of relaxation in front of the TV, which was still tuned to one of Standard's bow-hunting programs, he heard the Chief welcome the crew from the news and show them where to start setting up. It was all of two minutes later that the pert blonde barged into the back room and said "Are you Jason Mondy?"

Like a grinning army general, she coached him on how to smile, which stance she would let him use on camera, what questions she was going to ask, and how he shouldn't talk too loud or try to mimic her professional tone. Jason didn't care, so things didn't come to a head until he refused to take credit for the save.

In the end, he side-stepped the hero question and gave credit to all the other members of A-Shift by name. He enjoyed watching the burn in her eyes as he listed each person, and so he went one step further. "There's going to be a fund-raiser at Salzone's tomorrow evening to help the Thurlow family find a new home and replace the precious things they lost. We will all be there, and hope everyone else will come, too."

Maybe he'd gone too far with the "precious things"; the blonde held her smile, but she was mad. Right then, the bell went off.

And he was out of here.

With a few quick steps, he ran for the house and heard her pert voice at his back. "As you can see, local hero, Jason Mondy is off to fight another fire. Who will he save today?"

Bitch.

Chapter 3

Jason

Two weeks later, nothing had changed. Except apparently he'd gotten grumpy as all hell.

"Take the damn dog, Mondy." Wanstall had practically yelled at him—as well as anyone could yell through a mask in a barn full of smoke.

He had come out of the red and white double-X doors in full gear, the squirming puppy tucked under his arm, and as soon as he had cleared the billows of smoke that followed him, he instantly became blind.

"*Sonofabitch*" rattled in his head while the rest of him fought not to tell the photographer what he thought. He saw Chief Adler direct the man not to take flash pictures and distract the firefighters. The man with the cell-phone camera immediately apologized, though it was about as sincere as snake oil, for he immediately turned away and got video of the barn with smoke pouring out every crevice. The people from nearby houses gathered to watch the action occurring in the pulsing red glow of the fire trucks' lights cutting through the dusk.

Honestly, the barn fire simply looked worse than it was. One truck could have handled this. Some old woman in a wheelchair had called the fire department because she saw smoke in her yard, and Fire Station #2 had stopped it before it became more than a campfire. At this point everything in the barn was wet, and Adler was already starting the arson inspection. But Jason and Missy had found an old-fashioned magnifying glass right next to the hay bales they'd put out.

The barn was mostly empty. The woman seemed to think maybe her young grandson had bumped something in there when he visited. But mostly, she'd caught it before it got bad and all she had suffered was some damn smelly water and smoke damage and the loss of two hay bales.

They had pretty much known that before going in. And—wanting to burn off some of the crap that had been eating him—Jason had volunteered himself and Missy to go back into the barn and see if they could find that seventh puppy.

The little thing was squirming and trying to lick Jason's smoke covered gear, which meant that it had no real damage. What it also didn't have was the ability to fix what was gnawing at Jason.

And what Jason did have was a pesky amateur photographer snapping another picture just as he handed the puppy to the little old lady in the wheelchair. What a fucking photo op. He should have put his arm around her and asked if he could get the photo framed.

There wasn't a lot going on in Southfield these days, so the barn fire would be news—as would the hero fire-fighter saving puppies.

Right now, he really hated that dog.

No good deed goes unpunished. It had been his mantra for going on two weeks now.

If anyone else had still been in or near the barn, the Chief would have had his attention there. But Chief saw the yahoo taking pictures and shut him down before Jason snapped.

People didn't need their tragedies documented. Didn't need their tears filmed and posted on the Web. From the moment he'd entered the job, there had been "public persona/customer service" training. More and more, the likelihood of things turning up online had gone from being "possible" to being a question of *how many* videos would get posted.

"Mondy."

The single word in the Chief's gruff tone told him that probably everyone could see his non-customer-service face. So he gave a curt nod, then listened to the Chief politely explain to cell-phone man what an ass he was being.

It took about an hour to clear the equipment out. Adler and Captain O'Casey filled out forms and did preliminary interviews of the old woman and her son. They sent Grimsby out to check through the lookie-loos to ask each if they had seen anything, and direct them to get in line to file a statement.

Finally back at the station, they re-stocked. Kept the used tanks out to be re-filled, and ran a full check of Engine 2 before they showered.

He had followed every protocol, had refrained from hitting the moron taking pictures, and had done all the proper post checks. So he was surprised when the Chief came into the break room and tapped him on the shoulder with the side of his fist. "Talk to you in my office?"

Normally the Chief didn't hang out in the evenings. It was a small town, so when there was an actual fire, he came out and handled at least the front end of the arson investigation. But why he didn't head home to his wife and big screen TV and save the paperwork for another day was just as surprising as the fact that he closed the door behind them.

Settling uncertainly into the guest chair, Jason began to worry.

Chief spoke first. "Don't look at me that way. You aren't getting written up or anything."

"Oh-kay . . ." *Then what was this?*

"Look, Mondy, I need you to be our golden boy right now."

Why? There had been no proverbial "golden boy" position before now. And if there was going to be one, why not Weingarten? Just because he was gay didn't make him any less "golden". In fact, Alex Weingarten literally *was* golden—blond hair, mild tan. And he could pull off PR like no one's business.

"You got elected to the post when you and Wanstall found those kids in the Thurlow house. You didn't let Missy carry one of them and so now you hold the post by yourself." Chief sighed.

"It's not that I didn't *let* her carry one. It's that we had two kids and didn't know our way out. First man into fire shouldn't have a child under his arm." It was standard procedure and logically sound. Lord knows he wasn't trying to be a hero.

"That's all true." Adler leaned back in his big leather chair. "And it doesn't matter. What's done is done. All the Thurlows are fine. And thanks to Standard, even the kitten is out. We came out of that one gleaming like chrome. And you're the one they all want to talk to. You're the one they want pictures of, and you're the one who came out with a barn puppy today."

Jason shook his head.

"Look, Mondy, if you don't want to be a hero, don't volunteer to go back for the puppy. So when they want your picture handing the cute dog to the sweet little old lady you smile for the camera next time."

"Yes, sir." His jaw was clenched, though he knew the Chief was right.

"It gets worse."

Well crapdamn.

Adler continued. "There is some big shit rolling down the pipe in our direction. We need you out there making good with the community."

"What is this 'shit'?" He asked it even though he didn't expect a real answer.

And he didn't get one. "I'm not at liberty to say."

But a thought crossed his mind. "Am I making pretty so that my job can disappear? Are we getting absorbed into some new super-district?"

He was leaning forward in his seat. With the government the way it was, fire houses weren't funded the way they were in "the old days". There weren't spare firefighters or sub positions open anymore. Not that he'd seen any of that in his time.

"No, nothing like that. Your job is safe."

There was something about the way Adler said it, something that made Jason's head tip to the side. "*My* job? But not *everybody's*?"

"I'm not at liberty to say."

Holy.

Shit.

And before that thought could loop back around and smack him again, the Chief added. "And neither are you. If I get any wind of you spreading rumors and creating panic, I will have your head."

Then the chief leaned forward as Jason absorbed that last bit. "Trust me here. I'm on your side. All of your sides. And it's not going to be bad for us. Or it shouldn't be. *If* we can go into this golden. You being "photo-op boy" is step one. We're going to have barbecues, and Wanstall, Weingarten, O'Casey and Connelly are going to go out and equal opportunity us to death."

Holy. Shit. The thought flitted through his head again. And surely the Chief could see it. He'd never had a good poker face.

"Bottom line is that I need you out there pulling kittens from trees and helping LOLs across the street every chance you get. Can you do that?"

"Sure, Chief."

"So why are you being such a butt? You not sleeping? Doesn't look like you are."

Nice segue there, Chief, he thought to himself. Maybe that's what this was really all about. Sure, they needed Golden-Boy-Jason to be "game on", but what the Chief really wanted him in here for was to find out why his ego wasn't headed on the upswing from all the attention. And if there was one thing he'd learned in seven years in this house, it was that you couldn't bullshit the Chief. So he just said "That's about it."

"Nightmares?"

"Yes. I still seem to fall asleep easily. But they wake me up, disorient me, and disrupt my rest." He didn't add, *maybe that's why I'm cranky lately.* But it seemed like perhaps he should, because if he didn't come clean to the Chief's satisfaction, he could get his ass thrown into counseling. And just the thought of that was enough to make him shudder.

After looking pensive for a moment, and therefore greatly concerning Jason, Chief said, "You don't usually have a problem leaving it at the job. Do you know why this one's different?"

"Not really."

"You don't think it has anything to do with your fire as a kid?"

That's what it all came down to in this house: Chief knew everything. At one point, when Grimsby had been spanking new, he had accidentally watered his own shoes, then landed his backup pair in a fantastic cow pie at the next call. Chief had approached Jason and asked if he minded lending Grimsby his spares so no one had to smell the kid for the remainder of the shift. That had been telling. Not only did Chief know Jason's shoe size, but he knew Grimsby's—after less than a week on the job. So it was no surprise that he knew about the fire that had probably started Jason on this career path.

Jason answered the only way he could. He shrugged. "Doesn't feel like it. This was two boys sticking together, I was by myself. Thing is, we pull a live save a couple times a year. I've done it a few times myself. But this is the first time it seems to have followed me home."

"It can be anything that triggers it."

"Sure, but why not the ones we didn't save? If I had a problem, I would have thought that's where it would come." He shrugged again. All he knew was that he was having stupid dreams. Everything was wrong in them. If his dream-self had any sense he'd tell the fire where to stick it and roll over and get some good rest. Instead he woke up drenched in sweat, with full memory of being terrified of things that couldn't ever happen. It would only be more disconcerting if he was having dreams where he was afraid of Chihuahuas or house cats. Or Jell-O.

"You sure it's not about the fire when you were a kid?"

"No." How could he be sure of that? Jason shook his head. "Of course it could be. But I dream that we don't get the Thurlow boys out because they're already dead when we get there, or something like that. My fire as a kid was in an old, run-down house. I was under a bed, not in a closet. I was alone, I was happy to see the firefighters. Yes, I was a kid rescued from a burning house, but that's not what I'm dreaming about. And that's not what's . . . waking me up from the dreams." He'd almost said "what's scary" but it wasn't.

"Well, I still have the occasional nightmare from some of my worst."

"What's that, Chief?" It was a blatant attempt to change the direction of the conversation. And also to learn a little more. He knew a great deal about some things about his Chief—the man lived in a nice house, had two adult children, and made a mean barbecue pork—but there were other things, usually about the job, that none of them knew about him.

"Worst of the worst?"

Jason nodded.

"It was about twenty-five years ago. I was pretty green. I was at a fire house just outside Montgomery and there was an apartment fire in a bad district. The building was a mess, not up to code, a death-trap. You know."

And he did. People didn't think much of those fire inspection certificates in public buildings, but they should. Jason nodded, and the Chief continued.

"A lot of people were out, the police were there corralling the live ones. There was a lot of screaming about people still inside, and a lot of them—closer to the source—were already dead. But my partner and I were doing a sweep and found this little boy, maybe five or six. He comes running through the flames to us, and he's screaming. He's petrified, fights us the whole way, but we grab him and haul him out, glad to have what's likely the last live one."

It didn't sound like too bad of a story. But anything could give a man nightmares on this job.

Chief wasn't done, though. "Thing was, when we got him outside, someone finally heard what he was yelling about. Our gear back then sucked for hearing, so we had no idea what he'd been saying.

"Turned out, he'd left his brother behind and was yelling at us to go get him."

"Holy shit, Chief."

"Yeah, well, it gets worse. My partner—Jacob Strobel—"

And right then Jason knew. You didn't give a firefighter's full name unless it needed to be remembered. *Shit*.

". . . went back in to get the brother. Finally found him, but he'd inhaled too much smoke. And so did Malloy. He died two days later from burns and lung damage."

Shit shit. Even the kid didn't get out. And Jason still had to ask. "Why didn't someone else go in after the brother?"

At least that made Adler laugh, even if it was just a wry sound. "Gear was so different then. The place was a burning maze and we went in with rope. No one GPS'd us. So we were the only two who even had an idea of where the brother might be."

Jesus. He'd known that things were changing—improving all the time for the stations who could afford the latest in gear, which was nowhere close to even half of them. But he hadn't thought that Adler, just twenty-five years ago, was still on the archaic system of running rope, Hansel-and-Gretel style, to get back out. Add in the asbestos and it's a wonder anyone survived a fire.

And Jason found himself saying what people always said, useless as it was. "You did your best, and saved the first brother."

"Yeah. I have a couple others that still wake me up sometimes. A boarding school for the mentally challenged. They were strong like adults, but fought like scared kids, and there weren't enough of us to get them all out. Some of the teachers ran and didn't take any of the students with them. Then there was a brick building in Montgomery years ago, and I swear I saw a kid in the window. I heard him scream, so I looked up. He was about five stories up. Flames burst out the window where he was, and no one ever found anything."

Jason nodded. Hell, there was no way he was going to sleep tonight. *Thanks, Chief.*

"Point is, you'll have these. And you have to find a way to sleep after. Your mother still lives around here, doesn't she?"

"Outside Huntsville, sir." He saw where this was headed.

"That's not too far. Would staying the next two nights with her help? Going home sometimes does."

He nodded. He had his old room there, still decorated with sports heroes and the occasional gap on the wall where a few years ago he'd finally taken down incredibly out-of-date posters of Kelly LeBrock and Carol Alt. Most importantly, he had a mom there, who would get up at an ungodly hour to feed him and get him back here for eight a.m. line up.

He nodded again. He'd eat well, see some old friends, and if he slept better, too, that would be wonderful.

Chief leaned back, looking content that he'd done what he could. "So call her now. Head home tomorrow morning when you get off shift and see if you can get some sleep the next few nights."

"Yes, sir."

That was the end of it. Ignoring the Gilford fire paperwork, Chief stood up and grabbed a few things off his desk. Still in his civvies—the badge clipped to his pocket the only thing identifying him as Fire Chief of Station House #2—he headed out the door and closed it behind Jason.

Jason followed him through the break room, where Adler announced to the lazing crew that he was headed home to his lovely bride. There was a chorus of "goodnight" and "see you tomorrow, Chief". But Jason didn't stop. He went all the way out the back bay and waved as Adler drove off.

Then he pulled out his cell and hoped his mom hadn't turned in for the night.

When he hung up, he went back into the house where the Engine 5 guys were watching *Jeopardy* and getting every obscure answer right. Wanstall had her mouth open in shock and Grimsby looked like he thought he might be in the *Twilight Zone*. Merriman was snickering and ruining it.

But Jason liked Stephen Grimsby and called off the dogs. "They saw this episode earlier when you were out on a run. It's a re-run. That's why they suddenly all became such brainiacs."

Missy finally dropped her gape-mouthed stare and laughed, "You fell for it."

Grimsby hung his head in shame, "I did."

The others all cackled a bit, then changed the channel. Jason didn't see who was in charge of the remote, but the channels stopped on *Sweet Home Alabama*.

"Seriously?" He swept the room looking for the culprit. But no one took credit for it.

∧ ∧ ∧ ∧ ∧

His old red alarm clock read 7:33 when his eyelids finally pried themselves open. Struggling from under the weight of unfamiliar covers and the deep, drugging sleep he was emerging from, Jason pushed himself to breathe deeply and open his eyes all the way.

It took only a moment to get his bearings: the sights, the smell, the feel of the last dying light of day slanting through the window. His first thought was that the Chief had been right, coming home had helped.

There was no fire in his dreams, no dead people, no remorse or regret. In fact, the only problem had been that he had slept too well. What finally dragged him from the last clinging layers of sleep was the smell of pork chops. He struggled to get out from under the layers of covers, to plant his feet on the floor and finally to stand.

Still fully dressed from when he fell into bed, Jason washed his face and headed downstairs following the smells. As expected, lifted lids revealed fresh snapped green beans and his mother's fluffy, white mashed potatoes. He nearly groaned aloud.

"There you are!" She came up behind him, slippers on her feet, jeans and a sweater set finishing off the look that was his mom. She still had on her pearls from some earlier meeting.

Turning, he hugged her and kissed her on the forehead, she was so much shorter than him. "Hi, Mom. It's good to be home."

She served him about three times as much as she served herself and didn't comment on how late he'd slept. They sat at a table with a linen cloth and a centerpiece and ate off of her 'everyday' china. She asked about Kelly, and he simply answered that they'd broken up.

He asked about her work and was surprised to find she had a real part-time job. "With Child Protective Services."

"Mom, that must be hard." He was shocked. "Why the switch? I thought you liked the women's shelter."

Merry laughed. "I did. In fact, I did my job so well I made myself obsolete. We raised enough awareness that they had almost too many volunteers. So I went where I was needed and made the plunge."

He didn't comment that her phraseology was off. And he wasn't sure which plunge she was referring to—taking a paying job or working with foster kids—so he ignored it. "How do you deal with it?"

She smiled again. "I talk to prospective parents . . . about adopting older kids. I got certified and I do home inspections, help get kids out of the system."

His heart rolled over in his chest. "Wow."

She was tearing up, her hands trying to wipe her eyes and grab his hands at the same time. "Adopting you was the best thing that ever happened to me. It's hard, but I like what I'm doing."

Then she deftly changed the subject on him, her tears vanishing with the new direction. "So what has you heading up here on short notice and sleeping eight hours during the day? Kelly?"

He shook his head and looked at the old scarred table top. She could afford a newer one, but like him, she used things until she couldn't any more. Or maybe he was like her that way. "I don't think it was Kelly. That's probably just a coincidence. There was a fire. And though I'm not having real nightmares, I'm not sleeping well."

"I saw the pictures."

He startled, looking up at her again. "You did?"

Looking at him like he was being silly, she spoke the same way. "I have a search engine email me whenever anything comes up on you. I saw it. I saw the puppy, too."

Jason couldn't help it: he laughed. His mother was reasonably tech savvy. Who knew? "Yeah, I don't know why it's happening now. I've been on the job seven years. I've had two promotions, I'm better than I ever was before. I'm about to test for 'firefighter three'. But that eight hours I just slept was the best I've had in nearly three weeks."

She looked away just as something passed across her face. Then she stood and started putting away the dishes. "It's going to mess up your sleep pattern. You'll never sleep tonight."

"No different than any other night." He shrugged and helped her clean up.

They watched *Jeopardy* together and she mopped the floor with him. Then he went out for a late night with a few friends who had either stayed or somehow come back to Madison. But they all had jobs to get to in the morning and the night didn't last long.

Two beers and some catching up and then he was alone in a bar in a town he used to know. But like an old friend, it had changed a bit while he was away and so had he. Realizing he didn't fit, Jason headed home and crawled under the old blue covers again. Sleep came quickly, but not well.

At three a.m., Jason gave up and headed downstairs. He was microwaving a plate of leftover pork chops when he saw his mother sitting in the living room chair in the dark.

Though the microwave dinged, he went over to her. The closer he got the more he realized something was wrong. She was silently crying.

"Mom!"

Instantly he was down on his knees. She'd done this once before, when he had come home to find his father had died of a heart attack less than an hour before. "Mom, what's wrong?"

He didn't want the answer, but pushed anyway. He'd rather know, even though his stomach rolled and his brain started shutting down in preparation for whatever bad news she was going to give him.

"Mom, are you okay?"

"Yes." Then she realized what she'd done and back-pedaled. "I'm not sick, it's not like that. But I've kept something from you . . . for twenty-six years."

Twenty-six years was as long as he'd known her. So if his mother had kept the secret for that long, then she'd *never* told him, and that meant it must be big.

Jason let go of her hands and rocked off his heels to a standing position. He knew it was wrong to tower over her. Regardless, he felt the adrenaline, the need to be poised, ready. A low-grade chill settled into his system, probably so the shock wouldn't be as great when it hit.

Though Merry started talking, her thoughts wandered and she didn't say anything of real value to him. At least not at first. "It's this training with the foster care program. You know you are the best thing that ever happened to me. Right?"

He nodded. She loved him. He didn't doubt that, but it didn't stop the ice that was forming in him.

Her disjointed sentences continued and her tears could be heard in her voice. "I think maybe I didn't take the job with Child Protective Services for so long because I was afraid I'd find out that what we did was wrong. It never sat well with me, what we told you and I only did it because they insisted it was the best thing for you."

"Who?"

"The workers on your case." She looked at him, her eyes wet, and she looked so sad. "They insisted you shouldn't know because we couldn't change it." She sighed deeply. "I have access to some old records now—through my new job. So I started digging. I'm trying to make up for what I ruined."

Jason didn't speak because he didn't want to say something hurtful. She was the only mother he knew and she'd never made him feel less-than for being adopted, for not being born of her, for not being there from the start. Instead, from the day they brought him home at age seven, they wrapped him in safety and home. She told him that she fell in love with him the moment she saw him in the foster center, a scared angry boy in need of a family. But now she said she'd held something from him. Something she'd held back the whole time he'd been part of this family. As far as his memory went, this family was all his life—and he thought again that it must be something big. So he waited.

She took a deep breath and he felt the chill dig in a little further.

"The fire you were in as a boy, the one that took your mother's life . . . your memories of it aren't entirely correct." She sniffled. "Some of that is my fault. I told you wrong things. Some of it, I let you remember wrong."

"Like what?"

"Let me tell you what I know. Turn on the light."

He did. Merry moved then, to sit at the table, and he saw she was clutching a small stack of papers. Jason wanted to rip them out of her grasp, but forced himself to have patience. He knew she would dole them out as she saw fit and patience was a lesson she had drilled into him from childhood. It was a shame it never took.

She put her hand across the top sheet, preventing him from reading it. "Your fire wasn't in Birmingham. That's where *we* lived, we came to Montgomery to get you. I've heard you tell people you were in a fire in Birmingham, even when you were a teenager. You'd been in the Montgomery foster system for about three months when we adopted you. That's where you were from."

That wasn't so bad.

"I snuck into the records office there when I visited and I pulled some more information for you, just in case you want to know."

"Tell me."

She started handing the papers over. "Your birth mother's name was Alcia Mallory. I've heard you tell people you were in a 'house fire' but I don't know if you were using that term generically – like the-place-you-lived-in-had-a-fire or if you really thought it was a house—"

"It was a house." He remembered that.

"No, it wasn't. It was an old apartment complex."

Oh.

He didn't know what to do with that. His mother had sounded like she'd created some big betrayal, but what did it matter if it was a house or an apartment? It only suddenly made more sense that his birth mother hadn't escaped the blaze and that he'd needed a firefighter to pull him out. No grand back-stabbing there.

His birth mother's name didn't mean much to him either. He'd probably called her 'mom' or 'mommy' and it was possible he'd never known her actual name. It didn't trigger any repressed memories either. He still didn't remember the woman.

"This is so difficult." Merry started to cry harder, and the words came out of his mouth before he could stop them.

"It's okay, Mom." Even though he knew it might not be. Clearly, this wasn't really about the difference between a house or an apartment fire—more was coming.

"No, it's not. I have been grateful that she died. I knew it was only because of her death that I had the son I wanted."

"You didn't kill her, Mom." Though the way she was crying caused a small sliver of doubt to push its way into his brain.

"No, but to be grateful for another woman's death is so wrong."

And there he stood, artfully soothing his mother, a woman who was holding onto things she hadn't yet revealed. But he kept his voice low and offered the consolation she needed. The detached part of him wondered if she knew she was requiring a toll from him. He would have to ease her conscience before she would tell him the secrets she'd kept. So he did it. "If something had happened to you, and I was put back into the system, wouldn't you have wanted me to be with someone who was grateful you had died, so that they could raise your kid?"

"I guess so." It seemed his words worked and she was mollified enough to continue her confession. She pushed a photocopied page at him; it held part of an old newspaper article. "This is the story from the fire."

Jason figured he'd read it later, but she sat, expectant. Picking up the page he scanned it.

The Pelias Street apartment complex had caught fire late on a Tuesday evening twenty-six years ago, killing fifteen residents. According to the article, this made it the deadliest single fire in Alabama in over twenty years. The building was not up to code and Jason knew that spelled death-trap. He had been even luckier than he had known all these years.

His mother watched him and handed him another photocopied page where the article continued. All the residents that survived had gotten themselves out of the building before fire trucks arrived, except for two boys.

His heart sank. One of those boys was him.

Several hundred residents in the building and only *two* saves.

The story went on. A firefighter had been severely injured pulling the second boy from the building. Both boys had been treated for smoke inhalation, one suffered from asthma and his lung damage was extensive, he wasn't expected to live through the night.

That hadn't been him. He didn't have asthma.

It wasn't until the end of the article that he caught it: the boys had been brothers.

Chapter 4

Jason

"Are you sure this is *my* fire, Mom? Holy shit."

For once she didn't scold him for his poor language.

"Did Dad know?" He didn't have to add *"about my brother."*

She nodded. "It was only about three weeks after that when we brought you home and started the adoption proceedings. Your brother was dying. His lung damage was too severe. You didn't remember any of it and they told us that was best. That you didn't have a brother now and if you asked we should just say you were an only child."

"What? Really?"

"The ideas were very different then. I've had recent training to counsel the families to find nice ways to be honest. Now we're supposed to tell the kids that their mothers were meth addicts who left them in a trash can. But then . . . then we were told to paint pretty, non-traumatic pictures for you . . . they said you didn't remember, and we shouldn't make a good thing bad."

"He died?"

She nodded, but then spoke. "I never checked."

"What!" He hadn't realized it but he had begun to pace. "Why?"

He had no right to get so mad at her when he hadn't even remembered the brother himself. Obviously, he'd been badly traumatized by the fire. But, still . . .

His mother cried harder. "He was supposed to be dead. And I was afraid. Afraid you'd be upset, belligerent about it if we told you. We couldn't bring your brother home. Your Dad checked. He said . . ."

She stopped.

"What, Mom? What did he say?"

Jason strained to make out her words through the wracking sobs. She grabbed at his hands and looked him in the eyes. "You have to understand, we would have taken him. We would have loved to have more kids."

He nodded. None of that made a difference now. Now he simply needed answers. So he waited her out while she sniffed a few times and became just a little more coherent. "I took what he said to mean your brother was dead, and it was easier to deal with that way. But he said we wouldn't be able to bring him home with us until he was in a box."

Jason felt his head reel. His brother—the one he hadn't known about until tonight—was gone. He sat down hard in one of the chairs.

She nodded at him. "It was easier to believe he was already dead, so I did. Your father made it clear that he wasn't far from it. But I didn't follow up again and if your father did, he never told me."

"So you have no proof that he actually died?"

"No, but you can't believe he lived. Don't go looking for him like that. He was a kid with asthma who had smoke inhalation severe enough to kill a healthy adult."

His eyes narrowed. "Are you trying to keep me from following this? Is there something else you aren't telling me?"

"No!" She was emphatic, looking him in the eyes again.

In his line of work it was important that they be able to spot liars. Knowing who was high and who wasn't, or that what you were facing wasn't just a run-of-the-mill kitchen fire could save a life. Who would have thought it would be just as useful in shaking down his own mother?

Merry spoke again before he could. "I expect you'll follow this through. I know you. And maybe I'll sleep a little better knowing you found everything. But I've seen the foster system's record keeping. Today it's merely horrible. Twenty-five years ago, it was beyond abysmal. It was on paper stored in boxes in basements, and there have been floods and fires and . . . The best you'll find are some documents. You won't even get a grave to visit."

She sighed. "That's what I regret. That your memories of your first family are buried in you somewhere and we didn't even let you say a proper good-bye to the mother and brother that you had."

"I'm still going to look."

"I know. I want you to." She shoved another paper across the smooth surface of the table. "It's pitiful, but it's a start."

With its blue scrolling around the edges and the raised seal in the lower corner, he recognized it for what it was even before he read the title across the top—Duplicate Birth Certificate, Baptist Hospital, Montgomery, Alabama. Jason Mallory.

For a moment he ran his fingers across the page before he read the rest, knowing his life would never be the same.

^   ^   ^   ^   ^

His mother had gone to bed, but once again rest eluded him. Here it was, almost tomorrow and he was still wide awake. So he got up, started with the methodical.

Downstairs, he hopped on his mother's lone computer. A relic from a simpler time, the monitor was deep and beige and vented all down the side. He'd considered upgrading her system for Christmas, but with the loss of Kelly's half of the rent this wasn't the year for it.

On the other side of the wall, Merry Mondy still held to routine. Up with the dawn, she was always dressed and ready to start the day long before it was really ready to start itself. Just like always. Just as though she hadn't dropped a bomb on him last night and left him with nothing but some grainy photocopies and a birth certificate.

The computer chugged—an actual physical noise, a complaint about the work it was doing. The hourglass on the screen wasn't even in the right resolution, her system was so old.

As soon as his screen loaded, he searched.

Chug, chug.

She'd be forced to buy a new system if he broke this one. And breaking it was tempting, the search yielded nothing he could use. No way to find his brother or even himself. He had his first and last names on the birth certificate and only the knowledge that no middle name was filed for him. He knew his birth date, his age, mother's name, hospital, city, state . . . everything. Hell, *he* was the person he was trying to find and still he couldn't find anything.

While the behemoth chugged slower and slower with each task, as if the machine could actually get tired, he called out to his mother. No "good morning," no real greeting. He didn't have it in him. "How did you get this birth certificate?"

It looked worn and aged, as though she'd had it on file for years.

It turned out she had.

"It came with the adoption papers. I know you can write away for them and request copies."

Great. The patience the universe was trying to instill in him continued to evade his efforts to grasp it. Just then the search engine popped up another list from his second request. It gave him the highlighted link to a page that demanded a load of personal information and then merely connected him to another list.

He shook his head and things clicked together. The torturous noises and the smell of coffee sent him on one last search: the nearest coffee house with high-speed Wi-Fi. He could make phone calls without his mother over his shoulder. Get a latte just the way he wanted it. Get out of this house and away for a while.

Ironically, the wired, low-speed internet his mother favored took five minutes to find said high-speed coffee house and he managed to put on his shoes, gather his laptop and tell his mother he was leaving all before he knew where he was headed.

In his car, he punched the address into the GPS and made it to Slow Brew a few minutes later. Taking a few minutes, he scouted out a table. He wanted to be able to make phone calls about his and his brother's birth certificates, and that meant he needed to be away from the low hum and the open ears of the Madison crowd.

Five minutes later, he was up and running, latte in hand and websites popping up quickly. He searched the last name "Mallory," but what little he knew of his original mother was that she was single and had no family to take in the boys. She'd died twenty-six years before, un-wealthy and off the modern-day grid. There was no trace of Alcia Mallory online. His own birth certificate did list her DOB and birth state. So that might be of some help. But the line for his birth father's information simply stated the word *unknown* in each blank.

An hour later he was desperate, tired, and out of options. Birth certificates couldn't be read, found, or even requested online. He called Baptist Hospital where he'd been born and spent thirty minutes on hold getting transferred to records, then sent to the archival holdings office. There he was told he could only get access to his personal birth certificate and that they would be more than happy to email him the form that he could fill out, print and send in with nine dollars to get a duplicate copy. Which he already had. They could not give him his brother's birth certificate nor find his mother's. They could not / would not even tell him even if Alcia Mallory gave birth to any other children at this hospital. And had no idea where else he could look for this brother he seemed to have misplaced.

Jason tried another tack. Or he tried to try.

Searching for "Alabama Child Protective Services" yielded ways to calculate what he should owe in child support based on the number of children and mothers he was paying to. Searching "CPS" at least got him to the place he needed.

Deciding not to waste any more time, he cold-called the Alabama office. There were contact numbers everywhere except the Family Services division. He was sure he had the wrong office, but at least it was in the right location: Montgomery.

So he asked the same questions there, the dregs of his latte growing colder as he waited on hold. This time the man on the other end of the line was at least sympathetic to his plight and ultimately suggested Jason come into the office and file a form requesting information.

Of course, it all came down to the idea that he should just go to Montgomery. What was normally a two-hour drive from Southfield to Montgomery was nearly three and a half hours from Madison. There was no way he could go today and be back for his mother tonight. He needed to be here to show her that, though there were hard feelings, he didn't hate her. That he was trying to be a real man and understand what she had done. Why she had done it.

In his own head though, there was no logic to it.

Why would you keep that kind of information from a kid? When they found him, adopted him, he'd had a brother no more than three months prior—a brother that he didn't even know if he'd seen again after the fire. Jason assumed the brother was removed from the scene via ambulance, as that was standard protocol.

But standard protocol today was so different from then. Though he'd lived in this "different time", he had no adult perspective on it. Maybe it *had* been the culture back then to tell kids what you wanted them to believe, though he certainly wouldn't have expected his mother to lie to him.

The man's voice from CPS broke through Jason's wandering thoughts. Getting the exact address, he typed it into a note document, his head swimming with thoughts and problems. But he thanked the man and assured him he'd find the time for a trip to Montgomery as soon as possible.

With his thoughts still muddled, he returned to the counter where he ordered a sandwich and a refill on his latte. He was back at his seat, sipping the piping hot mix before he realized it didn't really go with roast beef and cheddar.

He was fucked.

His brother was dead. All he wanted to do was find out when and how and be able to close the book on it. Partly for his mother, but mostly to soothe his own churning feelings about a brother he'd completely forgotten.

The man at CPS had thrown some daunting walls in his way.

He had only his own information: driver's license, social security card and—thanks to his mother—birth certificate. He had nothing on his brother, not even a name.

Jason nearly groaned out loud into his hands. He didn't even know if the boy was older or younger. He was so fucked.

Unless he decided to give up.

It was an appealing option and one he began to weigh heavily.

He'd been at this for three hours and all he had to show for it was a catch 22 list of things he needed, each of which he couldn't find without finding a different one first.

He was sitting there in a daze when he heard the voice. "Jase!"

Turning, he saw a smile that he knew but couldn't place.

The voice didn't help either, nor did the words. "Long time, no see. What are you doing here? I heard you were fighting fires in Birmingham."

Dave Hauser. The name came rushing back as did all the stupid shit they'd pulled as teenagers. For a while he managed to forget what he'd been looking for.

PHOENIX

^ ^ ^ ^ ^

The offices of the Child Protective Services department were housed in one of the big gray buildings in downtown Montgomery. He badly wanted to disregard the whole thing. No searching for dead brothers. No need to find out what had happened. Just wait it out until the itch finally faded. Sadly, it didn't work that way.

The itch got worse. But he had no clue where to start. He didn't remember this brother at all.

Staying in his bed, late into the morning, Jason had repeated all those things to himself and still been completely unable to shake the need to search, to start, to do something. No matter how casual it sounded, no matter that he didn't remember, he had a brother. Or he'd had one.

Having lost his father, and gone through what was required to get himself together after that, Jason knew he had more to do. And he wasn't stupid. What seven-year-old kid can't remember his own brother? Even a brother you hated, you would remember. So the only thing he could imagine was that it had been pretty bad—whatever it was that had shut out that part of his life. He had no mental images of his birth mother or the brother. And that was wrong. It had been wrong of his mother and father, and all the social workers involved, to think he should go on with a spanking new life without any of those old memories.

Still, there was every possibility that he was opening the doors to a class five shit-storm. Who knew if his brother had saved his life, and died in the fire to do so? His brother may have been no more than a toddler—Jason figured he was at least that old since the article didn't list the hurt boy as an infant. It was possible his birth mother was a down-on-her-luck princess just trying to get by and keep her kids together. Or she may have been an abusive alcoholic or trying to sell the kids for crack. None of it rang a bell.

So searching for answers wasn't in any way guaranteed to be a good thing. And it wasn't like he didn't have a lot else on his plate these days.

His apartment still had a strange vibe to it. It just wasn't quite right—almost like walking into your place after you'd been gone a week and left the heat off. Only it happened every time he walked in. His dreams still harbored things he couldn't explain; they no longer scared him but nonetheless kept him from being really rested. And standing here outside the big Montgomery city building and readying to go in and find out what was behind door number three was another good excuse for the churn in his stomach.

Pushing through the heavy door, he walked from the relatively warm day into the cold, colorless smack of industrial government. A security guard made eye contact with him and nodded. It was a trick Jason knew from training—people who made eye contact were less likely to rob the place or hurt someone. Did that mean the guard found him suspicious, or was the middle-aged woman in line behind him getting the same treatment?

He didn't ask, just put his things into the bin he was handed and passed through the metal detector before putting his pockets back together and shaking the vague sensation of being violated.

Jason headed for where he thought the CPS office would be, keeping a tight hold of the manila envelope where he had stashed the papers his mother had given him. Ten minutes later, he was hopelessly lost. Though the suite number started with 12, it wasn't on the twelfth floor. That floor was a maze of other suites—including a DMV ticket office and an anger management class, which he was afraid he'd have to visit if he spent much more time in here.

After prowling the whole floor and returning to the ground-level entrance to check the listings—where he didn't find his office posted at all—Jason gave up and asked the guard for help.

Apparently, they were protective of Child Protective Services. The place he wanted was just down the hall, then down two floors to a basement walkway to another building, then up to the second floor there. He was surprised he got in without a personality inventory and lie detector test. But when he opened the heavy door, he saw that the people already in the waiting room didn't look much different from the homeless people camped just outside the building. In his clean jeans and snarky T-shirt he looked as out of place as if he'd been in a suit and tie.

Sitting in a sturdy steel chair with his paper number clenched in his fist, he listened in to the conversations at the desk. One bedraggled woman waited ten minutes to get called to the window to hand in the results of a drug test. Though the place was bleary, the girl behind the counter said brightly, "Theresa, three more and you can appeal to get your kids back. I'm really proud of you."

Several others dragged themselves out of the chairs and to the counter in turn before an angry man barged in and demanded to be given his visitation rights back. Even Jason knew it was stupid to think the older woman who was working that window would have any control over that. The inexplicably cheerful younger girl left her post and came up to stand behind the first woman, who told the man in no uncertain terms that he was not allowed to see his kids anymore, supervised or not. Two other employees were moving from the back of the office to lend any needed support and Jason was already on his feet as the man began the lunge across the desk.

Luckily, the idiot had pulled his right hand back for a bully-style haymaker and Jason caught it. "Sir, you might want to re-think that if you want to see your kids again."

For his trouble, he was yelled at. "I don't need some prick like you telling me I can't see my kids!!"

The man's eyes were bloodshot, his lips cracked and his face red and he looked like he was on the bad side of a three-year bender. But he glared at them all before turning and leaving as angry as he'd been when he came in.

The older gentleman behind the counter gave Jason a hard look. "You shouldn't have gotten involved in that. We had it under control."

Like hell you did burned a quick path through his brain, and was rapidly followed with the clear knowledge that he didn't belong here. There was no way the four feeble employees behind the waist-high counter could have taken on that half-crazed asshole. And the concerned looks on the faces of the two women at the counter agreed with Jason's assessment.

But he shouldn't have stepped up—because he shouldn't have been here in the first place. This is what his mother and father had saved him from. He didn't have to be here. He didn't have a history like this, didn't have a father who beat him or a mother's boyfriend who drank and yelled at people. He had a warm home and lots of support.

He was shaking his head as he turned to leave. The whole thing was a stupid waste of time. But the voice caught him. "Thank you."

The inexplicably cheerful girl was blonde and rounded, with a sweet smile that didn't seem affected by the gray, industrial atmosphere or the dead-behind-the-eyes people she worked with. "What can I help you with? You must have come here for something."

And wasn't that the truth? No one would come here without good cause.

Once more acknowledging the pull that he'd been feeling, he went to the desk and gave his all to the crapshoot. "I'm looking for my missing brother."

Her eyebrows shot up. "We don't deal in missing persons, unless it's one of our kids in state custody."

"That's just it. He *was* in state custody—about twenty-seven years ago." And he waited while she processed it. He figured that would be the end of it. Game over. He'd done what he could.

But she asked, "What else do you know?"

"Not much."

A soft laugh came out of her along with a smile completely out of place in this hellhole. "I have a lunch break I'm already late for. You helped me; I'll help you."

"Okay." It was all he could think of to say. He'd already eaten lunch, but he'd driven all this way and it seemed that he wouldn't be giving up today.

A mere five minutes later they were sitting at a metal table in the courtyard. The traffic out here was a mix of cops, lawyers, judges, the upward and the downward. They ate artisan sandwiches from an upscale food trailer and tried to ignore the wind. Well, she ate. He picked at his food, having gotten it only to keep from making her uncomfortable.

Quick introductions revealed that she was Aida Jones, a graduate of the foster care system now holding a master's in social work and valiantly fighting for the underserved. He thought she should come play "golden boy" for the SFD; she made him look like a self-serving slacker.

Despite her being a total stranger, he told her everything. Again, he was struck by the feeling that it wasn't personal information he told—just facts that didn't have much to do with him. It felt the same as if he were looking for a part for his computer.

Her sandwich had disappeared as she nodded and took notes. She'd carefully copied information from his birth certificate—his name, his mother's, birth dates, and locations. "When were you in the system?"

"Twenty-seven years ago. Probably only for a few weeks." He slipped the birth certificate back into the envelope, hoping to remove it from range of the ranch dressing dripping off her sandwich. He switched it out for the paper copy his mother had made of the article. "This is the fire where my birth mother died. This article is really all I know."

She scanned it, and he felt the need to fill the empty air. "It would have helped if they'd put his name in the article."

Aida's smile was genuine if a bit sad. "It's illegal. They can't reveal the names of minors. And this search of yours is going to be difficult. The courthouse has been destroyed twice since you and your brother were wards of the state. Katrina did some real damage here, and in '96 we had an F2 tornado come through that took out an old archival records building."

"Shit." Though it was under his breath, Jason still apologized for it.

"No worries." She even smiled at him. "Here's what I can do: I'll see if I can get a name for you. But I'll want to run a full background check on you first. I'll need driver's license, social security, copies of all this."

This, at least, he was prepared for. "That's not a problem. I'm not sure why you're so concerned about me finding a document for a dead person, but it's fine."

Her head tipped. "You weren't in the system long enough to understand the security. One of our employees helped a woman find her missing sister's kids. But the woman wasn't the sister. She was the girlfriend of the birth father of the kids. He used the information to shoot the foster family and kidnap the kids."

Well, crap. No, he clearly hadn't been in the system very long at all. That hadn't even occurred to him. "I'll get you anything you need. I am who I say I am. I'll even pay for a full background check."

Though the moment those words left his mouth he wished he could pull them back. It was stupid to offer to pay for anything. He'd be barely eeking by on his rent. He could pay for things later, next spring. And having a legitimate excuse to put off this needle-in-a-haystack search wouldn't hurt him any. But she refused him, saying it was a conflict of interest, and she'd do the search herself on her system at work.

With that, she stood and announced she should get back to work. Deftly, she gathered her trash and eyed his as he threw out most of the sandwich, uneaten. But as he started to thank her and go, she insisted that he follow her back upstairs so she could copy all his info.

Like a lost dog, he did—back through the maze of corridors, each one bleaker than the one before. He stood at the counter while she disappeared into the office with the envelope that contained all he knew about his brother. Jason was surprised to find he felt the loss of it, a fear of the information being out of his reach.

But Aida gave it back with a smile and a card with all her contact information on it, including her cell phone number which she'd hand-written on the back. It seemed a bit much in exchange for stopping an idiot who was probably too drunk to hit with any force. But he didn't look gift horses in the mouth.

Jason thanked her and finally left the building, ready to fetch his car and begin the drive toward home. He still had to put in two hours at the Thurlow rebuild. The Chief had all of SFD on a rotation there and today was his day. He couldn't be late.

But even with the weight of time starting to bear down on him, just outside the office he stopped and gave in to the need to open the manila envelope and check to see that it was all still there.

^ ^ ^ ^ ^

The Thurlow house had been the usual hive of activity, the late afternoon weather perfect for stripping shirts and swinging hammers. But the SFD had been given strict instructions not to strip shirts. So Jason had held the fabric away from his skin as much as possible to let his torso cool a little.

Jesus, playing golden boy sucked.

He spotted Jack Standard across the way doing the same thing, though other men on the build were naked to the waist. Chief had made it clear that they were to have the official T-shirt on at all times. If they stripped, they lost advertising for what wonderful people they were. Calculated, yes—but the Chief was right, they needed it. Jason also figured they didn't need the negative publicity that would come from everyone seeing Standard's gut.

PHOENIX

The Thurlows were always on the site. Mrs. Thurlow manned a grill while the kids ran hot dogs, burgers, and drinks out to the guys.

Jason was enjoying a short break on the edge of what would be the new front porch when a pair of leather, high-heeled boots planted in front of him. They were out of place in the sooty yard, and they squared up, toes pointed straight at his. So he did the only logical thing and followed the long thin legs in impossibly tight jeans up to a clingy shirt that showcased a great set of tits. He considered stopping there, because he recognized that necklace. In fact, he knew exactly what it cost and he was hard pressed not to ask for it back.

"Hello, Kelly."

"Jason." Her hip jutted out and she held out a can of Dr. Pepper.

He debated taking it then figured it was sealed so there wasn't much she could have done to it. But he didn't open it right away. Giving the can a hard shake was too easy and not beneath her. "Thank you."

The words galled him, but he said them anyway, hoping she would leave.

She didn't. "Did you miss me?"

Holy shit.

As if her leaving the way she had didn't make it undeniably clear that he had no comprehension of the female of the species, the fact that she would even ask him that let him know he was far worse off than even he'd known. What was he supposed to say here?

So he shrugged and let Kelly fill that in to mean whatever she wanted it to.

"I needed to get your attention."

No shit, Sherlock. "Well, you got it, and then you lost it again. What do you want?"

He made the mistake of looking up at her face. A small, half-grin pulled at the corner of her mouth. He used to think it was sexy, until he saw past the surface and realized it was actually pretty psycho.

"I could come back if you wanted me to."

At least that he knew how to respond to. "I don't." And he aimed the top of the can in her direction before he opened it.

Sadly, it did not explode everywhere.

The younger Thurlow boy chose that moment to come up to them. "Hi."

"Hi." Jason smiled back at him and thought *good timing, kid.* He'd learned early to respond to kids only as they spoke to him—which usually meant short sentences, low-level topics and answering only what was asked. The few times he'd tried to have a real conversation with a child it had gone badly. So he waited for Henry Thurlow, three-year-old, to make the next move.

Henry did. "You're my fireman."

"I am?" *Did firemen belong to people?*

"You saved me." Henry smiled and held out a can of Dr. Pepper, apparently not seeing the one Jason already held.

Jason grinned and tried to be subtle about slipping the other can aside. "Thank you. Did you know that I carried you, but Ms. Wanstall actually saved you?"

He nodded, a short, sharp burst of movement of his head, then smiled again, small teeth with even gaps showing in his chubby face. "Missy finded us."

"Yes, she did. We were all stuck in the fire and Missy got us out."

Henry pulled back and looked at him sideways. Frowning harder, he stepped back, directly into his six-year-old brother, Ben. Wrapping his arms around the younger one, Ben looked at Jason. "He still has nightmares about being trapped. We just say that Missy found us."

Oh, good. He'd shut down another conversation with a kid. The only sentence he'd uttered and he'd reminded the kid that he nearly died in a house fire. *Way to go, Mondy.* But he looked at Ben and tried once more. "How about you?"

"I'm okay."

With a sigh that she had to wait or that she wasn't the center of attention—Jason couldn't tell—Kelly picked up his discarded Dr. Pepper and took a drink. Then she spoke right over the kid's next words. "You need me, Jason. Even if it's just to pay the rent."

Then she set the can back down and walked away, hips ticking like a metronome. Jason had to wonder if the next girlfriend would be any better. Kelly wasn't the first woman to walk out on him, just the most recent and most dramatic.

Southfield Fire Station #2

Shift	A	
	O'Casey	Captain
Engine 2	Standard	Engineer
	Mondy	FF2 / EMT
	Grimsby	FF1
Rescue 5	Wanstall	FF3
	West	FF2
	Merriman	FF1

Chapter 5

In his usual spot at the dining table before his day began, Jason waited while C-Shift wound down. Bruce Connelly and Alex Weingarten both walked by as they finished up their duties to head home. To his surprise, he watched as engineer Lex Maynard came by afterward.

Maynard's eyes followed the two men in front of him and his brain followed its usual track. Connelly was sticking close to the queer, making sure his little friend didn't get any crap for being less-than. Maynard sighed; it wasn't that Weingarten or Wanstall failed at the job . . . they just couldn't do it as well. They needed real men in this place. Take Johnny Forman, he was young but he was learning. Unlike Wanstall, he still had musculature to develop—and the kid had walked in with a nice set of mechanical skills that went hand-in-hand with his redneck accent but were incredibly useful.

Since being hired, Forman had proved useful by patching the trucks numerous times and even fixed the old 1970s two-way radios that remained in dispatch long after the job of fielding incoming 911s had been centralized to the police station. The old dispatch office was reduced to a space for filing forms and gazing out the window. Which, honestly, was where Maynard would have found the most use for Wanstall or Weingarten.

He knew when he was Captain he could make certain he didn't have any "girls" on his shift. And when he made Chief, he could get them and their accompanying rules and regs out of the house.

He burned a minute and spoke to Mondy. *"Birmingham News?* Anything good?"

The local paper was always around, but Maynard never read it. Nothing happened in Southfield, and the news channels always made things red, white and blue.

Mondy held up the page he had been looking at. "Oh, just an ongoing series on the state of firefighting in Alabama. Apparently it started with the article that guy did on me." He flipped through a few pages of the paper. "Jernigan. He was the only decent interview I did."

Regardless of Jason's last statement, the article could be concerning. "What does it say?"

Mondy flipped through it, pointing out a few spots. "It says we're underpaid and underfunded in general. All true. No real spin on it one way or another."

That was good.

Mondy continued. "It does comment that the money in the stations clearly goes to equipment and upkeep of the firefighting gear—he comments on the cheapness and age of the kitchen and says Southfield is indicative of the state of the other stations he'd been in. Though he adds that our trucks are in better shape and we have more up-to-date equipment than Birmingham—which is clearly poorer than us."

Maynard snorted. "That's hard to believe."

"Tell me about it." Mondy flipped to where the article continued. "It says that the Birmingham stations are much more homogenous, and that Southfield again stands out for having a more representative mix from the community. He cites two African American firefighters, one female and at least one openly gay male."

And that was a problem. Maynard didn't have an issue with color, he wasn't a bigot. As long as a man was useful and did his job well, all were welcome, but idolizing the "girls" was bad. And this journalist was putting a spin on that.

But it was nearly time for the official shift change, and Maynard was finishing a double and ready to get out. He'd had precious little sleep during the last forty-eight. His wife would have a big breakfast waiting when he got home. His girlfriend had stopped by for a quickie in the back room last night and life was good.

Out in the truck bay, he took a spot in a rocking chair and was happy that, unless a four-alarm went off, he was done.

A-Shift came in, the six of them lining up in front of the near wall and standing at attention. No pre-ordained order to the line, but otherwise neat as a pin. Chief Adler walked back and forth with his clip board, inspecting his men and looking at his watch every few seconds. They all knew what he was looking for.

The lineup board on the wall had already been changed to reflect the new day. And Chief methodically handed out assignments to A-Shift members, but none of them moved. None would, until they were dismissed to get started.

Minutes ticked by. Though C-Shift was finished, they all waited.

"Chief?" It was Maynard who spoke up. He hated a useless man.

Adler nodded at him and he continued. "According to my watch, it's five after eight."

Several voices chimed in after him in agreement—Weingarten, Connelly, and Bender. No one from A-Shift said a word.

With a sigh, because he would carry the burden of this, Adler nodded. "It is. It's officially five after."

It was Grimsby who broke rank, running to the back bay doors and scanning the parking lot. He trotted back to the lineup and shook his head.

No one started it, but a chorus of under-the-breath "yay"s and even a "thank you, baby Jesus" came clear.

It was Wanstall who asked, "Is it official, sir?"

"Yes, ma'am it is." Then Chief turned and asked C-Shift, "Who can stay?"

Connelly's hand went up. A single guy with a house full of roommates, he was ready to go again, ready to pick up the overtime others left lying around.

Adler turned to the board and grabbed Connelly's tag, using it to replace Merriman. He had just put the offensive tag into his back pocket when the rookie came in, red-faced from the short run from his parking spot. "I'm here, Chief."

Adler looked grim. "Not in time, son. Follow me into my office."

Geoff Merriman followed Chief Adler, plagued by an air of dread. His head hung; he knew he'd screwed up. He'd be suspended again for sure.

So he was shocked when Chief Adler sat him down and said point blank, "We're letting you go."

He blinked a few times. "You're *firing* me?"

"Yes, son. You are at your fourth suspension in less than that many weeks. It's not even a five-day job, Geoff. You can't do that."

"I do good work. I'm trained." Merriman was obviously starting to fray at the seams, and frankly Adler was glad the door was closed. "You can't fire me for a little tardiness. None of that was my fault."

He leaned forward. "The truth is: this fire district is privately run, no union. That means three suspensions, especially in such a short period of time, will get you let go. Secondly, to appeal, you'll need letters and statements from your fellow officers. I don't think you'll get them."

"What?!" Merriman leaned forward in his own seat, but for an entirely different reason. "They will. They like me."

"It has nothing to do with 'like'." And, no, they didn't like Merriman.

Geoff Merriman stood now. "You can't fire me just for being late!"

Right then the bell went off, and the Chief stood up and sighed, leaving Merriman waiting in his guest seat. He took the call—EMS, teenage girl fainted at a slumber party, possible seizures—and sent Rescue 5 out after it. He subbed Mondy out for Wanstall. Mondy was EMT ranked, necessary for this emergency run that had nothing to do with a fire and had nothing they could bill for.

It was nine minutes later that he came back into his office only to find that the newest reject from the Southfield Fire Department had been stewing the whole time. "I'm highly trained. You can't fire me."

Okay, game over. He'd tried. Adler had wanted Merriman to have a come-to-Jesus moment, but nothing was going to make the kid understand what he'd done and what he hadn't. "I can, and I just did. You have fifteen minutes to clear your things."

"I'm appealing this."

"You're welcome to try, son." It would never go through.

Merriman didn't move from his spot. "I'll get you fired for this."

PHOENIX

Useless threats from a fireman who was neither good in a fire nor good at being a man. Adler stood stoic. Now he had to wait until the kid got the hint and left. Then he'd have to wait some more and see what kind of shit blew back from this. Because some would.

If Merriman found out what was coming, he just might have some kind of foothold for a real appeal. It could stink up some of the golden buff he, the Chief of Police and the Mayor had been working so hard for.

And, their time frame had just bumped up. By about three weeks.

He waited as patiently as he could—Merriman was too slow at this, too. The Great Grape took twenty minutes to clean his locker and try to catch any of his fellow firefighters to see if they'd back his appeal.

The men dodged. It was Wanstall who didn't take that shit. When Merriman caught her eye and told her what a good friend she was, she answered point blank, "We aren't friends. We are co-workers in a very dangerous job. Though we don't agree on a lot of things, I trust any of these men in a burning building. But not you. I won't help you appeal." Her only concession to him was the mildly softening, "I'm sorry."

Chief Adler watched as the kid shoved his few things into his battered old car and peeled out of the lot. Then he turned and closed his office door and privately conference called the city leaders to tell them that it was time to put things in motion.

∧   ∧   ∧   ∧   ∧

It was nearly a full week later that Jason sat at the long laminate table in the dining room with the *Birmingham News* and a notepad.

A small article on the state of fire fighting in Alabama was positioned in front of him, and beside him was a copy of the *Southfield Press* with a big picture of the crews fixing up the Thurlow home. There was a second picture of just him, big as day, splashed across the front page. The only good thing he could say about it was that his Oakleys were on, so you couldn't see his eyes. To his own view, his smile looked entirely forced, but maybe that was because he knew it was. He hoped no one else noticed. A fake golden boy wasn't very golden.

Alex Weingarten came up and sat beside him, "Hey, pretty boy."

The sound burst out of Jason's mouth. *"You're* calling *me* that?"

Alex pushed his honey-blond hair back, though he didn't need to—it stayed perfectly in place all by itself. His grin was white and straight, his blue eyes piercing and his face almost too perfect. "I know. Why am I not on the front page?"

Then he answered himself. "Oh yeah, because I'm not girl bait. And I'm not the hero of boys and kittens everywhere."

Jason grumbled. "Puppies. It was a puppy. Screw you, Weingarten."

"You're not my type." Alex smiled.

Fuck it. Jason sat for a moment. Alex's smile went to his eyes. And it didn't take a genius to know it was because of Leo. Alex had it rough – he was a gay man for starters, so his dating pool was smaller. He was a gay man in Alabama, so shrink that again. He was in a man's man type of job, *way to bring on the pain* . . . and yet he had everything.

Jason had none of those barriers. So why had Kelly cleared out without even a warning? And why was he in a bad mood about everything?

So he did the one thing he could think of. "Alex, tell me what you would do . . ."

Luckily, Weingarten didn't start in about hair gel and tooth whitener. "What?"

"You know I'm adopted, right?"

"Nope. Didn't."

And that's why everyone loved Alex. Through all the "being himself" and being openly gay, the man was a straight shooter.

"So, my birth mother died in a fire when I was seven, and that's how I got to my new family. I don't remember any of it. I have no memories of my birth mother and apparently the memories I do have are partly false. Then, a week ago, my mother breaks down and tells me that I had a brother who died in the fire. So what do I do?"

"Oh shit. That was a bushel in a basket." Alex pushed his hand through his hair again, but this time he was thinking. "You mad at your mother? Your adoptive mother?"

"Not really. I mean, yes, I wish she'd told me. But something's nagging me."

"What's that?"

Jason sighed and Alex unconsciously mimicked his stance, waiting. "She knew I had this brother all along."

"And *you* didn't?"

"Nope. No memories of him whatsoever. I don't even know if he's older or younger."

That was tough, and Alex didn't know where to go with it. He knew what to do with people not breathing and when things were on fire. He knew what to do with Leo and what topics to avoid with his own father. He'd worked hard for that balance. But this was in left field. "Does your mother know? Can you find out?"

"She didn't say. My mom and dad supposedly knew about him, but only that he had bad asthma and severe smoke inhalation. Which is why they didn't adopt him, too."

"So they didn't take him because he was *damaged*?" Alex was a bit taken aback by that. He and Leo had been looking into adoption . . . There were too many throw-back kids out there.

"No. They said they couldn't – he was basically dead." Jason spilled it all out. About the article, about the birth certificate. And the trip to Montgomery to start the grueling paperwork that would yield nothing.

Adler walked through the main room then. It was nearly time for the big meeting he'd called. All three shifts were in house for it, and so were the guys in the other two houses. This was the big change, why they'd had to work for the golden-boy image, and why Jason couldn't take time to focus on what was bothering him.

"Okay. I need everyone!" Adler's voice reverberated off the painted cinderblock and his eyes did a quick sketch to the side to look at the bell. If the damn bell went off now this would suck worse than it was already going to. He started counting heads.

Jason did, too. While he had been picking Alex's brain, the room had filled up. Connelly was now sitting on the other side of him, and he had no idea what his friend had overheard. Grimsby and Maynard didn't have seats and were leaning on the few open spaces along the wall. The TV took that moment to blink out, the remote in some unseen hand. Everyone was here, except the now permanently absent Merriman.

Adler looked around one last time, he knew this was going to blow. But he knew if he didn't get started, one of the other stations would finish first, and then his guys' cells would start ringing, so he opened his mouth and started to talk. "There are going to be a lot of questions. So let me get through what I can and then I'll answer what I know."

He glanced quickly at all the wary but nodding heads. The fan was spinning and the shit was on its way. There was a rough six months coming.

He started again. "You all know that we are a privately contracted fire department hired by the City of Southfield. Which has its benefits—"

"Merriman!" Came out as a cough to his left, and a few chuckles followed, but a dirty look put it all away.

"And detriments. One of which is that we are first responders by contract on nearly every EMS call. We hand those patients to the ambulance for transport and we can't bill for any of it. That affects your work-for-pay-rate. Delta Cross—our private owner— put in a bid to get the EMS contract for the city. We won it. In a few months, Gold Standard will no longer operate in the City of Southfield and we will become Southfield Fire and Rescue."

Voices started piling up on each other.

"We don't have the man power."

"Will we get new trucks?"

"Where the fuck will it all go?"

So Chief waited, raised his hands, palm out and let it all roll off. He tried not to listen to the questions yet. Once it was quiet, he dropped the bomb.

"Your jobs can be safe."

It started again.

"*Can* be!?"

"What the fuck, Chief?"

Adler did what he did best: exerted whatever calming force he could and waited. But it was like getting a word out in the middle of a flock of geese. "There will be a greater number of positions available, but there will also be a greater need for EMTs and paramedics. If you all don't train up, some of you will lose your jobs to new-hire firefighters with EMS training."

This time the crowd stayed silent. To a man they were assessing their spots, wondering if they would be one of the ones to go. "The city *can* keep all of you, but you all pretty much have to work together for that to happen."

He avoided looking at them as heads swiveled and they all checked each other out—would they be a team or not? He picked up his clipboard. It was the typical rock and hard place. He couldn't have sent his men out to get training until they got the contract approved.

"Here's the math." Adler's voice drew their attention to him again. "We have five with EMS training. We need fifteen. We have four open shift spots, which we will not necessarily be waiting to fill. Follow me."

And they did. Like willing puppies or lambs to the slaughter, none of them were sure.

He led his men into the training room, where he had a whiteboard that he'd drawn up in his hideous scrawl just before coming in here. Faster than ever before, they took orderly seats at the desks and the extras positioned themselves around the periphery, all mouths quiet for once and twenty pairs of eyes focused on his red-marker chart. No one could actually read it— he'd almost been sick while writing it, he hated the thought of letting any of his men go—but they could follow the idea of it.

The questions became more orderly, hands were raised. Adler had pulled the magnets from the front assignment board and started sticking them to the board around the sketch he had done. He put Maxwell in the guaranteed job of Paramedic and wrote in a new name—Ryan Donlan / Engineer-Paramedic. He explained that he'd already hired the man and that would help lift some of the pressure off the remaining guys. He didn't tell them that Donlan was old school Irish from Boston with a thick accent and a hard line. They'd find that out soon enough. They couldn't be picky, they needed Donlan. They'd find that out soon enough, too.

That left four open Paramedic spots . . . where he bumped Mondy, Weingarten, Railles, and Baxter. He looked each of those four in the eyes for a second. "You guys have the power to help save the house."

They waited. "You can sit where you are and take the EMT spots. Delta Cross believes in seniority and works to keep employees whenever possible. And we'll hire in more Paramedics and Advanced EMTs." He turned his attention then to the others. "If that happens there will be no more EMT positions still open to train into, some of you non-EMS-trained guys won't have jobs in four-to-six months. If all the EMTs train up to Paramedic, then some of you can train up to EMT and we should be able to get a stay of execution if you are on your way to Advanced EMT, then we may be able to save everyone."

The four EMTs looked back and forth at each other and Adler spoke again before they could. "There's a class coming up. You all have pre-paid training spots in it, courtesy of Delta, if you wish. It will get you certified in time."

Adler pulled the other magnetic names from the pile and put them on the board one at a time. He piled them down near the bottom, crowding them around the open spaces—where there were more names than positions—and well below where the open EMS spots were listed. Saving everyone only worked if everything went according to his master plan.

At Station House #1 he was using this as leverage to remove two firefighters he didn't want on crew. And there was a huge possibility of some round-robin bumps: guys coming from Stations #1 and #3 and others moving from here to there, to help even out the numbers. He'd just gotten that possibility out of his mouth when he heard the phone ring at the front of the building.

Shit.

He saw his own thoughts repeated on each face as he turned to get the phone. Just then, the printer started to chug. Central dispatch had them ready to roll. He listened to the info and yelled down the hall—for once no one had followed him in here to see what the call was for. "A-Shift, ready to roll. Flames on the west side, need Engine and Rescue. Suit up!"

Shit. They had spent morning rounds on the coming shit-storm. They hadn't cleaned up; they were on C-Shift's backup air tanks and yesterday's safety checks. He watched as they poured into the bay, pushed legs into puffy dull yellow pants and dark gray boots, pulled the wide suspenders over their shoulders.

C-Shift came out to run a few checks as A readied to load in, and B—bless them—handed out the back-up tanks and started running checks on the non-use trucks.

They'd gotten an assload dumped on them this morning. And it had been after his men had worked for free for the Thurlow fund-raisers, bought teddy bears and toys from their own underpaid pockets for the kids. And most had come, hammer-in-hand to help with the rebuild of the house they saved from fire, but finished off with water and foam. Wanstall, O'Casey, Weingarten and Mondy had all done extra interviews for the Birmingham paper and anywhere else they had managed to get a little extra positive press. They had put on their golden faces and gotten the possibility of lost jobs in return.

The Chief stood back; he was going out on this run, too. They would all be leaving, doors slamming, horns honking, in under a minute—ready or not. He hadn't gotten to tell them yet that there would be money for some to get trained up. That there wouldn't be a loss out of pocket. For those who made the cut, there would be raises, and those could be substantial if a rank level increased.

But the bell had come. And when the bell went off, nothing else was as important.

A girl at Delphi Coffee across the street straightened and waved at the trucks as they did a gravity-defying bounce out of the drive. She didn't understand what they were headed to and she smiled.

As they pulled away from the station house, Alex Weingarten turned to Jason. "So, your mother said your father checked on the brother and said he was dying?"

"Something like that." Mondy didn't think anything of it. His head was in the game, his eyes scanning the side roads with Grimsby, keeping a look out for traffic and stupid people.

"Well then, it sounds like you're going to be busy. You and I have Paramedic rankings to get in record time and you need to find out about your brother."

Mondy shrugged. "I'm not sure it's worth the time. Especially not now with all this."

Weingarten changed tacks again. "Did you know about this? About the EMS stuff?"

"No. Only that something was coming. No clue what though."

"You have to go to find your brother." There were too many things going on, Alex didn't even try for a segue.

"He's dead." Mondy watched as people pulled patiently to a stop at the insistent blare of the horn, or jerked to a dead stop—shocked that a fire truck was right in front of them. "He already had asthma and he suffered severe smoke inhalation. You don't survive that."

Weingarten muttered a curse under his breath as he laid on the brakes and horns at an old man trying to cross the street in front of them. "But from what your mom says, it sounds like he was still alive three months after the fire."

Chapter 6

Jason

Two days ago, Chief had pulled him in to the office for a discussion—in fact, Jason suspected that Adler had a serious heart-to-heart with each of them. He already knew that Alex's conversation had gone much the same way his had. That the EMT licensing he had afforded him a guaranteed spot on the new team, but if he advanced his status he could get higher pay, climb the ranks and save the jobs of some of his fellow firefighters.

So, no pressure there.

Chief had leaned back and begun counting off what they needed, "Two Paramedics, an EMT and an Advanced on *each* shift—"

"Holy fuck, Chief. That's all of us. So the EMTs all have jobs and the rest are S.O.L.?"

Adler had ground his teeth just a little, having probably explained this several times already. "Of course not. Not if everything goes according to plan. I'm trying to keep all of you. Inside probably four months, Gold Standard EMS will close its doors. We will be purchasing fully equipped EMS vehicles, to have two per station, for medical runs. We'll be adding a full position to each shift, so we'll be running three vehicles—a rescue, an EMS and an engine, with a two, two, three set-up plus a captain."

The Chief had waited a beat and Jason back-calculated the timing. This was why the Golden Boy campaign had begun. They were taking a spate of EMS jobs away and killing a local job source. Not that the EMS stayed busy. They'd been downsizing recently due to the fact that the FD was truly the first responder in the area. Then his thoughts darted from the generic to the specific: he could get certified as Paramedic Three in the next few months. He could do it.

His brain still churned from the thought.

At least he didn't doubt his ability to pass the class. Railles was a wild card in that respect—he had an innate ability to size up a situation and nearly psychically diagnose what a patient needed, but he struggled with the material.

Now, in a nearly identical outfit to the one he always wore off duty—jeans and an SFD T-shirt—Jason headed to Jefferson State Community College for his class. It had been a while since he had been in a classroom; that alone would explain the odd gnawing in his gut. He was just walking through the front door when a hand clamped around his arm and spun him.

Hopped up on a long, stressful day and an unreasonable amount of caffeine and sugar, Jason swung.

Luckily, Alex had anticipated it and ducked. "Look, I'm trying to stop you from making a mistake."

"The mistake of being on time?" There were just a few minutes left, he didn't want to be late the first day.

"You're wearing an SFD shirt. You don't go in like that."

"Why not? Am I on the skins team?"

Alex was dragging him back out to the parking lot and ruining the fact that he had made it with enough time to spare that he didn't have to worry about being late. Now he was going to worry.

"No, but you are *not* on the SFD team. Not tonight." He was unlocking his own car door, a small green Jetta that screamed 'Alex' in ways that nothing else could have. "This class is likely taught by a former EMT, our classmates will be EMTs, and we are here to take EMT jobs. Peel."

Shit. Could he do nothing right the first time today?

Still, he didn't just strip down in the lot at the Community College until he saw Alex pull a short-sleeved button-down from the several that he had on hangers in the back seat of the car. It took two seconds, though, to see the light, and Jason yanked his SFD shirt over his head, tossing it into Alex's car just to get back at him for being right.

As he buttoned up, Alex commented. "Hey, I don't want the wrath of the teacher. I suspect they'll already know who we are and why we're there. But I won't be the one to advertise it to the whole class. Chances are this is going to be a bitch for us."

Jason buttoned the shirt and realized he hadn't even thought that far ahead. In fact, he could have walked into an ambush tonight and never seen it coming if not for Alex. He wanted to tell his friend thank you, but all he could say was, "I look gay."

"Yes. That means you look nice, so man up. It just doesn't look like your usual craptastic-wear."

"I just don't want to look like I—"

"I'm sorry. Were you really considering trolling for ass in your *career advancement class* that the whole house is depending on you for?"

He pushed Jason between the shoulder blades, directing him and his borrowed button-down toward the front door. "Yeah, I didn't think so. So wear your gay shirt with pride."

In the end, Jason realized Alex was right. The teacher was an older woman with a short cap of tight gray curls. She wore an old EMS embroidered polo, but the pants and shoes looked just like she'd stepped out of an ambulance. And on each sleeve was a 'paramedic' patch. Not just one sleeve, but both. This one was EMS coming and going. She gave them dirty looks throughout the class and called on them whenever she thought they weren't paying attention.

Alex managed to smile each time, as though this was a game. But Jason simply answered the questions and tried not to argue when she told him that a field maneuver they had performed wouldn't work. He wanted to say "Let me call that guy and tell him that he's dead then. I'm sure he'll be interested in hearing that." But he didn't. It was probably the three Dr. Peppers in his system. He kept telling himself that.

The three-hour evening class was awarded no reprieve for it being the first session. And the whole class spent the evening being mildly scolded for not reading the whole first chapter between when she mentioned the book they would be using and when she started asking questions about it thirty seconds later.

So Jason was dead on his feet when he opened his apartment door, the sugar and caffeine long since having left his system bottoming out of a full-scale crash.

That was probably why he didn't see her at first. Why he nearly jumped out of his skin when she said, "Hey, baby."

PHOENIX

∧   ∧   ∧   ∧   ∧

Jason woke thankfully alone and startled that he'd actually drifted off. He vaulted from the bed, stopping only to brush his teeth thoroughly before stripping and walking into the shower before it was fully hot.

Jason dried and tried to dress in something that didn't identify him as SFD—a task that was surprising in its limitations. Even many of the plainer shirts that he owned were Ts or jerseys with the logo or prints from some SFD event or other. He stared into his half empty closet and frowned. Did this mean he had no life? Unlike most on a regular nine-to-five he didn't work five days a week but only two or three. So logically he should have more street clothes than the average person . . . not less.

Pulling an unmarked long-sleeved shirt from the very back of the closet, he pushed the thoughts away in favor of studying for his Paramedic license. Even without the logo on his clothes, without the big SFD plastered across his chest, his teacher disliked him. Well, Alex, too. To add to the issues, they disrupted the schedule, constantly changing nights. SFD had spots in several of the classes, and they made sure each firefighter attended each class session, but with the rotating schedule, no one could commit to just Mondays or just Tuesdays. The EMT classes had even more firefighters in them trying to get ahead or keep their jobs and in general having to run to just stay steady.

Jason didn't mind it though. He ate the sandwich he had piled high and re-scanned the chapter they had covered in the last class. Seeing how the teacher was on his case, he started on the next one too. Absentmindedly, he chewed and read, turning pages and not taking any notes.

He had just finished the chapter when he realized that it was time to head out, so he gathered his things and went off to school. He had hoped to be studying arson investigation and other inspection-oriented things, but the Paramedic material was interesting and would lead to an immediate pay raise. That was hard to shake a stick at even if his instructor was a bitch. But the class was paid for, and as long as she didn't misinform them, he'd test out just fine.

He paid as much attention as he could throughout class, but his brain was out in left field. He needed a roommate in a bad way, and he had no clue how to find one. Other than women he was sleeping with, he hadn't had a housemate since college when the school matched him with someone. He would have to ask Alex . . . Alex would know.

Jason looked over at his friend, who was actually paying attention to the class.

Shit. This was important. He tried to focus.

But before long he realized that his thoughts had wandered off again. He was plotting out going back to school. Real school. He could study criminal profiling, and take some of the courses that the cops took—those who wanted to make detective and had degrees in criminology and criminal justice. Or he could focus on arson-based forensics.

Before he realized it had happened, class was over. He had participated a little and watched more, but couldn't quite say what had been covered. As they hit the parking lot, he asked Alex if he wanted to head over to the nearby bar for a beer.

"Seriously?" Alex raised one eyebrow. "You want to get a depressant after that class? Were you paying any attention?"

"Not really. So, you want to go?"

Alex shook his head. "Leo's waiting on me and I'm beat. He decided to take the day off and go antiquing. I had to smile all day and pretend that I think pie-crust tables would look great in our living room. Which they will, I just don't care."

Jason nodded and wondered if the EMT class was out yet or not. For a moment it occurred to him that aside from Rob Castor he didn't have many friends outside the SFD. And Rob only partly counted. As a police officer he was in a similar job, and the police station was located across the street behind the fire house. When he counted it out, he was coming up pretty lame. "Alex, hold on a second. I need your help."

"With beer?" The other man, already seated behind the wheel of his car, looked skeptical.

"No. How do I find a roommate? I need to pay my rent."

"How did you find Kelly?"

This time it was Jason who looked at Alex funny. "I picked her up in a bar, then dated her, then slept with her. I don't have that kind of time."

"Yeahhhhh." Alex drew the word out. "Because it's the *time factor* that dictates that you shouldn't do that again, not the absolute horribleness with which it turned out. How did you find your other roommates?"

"Same way." He felt sheepish about that one. But if he could have found another roommate by himself, he wouldn't have asked, now would he?

"Oh dear God." Alex took a deep breath. "This is such a bad idea."

"What is?" Jason was standing in the open doorway of the car, his arm propped on the driver's door, leaning down.

"How long do you need the roommate for?"

He shrugged again. "Three months? It could go longer if it works out, but I think I'll want to move to a new place when the lease runs out."

Another sigh from Alex, and Jason began to worry. But before he could do anything, Alex asked another question. "What do you want?"

"Meaning?"

"How much money? Bills? Do they get the whole second bedroom? They get that bath right?"

Jason hadn't thought about that and he hesitated. "Just under half the rent? Plus half the bills?" He guesstimated a number and realized he really hadn't thought this through at about the same time he realized that he was very late on that train. There was every possibility that he wasn't going to get a roommate at all and he'd just slowly drain his savings. *Crap.*

Alex was nodding to himself before he started speaking. "I'm only doing this because I am a real friend and you have no sense whatsoever for this. I'll find you a roommate."

"What? What if I don't like them? Or they run off with . . ." he couldn't think of anything, wait, "The TV?"

With an *are-you-kidding-me?* look on his face, Alex just stared. "And this would be any worse than your last choice for a roommate how?"

Jason nodded. "Okay, good point. I'll agree to take whoever you find."

"I need a little time, Leo will help. But I'm on it." Alex reached out for the door handle. "Now get out of my way. I'm going home."

"Thanks, man." Jason backed up and grabbed his books from where he'd stashed them on top of Alex's car. He was halfway to his apartment before he thought to stop at the grocery store and grab some beer. With the way he'd slept today, it wasn't like he was going to get any sleep tonight.

A little while later he let himself into the unit. Scanning the place for unwanted visitors, he balanced a carton of his favorite pale ale on his arm and cursed himself for not getting a book bag. The first thing he saw was the message light blinking on his phone.

He scowled and hoped it wasn't Jernigan. Why the man kept calling for more interviews was a mystery. But it didn't change the fact that Jernigan had interviewed him three times already for his newspaper series.

Jason put the beer in the fridge and pulled one out. He opened it, drank half in one gulp and turned on the TV. Halfway through watching his recording of *Jeopardy* he swore and got up to play the message, just to keep that stupid little light from blinking at him.

He hit the button.

"Hi, um."

He was startled by the sweet voice and the hint of recognition at the back of his brain. He waited.

"This is Aida Walters and I hope I've reached Jason Mondy." She paused again and he took that moment to place the voice to the face of the woman at CPS in Montgomery. His breathing stalled and he waited.

"I don't want to leave a message, in case this isn't the right person. But you can call me back tonight or tomorrow. Thanks."

With a long beep, the recording stopped.

Shitshitshit.

She had something. That's why she called. He needed to call her back . . .

Setting the beer there on the bookshelf by the phone, he bolted for the kitchen. Where had he stashed the card with her info? He'd taken it out of his wallet, he remembered that much.

He jerked open the junk drawer and his fingers raked through the crap there. Pencils, sticky notes, ketchup packets . . . but no card.

With a blink he slammed the door and headed for the other end of the apartment. He'd put it in the manila envelope. For now that was where he had everything associated with his search—all three pieces of paper and one business card.

Fishing it out, he then turned and went back to the living room to call. He was halfway through her cell number when he hung up and checked the machine for the time he called. It was nine-thirty now. That wouldn't be too late. Would it?

He played the message again. Aida had called just over two hours ago. But Jason took a deep breath and dialed anyway. Most people were still up until ten, right? His mother would have killed him if she knew, but that was true for a lot of the decisions he made.

The phone rang and rang and rang and he was sighing in frustration, feeling bad that he'd called after she'd gone to bed when he heard the *click* and the out-of-breath "Hello?"

For a moment, he simply didn't know what to say. How do you ask someone if they found your dead brother? "Um."

Then he got his shit together and acted like a grown-up. After introducing himself and listening to Aida apologize for being on the other end of the house and not getting to the phone in time, she told him to wait while she grabbed the information she had found.

Jason heard the phone tap as it touched down on the surface of her table or desk, he heard her feet and he waited, knots growing in his stomach. If he was lucky, she would give him a cemetery and plot number. He could even drive down tomorrow and pay his respects . . . if he was awake.

She came back to the phone, and he steeled himself with a deep breath.

"Okay." No matter what she said, her voice sounded too sweet for the job she had. "The records were partially destroyed in the tornado I mentioned. I'm sorry about that."

She sounded wistful, as if the tornado were somehow her fault. "That's okay. Did you find anything?"

"Yes, not a lot, but something." She shuffled some papers. "I found you. You Jason Mallory, born in 1979, were admitted as a ward of the state on July 29 of 1985." She paused. "You should write that down. I'll email you copies of what I have, but you should record that."

He bolted the three steps it took to get to the junk drawer and pulled out pen and sticky note and started scribbling.

"FYI—that's one day after the Pelias Street fire that took your mother's life."

Yes, it was. He had seen that date on the copied article but didn't think about it. "Thank you."

"I'm not done. I don't have anything on your brother except—"

His stomach clenched.

". . . that you have one. The papers mention Mother: Alcia Jean Mallory aged twenty-five. Father: unknown—although I'm guessing they got that off your birth certificate. And brother: name unknown, age four."

Holy shit.

"Name unknown? Was this all on the same record? Why would no one have known his name?"

"That I have no idea about. I've never seen anyone listed as 'name unknown' before. But that's exactly how it is here. I'll send you the copy."

"Thank you. It's not that I don't believe you."

He could hear the smile in her voice. "I know. But I'm going to send them to you via email for your records."

He rattled off his email address, then asked, "Did you find anything else?"

"Sadly, not yet. And I don't know if I'm going to. It's really hard to track an unnamed kid through the system after the records got blown to kingdom come."

Dead end. He should have known. *Shit.*

"Wait, wait! I *do* have one other thing. The officer who turned you over to the state was a patrol officer named Richard Candless. But he only handed you over, not your brother."

"Why not both of us?"

She sighed. "Honestly, and I'm really guessing here, I think you were split up before you were handed to the state. Maybe even got separated at the fire or in the hospital. That would explain at least some of the lack of info on him. But that's pure speculation on my part."

Like it mattered. "Well, thank you for finding that out."

"Hey, you checked out as legit. I'm glad to help where I can."

He nodded to himself and pinched the bridge of his nose. "For what it's worth, thank you."

" 'For what it's worth'? What do you mean? You have enough now to keep searching."

"What?" His head snapped up.

"Well, see if you can locate Officer Candless. He might remember something. You may be able to find your brother's birth certificate online. You have the year and mother's name. It was probably in Alabama—most people don't move out of state before age four—and he was probably born in the same hospital where you were born. You had your birth certificate so you know that. You'll probably have to pay a fee to see it. But if it were my brother, I'd pay it."

She was right. He'd given up far too easily. "Wow. I hadn't thought of that."

Aida laughed. "I live to serve."

"Thank you."

He was about to hang up when she started speaking again. "Oh, and I was thinking, since you're a firefighter and all . . ."

"How did you know that?"

She laughed again. "Well, your shirt said 'SFD' when you were in here, which is usually a fire department, then an Internet search turned up a handful of articles on you. You're quite the hero."

Jason cringed. And there he was, again haunted by his incredible lack of wardrobe—which he would be fixing right away—and by the articles about him—which he would likely never be able to fix.

"Anyway, since you're this hero firefighter, I was thinking you might consider finding the firefighters who handled the Pelias Street fire and see if they knew anything. It would mean another trip here to Montgomery, but my guess is that you'll have quite a few of those before you find him."

Wow.

This was so far from the cold trail he'd imagined it to be. Aida was just a font of good ideas. He thanked her about five more times before he let her hang up. And within three minutes of finishing the call he was online.

He found sixteen records of birth for male children with the last name "Mallory" at Baptist Hospital in 1981, and another twenty-three from 1980. At forty bucks a pop, he couldn't order them all. But there was a good chance he could narrow it down.

He hit another site that gave him not just the fact that there were that many of them, but had first names listed, too. It cost him thirty bucks to become a "member" at the site, but that was okay. Alex was going to find him a roommate, and he would have the money for this search. He entered his credit card info and hit "submit."

The list popped up, name after name. Jason stared at it, open mouthed. Maybe he *could* find his brother.

Leaning back in his chair, he had to remind himself that for all his searching, if he was lucky he would find a death record of a little boy who had died in state custody with no real burial. He had probably been cremated; there was likely no headstone or even a person who could say where they had scattered the ashes.

But he had a trail now. Thanks to Aida, whom he now owed far more than a food-truck sandwich eaten in the wind, he had something to go on.

It was three a.m. before he had exhausted his abilities online. He didn't think he'd be able to sleep. But he had to. He had to be awake in the morning for his shift. He had to be awake enough the day after that to go to Montgomery. He simply couldn't screw up his schedule like this.

So he did the one thing he could think of.

He hit the fridge and downed two beers in rapid succession. Jason then changed into sweats and parked himself in front of the TV with a third beer. Programming sucked at this hour, no matter how many channels you had. He tipped the bottle up, hoping to drink himself into some sleep.

Southfield Fire Station #2

Shift	A	
	O'Casey	Captain
Engine 2	Wanstall	FF3
	Mondy	FF2 / EMT
	Grimsby	FF1
Rescue 3	Standard	Engineer
	West	FF2
	Donlan	Engineer/Parmedic

Chapter 7

Alex Weingarten walked up to where Jason sat at the dining table. Though he was reading the paper like usual, he looked like shit. Alex said so.

Jason didn't even bother to deny it. "I'm not sleeping, and I spent two hours the other night convincing Kelly to leave the apartment."

"What?" Then Alex realized that there was something more important here. "You *did* convince her, didn't you?"

"Yeah, but I think her new boyfriend kicked her out and she didn't have anywhere to stay." Jason almost looked unhappy about that.

"Oh, don't fall for that, bud." Alex sat back. There were just a few minutes here before shift change and he wanted to hear the whole thing. He worried about Jason. How was it that Alex—a gay man, who could happily live the whole of his life on a planet with no women—understood them so much better than Mondy?

"I didn't. I told her she had all her rent money to put toward a hotel. She played the 'my name is also on the lease' card then."

"Crap."

He sighed and nodded. "So I played the 'I'll make your life a living hell if you stay' card. Then I threatened her if she tried to take anything and I threw the deadbolt after she left."

Jason looked sad. Worn out and glazed over. Alex didn't ask about Montgomery. He hadn't had a chance to yesterday and it looked like it would wait a little longer. But Jason was on the short path to eternal grumpy bachelorhood or else to becoming the man with a new wife every decade and more alimony than paycheck. Neither of which was a good option. He was getting ready to offer

79

Jason lessons in the way of womankind when his friend spoke again.

"I really thought I'd seen the last of her at the Thurlow house."

Well, crap. "What?"

Jason explained how she'd shown up there before surprising him by being in the apartment when he got home from class.

This time he voiced it. "Well, crap."

Kelly wanted Jason back. Which meant she hadn't really wanted to break up in the first place. She'd just wanted his attention. And Jason hadn't had it to give. Somehow Jason expected a woman to have no purpose in his life but to be a "woman" —there for sex and outings—and only performed the rote motions of couplehood. Alex gave Jason a long hard look and was suddenly very grateful he was gay. He almost laughed out loud at the thought that his homosexuality bothered the other firefighters—as if he would even have a crush on any of these bass ackwards Neanderthals. None of them held a candle to his Leo.

He asked the last important thing. "Did you check the apartment?"

Jason nodded. They both knew Kelly could do a lot of damage. "Whole thing, top to bottom. Had me up another hour after she left. Three days - haven't found anything. Guess she didn't fuck it up because she thought she'd be staying."

Lovely. Mondy wasn't even talking in complete sentences anymore.

It was time anyway. "Let's get out for lineup. And once you get your chores done, you should take a nap."

One eyebrow quirked at him. "What am I, three?"

"With your taste in girls? Yes."

In the bay, Alex leaned against the wall, ready to go home, while Jason took the end of the line. But no one paid attention. All eyes were on the new guy—Ryan Donlan.

They'd heard about him. Down from Boston—clearly, as he wore a BFD shirt even now—late forties/early fifties, Engineer, Paramedic. And he'd just jumped line to the Captain's position.

Donlan wore his hair military short and his expression military stern. Though his pants, shoes and belt all looked regulation, that BFD shirt was out of place. Adler was going to get on that in a minute. Right now, it was time to throw the new guy to the fishes and see what happened.

With Donlan the shift maintained standard seven men. But Donlan was only just beginning to learn his way around the station—by Adler's count that meant he could now find the toilets and the fire trucks and not much else. Then again, they'd had Merriman on this shift and he'd known where everything was and had still been close to useless. So Donlan was a step up, content wise. It was all just a question now of how old-school Boston was going to mix with Adler's progressive Alabama fire house.

Game on.

C-Shift waited in the rockers and against the wall—all of them watching while A lined up. They'd all seen Donlan's name on the board, and by the look on Donlan's face, so had he.

Chief wrote his check-marks on his daily list, uniforms: clean and pressed. Shoes: all black, good treads. Hair: short or out of the way. He'd had to make an exception for Wanstall, but she always had her hair up in braids or in a knot on the back of her head, and it was less of a risk than Merriman's yahoo locks had been. The checklist served as a tangible record that his men were always on track. That—if anyone should look in the future—they'd see he'd run a tight ship at all times. Donlan fit right in, in this respect at least. Adler handed out the daily assignments.

He'd waffled between having Donlan on cleaning duty, which he could accomplish without much supervision, and putting him on truck inspection. "Standard, you and Donlan are on inspection of both trucks."

Standard nodded.

Adler nodded back his thank you. It would be extra work for Standard, but his obsession with precision and rules was a blessing here. There would be nothing missed as Donlan was walked through his checks on the first day.

Chief cleared his throat then got down to business. "Gentlemen, I'd like you all to meet Ryan Donlan, from Boston FD with twenty-three years on the job. You know he has Paramedic training, so he'll be on all our EMS runs today."

He refrained from adding "and he's saving some of your jobs".

Then he turned and reversed the introduction, going down the line of his own men. "Donlan, meet A-Shift. Wanstall is driving Engine 3 today with Mondy and Grimsby. Wanstall and Mondy had a live save of two young boys about a month ago. Wanstall has the best nose in the house for clean air and Mondy is our resident brainiac. He'll whip your butt at *Jeopardy*, but he'll make your life easier around here. He designed the bay layout and will likely be helping us with the new EMS layout."

Down the line he went. Grimsby was his go-to guy for water rescue; a certified scuba diver and amateur rock-climber, the kid could get anywhere. He put Standard's meticulousness in a helpful light for Donlan for the day, and added Kellan West's ability to never make the same mistake twice. He ended with O'Casey—who never lost his head and thus was a highly decorated vet who had teamed in big and small firehouses alike (a fact that Adler thought would help Donlan accept the black man as his boss).

He felt like a proud papa—a papa trying to piece together a step-family. He looked at them all. It wasn't a brotherhood. At least not until someone died or got close to it, not until they were all in a building ten seconds from flashover. Brotherhood had to happen then. And so the Chief worked for it now.

"Donlan, follow me for a minute."

With a sharp step, Ryan followed him around the corner and into the office. Everything was standard—cinderblock instead of the old-city brick Donlan was used to. It looked cheap to his eyes, 1970s instead of 1870s. No craftsmanship, no style. But they had space the likes of which he had never seen. The sleep room didn't even have bunks, though he'd probably still automatically duck his head when he came out of a dead slumber.

He thanked the Chief again, and accepted the SFD polo shirt he was handed. His own button-down blues had not yet arrived. He reached for the hem of his shirt then thought better of it. Stripping to the waist in the Chief's office might not be okay in the South. They had a lot of odd sensibilities here he wasn't sure of. He was just as unsure about putting his life in the hands of a man with a drawl. But sooner or later one of these slow-bred Dixie boys would have his back, like it or not.

Part of the odd sensibilities were because of the girl and the gay, he knew. The girl was easy to spot. The gay he hadn't found yet. And if he didn't ever, that would be okay with him. As uncertain as he was of working with rednecks, he was even more concerned about these other two. Time would tell.

His name was already tagged on his locker and he'd stashed his things in it, even though a faint odor of bubble gum that he found unmanning lingered in the metal. Hopefully, it would fade.

Back out in the bay, he stuck by Jack Standard. Slightly overweight and a little too stiff for Donlan's tastes, the other firefighter went through every piece of equipment on Rescue 3. Bright and shiny, this truck was about ten years newer than the re-furbs he'd been driving in Boston. Southfield, backward as it was, had fully up-to-date equipment that he worked to memorize. Fire trucks weren't standardized, so each one had to be learned. Donlan focused on obvious basics and commonalities.

Standard looked up at him in the middle of a tank inspection and asked point blank. "Why Southfield?"

That, at least, he knew the answer to. "My wife's folks wanted to retire to somewhere warmer. It seemed like a good idea at the time. We just didn't realize that meant *we* had to move here, too, when their health started failing."

So here he was in the land of cotton. When was the bell going to go off? Would he ever adjust to this slow Southern life? They talked slow, they moved slow, and apparently even their emergencies bowed to that Dixie dictate. They were halfway through inspecting the second truck when he finally got his wish.

From where he stood he saw the Chief go into the dispatch room and pick up the paper off the printer. He gave a thumbs-up to both Wanstall and Standard; both trucks would be going out.

As he watched, the pace changed on a dime. Within a blink or two, Mondy and West were in the fire-retardant pants, wide suspenders over their shoulders, jackets in hand. While he'd been watching the Chief, Standard had gotten in gear too, his jacket already on and getting buttoned. The only thing he didn't do was don his mask, and Donlan thought that may be because it was against the regs to drive with it on.

Realizing he was late to the party, he yanked his gear off his pegs and hauled himself into the seat behind Standard just as he put the truck in gear.

Standard looked back to check on his new charge; likely the new guy was just along for the ride on this one. And though he didn't have his official shirt yet, he wasn't without gear. Just in case this really was an all-hands-on scenario.

And the fact that two trucks were going out to the very middle of Southfield meant that nothing good would happen there today. Hitting the siren, Jack watched as Rescue 3 went out first, then he added the regulation single honk at the two cars that had stopped for them, even if the one was well over the line. He headed straight across the intersection and into the portion of town he privately referred to as "Hell."

It was only ten short blocks from the fire house, and the area was split by a line dividing the Station #2 and #1 territories. Though this was just barely inside their jurisdiction, they owned the whole problem.

Three blocks away the guys could see a column of thick gray smoke. It was Donlan who spoke up from the back seat, "Tell me that's the right address, and not something else."

West answered him from the front seat without turning around. "Yes. Thank God. This neighborhood—you just can't tell."

As the truck pulled closer, driving got harder. In spite of the clear fact that something nearby was on fire, the residents came out and impeded progress. Two twenty-something men walked slowly across the street while Standard stopped, honked repeatedly and swore under his breath. This happened again at the second intersection, and Kellan West hoped the other truck was having better luck—there was a reason they had taken two different routes in.

They rounded the last corner, a tight turn that required the cooperation of the other drivers on the road. They didn't get it— the residents just stood on the street and watched as Standard maneuvered the truck into a spot that was going to be twice as difficult to get out of as into.

Kellan climbed down and surveyed the situation even as Standard put the truck in gear. He was heavily clothed, in his buttoned fire jacket, with his helmet on, mask around his neck. He wasn't the biggest guy, but he was tall enough. Still he wasn't overly comfortable walking into hostile territory like this.

The fire came from two cars hopelessly entangled in the middle of the street. Looked like a head-on collision that had burst into flames. But cars didn't burst into flames. In fact, when he looked a little closer he could see these two were burning inside, outside, and in glowing ribbons on the ground around them—but not from the engines or trunks, the two places a car might actually catch fire.

Heads swiveled to him as he approached.

In spite of all the gear, he heard Standard and Donlan coming up behind him and he was grateful.

It was Standard's voice that came over his shoulder, asking the protocol question. "Is there anyone in the cars?"

No one answered. But there wasn't anyone inside, and if there had been, they weren't anybody anymore. Flames licked out the broken windows and dripped from the bottoms of both cars. The burning lines of fuel around the ground were indicative of an accelerant—like someone had doused both cars and trailed it around the perimeter to light it.

It looked so deliberate that he had to wonder who had called it in?

All around him people came out of their dilapidated homes and stood looking at the firefighters, arms crossed, shuttered expressions on their faces. Most were African American, most were in old clothing, and most weren't dressed warmly enough for the slight chill in the air. In spite of it being a regular school day—as far as he knew—he saw three kids ranging in ages from elementary to high school in the small crowd.

Engine 2 pulled up and spilled out Wanstall and Mondy in perfect sync. Grimsby came out of the backseat a moment later. The other FF1 was more like him, lacking that fluid movement that was born of years of moving in the heavy gear. Lacking that ability to just walk into this goatfuck, because that's exactly what this was. Mondy and Wanstall looked like they were at a little girl's birthday party and wouldn't look otherwise until it truly became a goatfuck, never mind that anyone with eyes could see it coming.

Standard and Donlan passed him, wading into the scene with that same casual air, though Donlan looked a little more reserved. Whether that was because he was the new guy or because he saw that this was a hand basket with the one-way ticket to hell, West was unsure.

Mondy smiled. "What's going on here, folks?"

One large man came out of the crowd. "You stupid? There's two cars on fire."

"So there is." The smile didn't falter. "Do you know how it happened, sir?"

"Don't need to." The man stepped up, crossed his arms and made Jason Mondy look small. "There's a fire and you're a fire man. Why don't you put it out and go home?"

"Sir." Wanstall strode into the fray and beamed at the man like he was the president. "We need to know how the fire started so we can put it out."

That was kindof bullshit. They could douse this. And they would. But still, the more they knew . . .

Kellan headed back to the truck and started pulling the small hose. Donlan came and helped him hook it up, got the water running, and together they hauled it the short distance from truck to blaze.

He was about to start the flow when he heard the crack of a bullet and about pissed his pants.

Mondy and Wanstall turned as a unit and dove for the ground. Grimbsy looked to be heading for the protection of the truck, and Donlan just muttered, "What the fuck?"

It took half a second to see that Mondy and Wanstall were not diving for cover, but running triage on the man on the ground. A fresh red stain spotted the front of his shirt around the neat bullet hole, but behind him on the blacktop a pool of blood spread like a living thing. It seeped into the cracks and potholes and wound around rocks and debris.

"Don't."

A new man, dressed in new jeans, button-down shirt and a jacket too nice for this neighborhood stood with the gun in his hand, still pointed at the downed man and far too close to Mondy and Wanstall.

Gunfire wasn't uncommon here, but it wasn't rampant either. That didn't matter—they were clearly balls deep in it now.

The muzzle of the gun wavered and Missy looked up at it. For a moment, she caught the view right down the barrel and felt everything inside her shut off. She froze, unsure what to do until she saw Jason start to put his hands up and back away from the man on the ground. Unconsciously she mimicked his movements until she was doing the same.

Damnit. She wanted fires. She wanted to help. These people wanted to watch these cars burn. SFD wasn't wanted here and no one should have called this in. She wanted to say "sorry" or "okay" or something equally inane, but in the face of the gun she couldn't find her voice. The only betraying motion was the sideways flick of her eyes.

She'd felt a faint pulse from the man on the ground just before she realized the gun was on her and Jason. Though the pulse meant she was supposed to help, she soothed her conscience with the fact that this man had little to no chance of survival even if a Gold Standard ambulance pushed him in the back and sped off at this very moment. With the gun on them, he wouldn't get help today.

So she stood and tried to look around . . . the cars still burned. Though the accelerant was mostly gone now, the insides caught fire quite nicely and the gray smoke now poured out. People were coughing, and breathing was becoming more difficult but no one backed away from the fire. No one backed away from the man with the gun either. They all stood stock-still—as did SFD—while the man who was now in charge of the scene stepped up and quickly put three more bullets in the man on the ground.

Missy felt her whole body flinch with each retort of the handgun. Jason didn't. They both kept their hands in the air.

"Are you done, sir?" Mondy asked in a very conversational tone. Missy hoped he'd crapped his pants inside the gear; there was no way he could be that cool.

"Maybe." The man didn't lower the gun or even remove his finger from the trigger. But he did look at Jason with an I'll-decide-when-I-decide expression.

Though his hands stayed in the air, Mondy took one ballsy step forward, and Missy was simultaneously afraid he'd try to hero-up by taking the gun and pissed that Mondy was the one with the brass balls. Time to grow her own pair.

She breathed in and found her voice.

"Sir?" The man with the gun turned to face her, but he didn't raise it or aim it. That didn't seem to keep her heart from trying to get out of her ribcage, but she managed to keep her voice regulated. "Is it okay with you if we put out the fire now?"

"S'ppose."

Missy raised her eyebrows. She was either going to get shot or not. "I'd like more than a 'suppose.' I'm not keen on any of the SFD winding up like him." She moved one hand to slowly point at the dead man on the ground and wondered when she'd become callous, too.

The man with the gun laughed at her. And that made her mad.

"Okay. I promise not to shoot any firefighters."

She nodded at him then turned to Kellan West who was still standing near the truck with hose in his hand. Donlan was more out in the open, poised at the edge of the crowd and Missy nodded at him, too.

She wanted to worry about how he felt taking orders from a girl, one he outranked at that. But she also wondered if he was going to pack up and leave after today.

West and Donlan moved toward the cars, small hose aimed at the fire. It hit the cars at high speed and bounced off in all directions. The crowd looked pissed and finally backed off.

Missy wanted to tell them to suck it up and stop setting shit on fire but that wasn't protocol, and though she and Mondy now had their hands down, the gun still made her nervous. As she watched, West inadvertently banked the water off the car in such a way as to douse the gunman who immediately became enraged and turned at him.

"Hey!" Missy yelled to get the gunner's attention. She was getting ready to yell out "You promised!" as though that would mean anything, when she heard O'Casey behind her.

Captain and the Chief must have pulled up at some point. But she didn't know where they had come from, and she didn't think it was worth it to take her eyes off the gun to find out.

O'Casey's voice startled her. "Conrad."

The gunman turned.

Oh, this was not going to be good. Captain knew him.

O'Casey walked up the old street, his eyes seeing both what it was and what it had been. It had been a nice little enclave of lower middle class, mostly African American families, when he'd lived here. His folks had left after he'd passed fire training and moved into Birmingham for his first job. What had happened here in the fifteen years he'd been away in the city was sad. What had happened with Conrad was clearly worse. He'd gone to kindergarten with this man.

"Lee?!" Conrad turned to him as though this was a grocery store and they were old friends. O'Casey knew the other man still lived in town, mostly because his name showed up in the police reports more often than not, and was almost shocked that the other wasn't in prison. Clearly he should be.

"You're a fireman? Shit. Thank God you ain't cops."

Well, that wasn't going to fix anything. The blue would be here any moment now. And Conrad wasn't going to fare well if he was still here. From the look that crossed Conrad's face, he could hear the approaching sirens.

"Shit." He looked back at O'Casey getting angry now. "Did you call me in?"

O'Casey put his hands up and wished he had suited up for this one. The gear would at least help slow a bullet, but instead he was in his dress uniform, just pants and a button-down. "Didn't have to call it in. Gunfire just brings them out."

"Fuck." Conrad shook his head and turned to move.

During the short exchange, Mondy and Wanstall had moved closer to Engine 2, West and Donlan were on the hose and exposed in the open. It was also noisy up by the water; they might not hear the sirens, and they were only passively watching Conrad and his gun. They needed their attention on the flames, which could be just as dangerous as the man with the weapon. But O'Casey didn't like where this was headed. "Can you put down the gun? These are my guys."

But Conrad didn't. Instead he gestured with it. "Yeah. You got a girl, too." He smiled.

The sirens were still out on the main road, but this neighborhood was a bit of a maze, streets stopping in dead ends, roads that didn't connect. It could be a while before the police showed their faces. In his head O'Casey swore vehemently.

Still, people stood around. Apparently, they had faith that Conrad wouldn't shoot them. Or they were too afraid to move. From the wary looks on faces and how the crowd had backed slowly away, it looked more like the second.

Conrad grinned.

And it took only a split second for everything to go to hell.

A loud cry came from somewhere in the crowd as gunfire came again, this time rapid and repeating. Conrad danced to a scream of "that was my brother" as bullets riddled him, his gun hand flopping but not letting go.

O'Casey—knowing his reactions were too slow to do any real good—dove for the ground. And in the instant he was falling he watched others doing the same. The crowd screamed and ran, and out of the corner of one eye he saw a young child being pulled along by the hand. It took so long to hit the ground that he had time to lament that kids saw this and that the old neighborhood was dead. The hard dirt and brown grass came up and assaulted him in a full body slam for which he was profoundly grateful.

He heard a voice shout something like, "Whoa" or "Hey" but he couldn't tell.

Then the gunfire stopped.

And as O'Casey lifted his head he saw the stupidest thing he'd ever seen.

Donlan had a man from behind, his beefy arms wrapped around the gunner's, locking them straight up. The hand which held a small boxy black gun was supported by Wanstall, who must have crossed in *front* of this second man with a gun in order to point his arm at the sky. And Mondy, being the tallest, was grasping the gun by the back and pulling it from the perp's grip.

"Holy shit!"

He didn't realize he'd screamed it until he stood up and was walking up to where the three had the man contained. He scanned the scene. West and Grimsby were standing up on opposite sides of where the cars still burned. Chief was walking toward the spot where Conrad had crumpled. He kicked the gun away from the dead hand, but then thought better of it and picked it up, instantly dropping the clip out.

On the other side of him, Mondy hit the ground and began emptying what was a small machine gun. With hands that were growing ever more unsteady, he dumped bullets, shoving them inside his gear and into his pants pockets in a hazy effort to disable the weapon. Wanstall increased her grip on the second assailant's arm and Donlan managed to get his hands behind the man's neck, aiming his head down and immobilizing him somewhat.

Just then, two police officers showed up, guns drawn, badges flashing. They walked in that crouch they often used and O'Casey's heart lurched as he felt another gun aim at him. However momentary it was, it wasn't a good feeling.

He saw the Chief scan the houses and he did the same, looking at windows and around edges, waiting for the next person to pop out.

Car doors slammed and the sirens became a full wail, as police flooded the scene. They joined him and Adler in scanning the area, which was now blessedly empty.

Adding insult, two Gold Standard EMS vehicles chose that moment to come careening to a stop. The EMTs scanned the scene from the safety of the trucks before they hopped down and rushed the two dead men.

About time.

It didn't take long for them to declare the two dead on site and they started scouring the dispersed crowd looking for injuries to haul in.

The police pulled the flailing machine gunner from Donlan and Wanstall's grasps, at which point they both hit the ground with their butts and started breathing heavily.

Missy leaned her head forward and tried to put it between her knees. She wasn't a pretzel on her best days and covered in gear it was even harder to fold up, but she forced it. Though she wasn't an EMT she knew this wasn't as effective as if she was in a chair, but—God help her—it made her feel better.

Twisting her head sideways she sneaked a peek at Donlan. "You're white as a sheet. Head down, buddy."

He blinked at her twice before deciding she might have a good idea. As soon as she saw him duck, she went back to breathing. She thought she heard Donlan mutter under his breath "oh shit, welcome to Southfield".

Mondy beat her to a reply, "Hey Donlan, you should know this is highly abnormal."

Donlan's head didn't lift either. "Yippee."

Missy rolled her head the other way and caught sight of Jason. "You should put your head down, Mondy."

He was just starting to when Rob Castor came up. "Dude, give me the gun."

Jason, still shaking, just looked up at his friend and handed over the small machine gun he only just then seemed to realize he was still holding. Then, he reached into his pocket and started pulling out fistfuls of the bullets he'd cached and pouring them into Castor's unready hands.

The EMTs came by and checked on each of them. Jason was having his arms inspected with little common nicety when they heard one of the EMTs shout out, "Got one!"

Mondy and Jason snapped their heads up to see the EMT that shouted standing over O'Casey. The Captain had O'Casey's pants leg lifted and even from the distance it was clear that blood was running freely down his leg.

Despite his age and slight extra girth, the Chief was already on his way to stand over them. His hand was up, palm out, motioning for the trio on the ground to stay. And even as he looked at O'Casey, he turned to West and Grimsby and pointed to the still-burning cars, motioning for them to resume putting the fire out. The one thing they were *supposed* to be doing here, and they were down to their two junior members.

Chief stood over O'Casey and the blue shirted med. "What is it?"

"Bullet wound is my guess." The EMT spoke tight-lipped to the Fire Chief. It was clear that they all had heard about the future of Southfield Fire and Rescue. Though the numbers weren't large, there were enough EMTs who were firefighter drop-outs to be problematic in general. Now SFD was taking their jobs. None of it played well.

Though O'Casey was bleeding profusely, it looked like he'd just been grazed. Chief spoke to the EMT, "Get him to the hospital."

He took a moment and shook O'Casey's hand, as much to assess his status for himself as to thank him for his work here. He watched as the EMT called another over and put his Captain on a wheeled gurney and rolled him into the back of the ambulance. Then he turned and started swearing like a sailor.

It was absolutely the wrong time for him to be out a captain. It was the wrong time for SFD to be in the middle of a gunfight. It was the wrong time for his men to be at the mercy of Gold Standard EMTs. But that's what it was.

He watched as his two newest men handled the car fire with aplomb. They were well trained, as practiced as could be. And it took only a second to recognize them in their full gear and masks.

Putting out the car fire went on for a while. Every time the two turned off the hose and checked, they discovered something else was still burning—something in the engine still had a tiny flame; a Duralog in the trunk still smoldered; rubbers and resins still dripping, flaming from the bottom of one car or the other.

Mondy, Wanstall, and Donlan sat at the edge of the scene. By then, all three had lifted their heads and were watching the other two do the work. Periodically the water bounced off metal and hit them, but they didn't move. They just stayed like statues and for once didn't shout advice to the newbs. The only thing they were missing was having their hands at their faces in the classic see-no-evil, hear-no-evil, speak-no-evil poses.

For a moment Adler smiled to himself at the image. Then he watched the cops crawling on the scene. They interviewed Standard as he worked on the trucks, attempting to put things back in order and inspecting for damage. As Chief watched, he saw Jack frown and run his hands across a low panel. Great, there were bullet holes in his truck.

The boys in blue knocked on doors with as little success as the SFD had. No one had spoken until the first gunner had recognized O'Casey. And given the shit-fest here, they were all going to be giving statements to the police until they were as blue as the cops.

Though Adler never would have normally done this while on scene, he felt he had to. Opening the small back door of the truck, he leaned in and pretended to find something on the floor. With his head shielded by the vehicle, he pulled out his cell phone. God bless technology, he was grateful he had the number he needed at hand. He dialed it up and worked his way through a quick introduction.

"If you drive quickly, you can get here before we leave."

Chapter 8

Jason

He left the fire house as fast as he could the moment shift ended. And it still wasn't fast enough. Donlan trailed him out the back bay doors as though Jason wasn't exiting at near warp speed. He called out to Jason's back, and it was sorely tempting to ignore him.

"You got some brass balls on you. That was pretty impressive today."

And with that volley he had no choice but to defend himself the way he had been doing pretty much since the moment the shit had hit the fan yesterday. "No, I don't have brass balls. What I have is sheer stupidity when I get scared."

He never should have approached that man with the gun, never should have talked to him. And he still wasn't sure that the first man would have suffered the extra three bullets if he hadn't opened his fat mouth. And though he kept trying, that was a tough pill to swallow. He kept reminding himself that the man likely would have died from the first shot. It had been at a close enough range and well enough aimed that it probably would have done the trick all by itself. But the "likely" and "probably" part there were going to keep him awake. He knew it.

He'd been hounded the moment the press started showing up at the scene. The *Southfield Press* came as soon as the area was clear—which was pretty much to be expected. In fact, they had probably been listening to the police scanner and just waited until the gunfire was shut down to pop their nosy little heads up.

No, it was the nearly simultaneous arrival of the *Birmingham News* that put them all on edge. No one in this neighborhood would have called them—the last thing these people wanted was cops and press. And what was the likelihood that the big *Birmingham News* was listening on little Southfield's scanners? . . . So how had they known?

The same guy, Clark Jernigan, had come with a camera man in tow. He was clearly their fire house correspondent. The camera man had shot continuous video of them cleaning the area and investigating the car. And Jernigan talked to each of A-Shift, asking what happened and what they'd done. But he'd focused on Jason. Not because Jason was anything spectacular here, but because Jason had been the focus before and Jernigan said the continuity made for a nice story.

Jason had been looking through the cars, clipboard in hand, searching for points of origin for the fire and diagramming out what he saw. Chief knew he liked doing it and threw him what he could. Then Chief would make his own notes, compare the two, and see if either of them missed anything or disagreed about something.

So to have the Chief pull him from something important to have a little chat with Jernigan and play golden boy yet again—all while he was crashing down from a mean adrenaline rush—only pissed him off. Playing golden boy sucked.

And even though it had all been over more than twelve hours ago, the irritation still clung, still oozed from him. And he felt it start up again each time Donlan spoke. Which he kept insisting on doing.

The other man just folded his arms, the two of them facing each other in the back parking lot, "Looked like sheer cajones to me. I'd be proud to have you at my back."

And though he'd eaten enough to combat the crash but hadn't had enough time or sleep to fight the anger, Jason quit holding back and let fly at Donlan. "Well, it wasn't all me. Don't believe what you read in the papers. Did you tell Wanstall that, too? Or do you have a problem with her?"

Donlan nodded. "I thought I might. Honestly, I would never have voluntarily joined a house with a woman or a gay. But after today I have to say that Wanstall has cajones as big as yours."

"Did you chase her down and tell her?"

"Not yet. She's still inside. But I am going to. That was fucking impressive today." Donlan crossed his arms. "I was worried it was going to be slow here south of the Mason-Dixon line."

"Well, it was an aberration."

Donlan just nodded. And Jason was ready to turn around and stomp off when Donlan's voice stopped him again. "Chief said you're the smartest one."

"No he didn't."

"Close to. Then you proved it."

How? How had he "proved" it? Jason kept his face impassive. "I can't fix the trucks to save my life. And I'm too big to go down the rabbit holes. So I'm not sure what use it is. And winning at Jeopardy is one of those skills that doesn't really get you anywhere." He'd wiped the floor with the rest of the station house that night, quite the dubious honor.

Donlan nodded. "You got your eye on Captain?"

It took just a moment to process what Donlan's clipped speech and phrasing meant. "No." So that's what this is all about. Jason spoke again before the other man could grill him. He just wanted to get home and get some sleep. "Fire Inspector."

He watched as it sank in. Donlan nodded.

And just before Jason could get pissed at him again, he crossed his arms and looked out into the field behind the station house. "It's not as bad as I thought it would be. Thanks."

Jason opened his mouth to comment on the double edge there, but once again, Donlan beat him to speaking. "I'm going to go find Wanstall and tell her I appreciate the cajones she exhibited today."

Jason wasn't sure Missy would appreciate being congratulated on having "cajones," but he was done with the conversation. So he finally turned and left.

A short time later when he found himself in his car at a drive-through window and not quite sure how he'd gotten there, Jason took a moment to take breath and think. Just then, the teenage boy at the window handed him a paper sack and thanked him. Jason had no clue what was in the bag.

It was a biscuit sandwich, which wasn't a surprise. Because it appeared he'd bought it and because he was hungry, he ripped through the paper and started eating. The sandwich was gone by the time he pulled into the spot under his apartment building.

Rent was due in three days. Though he had his half and some extra, he didn't really have all of it. He could pay the whole thing but it would interfere with the exorbitant cable and Internet bill for the super-high-speed stuff that Kelly had insisted they needed. They hadn't been in this unit for a full year, so he wasn't able to change his service to help reduce the bill. What he needed was a roommate. A quiet roommate. One who didn't want much and who had a lot of money. For just three months.

Jason went straight through his front door—which the super still had not had re-keyed—and plowed his way directly to the bed. He didn't shower or even change clothes, just fell face first on top of the covers and prayed for the sleep that had been eluding him.

∧ ∧ ∧ ∧ ∧

He woke up curled into a ball and hanging off the side of his bed. His bare feet were cold and his mouth felt horrid and tasted worse, but he'd slept. Though his head felt as cottony as his mouth, Jason pushed himself upright and headed for the shower. He passed his alarm clock on his way into the shower.

8:38 a.m.

That was okay. He'd been in and out all day and night, but he'd finally had enough sleep to be worthwhile, and it was still early enough to get to Montgomery and see what he could dig up.

Three hours later, he was almost to the other town. He'd showered and dressed in an SFD shirt—this time he wanted people to know what he was. He hoped to play on the whole "brotherhood" thing if he could; maybe Officer Candless would be more willing to talk to him.

There had been only one Richard Candless listed in Montgomery. It hadn't been the right person. But after trying two R. Candlesses, he'd struck gold. Or at least silver. Roger Candless was Officer Richard's brother. Though Roger wouldn't hand out the phone number, he took Jason's. Yesterday Richard Candless, retired police officer, called him back and agreed to meet for lunch.

As he pulled into the lot he saw that Jack and Debby's diner looked just as Candless had described it. He could only hope the man was as accurate about himself. Another glance at his phone showed him he was somehow fifteen minutes early. Which was pretty impressive, since he'd gotten to the edge of Southfield, then had to go back for the envelope with all seven of his papers in it now. He hadn't thought he *could* be early.

Crap.

He didn't want to go in and wait. He wanted to walk in, see the other man, and get started. And he didn't have anything but his envelope with him.

Jason didn't park.

He was in another city for the second time in two weeks. He'd invested hours in this already. He was onto his second interview—if he counted Aida as the first—and he was hoping he'd have another two or three by later today if the guys at Montgomery Fire Station #6 were willing to help him out. Especially if any of them had been there at the Pelias Street fire. But being twenty-seven years in the past, that was unlikely.

So he needed materials even more.

His phone found him a nearby office supply store and he purchased three pads of paper in different colors. A set of pens. A set of manila folders. He had highlighters, pencils, and a block of sticky notes before convincing himself to stop. On the other side of the store he found a laptop bag, too. Then he pushed through the checkout and out the door.

Arriving back at the diner, he took just a moment to throw all his new supplies into the bag and tucked in the manila envelope, too. Then Jason slung the whole thing over his shoulder and walked into the diner.

It was official. He was serious about this. He was going to find his brother. Or at least find out what had happened to him.

The retired officer was easy to spot. Candless was in his sixties, sitting by himself on the far side of the diner. Looking much as he'd described himself to Jason, he was easy to ID from the shirt bearing the Montgomery Police Department logo. Clean and upright, and looking to be in general good health, the older man was clearly in the early stages of what appeared to be arthritis and his hair was in need of a cut.

There was no way not to compare this man to his own father. A man who had been hale and hearty until the moment he died. A man with a clean pressed wardrobe, a look of contentment that Jason had never placed before, and the air of family.

He approached the table and held out his hand. "You must be Officer Candless."

"Lieutenant." He stood and met Jason in a hearty handshake that was younger in feel than the man appeared to be. "You must be Jason."

"Yes, sir." He slid into the opposite bench and waited a moment as Candless signaled the waitress to come over. Jason ordered a coke and let Candless recommend the cheeseburger and fries—which the older man described as "greasy as hell" and "best in town" all in one breath.

As soon as the waitress left, Candless looked at him. "Are you new to this research you're doing?"

He had to laugh. "Yes, how can you tell?"

"Tag's still on your bag."

"Yeah, I'm just getting started, but I'm really hoping you can help me." He rummaged around, pulling out some of what he had and organizing as he went. He pushed the article on the Pelias Street fire across the table just as his coke arrived. "I'm hoping you remember this."

Candless scanned the article. "I'm not listed here. How did you find me?"

Not the instant recitation of useful information that Jason had been hoping for, but exactly what he would have asked had he been on the other side of the table. "I went to CPS here in town. I know I was in the foster care system. Your name came up as being the one who signed me into state custody."

For a moment, the two men looked at each other. Jason was suddenly struck by the fact that he wasn't meeting a true stranger, but a man he had met before, one who had ushered him through probably the most difficult thing in his life.

Neither spoke for a minute.

"You're the older brother?"

He nodded, unable to speak. It was the first time he'd heard himself referred to in that way. He was *the older brother*—something that he'd only found out recently. But there was a difference between his mother saying he *had a brother* and Aida telling him his brother was *four* to actually *being* something—to being *the older brother*. Maybe he shouldn't say yes; clearly he hadn't been a very good one. He'd forgotten he'd *been* a brother until this very moment.

The burgers came out just then, giving them both a moment's reprieve. Lieutenant Candless took a big bite of his before he asked, "So if you know all that, what exactly is it that you need from me?"

Jason swallowed and realized he should have a notebook handy and that he shouldn't drip cheeseburger juice on his notes the first day. So he hauled out pad and pen and set them at the edge of the table. "Well, for starters, I don't know my brother's name. Do you remember it?"

"Never heard it." He took another bite.

"He's listed as 'name unknown' on his documentation into state care. Do you know why that is?"

Candless nodded, but then contradicted himself. "I can guess. He didn't speak. At all."

Jason set down his burger. "What? How?"

"He had smoke inhalation, so he didn't speak. But he didn't even try. I guess his throat hurt from all the screaming, probably swollen from the smoke damage, too, that he just quit."

"The screaming?"

Again Candless nodded and Jason realized it simply meant there was an answer, just not that the answer was in the positive. "You were screaming when they pulled you out. You were so hoarse that for a while no one understood what you were yelling about. They didn't understand immediately to go back for the brother."

Somehow, the disconnect of saying *the brother* made it easier to take. Though Jason still couldn't fathom how he'd come through the fire and didn't remember any of it. "So I was rescued first? And they went back for my brother?"

Candless continued. "The firefighters said you found them and they hauled you out screaming. Then they finally got you calmed down enough to understand what you were yelling about and they went back for your brother. I was there, it took a long time before they came back out with him."

"Why was that, do you know?" He had started jotting things down, not that he thought he would ever forget this conversation, but he wanted a record. At the top of the page he wrote "Lt. Richard Candless," the date and even "Jack and Debby's Diner, Montgomery."

"Lots of rooms, lots of units. It was a big apartment building. It was a long way in and back out. That building was falling down long before it caught on fire."

Nothing the man said contradicted anything his mother had told him or what he'd read in the article. Jason lifted the page and started a to-do list, adding "check paper for follow-up story on Pelias St fire." Then he asked another question, "How was it that you were the one who signed me over to state custody?"

Another nod, but he knew now not to expect anything because of it. "There was a young female officer there who watched you at the scene. If I remember right, you were given some oxygen from a tank there at the building, but your brother was taken to the hospital right away. His injuries were life threatening. You screamed for him then, too. I remember that."

Jason didn't.

And he got hit again by the fact that this man was telling him about the last moments he'd ever seen his brother. But he didn't say anything to that effect, and Candless kept talking, his burger now gone.

"You stayed at the building while it burned. I think you were waiting for your mother. All the neighbors stood around and watched it crumble. They didn't have anywhere to go. It wasn't a wealthy neighborhood, you understand."

Jason only nodded. He did.

"So it was dawn before we had the Red Cross come in and some social workers, too. You went to the police station in the back of my squad car. I filled out the paper work once we got there and the social worker took you from there. That's the last I remember."

Jason asked a few more questions, but Candless didn't have the answers. Like what hospital had his brother been taken to? Did he know who had done that paperwork? He thought up a few more questions as he paid the check, but none of them helped. Candless had told everything he had and he was shut down like Main Street at midnight.

In the end, Jason shook his hand again. He handed over a sticky note with both his home and cell phone numbers and asked the older man to please be in touch if he remembered anything. "Can I contact you again if I have any more questions?"

"I suppose." It was accompanied by a shrug. "Told you what I know, though. Don't expect to remember anything else."

Though that last statement rang as a little odd, Jason took it at face value. The man had managed to tell quite a bit and yet so very little. As he drove away from Jack and Debby's Jason reviewed what he had learned. He knew why his brother had been listed as "name unknown" —he couldn't speak. And Jason, at seven, apparently hadn't been more forthcoming, though that was understandable since it seemed he'd been screaming most of the time. First to get his brother out of the burning building, then probably because he was being taken away in an ambulance.

Apparently, flat-out screaming had been an appropriate response—he'd never seen his little brother again. Even in memories, because he'd lost those, too.

Montgomery Fire Station #6 on Gold Street was his next stop. Just half a mile from the address the Pelias Street Apartments had occupied, it was the nearest fire house and most likely the district that would have been on call twenty-seven years ago.

Finding the house with relative ease, he drove slowly in front of it. It sat on a corner, the truck bay a full two stories tall, but the rest a simple one story. Though much was like his own station house, it had some revealing differences: siding ran vertically on the front, but only the front. Even the slightest glance around the side revealed the façade was just that. But it was inviting, with large, tinted square windows running across what looked like the lobby and front offices.

Since he knew better than to park in the wide sloping driveway as people were often wont to do, he pulled up behind the station house and parked in the farthest open spot. From behind it was much more industrial looking, the back bays wide open but seeming a bit off, being the opposite orientation of his own station house. He came in looking for anyone but found the bay empty. They might be in the back doing some kind of classroom training.

Jason was reaching for the door that led into the house when he noticed the two empty spots. Two missing trucks meant there was every possibility that no one was here. He knocked anyway, not willing to walk right in to someone else's fire house. He was an unknown factor; he hadn't even called ahead because he hadn't known how long his lunch with Lieutenant Candless would go.

No one answered the knock.

He waited a moment and knocked again, getting the same non-response. So he headed out to his car and pulled out of the lot. They could be on the scene of some call for a while. So he wound his way back out to find a gas station. He didn't have enough in the tank to get home and he decided to kill time and wait.

After filling up and coming back, the place seemed just as empty as before, so he pulled up a search on his phone and found some restaurants in the downtown area. If Alex didn't come through with a roommate, then he was spending money he didn't have. But he'd already spent money he didn't have—the birth certificate website, the ancestry site, lunch for Candless. So far it didn't add up to anything astronomical, and if it started to, he'd have to re-assess what he was doing. He might even have to call off the dogs, because he was really only looking for records of what had happened to a boy he didn't remember who had likely died a long time ago.

But the possibilities kept Jason in the car, parked in the back of Montgomery Fire House #6, waiting. He made several calls before trying Aida.

She answered on the first ring. "Jason?"

That caught him off guard. "You put my number in your phone?"

"No."

But at least she was laughing. *That was good, right?*

"You're the only person I know with a 205 area code who *isn't* already in my phone."

"That makes sense." She'd thrown him.

"So, did you find anything out?"

There was his thread. "Actually, I'm doing that right now. I'm in Montgomery. I had lunch with Officer Candless."

"Wow. You work fast!"

"I did what you suggested. I called him up and for the price of a hamburger, he told me what he remembered."

"Was it helpful?"

"Yes and no."

"You'll have to stay in one of the chairs."

He frowned. "I'm sorry?"

"Oh, not you. I'm at work though. Can I call you later?"

"Wait!" He gathered his thoughts and took a breath. "I have reservations at Sinclairs tonight. Will you join me?"

"What?"

"I owe you dinner at the very least, and I can update you and you don't have to miss work. Seven?"

He waited.

Then, suddenly, Aida spoke again rapidly. "That would be really nice. I love Sinclairs. I'll meet you there at seven. I have to go."

She managed to squeeze out one quick "thank you" before she hung up on him. And there he was, sitting in his car, stalking firefighters in a strange town. Having just asked out a woman who might have a boyfriend and who wasn't his usual type. She wasn't the super-model wannabe that his exes had all been. Not the kind he could pick up in a bar, but she was pretty and smart and he owed her dinner. And if she had some body builder boyfriend or it just all went to hell, at least he wasn't even in Southfield for anyone to see.

It was another thirty-five minutes before the trucks rolled in. He was playing a game on his phone when he was startled by a knock on his window. He looked up and then lowered the window.

A burly man probably in his fifties leaned down. "Can we help you with something?"

It wasn't the most friendly question or tone, but Jason expected no less. He *was* sitting in his car in a lot where people didn't park unless they worked there or were fucking someone there. He was neither.

"I hope so." Jason turned slightly, hoping the SFD logo on his jacket would help out. It did.

"You're fire?"

"Yessir. Southfield. Outside Birmingham."

And that was all it took. He wasn't welcomed like a prodigal son, but the doors were now open. He stepped out of the car and introduced himself, then met Shift Captain Robert Gallow.

He was in the break room, getting introduced around before Gallow asked. "So what brings you by for a visit?"

Jason addressed the room at large. "When I was seven I was in an apartment fire here in Montgomery. My mother died and I was adopted, but I lost my brother in that fire."

All the faces turned reverent and solemn, just for a moment. One man looked at him, "You got out?"

"I was a live rescue."

That started a few murmurs and nods, "And now you're one of us?"

"Yes, sir."

"Hm." But there was no other response. Jason didn't let it get to him. He went on to explain what he knew, half of it things he had learned from Candless just an hour or so ago.

Around him faces turned thoughtful. One voice piped up. "When was it?"

Jason looked at him. "It was the Pelias Apartments fire. July 28, 1985. Did anyone here work that fire?"

They all quit looking at him and started looking at each other.

He frowned. "This is the closest station to that address. Is it districted somewhere else?"

Districts were crazy things, sometimes cutting down the center line of roads or worse, sometimes with donut holes owned by other districts. Who knew which house owned the Pelias fire.

Gallow took the lead. "This house wasn't here then."

"Oh?"

"Yeah, that's why we are number six in between numbers two and four. This was built in the late nineties."

Jason hadn't caught the numbering, but he should have seen that the architecture here was all off—this place had clearly been built in the nineties. "Do you know where I can find the house that ran that call? Or better yet, someone who worked it?"

Heads swiveled to Gallow, who appeared to be the oldest. Several asked him "weren't you around here then?" and "didn't you work that one?"

Gallow looked at the ground and shook his head. "I didn't work that shift."

Jason was getting ready to ask another question when one of the younger firefighters said, "Let me introduce you to the Chief. He can figure it out for you."

Though Chief Barrett was kind and tried to be helpful, he started off with a laugh. "Wilson here thinks I'm older than dirt. And he only has one of his facts right. I wasn't here then, I did all my work in Mobile before this house opened. So I wasn't in town for your fire."

But he showed off a nearby wall with a ten-by-ten map that showed all the Montgomery districts by color code. Pelias Street was districted to Number 6, but the chief pointed to another house. "Number Two there would have handled that fire in '85, I think. You gonna head over there?"

"If you think I should?" Jason stuck his hands in his pockets, unsure what he'd do if the Chief said 'no'. It would be a great excuse to quit, but he didn't want to quit now.

"Sure."

Hiding his relief, he unclenched his hands in his pockets.

Chief continued, "I can call over there, ask if they're in. See if anyone is around who worked then?"

Startled, Jason just nodded before he managed to get out a "thank you, sir."

The Chief waved him back into his office and Jason added 451 Oracle St into his phone. He only half listened as Barrett worked out some details.

"Chief says you should talk to Captain Grady there. He's on shift today. Both Chief Stevens and Captain Grady worked that fire, they'll be glad to help."

Finding Fire Station #2 wasn't hard. As he passed the front, he saw what he'd missed at #6. This house was brick fronted, the windows had white wood casing. The grid on the window resembled panes of glass and actual sills sat at the bottom. This house had been around for a while.

The whole thing was two stories tall and as he passed in through the back bay he went past a pole. His eyes shot up, following it where it disappeared into the ceiling, just under the top landing of a new addition of a long staircase complete with speed rails. The pole was just there for old times' sake maybe.

Another older man came out the door as Jason came in. The security cameras along the back bay had been hard to miss as he'd walked up. It looked like all the trucks were in, but that didn't matter much as the white shirt identified the Chief and that meant this man was Stevens.

After a quick handshake, Jason was ushered in to the break room where the Chief announced his presence. "This is Jason Mondy, he works over at Southfield FD outside Birmingham."

There was a chorus of hi's and oh's and the Chief turned and whispered, "I'm about to embarrass you, son."

Then he announced, "I've been reading about this guy. He and his partner pulled two young boys from a house fire, saved both kids. Their crew even saved the kitten."

The murmurs became more positive now, changing to "nice" and "congratulations" even as Jason wished he could become invisible. But he needed the info here so he waited. And sure enough Chief Stevens wasn't done yet.

With a pause, he turned and stared at Jason. And if Jason was correct, the old man got a little misty looking, but he turned back to the gathered shift before it was possible to be sure. "Mondy was a live rescue as a kid, right here in Montgomery. I haven't seen this young man in twenty-seven years. I worked the fire on Pelias Street. You lost your mother, didn't you?"

Jason nodded—it was all he could do.

Holy shit. This day was going to knock him on his butt.

"I'm sorry about your mother, and your brother, too from the sound of it." The Chief *was* a little misty around the eyes. "You're the only save from that fire." He turned back to the others. "This is why we do what we do."

Now they clapped. Came forward. Shook his hand.

It was embarrassing, Stevens had been right. But he smiled, imagining what it would be like to see Ben Thurlow in twenty-five years. He'd embarrass the shit out of him, too.

Only after he'd said hello to all of them did he see that Grady, the other man he was to talk to, had hung back a bit.

Chief looked at Jason again then. "Thank you for letting me do that. This is amazing."

He motioned for Grady and Jason to follow him into his office, but he kept talking. "Is that why you became a firefighter?"

Jason shrugged. "I guess. I'm sorry, but I don't remember any of you. I have no memories of the fire or of my life before I was adopted. My parents told me stories of how I'd been pulled from a burning building and saved for them. It was always what I wanted to do."

Chief patted him on the back before sitting in his big chair and directing him and Grady into the guest seats. "Well, maybe it's better that you don't remember. It was pretty traumatic. Now, what can Grady and I help you with?"

As forthcoming as the Chief seemed to be, Grady was just as much a closed shell, sitting back and letting the other take the reins.

"Well," Jason started the only way he knew how, "I'm trying to find my brother. I'm certain he died, but I learned earlier that he was taken away from the scene in an ambulance and that it was the last time I saw him."

He explained the documentation about his brother being listed as 'name unknown'. Then asked his questions, "I'm hoping to find someone who knew his name, so I can find him in the system. Do either of you maybe know?"

"Sorry son, I don't. Grady?"

"Nope." He finally looked up at Jason.

Chief nodded. "I was working the ladder outside at first. I think that's how you and your brother were taken out of the building. I remember being on the far corner and seeing the boy kicking and screaming—that would have been you—and we all cheered because we knew you were alive. But I had a hose in my hand and I was dousing another part of the building. Grady?"

The man just shrugged and shook his head.

They talked a while longer, and Jason realized his jackpot was anything but. They remembered him but had no clue about names. He was no closer to finding a lead he could follow. But he stayed and talked about it. He made some notes while the Chief waited patiently and Grady just flicked glances at the page as he went. But he asked what he could, hoping for *something*. Chief Stevens wound up telling about the fire and about how it had gone down.

"We had all our trucks out. Every man on shift." He sighed. "I remember we couldn't rouse anyone from Station #3 because they were out on some other run and we called in the Burkeville Volunteer unit from Hope Hull."

Jason took note. There might be others he could contact, maybe they would be able to recall a name or something. "Hope Hull?"

"It's a little town southwest of here. It's the Burkeville Volunteer Department that operates out of there. The Pelias Street area was poor, and the city hydrant system was bad there. There wasn't one in reach and the pressure was for crap. So we were trucking in water. We needed more than just one station house on it."

Jason nodded. Hope Hull was next on his visit list.

Chief continued. "The Burkville guys may be able to help, if anyone is still around from then. They lost a man to that fire. He got burns and inhalation and died in the hospital three days later."

Jason nodded, wanting to express sympathy, but he hadn't known the man, and it seemed these two didn't really either.

The Chief kept talking. "In fact, he and his partner were the ones who pulled you and your brother out of the building."

Jason suddenly sat up straight, his pen stilled.

"Um. I don't remember the other one's name, but we all went to the funeral for the one that pulled your little brother out. There's a big plaque to him over at Burkeville. I want to say his name was Jake Strider? No. Strobel. It was Jake Strobel."

Southfield Fire Station #2

SHIFT	A	
	O'CASEY	CAPTAIN
ENGINE 2	WANSTALL	FF3
	WEST	FF2
	GRIMSBY	FF1
RESCUE 3	STANDARD	ENGINEER
	DONLAN	ENGINEER/PARMEDIC
RESCUE 1	MONDY	FF2 / EMT
	BLOOMBERG	FF1

Chapter 9

Donlan looked at the rest of them. He thought he'd done a better job of getting to know them all than this. So how the fuck had he missed this guy Bloomberg? Had Chief Adler lost his ever-lovin' mind and put two new people on shift at once?

Adler walked in front of them and ran down his checklist as he always had, silent as he made his marks on his paper. The previous shift had a tradition of hanging around for check-in—with Merriman previously on A-Shift, C folks could often pick up some overtime by covering for his ass. Then they'd gotten extra for picking up the shifts after he'd been canned. But lately it had been crazy around here.

The gunfight in the "Ghetto Corral"—as they were calling it—had been a lot to take. Even for a seasoned veteran and Yankee.

So as C-Shift sat and watched the changing of the guard, today they were quiet. They didn't fidget and no one got up to leave. No one had anything more important to get to than what was happening right here.

Adler finished his checks and cleared his throat. Though they all waited for something miraculous, something that would explain the Twilight Zone feeling, he merely assigned tasks around the house to the incoming guys.

Jason stayed in line and wondered when he would get a chance to pull the Chief aside and tell him what he'd learned. But now wasn't that time, so he tried again to learn patience.

Adler cleared his throat.

"Tell me you all have been keeping your commitments out at the Thurlow house rebuild project."

There were a handful of nods, and West spoke up, a laughing tone to his voice. "What are we going to do when the house is done, Chief? Parade around with puppies under our arms?"

Mondy turned and glared at him. When the Chief glared at him, too, West shrank back a bit.

"Gold Standard has clipped two months from their contract. As of yesterday morning we are down to nine weeks to get ready to run a full EMS operation."

The line stayed stiff and straight and C-Shift had straightened up to listen. Though they sat instead of stood, they were now as military precise as the incoming guys were.

"All right, a good number of you yahoos took up the city's offer for your career advancement courses. All the EMTs are headed to Paramedic—which saves some of the rest of your asses. And we have the required four on the way to EMT and one on the way to Advanced EMT. That means we need to hire one more Paramedic, one Advanced EMT, and one FF 1 or 2. So that's what I'll be hiring. If any of you decides to flunk out of your course, you'll be the first one looked at to get dropped. You are warned. I already hired a 'one' because he costs less and what little difference there is of that budget goes to the rest of you."

There were a few nods.

"His name is Bloomberg—as you may have used your mighty powers of deduction to figure out. And due to today's new snafu, he'll be here in a few minutes. I expect you to teach him what he needs to know and not drive into any god-damned gunfights today."

As though that had been their fault. And "god damned gunfights" and "new snafu?" Missy flinched. She was a brave woman, but the Chief's swearing always made her nervous. She'd take a collapsing building at full flashover any day.

Still they were not dismissed.

Chief seemed to recognize this. "Wait. It gets worse. We are damned lucky that I already had an extra man hired and that he was free to be added to today's shift. The city just called and let us know that Gold Standard is suffering an overabundance of sick employees. In fact, not one single EMS worker in the city of Southfield has shown up for work since the beginning of their shift at seven a.m."

That was the first thing that created movement along the line. It rippled like a shimmer through the men.

"This is our chance to prove that we can handle all of the work. We have only two old ambulances in the district, so we will haul patients on backboards if we have to. We will staff every EMS run we make with the few medic-trained guys we have and make every effort not to get our asses sued right off our backs." Then the Chief started pointing at them as he spoke, and any relaxation of stance disappeared. "Standard, you are head of Rescue 3, as expected you are driving. Donlan—" He pointed again "will take lead at the scene but pay attention to Standard and what he says about local customs."

Standard nodded, only looking forward. Donlan, though he followed suit, wondered what kind of unholy clusterfuck he'd walked into here in Southfield.

"Mondy, you've got Bloomberg as soon as he arrives."

"Yes, sir." Was all that Mondy said.

It was only then that the Chief dismissed them, pinching the bridge of his nose between his thumb and forefinger.

This day could not get any worse, could it?

But they all knew from experience that it could.

Fresh out of the locker room, Bloomberg was in his uniform for the first time and looking like a high school kid rather than someone with an associate's degree and firefighter training.

Mondy checked tanks and was inspecting equipment on both Rescue trucks. Though it was clear to everyone he was a bit touchy today, no one knew quite why.

It was right then that they heard the phone ring. As Chief picked it up, the bell in the house went off and everyone looked up to see who was going on the run.

Chief pointed to Donlan and Standard, and everyone moved in tandem to get Rescue 3 up and running. By the time the two were out the bay door less than a minute later, they knew they were dealing with a hysterical mother and a choking child.

The horn honked twice as they rolled out of the station house.

Missy picked up her mop and Mondy went back to work on Rescue 1 now with Bloomberg right behind him. He let the rookie check one SCBA tank while he watched, made a correction, then looked up as the phone rang again.

This time it was Engine 2 that was headed out for a "small" kitchen fire. Rescue 1 stood ready to follow in case they got to the scene and radioed back that the caller had no concept of "small." Sometimes the caller also had no concept of "fire."

Jason was sitting at the break-room table when Wanstall, Standard, and Grimsby came back an hour later. He'd just hung up from an interesting phone call from Captain Smith from the Burkeville Volunteer Department. The man had said that he'd heard about Jason's visit and he'd worked with Strobel. In the end, he'd given no more information than what Jason already knew. But he wanted to check in and see if Jason had learned anything else about what had happened to him and extend his condolences.

Mondy closed his phone, thinking *not yet*, then he turned his attention back to work and to the three firefighters just returning Engine 2 from a small kitchen fire.

He sniffed the air. "I smell bacon."

"Shut up, Mondy." Wanstall shuffled past him. They all smelled like it. She explained that an older man had started some bacon on his stove and walked away to do something, then forgot that he was cooking. What the homeowner had by the time they arrived—aside from the phenomenal luck that he hadn't burned the whole place down—was about six strips of meat no longer fit for man or beast.

It was Bloomberg who piped up. "Miss Wanstall, I believe you're my perfect woman."

Everyone stopped dead to hear this. Missy stood in the center of the room, eyebrows up, a smudge of some kind of dark grease on her face. Her yellow fire-gear pants made her look like she had the ass of the Stay Puft Marshmallow Man. And all she said was, "Oh?"

"Yes, ma'am. You're real pretty. You're brave and smart. You'd leave the house for a whole day every three days and you smell like bacon."

Clearly, Bloomberg hadn't learned the cardinal rule of being new: shut up and step back. Listen and look, but don't say anything unless you have to.

In fact, no one said a word. You just didn't mess with Missy. She earned respect, you treated her with respect, and if all went well according to her plan, everyone forgot she had boobs and girl-parts. So all the jaws around her practically unhinged when she threw her head back and laughed. She howled while everyone else stood and stared.

Then she stopped.

"That's funny, Bloomberg."

"Thanks, Missy." His grin was shy, and it looked to the others like maybe he had a thing for her. Donlan thought to himself that after twenty-four hours it'd been clear to *him* not to do that. Bloomberg needed to learn fast.

Missy smiled back, a slow predatory grin. "It's 'Wanstall.' And if you call me 'Missy' again, I'll torture you until you leave not only this fire house but the entire profession, quivering like a naked baby in a bowl of Jell-O. Got me?"

Bloomberg snapped upright, fear in his eyes. "Yes, ma'am. Sir . . . Wanstall."

She smiled at him then. Sweetly. "Thanks, kiddo."

And off she went to shower, Bloomberg's eyes following her every move until she was out of sight. When he slumped back, it was Mondy who patted him absentmindedly on the shoulder. "You'll learn, little boy. You'll learn."

Then he checked the message on his voicemail. It was from Merriman. Though he put forth a well-composed plea, it was still a plea, and his voice still whined. Unconsciously mimicking the Chief, Jason pinched the bridge of his nose while he listened. He didn't know how to tell the kid that there was no way he could write him a letter of recommendation for an appeal. He couldn't in good conscience recommend that Merriman come back to work. So Jason deleted the message and set the thought aside.

It was one p.m. before the daily tasks all got finished and Chief called off the regular afternoon training in light of all the other crap that was going down that day. One by one about half of them went out to get lunch in some way or other. There was a burger run, a sub run and Bloomberg who wandered down the block and came back with a huge dish of ice cream covered in M&Ms and chocolate chips.

Donlan was the first to spot him coming in with his mound of soft-serve. "What's that?"

The kid smiled. "It's frozen yogurt."

"Seriously?"

"What?" Spoon nearly to his mouth, Bloomberg pulled his head back, like "was he going to get teased about this, too?"

Grimsby didn't say anything, but looked like he knew what was going down. And he should, he'd gotten this same lecture when he first came to the house, he'd just gotten it from Connelly back when he'd been on B-Shift.

Standard took up the reins. "Is that what you're having for lunch? Because I could have sworn we said you could go down the street for *lunch.*"

The kid nodded missing the stress.

Around the room a few eyes looked at each other. He had a long way to go, and they didn't have the space or time to deal with another Merriman. Maybe that was why they came down on him just a little harder.

Standard planted himself in front of the kid, his girth and broad shoulders giving him heft and intimidation factors galore. Bloomberg nearly backed up, but held on, only tipping slightly away from the senior engineer.

"From now on, when you get a chance to eat lunch, you eat *lunch.* It's not a sugar bomb. None of us can carry you if you pass out on the job."

Bloomberg smirked and took a bite and spoke through it, "I'm not going to pass out before dinner."

It became clear to all the others standing around that Standard was working to hold back from smacking the Styrofoam dish right out of the kid's hand. "When's dinner?"

"I don't know. Around five?"

"And what if we go out on a fire and dinner time doesn't come until five a.m.? And at four a.m. you're in a building at my back, and you can't cut it because you had ice cream for lunch?"

Finally, he started to catch on and show some remorse. But— as his youth would indicate—he didn't quite know when to call off the dogs and cut his losses. "It's not ice cream. It's frozen yogurt. It's low cal and has fruit sugars, so it's better for you."

Donlan came into the conversation again at that point, if only to keep Standard from going postal. "What's that on top of it, then?"

Bloomberg murmured.

"I'm sorry. I couldn't hear you." Ryan Donlan cupped his ear, leaned in close, and faked his sincerity.

With a deep breath, the kid found some balls. "It's M&Ms and chocolate chips. There's a Butterfinger underneath. It won't happen again."

Standard looked at him. "Damn straight it won't. You show up next shift with a packed lunch and dinner and if I don't approve it, you don't get to eat it."

For a moment Bloomberg fought his protest. Then he visibly swallowed it and said, "Yes, sir."

Then the bell rang and Mondy took him out on a run to where a sixteen-year-old girl had fainted at her friend's house. While Bloomberg's yogurt melted into soup where it was left on the dining room table, Mondy walked him through all the procedures.

The friend's mother had no medical authority here, but she pulled Jason aside and asked if he thought the girl might be anorexic or bulimic. He smiled and though he wanted to say "No shit, Sherlock" he told her that he couldn't diagnose anything at this point, but the hospital could recommend places to be evaluated.

It took two hours before they were on their way back to the station house. And Mondy drilled Bloomberg the whole way back—about minors, about parental consent, about all the phone calls they had made trying to get someone who was actually responsible for the girl to pick her up and get her to a medical facility. About how you couldn't say you thought she was anorexic or anything like that, but you could say that this random, unprovoked fainting could be a symptom of these certain medical conditions and show the mom a BMI chart and how her daughter ranked abnormally low.

He was just checking the kid for comprehension when he heard a weird noise and saw Bloomberg tense. "What was that?"

"Um." He didn't say anything else, but shifted a bit in the passenger seat.

"Was that your stomach growling?"

"Yeah."

After ascertaining that no, the boy had not brought any real food to the station house with him, Jason uttered a "fuck this" and cranked the wheel. Turning the truck into the nearest shopping center lot, he parked sideways and walked up to the Cheeseburger Chuck's, dragging Bloomberg behind him. "Do you have any money on you?"

After a brief nod, Mondy continued, "Buy a damn burger."

^ ^ ^ ^ ^

It had been a long day full of turnaround runs and barely enough time for dinner. Though the pace had slowed a bit after it got dark, by midnight half of them had crawled into bed. But there had already been some issues with that. The sleep room had nineteen beds in it, for eighteen men plus a spare. Until today, each man had his own bed that didn't get used by anyone else. That was a luxury that was over for now and would get worse as they filled in the new spots. Now they needed that spare bed at least every night, and there would be issues with seniority about who had to use a random bed and who got his own. Just after lunch, Chief had put a few calls out and Connelly had come in to grant a little relief.

They had enough people to run the shift, but still the pace had been challenging. And just after midnight, the Chief was still in his office reclining his chair back as far as it would go.

Adler didn't have a bed in the station house—he was one of the very few who worked a reasonably standard Monday—Friday shift. He had spent his day on the phone trying to figure out how long Gold Standard's "blue flu" was going to continue. And the city heads were all becoming concerned that they had underestimated the EMS business in town.

He wanted to go back over the projection and the write-ups they'd made. Wanted to know if today was just a heavy day— which happened—or if there had been a serious error in their estimates. But only time would tell. His head hurt from the inside out, and he tried not to think about it.

He could hear the faint strains of the romantic comedies that always seemed to mysteriously appear on the TV right around midnight. No one ever admitted to queuing up the movies, but no one ever changed the channel either, and Chief had caught each of them watching some piece of romantic drivel at one time or another. Right now it was a soothing sound, that drone of the audio, the rise and fall of emotional scenes.

He'd already made the rounds and seen that the night was passing normally and maybe he could finally go home. For a moment, the near silence allowed his brain to crack and fissure from the fear that they would have to re-petition the contract to get money to add another man to each shift. They had done all the math before they bid. He, Delta and the mayor had been stitching this deal together for months. Again he asked himself, Had they been wrong?

Again he answered. No. They weren't wrong. He'd stood out there just that morning and told the men that there would be growing pains while they did this. Yet somehow he'd gotten stupid enough to think that didn't apply to him. What a fool.

Oh well. All is well right this moment.

The thought had just passed through his brain when he felt the vibration, as though he could sense the signal coming through the wire. *Shit.*

And his phone rang. Not the normal station line—dispatch. "Yes?"

He breathed in and sighed it out and felt everything drain. Adler listened to the phone, and as he did he heard the bell ring in the main house.

The bell was loud enough to wake them all up—they were all tuned to it anyway. It took one look from the Chief to see that it was big. With no further information, everyone's eyes cleared and they all started to get in gear.

Though it wasn't daytime and no one had really been up and about when the call came, in a few minutes they rolled out both engines followed by Rescue 3. Mondy and Wanstall were in Engine 5 and almost to the location when she turned to him and recited the address, "Is that what I think it is?"

They had passed a small handful of cars as they drove toward the building. Normally it would be considered suspicious for someone to flee the scene of a fire, as though there was something to hide. But neither of them really thought anything about it in this case.

"Ho-lee shit." It was all Jason could say as they rounded the corner and caught sight of the blaze in the distance.

The building was the only one this far out on the street, set about thirteen feet beyond the city limits, and for good reason. No one wanted to be the business next door to "Different Strokes."

The engines pulled into the now empty parking lot, lining the trucks up like Rockettes. As Missy let herself down from the driver's seat she saw a group of forlorn looking people huddled on the far side of the parking lot. About seven girls stood huddled in blankets, apparently with little to nothing on underneath. Mascara ran down some of their faces, and most of them seemed to shiver in the night air. They weren't dressed for this. And suddenly Missy connected the big sign that sat along the roofline that said "lingerie" to the girls outside. They weren't just selling it, they were "modeling" it and providing whatever services might go along with that. Her stomach nearly turned over, and then she reminded herself that they were probably out-earning her.

She felt better when the Chief walked over to the crowd. Better him than one of the other guys. The rest of them hauled hoses and wished for a hydrant that wasn't there. They were all set up and still waiting for word that everyone was out of the building before they could start blasting with the water. One by one they all slipped their hoods on and put their face-mask straps into place. At the word, they'd start breathing filtered air.

Chief came back and pointed out best routes into and out of the building. "They're certain everyone is out. The owner says he did a whole sweep. But you'll keep your eyes open. The structure itself—the frame—is entirely metal."

There were nods, and air tanks were slowly turned up, breathing rates changed, and several of them looked over at Bloomberg, worried. Donlan was the last one to put his mask on. "Hey, Frogurt, this is your first big one. Stick close."

Fifteen minutes later, they had made a first sweep and were outside getting ready to start another assault on the fire when they heard the voices through their gear.

"Shit. Shit, Shit!" Immediately overlapped by, "We're coming out."

Just then, Mondy and Standard burst through the front doors and just behind them followed the roar of the flames as everything caught fire.

It seemed the critical point to make things spontaneously burst into flames was relatively low in a sex shop. Chief muttered "flashover," and went over to where his two veterans had finally come to a stop after jettisoning out into the parking area.

An hour and a half of hard labor passed before they were able to declare the fire under control. And it was another three hours before they could declare it officially out.

Though Different Strokes was now out of business for a while, and the question of how the blaze started was not being answered satisfactorily, there was no more fire. No smoldering ashes or lace-up heels ready to start anew when they turned their backs.

The police had arrived hours ago and the owner of the store, some guy named Robb, had greeted each of the cops by first name as though they were old friends. Some had the wherewithal to get embarrassed, though by the fifth or sixth time it was clear Robb was ragging on them. One or two officers had hung out, questioning the employees and sending most of the girls home for a hot bath and decent clothing.

By the time they rolled the hoses all back up and the trucks were packed, every single member of A-Shift wore the smudges of a fight across their faces and hands. Even Adler had geared up and gone in near the end, and he too had marks on his skin and his formerly pristine white shirt. When they left the scene to the police, who were stringing up yellow tape and turning away the few folks who were brave enough to venture close, it was less than an hour from the dawn.

Weary to the bone, they parked the trucks and slowly wiped them down. One by one, they finished up with checks and refills and headed into the showers. The Chief had retired to his desk, needing a shower himself, but unable to leave all the work to the men on crew. The trucks were like horses in the Old West—you needed them, they saved your life. And so, just like the Old West, it was horses first, or in this case, trucks.

Adler was just easing back into his chair, thinking that this was exactly the position he'd been in when that call had come in. He was swinging himself upright in an effort to fight bad luck when he heard more than saw someone come through the door.

It was Mondy, unshowered and looking even grittier than the Chief felt.

"Yes?" Even that single word was difficult to get out.

"There's something I wanted to tell you. All day. But I didn't get a chance."

"Hmm." If anything beyond one syllable was necessary he was going to need a wrench to pry it out of himself. Then he caught on, "No, Mondy, you don't have to play 'golden boy' and tell the papers all about the fire at the sex shop."

But that didn't seem to be what he wanted.

Paying no heed to the fact that he was filthy and the chairs were clean, Mondy plopped down and looked right at him.

Adler became very concerned.

"Chief. You remember that fire you told me about? Outside Montgomery, where you lost your partner?"

He nodded.

"Well, it turns out I was the boy you rescued."

Suddenly, Adler was awake. Fully awake. "*What?*"

"Yeah, my mother told me something about a month ago. That I had a brother in that fire. I didn't know." He looked away, his eyes turning sad. But then he pushed his expression back to something resembling normal and faced the chief again. "Anyway, your partner—Jake Strobel—was killed going back for my brother. I'm the one who sent him back in. I'm sorry."

"What?" Confused as all hell, Adler first addressed the concern he saw on his firefighter's face. "Strobel was doing the job. You know that. I know that, and somewhere, so does he. . . Now, are you really telling me that you're the kid we pulled out? The older brother?"

Mondy nodded.

"How the hell do you know that? You didn't know it a few weeks ago." He was searching for some kind of confirmation and hope that Mondy was wrong.

The firefighter fidgeted with something he held in his hands. Something he'd picked up from the front of the Chief's desk absentmindedly. Normally, that would have caught him hell, but right now it didn't matter. "Yeah. I didn't know I had the brother. And so I started looking for him. He's probably dead. But I found out the fire that killed my birth mother wasn't here in Birmingham like I thought, but in Montgomery. It was the Pelias Street Apartment fire in '85."

Chief felt his breathing slow. "You've been digging into it?"

"Yeah, well digging into what I can find about my brother. I went to CPS and then to the fire stations. I'm figuring on checking in with the police stations in Montgomery next. See if anyone knows anything." He shrugged.

Slowly Adler's breathing came to a complete stop. "Oh, God. That thing was a clusterfuck from the start. I don't know what the hell you've opened up, but you've just pulled an old scab off of something and it isn't good."

Mondy stared at him.

And Adler felt himself go ice cold.

Chapter 10

Jason

The others had wandered into the bunk room and gone to bed, but once again, Jason found he just couldn't sleep. For a while it had been the odd feeling of Kelly not being in the apartment. Then the bad dreams were probably because the recent happenings hit a little too close to home. Maybe that was why the Chief had only now told him the story of the rescue in Montgomery so many years ago. Maybe the Thurlow fire had sparked all of this.

The facts were that he'd been in a fire as a kid and he'd grown up to become a firefighter. So when he found himself on the other side of the story, something in his memory had started burbling up.

But now there were so many more things to keep him awake. Fidgeting in one of the easy chairs, he tried to immerse himself in a paperback. Though it was usually easy to do, tonight he couldn't get into the story. He read the same page three times before he gave up and closed his eyes. Hoping for sleep, and doubting it would find him, Jason let his brain wander.

He wondered if it was fate that had him wind up working in the station of the man who had rescued him, but quickly dismissed that. Southerners didn't tend to move far from home. He was proof of that himself; though he'd left the state a handful of times, he'd never lived outside its borders. So it was a coincidence—but not a completely strange one—that Adler had been at the Pelias Street fire.

That it had taken seven years to figure it out was odd. Jason had come to this house shortly after Adler had made Chief. He'd interviewed and been hired here before heading to the

Birmingham training program. Someone had suggested that he try out the smaller, privatized district, so he did. And he'd liked Adler right off.

Jason stiffened with the shock of that.

Though he still had no memories of Adler pulling him from the fire, maybe some part of him had recognized the man. A big part of his decision to come here had been the feeling he'd gotten when Chief interviewed him.

Holy shit. Things were becoming less and less coincidental.

Maybe Adler had recognized him subconsciously, too.

Jason just wished he could remember. While home fires were traumatic for anyone, they were the hardest on kids. Trauma could make people lose or bury memories. So it wasn't unreasonable that he couldn't remember. But logic didn't help him find his brother.

When the bell went off at six thirty in the morning, Jason volunteered for the run. He took Bloomberg with him to help an old man who was sitting on his front stoop, bag packed and waiting. As the two of them walked up, the man introduced himself in a tight voice, then stuck his hand out for a shake—even though he was already blue and couldn't feel his left arm.

Jason made Frogurt drive them to the hospital while he monitored all the symptoms he could. The ER staff ran out with a gurney and listened as Jason rattled off stats. It was clearly a heart attack, but only the doctor could say so. Within a minute, the man was loaded up and whisked away. Guiding Frogurt to follow the procedure, they got an ER staffer to sign off that they had delivered a live patient.

Frogurt commented, "It's like we're driving UPS. We just got our package signed for."

Jason couldn't help but laugh at that. "But our package was alive, because we delivered him."

"Yeah, but we still have a clipboard and still had to get that signature."

And for a while, his brain had been occupied with something other than conspiracy theories and coincidental ties.

He was just signing off on the paperwork he was re-doing after letting Frogurt have a try at it and waiting for the last thirty minutes of shift to magically pass when his phone rang. He smiled. "Aida."

"Hi." Her voice sounded somewhat shy.

"What can I do for you?" As soon as he uttered it, he felt stupid. He liked her, but he didn't know what to do with her. Though it was probably a good thing, it left him on uneven ground. He wasn't hit in the gut with that lust that he usually looked for. Jason put his face in his palm and was grateful she couldn't see him.

"I knew you would still be on shift and probably be up or I wouldn't have called so early."

She remembered.

"You caught me at just the right time."

"I was curious if you were still going to come down to Montgomery later today?"

"Oh." He'd forgotten all about it in light of what the Chief had said. "I don't know yet. Though probably not."

He was rambling a little. He had told her he'd be back—today in fact. She was right about the timing. But now . . . now he didn't know if he should go. And he knew he definitely shouldn't go before he talked to the Chief. "I'm sorry. Something came up here."

"No problem."

Silence filled the line for a moment and though he wanted to tell her he'd be coming down soon, he couldn't. Adler had gone stock-still when Jason told him that he'd been looking into the Pelias Street fire.

Jason hadn't yet decided if he was going to pursue the investigation. And if he didn't, then he wouldn't be going back to Montgomery. And he wouldn't see Aida.

She replaced the silence with something. Like most women he knew, she could do that. "Well, just give me call if you head back this way and if you want me to make dinner for you. I'll let you know if I'm free."

"I will."

They hung up. That sounded like she was inviting him to her place. But the "I'll let you know if I'm free" was definitely a note that she would not be waiting around.

He couldn't blame her.

When he looked up, most of the dreaded last half hour had disappeared, and he gratefully went to gather his things. He was ready to head home when Adler pulled him aside and told him that he would treat Jason to breakfast. It wasn't a question.

So Jason waited out the shift change. He sat through the assignments, watching as O'Casey handed the shift over to Bender. They all knew that no one had shown up to work for Gold Standard for three shifts now. It wasn't looking good. Then Adler told them he'd be out most of the day—sleeping. He gave everyone the "do the right thing" nod and left the building with Jason in tow.

Following in his own car, Jason wanted to be sure it didn't look like the Chief was dragging him out for a private chat—which was exactly what was happening. There was enough shit going on these days without adding to it, and it didn't sound like this should be something shared with anyone else at the station house.

Crapcrapcrap.

The Chief picked a sit-down diner favored by the older folks in town, reminding Jason that Adler wasn't just a boss, but a man of nearly sixty years. One who'd seen and done almost everything. Though they casually chose a table and ordered, his stomach was churning and the look on Adler's face didn't help at all.

As soon as the waitress left, Jason blurted out what he'd intended to ask calmly. "Did you hire me because I'm the kid you pulled from the fire?"

"I hired you because you had a good work ethic, wanted to come to Southfield and had rec letters from men I trusted. I didn't recognize you." Adler frowned. "Not even after seven years on the job. Did you recognize me?"

Jason shook his head, then amended the thought. "Not consciously at least. Even now I don't remember it. I only know what I've read and what other people have told me: the location of the fire and that the man who pulled me out was the partner of the man who pulled out my brother—Jake Strobel . And that Strobel died a few days later."

Adler sighed. "That's definitely me." Then he sat patiently while the waitress filled both their coffees and asked if they needed anything else. Even when she left, Chief stared into space for a moment before asking, "Why are you looking for your brother now? What sparked this?"

Jason almost laughed. "It's your fault."

"How's that?" At least Adler looked like he was taking it in the non-blaming way it was meant.

"After the Thurlow fire, you told me to go home and see if I could sleep in my old bed."

"The Thurlow fire brought it up? There were enough similarities, I guess."

Jason shook his head. "No, that fire just kept me from sleeping. Then you said I should go home. My mother had followed the reports of the Thurlow fire, so when I had problems she dumped all the facts she knew of the Pelias fire in my lap. Really just that I'd misremembered a lot of it and that I had a brother. I still don't remember him at all."

"Well, crap."

From the look on Adler's face and what he'd said earlier, none of this was good. But Jason still didn't understand *how* it was bad. "Look, I know my brother is dead. He apparently had bad asthma before the fire. They took him away in an ambulance and I never saw him again. I'm just looking for some record of his death. I feel bad that I don't even remember him. What's the problem with that?"

Chief gave a heavy sigh and his eyes squeezed shut like he was pained.

Then their food arrived, delaying any information yet again. They should have gone for fast food, Jason thought.

"The problem is that something was wrong with that fire. A few of the firefighters cried arson—myself included—and we were told the investigation was finished and the fire was ruled accidental."

"How is that—" He didn't even finish the sentence.

"They announced it before the smoke cleared. There was no way any legitimate investigation was run in that time frame. Which means it was shut down and we were told to shut up."

Jason's food suddenly seemed unappetizing. "There was a cover up?"

Adler shook his head but said, "I spoke up, but no one would listen. Not the police chief, not my chief. Then I was told—in no uncertain terms—that I appeared unstable. That I was obviously suffering the loss of my partner. I was sent to counseling."

Well, that sucked.

Adler continued. "I tried to tell the counselor that it was arson, but all I got was 'and why do you think that?' and 'how do you feel about your partner's death?' I knew if I didn't get out of there and fast, I'd lose my job."

"And why did you think it was arson?" Upon hearing his own words, Jason added. "Sorry."

The Chief at least chuckled a little. "Are you going to stop digging into your brother's death?"

Jason sighed. "Maybe."

Maybe it wasn't worth it. Likely all he would ever find was a death certificate; he'd never kidded himself about anything beyond that. He didn't even want a death certificate, what he wanted was closure. Maybe something that would spark a memory. But the memories he did have had all been buried. There had to be a reason for that.

Adler looked him in the eyes. "If you follow the trail to find your brother, you'll dig up things on the Pelias Street fire. I don't think people want them dug up."

Jason took a deep breath and nodded.

The Chief went one step further. "You can't look for one without the other. And if you look, you'll open a bad can of worms."

They left it at that. Chief picked up the tab and Jason left his plate half-full. By the time he had the key in the front door of his apartment, he'd made up his mind. It wasn't worth any of this coming back around.

He'd thought it through. And though he hated the thought that someone would get away with arson—murder, maybe—there was no way he'd find real evidence now. Even if he solved the whole thing, he'd likely just be left with papers that wouldn't explain what had really happened to his brother. Probably only a diagnosis—which Jason could already guess would be "smoke inhalation exacerbated by asthma" and a date of death.

Adler would likely get investigated. Not that anyone would find anything on the Chief. Mostly it would reflect badly on the department at a time when Southfield couldn't afford it. Hell, there was every possibility that Gold Standard would close its doors this week when no one showed up for shift. The three stations were already getting an extra ambulance in each bay, borrowed from nearby districts. B-Shift was running with full EMS equipment today.

No, it wasn't worth any of it.

And he had to stop anything he'd already stirred up.

So Jason got out the bag that had seen exactly one day's use and pulled out the phone number for the Burkeville Volunteer

Fire Department. He'd tell Captain Smith that he'd hit a dead end and that there wasn't anywhere else to look—which wasn't even much of a lie. But it should put some things to bed and quell anything he'd upset.

They answered the phone after two rings, surprising in a volunteer department. But Burkeville was one of the best.

"I'm looking for Captain Smith. He called me yesterday." Jason knew there was little to no chance that the man was in the station house two days in a row in a volunteer division. But he intended to leave a message.

He was told, "There's no Captain Smith here."

"Right, he was on yesterday."

"No sir. No Captain Smith has ever worked at this station to my knowledge."

"What?" Jason scrolled through his cell phone's call log. He asked about the number that he had been called from earlier. "Isn't that to this station house?"

Even as he thought about it, he realized that the numbers were drastically different, only the area code was the same. Like many older businesses, the call lines were likely off from each other only by one digit.

The voice on the phone confirmed that. "No sir. That number sounds like a number from Montgomery proper."

Jason heard his own voice trail off. "Oh. Sure."

He sat silent for a moment before something congealed in him and he began babbling. "I'm sorry. Is this Burkeville? I meant to call the Montgomery station. House Number Three. I just misdialed. I'll call them."

"Sure." The man on the other end seemed to think Jason was nuts. But that was expected because Jason sounded like he was nuts. He disconnected and sat down hard.

That call yesterday, the man had said he was from the Burkeville Station. Jason remembered, because he hadn't met a "Smith" when he visited. And when the man said "Burkeville" Jason had hoped it meant he'd have something useful.

So he sat on the arm of his couch and looked blindly up at his shelf where he saw the beer bottle he'd left there days ago. He must not have used the house phone since he'd set it there.

Absentmindedly, he reached up to grab the bottle and wound up knocking it over. The remaining beer spattered across the generic pale carpeting and didn't even have the grace to give up any fizz as it went.

Swearing to himself as he watched it soak in, Jason went to the kitchen for paper towels. It hit him then, there on his hands and knees trying to soak beer out of his carpeting, that he was incredibly tired. He didn't own a carpet scrubber—he didn't have pets or kids, so he hadn't thought he needed one. Unfortunately, there was no way he'd be able to get the beer entirely out.

When he turned to get a stray spot near the wall, he felt something in his pocket. Frowning, he reached in and fished it out. It was a bullet. Frowning, he patted down his other pockets but then remembered emptying out the automatic gun at the gunfight. Just holding the bullet in his hand brought on a small case of the shakes. Any of them might not have survived that day. And what he'd done was stupid, going after the gun like that. But he hadn't thought, hadn't been trained to disarm people, and he'd just reacted.

He sighed. The bullet must have gone through the wash in his pocket.

And he *had* survived that day. All of Station House #2 had. So he pushed it back into his pocket and left it there. Maybe his luck was okay. Then he looked at the beer on the carpet and thought otherwise.

He'd soaked more paper towels than he could count when the phone rang. For a moment, he stopped and sat back on his knees and listened to it ring. Whoever had said he was "Captain Smith" could be calling back. Jason had dialed Burkeville using his home phone. *Shit. That had been a mistake.*

But he manned up and looked at the caller ID. "Hey, Alex."

"I have a roommate for you."

"Really?" That was the first good news in a while. His fingers went into his pocket and around the bullet there.

"Of course. I told you I'd find someone. She's only in town for a little while, so the time frame is perfect. She'll move out about two weeks before your lease is up."

"Wow." Jason smiled to himself, then thought he must be more tired than he realized. "You said 'she'."

"Yes, I did. She's fantastic and can put up with you. She's Leo's second cousin." There was a smile in Alex's voice. "I've met her before and she just asked Leo if he knew of a place she could rent. It's perfect."

Maybe, Jason thought to himself. But he didn't have a lot of leeway and he couldn't afford to be picky. So even though she wouldn't be perfect, he would make due. And he would get his own life back at the end of the three remaining months, find his own place and be his own man again. "Okay."

"Whoa, Bucko. She wants to see the place first."

Jason turned down the offer of "now" and opted for "later"— after he got some sleep and talked to the Chief. He hung up with Alex, grateful that at least one of his many problems might be solved, and even if "she" was an unholy terror, it was for less than twelve weeks. He could do it.

After he gave up on the carpet, he called the Chief at home. Jennifer Adler answered, as he had suspected would be the case. He told her to wake her father.

Instead he got Abigail Adler, whom he told to wake her husband, but this time he apologized profusely. And when his boss came on the line sounding as though he'd been dragged up from under the ocean, Jason explained about the call from Captain Smith.

Adler had cursed loud enough and long enough for Mrs. Adler to comment on it from the background. And when he finished he spoke to Jason again. "Don't do anything. Don't talk to anyone today. Don't answer the phone for anyone calling back from Montgomery. We'll meet tonight and figure this out." He sighed and Jason could imagine him pinching the bridge of his nose.

"Yes, sir. Will do."

"I'm going to call the station and have them alert everyone that no one is to talk to any press or answer any questions about you." Then his voice got a little distant, but Jason heard the words clearly. "Shit shit shit."

He even heard Abigail again. "Michael, I don't think that's necessary."

Chief responded, "Trust me, Abby, it is."

Jason was starting to chuckle when the voice was aimed at him again. "If this blows wide, there are a fistful of murder charges to be handed out. This could get very ugly, very fast."

He sobered. "I'm so sorry, Chief—"

"You didn't know. You couldn't have. Hell, I didn't even know you were in my station this whole time. Look, I have to get some sleep and so do you. Call your police friend and set up a meeting for us tonight, somewhere not my house or yours. At eight. Leave me a message where. I'll be there."

"Yes, sir." Jason hung up in near shock. *Shit,* that "not at my house or yours" sounded as though someone might be watching them.

∧   ∧   ∧   ∧   ∧

Not surprisingly, Jason didn't think he'd slept. He wasn't stupid; he'd been in bed with the blackouts drawn and a lot of time had passed so he must have dozed. But he hadn't *slept.* He'd gotten up and eaten a bowl of cereal when his stomach had become mad at him for not finishing the omelet he'd ordered that morning. Then he'd crawled back under the covers and tried again, only to toss them back about an hour or so later, broken out in a cold sweat.

He'd called his mother. "Mom, I did something . . ." And he felt like when he was in elementary school and he'd had to come home and confess to his parents before they heard from his teacher. His heart clenched and his mouth had pressed together involuntarily. The thought that this search might wind up hurting the only person left on earth who simply loved him was more than he could bear to think about.

But for her own safety Jason explained about "Captain Smith" and that Adler had said the whole fire had been a clusterfuck— but he didn't use that word. He didn't tell her more than that, again, because he didn't want her to worry. For a moment, he felt like he was in a spy movie, then he simply felt afraid. She was really all he had left and she was older—older even than his friends' mothers had been.

Telling her what she needed to stay safe and trusting that she was smart, he hung up. Having taken care of the worry that had sent him bolting from bed, he tried again to sleep. He consoled himself that no "Captain Smith" had called her. No one had asked her about him or anything related to him. But the conversation had brought on a new set of concerns.

It was a good thing that Kelly had left. He needed to find someone better—someone who would really love him. Someone for when his mother finally left this life, so he wouldn't be all alone. He knew his mom missed his father terribly, but she made small statements about wanting to see her grandkids. He always joked that he was "nowhere near that" and she always left it alone. But her friends all had grandkids—some were even graduating high school. She deserved to see hers. And where girlfriends were concerned, he deserved more than he'd been getting.

His thoughts turned to Aida as he rolled over and pulled the covers with him, as though another position would make the difference and he'd finally sleep. He didn't know what to make of Aida. She was pretty enough. She was smart and fun to talk to, but she didn't make him want to peel her clothes and do the kind of things that would give his mother grandkids.

It certainly wasn't like she was repulsive; she did have moments of sexiness, and she'd talked about making him dinner. He had to wonder if it was code for him to stay over. And he had to wonder how he would feel about that when the time came.

That was a first in and of itself. He'd never turned down an offer from a woman he liked. Not before. Not that Aida had really offered.

He was awake when the alarm went off, and he rolled out of bed as tired as when he went in. But he popped into and out of the shower, dressed in clothing that didn't identify him as SFD, and again made a note that he needed to buy some clothes. Maybe he'd be able to now with the new roomie paying half the rent.

He made a sandwich and ate it on the way to the station to drop off his key for Alex. Alex and the new roommate would come check out the digs while he was out. Apparently, she wouldn't be in town again until next week. He didn't want to get a new roommate sight unseen, but he needed to meet with the Chief tonight, and wasn't trusting Alex the whole point of putting him in charge?

Jason pulled into Jenkins, a local bar where they could get a table in the corner, where the music was just a little too loud for anyone to overhear anything of importance, and where no one would think twice that the fire chief was meeting with a cop and the local ADA.

Sure enough, as Jason walked in the front door from the chill of the late fall night, he spotted Rob Castor and Bart English at a far table with tall glasses of beer already in hand. Neither of them wore anything labeling them as any kind of official, but Southfield was a relatively small town and people knew.

His own beer arrived just a few moments after he ordered it and Chief came through the door then, followed by Bruce

Connelly. The Chief ordered several appetizers for the table and Jason wasn't sure if the man was hungry or if he was just trying to make things look normal.

Adler turned to Jason and asked, "Connelly?"

"I've talked to him about some of this in the past. He's kept up with where I went and who I talked to, so I thought he might have some insight."

That seemed to be good enough for the Chief, which was a good thing since Bruce Connelly already sat at the table with a beer in hand.

For a moment they all looked at each other, then Bart English started, "Okay, I'm out of the loop. Catch me up on what's happening and why we need a clandestine meeting about it."

With a nod of his head, Adler passed that to Jason. He told about being rescued by Adler as a kid all the way through getting the call from a non-existent Captain Smith. Adler then hopped in.

"I worked the fire he was in. It stank of arson and the investigation got shut down, fast. The report was logged and the fire was ruled accidental in under twenty-four hours. I don't think the scene was even cleared when that paperwork was filed."

Rob Castor, ever the police officer, looked at Adler, "If you're so certain it was arson, why didn't you file a complaint at the time?"

"I did. I spoke to my Chief. He told me it was getting looked into. I later saw the official report that it was ruled accidental."

"You didn't protest?" Castor narrowed his eyes at Adler. They all knew Adler to be a straight arrow, but maybe in his younger days he hadn't been.

"I did. I filed an appeal."

"Can we pull it?"

Adler shook his head. "When I followed up, I found out that it had never been handed in. I was told to shut up. The reasoning was that I would stir up the press over nothing. That I was too new to know what I saw and that I was upset that my partner died. I didn't have a leg to stand on. It's always sat wrong with me." He shrugged.

The men all looked at each other. English popped a pistachio in his mouth and thought for a moment. Then he turned back to Adler. "What made you think it was arson? Wait. I need paper. . . shit."

Jason smiled. "One minute."

He grabbed the research bag from where he'd stashed it at his feet. This would be the second time he'd gotten to use it, and maybe the last. He handed over a full pad of paper and a pen.

"Thanks."

Jason nodded. "I have all my notes in here. My birth certificate and the duplicate of my brother's. Two articles about the Pelias Street fire."

Bart English started writing. "Did anyone die in the fire?"

"Fifteen people." Jason rattled off the number. He'd read it in the follow-up article. "That included the one fire department casualty—Jake Strobel—Chief's partner who saved my brother."

English shook his head. "There's a three-year statute of limitations on arson in Alabama—which is long past. However, with the deaths from that arson you're looking at second-degree murder. Which means the murder and any crimes associated with it have no statute of limitations."

There was a brief silence, and it was Connelly who finally broke it. "So, if it was arson, then there's someone out there who set the fire. Someone who can still be prosecuted for it."

English nodded. "And that someone is willing and has the means—or at least had them almost thirty years ago—to cover it up."

Jason felt his eyebrows go up, *Well, shit, when you put it that way*, he thought.

English turned back to the Chief then. "So first order of business is whether it was or wasn't arson. Why did you think it was arson?"

"You get to where you can recognize it after a while." But then Adler looked right at him. "This is going to be tough, kid."

After breaking his gaze with Jason, the Chief then looked at each of them. "I never told anyone this. Strobel and I were the only ones who saw anything, and he died before he could corroborate it."

Jason braced himself when Adler looked him in the eyes and apologized. "Son, I'm sorry."

Then he told the story to the whole group. "When we pulled Jason here out, he was screaming. It took us a while to figure out what he was yelling about. He was hoarse from the inhalation and he was a kid. He was yelling that his brother was still in the building and he kept screaming '187,' over and over. It took a while to realize that it was his apartment number.

"When Strobel and I went in the first time, we were just doing a sweep. It was an old building, not up to code. The fire obviously had multiple points of origin—almost a dead giveaway of arson."

Jason and Connelly both nodded.

Chief didn't look at either of them. "The start points were in the hallways and staircases. On several floors around the eighth. It made it hard for those residents to get out. In fact, all the deaths were on those floors, all the others got out."

Castor finally set aside his beer if not his thoughtful expression. "So Jason and his brother weren't on those floors?"

"They were."

Castor frowned. "How did two kids get saved from floors where the adults didn't?" He pulled the article over and scanned it quickly. "The boys were the only live saves in that fire."

"The adults who escaped kept their heads and got themselves out. Some got to the fire escape or climbed down balconies. The boys—" he tipped his head at Jason, but couldn't seem to look at him, "stayed low and hid in a closet. They stuffed clothing under the door and around the holes. Maybe learned it at some school event. We did a lot of those in those days.

"When I was in the building we counted the doors. 187 was on the eighth floor, but I never saw the door number. I knew which one it was because it was after six and before eight. The door was engulfed in flame. Though the fire from the ends of the hallways couldn't reach it yet, 187 was fully involved."

Jason sucked in a breath. "The other origin points hadn't met up yet?"

Chief shook his head. "187 *was* an origin point. In fact it seemed to have several."

"Then if the door was engulfed, how did my brother and I get out?" It didn't make any sense.

Another deep breath from the Chief. "We heard you screaming and pushed through the door. There were several points around the apartment, and even they hadn't all joined up yet. We didn't find you, so we went to the next unit—188. You came out the apartment door and ran smack into me, so I gave you clean air and we got you the hell out of there."

Jason nodded.

"But later, when you were still yelling, we realized we had to go back. You said your brother was in the closet. When Strobel came out, he told me it was the damnedest thing. That the brother

135

was in a closet but in 188 and that the closet was stuffed with clothing at the bottom.

"He said there was a hole in the back of the closet that led to another closet in the adjacent apartment. I'm guessing it was 187, he never got to say for sure." He finally looked at Jason again. "I'm guessing that hole between the closets was something you kids knew about and it saved your life. 187 was full of smoke—you would never have survived there."

An uneasy quiet settled over the table as Jason thought that the whole thing kept getting weirder and it wasn't worth it to dig everything up for someone who was already gone.

But Bart English started talking again before Jason could say so.

"So, we have fifteen counts of second-degree murder that someone is still willing to cover up. That's not good."

Connelly frowned. "How do we know this person is still willing? They might not even be alive anymore."

"Someone with a stake in it is definitely still alive. That person called Jason pretending to be this 'Captain Smith' and check up on your investigation. Impersonating a city employee is a crime." English polished off his beer as though this wasn't as incredibly disturbing as it was.

Jason leaned forward. "Why can't I just tell people that I quit looking? I can shut up and make the whole thing go away."

Adler shook his head. "They wrote me off when I was new. If I come back now and say Pelias was arson, it has a lot more weight. You were a kid then—nothing you said would have meant anything. But you're an adult now and a firefighter. This call from 'Smith' proves the ball is already rolling.

Adler swore under his breath and continued to look at his beer. "I don't think we can count on this person to stop coming after us even if we shut up. It's fourteen counts of second-degree murder and one count of first. One of the points of origin in 187 was the couch, and there was a person on the couch when the fire started."

Southfield Fire Station #2

Shift	A	
	O'Casey	Captain
Engine 5	Wanstall	Lieutenant
	West	FF2
	Standard	Engineer
Engine 2	Grimsby	FF1
	Bloomberg	FF1
Rescue 1	Mondy	FF2 / EMT
	Donlan	Engineer/Paramedic

Chapter 11

Jason hit the station house at his usual time. His sleep schedule was still out of whack, and he'd spent the day before in a bit of a haze. He remembered waking up and finding a phone message from Alex that he had a new roommate, though she had balked at the smell of beer. Jason didn't remember much else, having spent a good part of the day in a near coma and all night watching infomercials.

Trying to avoid thinking about the person on the couch in apartment 187 was futile. Though no one said so, that person was likely his birth mother. And it sounded like she'd been torched. His stomach rolled and he fought to not show it outwardly.

He was sitting at the table with the paper in his hands, thinking he was doing a good impression of normal, when Alex came around the corner. "Jason!"

"Hey, thanks for the roommate. Is she willing to pay half the rent?"

Alex laughed. "She wants a discount if it continues to smell like beer."

Shaking his head, Jason wondered why some things insisted on going wrong. Then he put his hand in his pocket and fingered the bullet there—others had gone right, and beer was a small thing. "It won't. I spilled a bottle. Hey, you have a carpet scrubber?"

"Hard wood floors," was the only reply he got.

But his roommate would move in early next week and as long as he didn't pour more beer on the carpet, she'd pay her share. It sounded easy enough. Weingarten disappeared to finish his work and Jason went back to the paper.

He was reading the *Birmingham News* today, the *Southfield Press* left behind in favor of bigger things. There was no piece on the ongoing state of firefighting in Alabama—which surprised Jason. If Jernigan wanted to write about it, then Gold Standard, which was finally back on shift, was a prime story. But today Jernigan was writing about bribery in the college football scene, and he made a nice tie to bribery in the government.

At least he was a good writer. And he'd been the best interviewer Jason had talked to. Not bubble-headed, not interested in sound bites that fit the story he wanted to portray, and not like the TV-station lady who was more concerned that wind might muss her hair than that anyone learn anything.

Still Gold Standard was a big story. Jernigan said he was doing an ongoing piece. So why not follow it?

Folding the paper back up, Jason looked at his watch and saw he had a few more minutes before shift started. Shuffling through the back issues didn't yield anything about it either.

Alex went by again, and Jason got up and followed him out for line-up. Connelly came out, too, and he and Alex plopped into two of the nearby chairs for the last few minutes.

Missy was sitting on a weight bench, ready for shift to start, Standard right beside her. She looked up, worried. "Has anyone seen Bloomberg?"

No one wanted another Merriman on their hands. But heads went back and forth until Connelly smiled. "No worries boys. He's been here for an hour, asking me questions and going over the trucks again."

"Holy crap." West looked surprised. Then again, maybe he was just concerned the new guy would show him up, something he'd never worried about with Merriman.

Just then, Bloomberg came in to a chorus of "Hey, Frogurt!" He blushed and started to protest, but then thought better of it.

Standard gave him a hard look. "Did you pack your lunch?"

Pressing his lips together, Frogurt gave a curt nod. "Yes, sir." He was learning, but then impulse got the better of him and he said, "It's in the fridge if you'd like to inspect it. I can pull up calorie and nutrition counts if you'd like . . . Sir."

Standard didn't answer.

What Bloomberg didn't know yet was that Standard's mild case of OCD meant he didn't forget much of anything. And he certainly never forgot when somebody mocked him.

Chief Adler came through the door then and they all formed their line while C-Shift finally relaxed. Without the need to run the EMS service as well, line-up was much less tense today. Chief looked like maybe he'd gotten some rest since Jason had last seen him at Jenkins. And even though they hadn't made a plan about what to do, they all seemed a bit more at ease.

Check-in proceeded like normal until Adler stepped back and grinned. "Today we have good news."

Everyone looked back and forth at each other, wondering what the news was. The line just moved their eyes, trying to maintain position and still see if anyone had a clue. Only Wanstall stayed motionless as Chief walked right up to her and stuck out his hand.

As the two shook, he announced, "Wanstall here just made Lieutenant."

"What?" "When?" "Wow." All overlapped.

No one had known she was headed up the ladder again. They only knew she hadn't applied for any of the EMS openings, maybe because she'd already been knee deep in another batch of classes.

The line fell apart then, the guys crowding around her as Adler grinned and pinned the silver bugle of her new rank onto her uniform. One by one, they slapped her on the shoulder, shook her hand, and a few even hugged her. Missy beamed. Ironically, it was one of the few times she let down her guard and looked like a girl.

The guys from C-Shift lined up to congratulate her as they headed out. After a few minutes, things returned to normal. A-Shift was off on assignments and C-Shift had all gone home—or so he thought—when Jason had his cleaning interrupted. Bruce Connelly was still there, waving a hand in front of Jason's face to get his attention.

Bruce smiled. "You're a million miles away."

Cutting the vacuum off, Jason shrugged. "A lot on my mind."

"Did you figure out anything about the Captain Smith problem?"

Jason shook his head, "But thanks for bringing it up."

"Look, I was thinking about it. You did that interview with the Birmingham paper and we all wound up talking to that guy. He seemed pretty solid to me."

Clearly, Jason didn't see where he was headed, so Bruce kept talking. "He's a researcher. He digs stuff up for a living. He's not associated with us at all, so no one will see him coming. Plus, I bet he knows a lot of places to look that we haven't thought about."

As Connelly watched, gears visibly turned in Jason's head. Dots connected. And finally he said, "Maybe."

"Well, just think about it. Maybe tell Chief, see what he thinks." He slung his bag over his shoulder, good deed done for the day. "It's just been brewing in the back of my head for a while. You might need some outside help now that this has gotten ugly."

Having imparted his wisdom, Bruce headed out the door and Jason had to admit, Connelly's idea seemed sound. When he finished, he went in search of the Chief to run it past him.

The morning had been blessedly quiet. Wanstall and West had taken Engine 5 out on a claim of actual fire, but it had turned out to be a neighbor's backyard barbecue. At nine thirty in the morning. With alcohol. And a bottle of lighter fluid.

Mondy was almost to the Chief's office when he got a straight view into the bay.

Bloomberg, who had been dutifully checking out the trucks and familiarizing himself with the equipment, now stood talking to a knockout redhead. She was smiling at him, her eyes glowing with admiration.

One deep colored nail traced down the front of his shirt, and it was clear even from a distance that Bloomberg's breath hitched. He wondered if anyone could see this. And he hoped they could—she was hot and all over him.

Clearly, she just wanted a firefighter, but she seemed to think he would more than fit the bill. In a breathy voice she asked him about the trucks, the gear, fighting fires. She hung on his every word, nodding sometimes. Then, when he ran out of things to say, the redhead walked around the truck, her high heels making her mile-long legs look even longer.

Bloomberg trailed close behind thinking he might get a woody right there.

Suddenly, she turned back to him, so quickly he nearly ran into her and revealed the extent of his interest. If she noticed, she didn't say anything about it. She only asked in that breathy voice of hers, "Do you think I could sit in the truck for a moment?"

"Sure. Sure." He answered too fast, trying to cover for what she did to him as she hopped toward the front.

Bloomberg had thought that was a feat in those heels, but then she hauled herself smoothly into the driver's seat without flashing him in spite of the incredibly short skirt she wore. It hitched up a little higher as she adjusted her seat. She giggled and rolled down the window.

He was about to say something, when she pulled the door closed and leaned out the window, one arm draped across the sill, a wide smile plastered on her face as she smiled at him. "Parker, right? Parker Bloomberg?"

He nodded, in awe that she remembered his name, in instant lust the way she let it roll off her tongue.

"Oh Parker, I'm gonna get you in so much trouble." She licked her lips, started the engine, and pulled out of the station house.

It took a second before it hit him that he'd just watched her steal a fire engine. She'd driven off with Engine 5. For a moment a thought passed through his head: Wanstall was going to kill him. She'd just made lieutenant, she was driving 5 today, and he'd let the hot redhead take Missy's truck.

Oh holy shit. As Bloomberg stepped out onto the drive he saw that the redhead—he didn't even know her name—was turning the far corner with the $700,000 dollar truck he'd loaded her into. He was dead.

"Frogurt! Where's our truck going?" Mondy looked at him curiously. "You don't just take the trucks out. Who's driving?"

He didn't know. Didn't have a clue what her name was. But she knew his—first and last, and she was probably convinced his middle name was "Idiot." "Um."

Wanstall showed up then, too, and she was furious. "It's my damn first day as lieutenant, and that's *my* truck you let that little trollop steal. Were you thinking with your dick, Frogurt?"

He couldn't think of anything else to say, so he whispered, "Yes."

They all stared at him for a minute, Donlan joining the party and looking disgusted. Finally, Bloomberg found his voice and asked, "What do I do now?"

Wanstall had turned her back on him and stomped off, her hands in fists, no longer his dream woman. Mondy shook his head. "You have to go tell the Chief what you did."

Fighting desperately not to piss his pants, he did just that. Marching solemnly into the Chief's office, he confessed, paying no attention to the fact that Adler was absorbed in something, and that he didn't seem upset. In fact, it took a moment for the Chief's words to set in. "Bloomberg, you're an idiot. Was it a redhead or a blonde?"

"Redhead." He croaked.

With a sigh of great weariness, Adler gathered breath then yelled, "Mondy! Radio our engine and tell Simmons to return our truck. Bloomberg here's about to have a coronary. Give the boy a break."

As he turned, Parker Bloomberg saw the whole shift gathered round, laughing hysterically. Mondy spoke and he heard it, though it took him a minute to process the meaning. "She's already on her way back. Just stayed out long enough for our boy to get worried."

Adler looked at him in sympathy. "She's from House 3. Oldest one in the book, kid. Works even better now that there's women in the house." Then he slapped Bloomberg on the shoulder and the young man tried to keep his knees from collapsing. But the Chief's next words made him feel better. "Someone pulled it on me when I joined. And I fell for a guy, not a badge bunny."

Then Adler sat back down and resumed his work.

As Bloomberg watched, A-Shift laughed and helped the hot, redheaded "Simmons" park Engine 5 like an expert. When she stepped down, still not flashing him in that short short skirt, he saw that her arms weren't buff so much as they were strong; her legs, too, had that sinewy look of an athlete. The only thing that made it better was that after hugging all the crew she turned and hugged him, too. "Welcome to Southfield FD, Frogurt."

Great, so that *had gotten around.*

At least she seemed softer than Missy. But her voice whispered in his ear as she held him close. "If you look at my ass while I walk off, I'll gouge your eyes out."

She waved and headed out the back of the bay to where she'd parked her car, completely unnoticed by him. Bloomberg turned to Missy, "Do you go to the other houses and pull that?"

"About once a year." She smiled and walked off.

Everyone dispersed then, and Mondy headed into the Chief's office where he closed the door before sitting in a guest chair and waiting for his boss to get a break.

Without looking up, Adler asked him, "What do you want, Mondy?"

Jason repeated Connelly's idea from that morning and together they came to the conclusion that Jason should call Castor and English and ask what they thought, then let everyone sit on the idea for a day.

Adler leaned back, rocking the chair a bit and finally looked at him. "It's your call. It's your ass on the line here."

"I don't know, Chief, seems like it's yours, too."

There might be some truth to that, the older man mused. If someone pulled the old paperwork, they might find something about him being vocal that it was arson. If someone remembered, then there was almost no avoiding the fact that they would remember him.

There was no keeping this quiet. There were five who had been at Jenkins the other night. It was hard enough to keep a secret between two. Not that it mattered. Apparently Mondy had been all over Montgomery asking questions and having no clue it could come back to bite him. But it could come back to bite Adler, too. Maybe it was best that they get Jernigan in on it. "We'll have to trade Jernigan."

"Trade?"

"He's not going to just do us this favor. He'll want to write it up. It'll be his Deep Throat."

"Crap."

But Adler could see that Mondy got it.

"I didn't want to, but we can pony up some interviews on the Gold Standard mini-strike." He'd have to coach the guys, but he couldn't sit on the old memories now. "The question is, are you willing to sell your story? That's what it will likely cost."

He sent Mondy off to think about that before turning back to his paperwork. He'd just finished his sandwich when the bell went off.

∧   ∧   ∧   ∧   ∧

Wanstall pulled back as the blaze reached out and hit her square on. Like tongues of heat, it licked at them all, making her previous feelings of being fried alive seem like a cool day in the park. Today she was a lieutenant; today she was in charge of more, responsible for more and honestly, it was a shit day for that to happen.

She'd had both West and Bloomberg under her wing earlier. But when this fire had been called in, Chief had rearranged them all. He put Bloomberg with Mondy and Donlan. As dangerous as this was, and as infrequently as they handled full-scale wildfires, she was glad not to have two new guys—make that two, new, *young* guys—under her charge. They didn't always have the best judgment or follow instructions well.

She reached out to her side, making sure her thickly gloved hand was in West's view as she motioned him back. He rammed the pick-ax into the hard ground one last time, making her question whether he got the signal, but then he yanked it out, turning earth as he went and retreated beside her.

With quick looks around, they walked backward from the fire line. Mimicking Wanstall, West looked left, right, and up, periodically searching for stray sparks and making mental notes on where the edge of the blaze was. Privately, he prayed that the dead line they had just dug would hold this time.

The flames were moving faster than they had expected; the wind had picked up at the most inopportune time. Still they had cut timber, turned dirt and poured out retardant for hours. There was nothing more they could do. Bear Mountain was on fire.

Chief called them back for a rest and regroup. He and O'Casey had their heads together at a table with a plastic-coated map spread out between them. With red and black grease pens they noted what was reported in, what they could see from the little satellite info they could pick up, and where they thought they could hold a line, any line.

Adler rubbed his soot-blackened face, smearing his sweat into the ash that drifted by and clung to exposed skin and every surface. It embedded itself into any technology left open. He was roasting in his PPE pants and jacket, but the guys had to be worse out there facing it. Remembering his days on the front, he kept his mouth shut and didn't complain. There wasn't enough time to complain anyway.

Twice now they had made a stand. Twice they had made a dead line to hold back the fire and twice the fire hopped the line. On this, their third attempt, the wind had picked up even more fiercely than before.

He hadn't called in reinforcements fast enough. They now had a full second shift worth of Station House #2 men, an engine each from Houses #1 and #3 and a small contingent of State Forestry Service staff providing support. It still wasn't enough.

They had seventy-two acres of mountain tree line and campground space fully involved. The people had been cleared but weren't out of the way, and random lookie loos were starting to show up. Adler fought the urge to swear, but if he did, it would surely end up online.

He sent Wanstall and West over to the State Forestry tent for thirty minutes. Mondy, Donlan, and Bloomberg were next. He made a note of the time and radioed to check their progress. Donlan responded.

The fire was moving east with the wind. But Adler knew that it would act like a petulant toddler, demanding what it wanted now and changing its mind on a dime. The only good news was that—according to Donlan—it had burned itself out as it had traveled. Which meant it couldn't double back. It *could* wrap around though. Adler and O'Casey put their heads together and mapped out what might happen if the wind changed, if it stopped, if it didn't.

A beautiful girl with wild brown curls and a State Forestry Medical shirt brought them water and energy bars. O'Casey was thanking her when she leaned in closer and spoke to them. "There's someone here with me who insists that he talk to you."

O'Casey looked up. Geoff Merriman stood there, hands behind his back and an expression on his face that spoke of trying not to smile.

"What do you need me to do, Captain?"

O'Casey felt his heart sink. Why had Adler hired the guy in the first place? The man didn't make many missteps, but Merriman was certainly one of them. "I'm sorry, there's nothing for you to do, son."

Geoff's round face hardened. "I know the trucks and the gear. I can help."

Actually, no, he couldn't. And O'Casey was not going to be the man responsible for that tornado of a legal problem. "I'm sorry, son."

Merriman stomped off, gone at least until he surfaced again, and O'Casey turned back to finding the strategies they needed to beat back this fire.

They worked tirelessly. Wanstall and West were treated for a few spark burns to exposed skin and they nodded to the State Forestry Medical workers who admonished them that they should know better. They shouldn't have taken any gear off until they were further from the flame area.

They sat in the shade of the pop-up tent, ate, drank, and helped when the whole operation had to pick up and move about two hundred yards farther south. At the exact end of their allotted thirty minutes, they went back to work, picking up chainsaws and a water hose, hoping for a chop-down and a controlled burn followed by a dousing. The dead line had to be wider than they'd made it before. They couldn't lose a third time.

Bear Mountain was a bitch to fight on. Not a real mountain at all, it was more a series of rising hills and valleys, covered in dense foliage. There were sheer rock cliffs and some of the most beautiful views in the state—unless of course there was a beast of a fire eating at you.

The animals had fled—the lucky ones. Each of the firefighters had seen the curled and charred corpses of more than one creature that had made the mistake of hiding rather than running. Luckily, none had been human.

Jason waited until he was well away from the burn to remove his mask and head cover. Both he and Donlan rubbed their faces and took a few deep, if not clean, breaths before hitting the relief tent, Bloomberg lagging behind.

Both men sprawled ungracefully in the uncomfortable folding chairs. They opened jackets and ran fingers through sweaty hair. As Jason looked up, he was handed a bottle of water by a rich-skinned woman with hair that bounced around her head in fat, dark ringlets. He thought the water looked more inviting than the all-business face with the dark eyes and professional mouth.

In a fit of discomfort, Jason slipped out of the rest of his gear and even his official button-down shirt. Sitting in his navy uniform slacks, SFD T-shirt soaked in sweat, with gear strewn in a haphazard circle around him, he finally accepted the water and chugged it. He balked at the blanket that was thrown over his shoulders a few moments later.

But the volunteer stood her ground. "It's fifty-five degrees, it's windy and you're sweating."

He glared at her as she re-draped the blanket around him after he shrugged it off. "Right, I'm sweaty. Therefore I'm hot. I don't need a blanket."

She argued right back. "You don't want to go into shock and be a detriment to your team rather than an asset."

He bristled. "I'm a paramedic. I can regulate my own body temperature."

"Even an EMT knows you never treat yourself. And you aren't a Paramedic, you're a liar." She pointed at his shirt insignia, her business-like expression from earlier morphed into stern taskmaster look. She then pointed at his shoulders, where he'd let the blanket slip for some much needed cool air. "Put your blanket back up or I'll have you yanked from duty."

"Wha—?"

"*I* am a disaster-trained nurse practitioner. I outrank you in this tent." She pulled energy bars from her jacket pockets and handed one to each of them with the admonition to "eat."

Donlan grinned and gave her a "Yes, ma'am."

Bloomberg stared at her retreating back and sighed, "God, she is so hot."

Mondy growled. "Shut up, Frogurt."

He started to stand, but the nurse turned back and glared at him as though she had eyes in the back of her head. "Sit down. You have twenty-two more minutes of break."

Fuck that, Mondy thought to himself. But he sat down and tore off the wrapper and waited out the interminable minutes until they were sent back out.

This time, Chief rearranged the groups. Replacing Donlan, he sent Jason, Standard, and Bloomberg around the backside and into the early burn area to scout and report back.

They re-engineered themselves back into their gear, and Standard insisted on checking out Bloomberg as though he was a toddler heading into the snow. The kid was mortified, but the senior firefighter didn't take notice. He counted off the various ways the gear sealed and made sure that Bloomberg had gotten each one correct.

With axes, two chainsaws, and packs of supplies, they started the hike around the side of the burn. They could have gone much faster if not outfitted in all the constricting layers, and it was a full fifteen minutes later before they rounded an area safe enough to pass.

They radioed their position and invested some time chopping a hold line so the fire wouldn't move any further south of that point. Then they continued on.

They had to walk farther than where they had visual on the old burn area before they could go past. Though there appeared to be no active fire, the land steamed from the recent attack. Blackened trees stood sentry in the stripped forest; only the occasional crackle of dead and still-dying wood told that this had been a thick, living sanctuary only a day before. Now the going was slow as they climbed over downed trees. Many had toppled and the sound of others breaking and crashing in the low wind could be heard from any direction every few minutes.

Standard made progress slow. He spot-checked section after section. Though it was regulation to do so, to make sure you never walked unaware into an area that had live embers or unstable ground, no one did the checks with the complete focus to regimen that Standard did. Time was of the essence, and as always there were the conflicting goals of total safety and stopping the fire. Most did visual inspections, but not Standard. He even took the time to talk Bloomberg through the steps. The inspection was not part of a firefighter 1 credential, but Standard was just that way: regulations and safety first for all.

They surveyed and called in what they observed. There was dead, black dry earth and the occasional steaming section of old forest—fat trees that had withstood eons only to be eaten by fire. They had been doused with water the SFD had trucked in.

Standard held his hand up and Jason almost laughed but held back; the open radios would have transmitted his mirth to Standard. The man looked like a jolly yellow elf with his puffy gear and his obvious tiptoeing through the deadlands.

The three of them stood silently, Frogurt having learned to wait patiently until Standard told him what he was listening for. Sure enough, his voice came over the speaker. "Do you hear the crackling?"

Bloomberg nodded, still not versed in the need to fully speak every response.

"That's the trees. The trunks are burned out and the wood that kept them steady and upright has lost all of its integrity. See how that one has already fallen and is braced against the other? Get back! Get back!"

Jason grabbed Frogurt by his gear jacket and hauled him away. Standard, having gone first, barely cleared the giant trunk as it crashed to the ground, black shards flying like shrapnel and pelting the three of them. One hit Standard square in the back and sent him sprawling.

O'Casey's voice crackled over the line. "Are you okay?" But they couldn't answer that yet.

Jason motioned for them to leave Standard face down, in case there was an injury, but when he started bitching, they each grabbed a side and hauled him up. He groused a bit that they screwed up and let the new guy get hit by flying trees, but he was unharmed. O'Casey came in clear, "Glad to hear it."

Bloomberg turned and stopped dead, probably seeing what Jason saw: that the tree had fallen directly where they had been standing. If Standard hadn't stopped and listened to every little fucking detail, he'd be standing three feet away from two dead firefighters.

The three of them looked at each other for a moment, Bloomberg audibly swallowed and Jason nodded at Standard, "Thanks, man."

But he was just doing his job and so they simply went further in when told to.

A single campsite sat in the center of the burn, and they searched for any information. The aerial shots were showing it to be the likely origin of the blaze. Charges would be brought if idiots had been burning a fire up here when the postings clearly stated conditions were dry.

Sure enough, there had been a fire. Standard was visibly disgusted but in order to bring the bastards in, they had to identify them, so he churned through the ashes of the camp.

The tent had been fire resistant and though it took some time, they found a scrap with a tag and the name "Tunstall" written in black marker. Standard found most of a hiking duffel, and inside the charred shell he hit pay dirt. Three wallets. As he surveyed the burn site, he thought it looked like three men had built a fire. At some point, the blaze caught the trees and went full scale. "Mondy, you want to be an inspector, what do you say?"

With broad sweeps and bends of his body because he couldn't completely swivel his head, Jason looked through things. "You can see the fire pit and it looks like it was dug fresh maybe yesterday."

Standard completely agreed. He also thought it was too close to the trees.

Mondy looked a little further. "It's also directly under the branches. Which is way too close. Sparks probably went up in the wind and caught this one . . ." he pointed one puffy gloved hand up, "or blew that way and caught the whole forest." He pointed over behind Standard and Bloomberg.

Yes, these campers were going to jail. Clumsily, he flipped open the wallets one at a time. First he got a face for Tunstall. The driver's licenses would be far more damning than a piece of tent tag with black sharpie writing. Standard smiled, they had the bastard. The next wallet was for a Robert Platt—both men were twenty something and looking stupid as hell in Standard's eyes. He flipped open the third wallet. "Son of a god damned bitch."

"What?" Both Mondy and O'Casey asked him through the comm at the same time.

He was sick to his stomach. "I got wallets in a backpack from the site. A Brad Tunstall, Robert Platt, and the third is for a Geoff Merriman."

"Son of a BITCH!" O'Casey nearly blew out their eardrums.

Standard watched as Mondy's face hardened from surprised to murderous.

They stood and listened to the heated swearing of Captain and Chief as they debated what to do. After a few moments and what sounded like a phone call—probably to the ADA—they instructed the guys to cordon off the area and flag the original location of the duffel for evidence.

Mondy listed their precise coordinates and Standard took point again as they went further along the burn path. With all the foliage gone they could see farther than ever. Standard paced them slowly through black trunks and piles of charred ground cover. There was a greater danger of sinkholes after a large burn; trees fell with frequency and the occasional animal survived or returned and was doubly dangerous.

Though the men could see blackened sky ahead where the wind had turned and was blowing the fresh smoke back their way, they had no peripheral vision. And no way of telling what direction they were hearing a noise from. An animal could come up behind them, and they'd never know it—except that right now there was a sheer rock wall at their backs. Standard turned to check it out.

PHOENIX

The burn had come up to the wall, then run along the bottom of it. Plants had clung to the rock face until yesterday, and it looked like the fire had used that tentative life to reach the top and start a new burn path there. He couldn't tell what happened beyond the upper cliff, only that blackened trees stood right at the edge and other branches reached into to his line of sight, rooted from somewhere beyond the rock.

Standard put his hand up.

Mondy stopped again, thinking maybe he heard something, too. They both scanned the area around them looking for the source of the deep groan. Frogurt caught on, and the three of them formed a wide triangle, faces out, as they searched in all directions for any danger.

The groan got louder and Standard saw Mondy turn as he did.

They were just in time to see the great blackened husk as it toppled over the edge of the cliff wall above and come down right on Bloomberg.

Chapter 12

Jason

Jason stuffed his hands in the pockets of his good coat and walked away from the service in silence. Bloomberg's mother was local and apparently her grief made her manic. Though they still used it some in the fire house, no one ever repeated the name "Frogurt" in front of her or any of his seven brothers and sisters.

Jason swallowed. None of them had known anything about his family. His father had died the year before, a police officer shot in the line of duty in Mobile. No one knew about all those brothers and sisters.

Looking to his left and right as everyone walked away in their Sunday best, Jason wondered what he didn't know about the others in his house. Sometimes a firefighter's funeral could be a lively affair: a life well lived, a man died doing what he did best and in service to others. None of that happened here. There was no trip to the bar afterward, no feeling of completion. Just the sharp twist of a short life, and man who wasn't quite a man yet— one who hadn't completed the tasks he'd set before himself.

Jason fought the pressure behind his eyes. Bloomberg had only been on his second shift. And he hadn't done anything wrong.

Well, he had, but Donlan had corrected him and Standard had flat out saved them all. Nothing could have been done about the tree falling from the cliff top. It was a crapshoot every day—a dangerous job and they all knew it. Bloomberg knew it.

And Jason kept repeating that over and over in his head as though it would make him feel better.

There had been no break. Though A-Shift had been sent home the next day as the fire was finally put out with the help of various state agencies, B-Shift had rolled in and been put on duty right on schedule. Today, C-Shift was on again, missing the funeral, but having their own shit day nonetheless.

He had barely made it through this. Dead on his feet from having worse nightmares than he'd ever had, Jason had held himself together with only the most precarious control.

As bad as this had been, he had no idea how he would make it through Connelly's funeral.

The key went into the ignition of his car of its own accord. Surely he couldn't do anything so complex as driving. But the vehicle maneuvered down the road toward his apartment, where his new roommate would be moving in.

In a show of royally bad timing, Alex had given her the key and Jason had agreed that today was as good as any before the week had gone to shit and today had become the exact opposite of good. No one even had the wherewithal to reschedule. Besides, the girl needed a place to live and he needed the rent. Postponing wouldn't bring his friends back.

Parking halfway up the block, Jason walked slowly home and put off the moment where he opened his door and realized he couldn't even control his own space anymore. As he trudged up the sidewalk he tried to block the mental image he had of some blonde with her hair in a ponytail, dancing stupidly to some horrible music piped into her ears while she rearranged his furniture.

Connelly would have had something to say. Connelly might have offered to date her. But not now.

Jason took the elevator, too tired to fight gravity and climb the stairs. Strangely, the hallway was silent and his apartment was closed up tight. No one was attempting to stuff a couch or bed through his front door.

His hand reached out and tried the knob, and he only prayed she could be quiet enough for him to get some sleep before he went back tomorrow and tried to do his job again.

Locked.

Maybe she hadn't come yet.

That was almost worse—it wouldn't be over. But he fit his house key into the bolt, turned it, and was greeted by the back of his new roommate's head.

The TV was on and people were acting . . . poorly. The *Lifetime* logo in the upper corner made him cringe. All he could see of the woman on his couch was a mop of tight, dark curls piled on top of her head in a haphazard fashion. She seemed oblivious to the fact that he had arrived.

But that assessment turned out to be wrong. The TV didn't pause and she didn't turn, but he clearly heard her voice. "Hello."

That was it. No "hey, roomie," no hopping up and hugging him while she popped her bubblegum.

Jason closed the door and hung his coat on one of the hooks he'd drilled into the wall a week ago. He noticed that only one hook had a jacket on it that wasn't his. In spite of several empty, waiting spots her hat was hung directly on top of her jacket.

Slowly, fighting through the lethargy that pervaded his cells, he wandered around the front of the couch to the phone that was blinking at him. If the roommate looked up from the TV, he couldn't tell.

In deference to her really bad movie, he played the message softly and leaned in to hear it. The tinny voice bothered him though he didn't have the energy to do anything about it.

"Hello, my name is Jack Deason the Third. I'm a volunteer firefighter at the Burkeville Station. I was here when you came in and I didn't know anything about the fire you mentioned. But I asked my dad, he volunteered here at that time and he remembers your fire. He said he wanted to talk to you. So I told him I would call and leave you his number."

Too rattled to write it down, Jason just pulled back and blinked. At the last minute he managed to hit the "save" button. Not that he would have forgotten the name.

His brain turned over, wondering whether Deason was another non-existent "Captain Smith" or if this time it was someone real. Maybe someone like Chief who knew something was wrong and wanted it fixed.

It was easy enough to find out if Jack Deason the Third and the Second actually existed. Jason bet they did – "Deason" was a much better name than "Smith" and why go to the trouble to make up two people?

But then his thoughts just stopped. His mental capacity hit the brick wall. He could find out later. No one was going to come here and . . . —he couldn't even imagine what they might come here and do, because they weren't going to do it. Taking a deep breath, which didn't help at all, he turned back to the problem he had to deal with right now.

His new roommate hadn't changed positions, didn't seem interested in him, and wasn't even eavesdropping on his phone messages. So he walked across her view of the TV before he thought about what he'd done and sat on the other end of the couch. For a minute he watched her watching television.

Tears ran down her face and she clutched a half-empty beer—not one of his—as though it was a beloved child. She didn't look at him, but said, "I'm sorry about your friends."

Jason nodded, then realized she wasn't looking at him at all, but at the overblown and poorly landed kiss on screen. The music swelled, all but swallowing his nearly whispered "thank you."

Facing front for a minute, he looked at the screen as a huge ring was pushed on a finger, eyes were stared into wonderingly, and the would-never-exist-in-the-real-world man said breathlessly, "I'll love you forever." The music swelled again and the credits rolled.

The roommate turned to him then, and something about her face was comforting. She wore no makeup, which was probably good. Jason had seen more running mascara today than a man should have to endure. Her brown eyes were large and sad. "I know you were with Parker Bloomberg when he died, and Alex told me that Bruce Connelly was your friend."

Jason nodded and put his hands on his knees to push himself up. It was time to go to bed and find out what happened if and when he slept.

She stayed him with an outstretched hand. "I'm Amara Bellamy. You don't remember me, do you?"

He was shaking her hand and displaying what pittance he had to offer in the way of smiles as she asked that question. He felt the frown play across his features and he shook his head.

"I'm the disaster-trained nurse practitioner from Forestry Service and you're the liar."

"Oh."

She offered the same half-hearted smile back at him. "Though Alex informed me that you aren't as much of a liar as I thought. You are an EMT and you're in Paramedic training."

He only heard part of what she said as his mind shuffled through the mental images. "You worked on Connelly when they brought him out."

After he and Standard had watched helplessly as a team rushed in to lift the tree from the crushed Bloomberg, they had hauled his inert form out on a stretcher. The probie had been gone from the moment the tree hit. There had been no chance of heroic rescue. None.

Slowly they had processed the body back to the main area only to find that the State Forestry Medical tent was in full riot. A man had been laid out on the table, Amara pulling burned and charred clothing from him. Layers peeled away from his back, thick PPE gear and thin cotton followed by thinner flesh. Face down on the table, the man had struggled for breath through damaged pipes and tissues.

She and her team had fought like demons to save the man that Jason, Standard, O'Casey, and Grimsby only recognized as one of their own. He'd been with Wanstall and Baxter. Jason had scanned the faces, trying to figure out who was missing, but it was no one from A-Shift. A handful of B- and C-Shift guys had come in for support; it could be any of them.

The nurse had finally tubed the man and breathed for him, though it did nothing. They all stood helplessly by because they knew what damaged lung tissue meant. They couldn't find a vein to run a line, and they couldn't add oxygen that way anyway.

Finally, Amara said something and her team had popped back, no longer huddling over the victim. At that moment, they ran out of ways to save him and started trying to make him comfortable. It was an impossible task and only lasted three interminable minutes before the patient gave up and expired.

It was only when the Chief ground his teeth and said "Connelly" that Jason hit his own knees.

And here he sat on his couch, while she drank a beer and watched his TV. This woman who had called a halt to rescuing Connelly. As he stared at her, she crumpled and cried, seeming to know what he was thinking.

"He had third-degree burns on half his body. The fire came up under his jacket. It fried his gear and then his lungs. He had his Oh-Two tank on and it popped and burned." She shrugged, whispered, "I'm so sorry. I did what I could." And downed the rest of her beer.

Then Amara sniffed and stood up. She was wearing flannel pajamas though it was still early evening. "I'll understand if you don't want me to stay. But I tried to save him."

Everything inside him seemed to fold in on himself and it was all he could do to say, "You can stay."

Pushing to his feet, he half-whispered, "I'm going to bed." His hand pointed to his bedroom as though she might be confused—or maybe it was him that was confused. Then he turned and walked away.

With no thought to anything but the pressure in his head, he stripped to his underwear, leaving the clothes where they fell before setting his alarm for thirteen hours away. He hoped he could sleep through them all.

∧ ∧ ∧ ∧ ∧

Work was slow and long, but Jason kept his head in the game. He reminded himself constantly that the family who had the car fire didn't know that he'd lost both a new co-worker and a good friend just three days before. They didn't need to know.

His smiles were forced and so were everyone else's. There wasn't much said, but everything got done. The tanks were checked—maybe with a little extra care—and put into place without fanfare, without the usual joking.

There was the occasional "do you remember that time Connelly . . ." statement. But they quickly became painfully apparent reminders that no one had those same thoughts to share about Bloomberg. He was new, and somehow—though no one could find fault anywhere—he was dead. In the absence of someone to blame, Bloomberg's death alone was evidence that they had all failed him, and A-Shift felt that deeply.

The Chief told them he was getting a flag made for the station house with Bloomberg and Connelly's names on it. He asked for input and ideas and got none. There was a standard to the memorial designs, and no one expressed anything resembling concern as to what it looked like. As long as it gave their names and made them heroes then it was good.

In the evening, when things were so slow as to be dead— Jason cringed at the very thought—Adler called him into the office.

"All the papers have the story. Of course the *Birmingham News* has given it to Jernigan as part of his ongoing series."

Jason nodded. That was not a surprise.

Adler continued, his voice perfectly modulated and somehow without any emotion whatsoever. Jason suspected that, like him, the man was drained and just pushing himself through the day. "He wants to do interviews. I talked to him about being respectful of the crew. He seems to understand."

Jason nodded. Time to be Golden Boy again. But he wondered, did Golden Boy appear stoic and simply state the facts? Did he accept the blame that he felt but couldn't quite shoulder? Or was he supposed to shed some layer of manhood and break down and cry?

At this point he was capable of any of the above and he was internally debating the wisdom of each when he realized Adler was speaking again.

"—come tomorrow morning at six thirty. He can talk to A-Shift and get B later in the day. But I was thinking you should get Castor and English together and we should all have breakfast after B gets in. I think it might be good to get Jernigan's help."

Jason nodded. In the same dull tones that Chief had used, he mentioned the call about the Deasons. Though he believed they were actual people, he had no clue what their motives were and he didn't know how to find out. He didn't have a covert bone in his body. He'd never played spy as a kid—he'd always been the firefighter. He'd been a firefighter/cop or a firefighter/explorer, but even as a child he'd never been able to cover anything up.

The Chief agreed with his assessment—both that the Deasons could have any angle and that Jason was not the person to try to figure it out.

"Chief, are we going to blindside Jernigan at the breakfast? I mean, he's here to interview about the . . . funerals. Or did you tell him anything else?"

"I didn't say anything. It's really your call. But I think maybe we *should* blindside him. Don't give him any time to dig anything up before he gets here. Or tell anyone something of value."

Jason nodded. "I also think that, when we sit down, we should just tell him a little bit about the story—no names, no dates—see if he's interested in helping before we give him everything we know." He paused. "Actually, it was Connelly who suggested that. I think he's right."

He couldn't tell if the Chief noticed that he referred to Connelly in the present tense. Neither of them corrected it.

Instead, they agreed on a course of action and then Adler got up to leave. He said good-bye to each firefighter personally before heading home for the day.

For a moment, Jason was envious. The man had a wife to go home to, and he obviously still loved her very much after thirty or maybe forty years. They had three grown daughters that Adler was crazy proud of, and he had a job doing what he loved. Every man in the house was part of Adler's extended family. Though the rest had hated Merriman, what the Chief had hated was firing him. He had to be heartsick at the thought that the police were now searching for Tunstall and Platt and Merriman. The trio was facing two second-degree murder charges.

Though it made Jason feel small, he just bet Merriman had talked the other two into lighting the fire against the local drought ordinance. He'd thought he was so knowledgeable; instead he was merely dangerous. They'd all mistakenly thought they were safe from him once he was gone from the station house. They were paying for that mistake.

As early as it was, Jason knew he couldn't go to sleep yet, so he pulled out his book and read the hours away. For a while he existed in a place where spies and ordinary men fleeing from secret government cabals kept him from his thoughts and held back the silence of the too-still fire house.

^ ^ ^ ^ ^

The following morning they all met at Bart English's apartment. Four men arriving at a bachelor pad at nine a.m. was odd, but then again the whole thing was odd. There was simply no way to make it look normal when it wasn't.

They came in four separate cars, from Castor's sleek chick-magnet coupe to the Chief's old Lincoln. They came with fast-food bags in hand and got buzzed in one after the other.

Rob settled them around the coffee table, not having enough chairs at his dining table to seat them all. He pushed his dog into the bedroom, and the creature whined while they got settled in, Jernigan looking around at them oddly while he set out a soda and a Styrofoam breakfast platter. He reached for his plastic fork and knife and started to cut his pancakes, but then seemed to think of something and set them down.

His eyes scanned the odd group. "Okay, I'm at sea here. Can we start with introductions? Do you all know who I am and what I do?"

The four others nodded almost in unison, and English took over while Jason shoved his usual breakfast sandwich into his mouth.

"You know Jason Mondy and Chief Michael Adler, right?" Jernigan nodded, still wary looking, still not touching his food.

"I'm Bart English, Southfield ADA and this—" he pointed "—is Rob Castor, local almost-detective with SPD. We're both personal friends of Jason here."

"Handy friends." The reporter still frowned at them a bit. "This is a suspicious group—and you made sure I was off government property. Honestly, just the professions gathered here . . . it's an odd mix. Want to tell me what's going on?"

English shook his head. "Not yet. We need to know if you're in or out before we give you all the details."

"Oh?" Jernigan's eyebrows finally rose and he set down his plastic ware, any interest in his breakfast gone. "Go on."

Jason chewed his suddenly tasteless food and thought that Jernigan looked like the game was now on.

English's voice filled in some carefully chosen details. "We have information on a forty-year-old fire written off as accidental. But we think it's arson. We want to look for proof, but we need investigative help. That's where you come in."

Jason almost opened his mouth to correct the date before he realized that it was his butt the ADA was protecting should Jernigan opt out. He took another bite and waited.

Clark Jernigan leaned back against the couch. "Okay, so I investigate this old trail you put me on, and what? I get to write it up if we find anything?"

Chief jumped in. "We'll all be investigating. We just don't have the skills or connections that you have. And yes, we'll give you the story once it's cracked open. But you have to agree to hold off on publishing things or sharing any of it until we allow it."

Jernigan was frowning again, but that changed to surprise as English reached out to the end table and grabbed several printed sheets of paper. "I wrote up a contract—a gag order—for you to sign before we tell you anything more."

Everyone turned to look at him.

"I'm a lawyer! Of course I'm protecting our butts. That's why I'm here, right?"

Jason laughed.

Jernigan didn't. "And my butt? How am I to know that I don't put in all the legwork, staying silent the whole time, and you all sell me out and the story goes elsewhere?"

Though Chief looked as though his personal integrity had just been maligned, English smiled. "I'm a lawyer, not an asshole. Contrary to popular belief, the two are not synonymous." He pulled out another set of documents. "These are to protect you." He scanned all of them. "This is why I made you guys pick up breakfast for me. I was typing these up. These bind us to giving the story exclusively to Jernigan in exchange for his work and silence until unanimous agreement to go public with it."

For a moment everyone looked at each other. Then they all nodded.

Jernigan read for a minute, then looked up. "This leaves the story exclusively to me. It doesn't state that I have to publish it through the *Birmingham News*. I could write a book."

English looked at them all, as though for affirmation, "We agree to give *you* the story. Once we go public, it's yours to do with as you wish."

Though Jernigan seemed to like the open end, he protested another part of the short contract. "You could learn what you want and sit on it forever. I do the work and you never decide to go public. So how is it determined when it's okay for the story to go wide?"

Chief wiped the crumbs off his hands and spoke up for the first time, "Don't worry, you'll get your story. We'll give approval when we have enough evidence to cover our butts. If we're right, people will go to jail. We *want* to go public with this. We just need to be safe."

It was clear they all needed a minute or two to stop and think. The others all polished off their breakfasts while Jernigan just pushed it aside to mull things over. After a minute he reached into his ever-present black messenger bag and pulled out a pen. Clearing a spot on the table, he signed both copies of the agreement English had written up for him and handed both to the lawyer to sign. There were spots for each of them, and for a while pens passed and names were signed, getting harder to read as each copy was John Hancocked.

In the end, English held an original set of signatures on each contract and everyone else had a signed version of their own. Jason looked at his page—this was the moment before they dove in, before the icy water hit them and the shock settled into his bones.

He was filing his own copy in his bag when the reporter took a bite of his now-cold breakfast before shoving it completely away. "Okay, let's start by being honest. I'm signed in, I won't talk."

Jason was ready to start explaining, but Clark Jernigan beat him to it.

"I doubt the fire is forty years old. I'm guessing none of you was alive forty years ago, except Chief Adler here. No offense meant."

"Can't be offended by the truth." Chief looked at Jernigan more shrewdly. Jason agreed with that assessment, especially when Jernigan talked again.

"That means the fire is more recent. I'd guess it's relatively recent, or you can't pursue any legal ramifications." He pointed at English. "Or maybe 'legal' isn't the issue. Someone famous is involved, and the court of public opinion will be enough, or—and this is the last option I see—the fire is older but there's a murder involved. That's the only way I can think that the statute of limitations hasn't run out yet and you have a legal leg to stand on."

He planted his hands palm down on his knees and gave them all a solid look. "Am I right?"

Jason figured the paperwork was signed so it was okay to speak freely, but just for reassurance he glanced at Bart who nodded a go-ahead. If the lawyer thought it was okay to speak, then everything that could be done to make sure Jernigan didn't take off with this had been done. "Yes, you're right. It's about me . . . and I guess about Adler, too."

He started to tell the story again, wondering how many more times he would have to do this. But Jernigan put a stop to it pretty quickly until he could pull out a small laptop and get his uneaten pancakes out of the way. While Bart English cleared everyone's trash, the reporter checked the coffee table for stray syrup or anything that would interfere with his electronics and by the time the ADA returned from the kitchen, the laptop was pulled apart so the keyboard could sit in his lap and a legal pad had joined his very expensive pen and now sat beside the propped-up screen. Jernigan typed something without looking at either the keys or the screen, and Jason took a moment to believe that they had pulled in exactly the right person to help them or to completely screw them over.

But Jernigan just said, "Okay, start again, please."

At least he was polite.

Jason told about the Pelias Street fire, Adler added parts about pulling the two brothers out. Jernigan's fingers were typing the whole time though his face registered open-mouthed disbelief at one point. He interjected with questions to Jason.

"You don't remember the fire at all?"

"No."

"You don't remember your brother? Or your mother?"

He shook his head, for the first time feeling as sad as Jernigan seemed to look about that. It was sad. But maybe he felt it because this was the first time he hadn't been so focused on finding the death certificate on his brother. Or maybe it was spill-over from the loss of two men within the last few days.

He wished they'd been able to postpone this until he was more together, until it didn't feel like he was telling something personal and maybe selling a small part of his soul. But he had no choice.

Jernigan wasn't here because they thought it was a good idea to get this into the paper. Or because they thought someone else should know about Adler's theories. He was here because Jason had received two calls from people following up on the little research that he'd done and at least one of those people didn't exist. And at least one other person had been flat-out murdered nearly thirty years ago.

Jernigan tried to hide his disgust when Adler mentioned the multiple points of origin of the fire—and that one of them had been on the couch, with a person there—but he didn't quite succeed. "I'm sorry, I sometimes do sports stories and the occasional humanitarian piece. Burned . . . corpses are a new thing to me. So you think this person was burned alive?"

Adler nodded.

"Was it a man or a woman?" He looked mostly at Adler but had a way of quickly sweeping his gaze around the whole group so he didn't miss anything. Despite the professionalism, he still looked like his stomach was rolling.

Adler shook his head. "Strobel and I couldn't tell at the time. The corpse was too badly burned, we had no training in that and we had other things to do. I'm sure the M.E. was able to tell from the autopsy, but I wasn't able to dig up the information at the time."

This time it was Castor asking the question. "We release that information to SFD and EMS all the time. Why couldn't you get it? Was it different then?"

Adler shook his head. "No, I'd just been shut down. Told that my 'fixation'—" he used air quotes, "on the fire was a sign that I was not psychologically fit for my job, and it was made pretty clear that if I went looking for more information, I'd never get cleared to go back."

"Okay." Jernigan picked up the pen and wrote on the paper for the first time. "That's job one: find out about who was on the couch. Chances are it was Alcia Mallory, but we need to be sure."

English spoke up again. "I tried to pull it, but I found out that getting the M.E. records from that year means I have to go through a person and request them with a reason for pulling them from the archives. So I didn't. I didn't want to alert anyone to what we were doing."

"Good." Jernigan typed more. "Has anyone tried pulling subsequent articles from the paper? They usually report the casualties at least as obituaries."

Of course. Jason wondered why he hadn't thought of that. "I looked for other articles, so did my mother—my adoptive mother. But we didn't find anything."

Jernigan's eyes narrowed. "Is she in on this, too?"

"No." Jason wanted to keep it that way. "She started the whole thing. She told me about my brother, and she pulled the first article, but she hasn't been involved since."

Jernigan tilted his head. "Your adoptive mother knew you had a brother before they adopted you, knew you didn't remember the brother, and didn't tell you about him?"

It was all he could do not to jump up and strangle the man. Maybe they didn't need him after all. Still. "My mother did exactly what the psychologists told her to do, over and over, even though she was convinced it was the wrong thing. She thought I should be told. She wanted to adopt him. But he died. She didn't do anything wrong."

The reporter's hands came up, palms out, for the first time leaving the keyboard. "Hey, sorry. It's just a sad story and odd that your adoptive mother didn't tell you about your brother even though she knew."

"Mother." Jason muttered the correction under his breath. "She's just my *mother*."

Jernigan either didn't hear or he chose to ignore it. "So who's working here? Is it just going to be me and Jason here digging or are we all diving in as researchers?"

Jason looked at Adler, then they looked to Bart English and Rob Castor . . . they all shrugged.

Castor chimed in again. "Either way. Whatever's best, but it seems to me we have a good group here, we have access to all kinds of information between the five of us."

"I agree. There are things you can each get to without alerting people as much as if a reporter requested information." He paused, then brought up what Jason thought was the most sobering thought. "My reasoning is that if one person does the research, that person is a target—the way it seems Jason here has become one. But if we all do it . . . well, there's safety in numbers, there's no way they can get rid of all of us, right?"

Chapter 13

Jason

Jason ate his cereal in silence. He also ate it while wearing pants and a T-shirt, which made him fidgety.

Amara had asked if they could pull the butcher-block table out from the corner so they could sit at opposite sides. In concession, Jason had held back a grumble about his space and his table. He was getting ready to tell her that he didn't expect them to share meals, when she smiled and ran her hand over the surface. "I just love butcher blocks like this."

Then she bent over at the waist and peered under the table. "It's a real butcher block, too, not just made to look like one. I like the mild scarring on it."

Damn her. He didn't give a shit about furniture. The coffee table was chosen because it held things up—including his beer and magazines and often his feet. He had picked out that couch because it was deep and soft, because of the extra length, and the fully padded arms. He knew he'd sleep on it sooner rather than later. His bed now had a metal frame, which held the box springs and the mattress. When he looked at it he knew his mother would cringe that there was no fabric covering all the workings. And sometimes the sheets pulled and exposed even the mattress. But he didn't fix it.

No, the butcher-block table was the one thing he loved. The one piece of furniture he had chosen because he liked the way it looked. So when Nurse Bellamy ran her unmanicured fingers across the surface and oooohed over the construction, he had agreed to pull it out from the corner. And here he was—eating cereal while nearly fully covered, across the table from Amara.

Her hair was piled on her head again. Somewhere in the curls was an elastic or barrette holding it up. For the life of him he couldn't see it. He'd studied building construction—enough to get to FF2—and he was studying it more on his own. Amara's hair seemed to defy every rule of construction he knew. It didn't even tilt as she leaned over the small bowl of oatmeal she seemed to consider a fitting breakfast.

She daintily finished it—which he thought was funny, because she didn't wear any makeup that he'd seen, called a six-foot firefighter a liar to his face, and had easily lifted her side of his computer desk when they finally moved it out of her room. As she rinsed the bowl, she turned to him and pointed at the book shelf. "Your girlfriend called last night. I left the message on a post-it next to the machine."

His eyebrows went up and the spoon stopped halfway to his mouth. "That's funny. I don't have a girlfriend."

His brain turned over. *God damn, Kelly*. Just when he thought she was gone for good.

Amara interrupted his funk. "Well, maybe you just dated her? She seems to know you and possibly expects something from you. Anita? Andrea?"

"Aida?" He hoped, then breathed a sigh of relief as she nodded and said "yes!"

She stood at the sink, one bare leg hooked behind the other. Why did she get to hang out in boxers and he didn't? She looked at him oddly until he returned the favor and asked "What?"

"Are you going to call her back?"

"Sure. Does it matter?" And why did it matter to Nurse Bellamy? So far she'd seemed to keep to herself; she asked him if she could watch his TV or stuck to the small one she'd parked in her own bedroom. She did a few things in the living area, like eat and cook, but she'd been relatively unintrusive. Which made him feel bad that he was charging her half of everything and she wasn't really taking up the space. But he wasn't pleased with this sudden push into his private life.

"I'm sorry." She held her hands up. "It's not my place. But you don't have a recording of how she sounded. She was really shocked that there was a woman answering the phone. So if you want to see her again, you should straighten that out."

He shrugged. He did want to see Aida again—he needed to see her again, but not for a date. Though a date wasn't out of the question, he had no clue where things might go or even if he was really interested in her that way. But Jason knew he had to change or he'd simply go through Kelly after Kelly, and eventually he'd wind up living alone in New York City with no furniture at all. Even so, he wasn't sure it was worth all the hassle to date Aida. She was part of the investigation into his brother and she lived several hours away.

Amara squinted at the shrug. "You know, I'm a woman."

"Really?" It was all he could think of to say other than "No shit, Sherlock." She was completely ruining his cornflakes.

"We talk to each other."

"I'm sorry? You're going to blackball me with all womanhood because I don't ask for a second date from a woman I saw once?" His head hurt.

"No, not at all. But when your next date asks me about you, what am I supposed to say?"

"Oh good god." He would simply stop dating for the next several months, until after Nurse Bellamy moved out. That was the obvious answer.

She held her hands up. "I'm sorry. It sounds like I'm going to narc on you to the girlfriend squad, and I won't. I really won't. But Alex said you needed a roommate because your last girlfriend walked out and took all the furniture with her. That sounds like an angry woman to me. And this one didn't sound much better."

Fuckshitdamn. She was right.

Jason smacked his elbows onto the table top and did a full double face palm. "Okay, Speaker for All Women Everywhere, what should I do here?"

"Tell her the truth without being mean about it."

He barked out a laugh. If there was any one thing he'd learned about women, it was that they did *not* want to hear the truth. "Yeah, I'll be sure to do that. Right before I decide to take up a second career as a soprano in the opera."

The phone rang then, saving him from getting further into this ridiculous conversation. He saw the number and answered it.

"Hey, Clark."

"Are we still set for today?"

"Almost." He answered.

They worked out logistics—Jernigan would drive, in case anyone recognized Jason's car or saw that his license plate was registered to Shelby County rather than Jefferson.

He hung up, but Amara's voice stopped him. "Was that about your secret club?"

"What?"

"Oh come on. There are five of you. The reporter Jernigan, your fire chief, and the cop and the ADA. You're on some mystery hunt and it's all very hush-hush." She grinned, clearly proud of herself.

She was a pain in the butt is what she was. "Don't you have a job to get to?"

Amara crossed her arms. "Don't you?"

"You know my shifts. You have since you first talked to Alex about renting my second room. So what about you?"

"I told you. I'm a disaster nurse doing my doctorate. I have a class to teach at five tonight, but that's it. Otherwise I'm working where and when tragedy strikes." She cocked her head as though that explained it all.

But Jason's eyes got wider. "So you came to Southfield waiting for a disaster?!" Then he thought about Bear Mountain. "Or do you attract them?"

There was no amount of rent money that would make up for having a crisis magnet in his house. His fire station wouldn't survive having her in town.

"*Yes.*" Strangely, the sarcasm dripping from her lips was a relief. "I came to *Birmingham* because the psychic hotline told me this is where I'd get the best paper for my thesis. I wound up here specifically because bringing trouble to you and your friends sounded just so appealing."

She stalked across the living room to the door that was now hers, muttering. "You don't need me. You have enough trouble with your secret boys' club anyway. Jackass."

Jason stood there staring for a moment after the door closed—miraculously without slamming. *Damnit.* She was right. Again.

∧ ∧ ∧ ∧ ∧

They'd come a long way since getting Clark in on the action. Though still business-like, Clark was now everyone's best friend. If they could find evidence of what Adler knew, this would be his big break. But the more Jason mulled it over the more he regretted selling the story of his brother.

He didn't feel he had any choice. After the call from the non-existent "Smith," there were no options but to move forward or wait for the axe to drop. And it wasn't just about him either. He'd unwittingly gotten the Chief involved, too. At least the other three had joined of their own accord—forming some kind of odd, adult "justice league" or just a boys' club as Amara had called it. Still, the necessity of it didn't make him feel any better about digging up his personal history for all to see.

He hadn't minded before—hadn't felt any connection to a family other than the one he knew. But since Bear Mountain he'd been feeling raw. And the thought of digging up what they needed on a dead boy who should have lived and been Jason's brother felt wrong.

Not "some boy." Daniel. Jernigan had found a name and a birth certificate. Almost exactly four years younger than Jason, Daniel Mallory had been treated for asthma at the Baptist Hospital ER. That was how Clark found him.

Jason now had a duplicate birth certificate.

And it had been Alcia Mallory who had died in the Pelias fire. On the couch. In the middle of a point of origin.

Somehow that made him numb. His mother had been murdered.

Chief pointed out that the other option was that she set a handful of fires around her floor, spiraling in to her unit, then doused and lit herself. They all agreed that was insane, and there was no evidence that Alcia Mallory had been insane. In order to do that, she would have committed a gruesome, painful suicide in front of her two young children. Children that there was no evidence she didn't love.

That was maybe the worst. He didn't know his birth mother *hadn't* been crazy, there was just no evidence that she was. He didn't know that she *had* loved him and little Daniel, but there was no evidence that she didn't. There wasn't much evidence of her at all. But Clark was working on digging it up.

They drove through a donut shop for a box of glazed and some coffee and arrived in Montgomery. While Jason sat patiently in the passenger seat, Clark navigated to the small house on Beech Street.

Chief Adler had helped them dig up info on Jack Deason the Third. He was on the roster at Burkeville, just like he'd said. Jack Deason the Second was retired FD from Montgomery and still volunteered at Burkeville sometimes. Lots of firefighters volunteered in rural areas when they were off shift, or once they retired, so there was nothing unusual about the story.

The problem was, there wasn't anything else to find out. There was no way of knowing whether Deason was one of the people covering things up or simply being helpful. So they sat and ate doughnuts and quietly sipped their coffee while they waited for Deason to leave his house.

Jason was on the border of just suggesting they ditch the idea about an hour later, when a big boat of a car backed out of the drive with an older man and woman in it. Jason looked at the couple in the car and then down at the photos Clark had printed up—they matched. Deason and his wife had just left home.

He turned to Jernigan. "Now what?"

"You stay in the car."

That wasn't a problem since the car was put in gear and moved forward. But it only went a few feet—out from the cover of the shrubs they'd been only partly concealed behind—and stopped in front of the house next to the Deasons'.

"Here." Clark handed him a pad and pen. "Write something, look busy, and wave and smile if I gesture to you. You're my associate."

With that enigmatic set of instructions, he exited the car and knocked on the front door of the neighbor's house. He spoke a bit, but was too far away for Jason to hear anything. He refused something the older woman offered him and gestured to Jason as he said he would. Jason nodded and gave a small, half-wave, feeling like a fool.

Then Clark thanked the woman and walked across the lawn to the house on the other side of the Deasons where the whole thing happened again, though the man at this door seemed suspicious and called his wife out to join the conversation.

The house across the street yielded nothing, but the process repeated next door until finally Clark came back and slid into the driver's seat with a grin on his face. "Well, that went as well as it could have."

"What was '*that*'?"

"Calling the district or the city and checking up on Deason would alert someone. So I told the neighbors that we were from the *Montgomery Advertiser*—which is partially true, I've had articles in their paper. I said Deason was a material witness for a story and we were checking his credibility."

"And that does what?"

"Only the first step. But the good news is that the neighbors say he's an upright man and that he would be a whistle-blower if he knew something was wrong."

"Oh, god. You asked that?"

Clark nodded and started the car. "Yes, I used that term exactly. And of the three I spoke to, one said she didn't know him well enough and the other two said 'oh yes he would.' Which is the best corroboration we're going to get right now."

They headed into downtown Montgomery and toward the big gray building that housed CPS. This time, Jason walked the maze of halls with confidence, leading Clark up and down elevators and along hallways mesmerizingly similar to each other.

Aida was expecting them, but as Amara had suggested, she seemed wary. He let Clark do the talking.

Aida nodded at them and got to work. There was a lot she could do now that they had a name and birth date. The two men stood silently at the counter as she typed away and printed out pages for them.

Jason had asked earlier if maybe they shouldn't go back to Aida, if putting in inquiries about his brother—about Daniel—would raise flags. But Clark didn't think so. He didn't think the cover-up was about the kids, but about the fire. And most of the people on the scene had been firefighters and EMS, not concerned with anyone's names, only that they got out and got treated for whatever they needed.

Aida came out from behind the dividers where she had been running a printer. She had a small sheaf of papers in her hand which she handed to Clark. All she offered Jason was a tight smile.

He offered a similar one in return. How could he say something to her with Jernigan standing right there? Though he wasn't sure that was the real cause—he didn't know what to say to her anyway. Maybe he should just ask her out again.

As they headed out toward the hallway he turned back and caught her eye, with his hand up in the old universal 'phone' symbol, he mouthed, "I'll call you."

Her nod was noncommittal.

They were two steps out the door when Clark turned to him. "Do you want to go back in there and ask her out to lunch? Can you eat within walking distance of here?"

"That obvious, huh? Don't we have other things on our agenda today?" Jason hated feeling stupid, and he was feeling stupid all around today.

"Yes, but I have to go by the pay phone and see what's near. Honestly, you shouldn't be with me. I'd hate for someone to recognize you."

"So, I stay and have lunch with Aida and you do recon then pick me up?"

Clark looked at his watch. "In about an hour?"

Jason agreed and turned around to head back into the CPS office, but Jernigan stopped him. "I thought I was paying attention, but seriously, how the hell do I get out of here?"

Laughing, and feeling better than he had in a while, he gave directions out of the building and went back in to see what he could do about Aida. He didn't know if she was what he wanted, but then again he'd wanted Kelly. What did he know anyway?

She was still wary even after he asked her to join him for lunch and bought her a plate from the cafeteria. The air had turned colder than last time and sitting outside wasn't much of an option. Though government cafeteria food wasn't what he would have done had it been a real date, Jason thought it was okay. Then he remembered she'd called and offered to make him dinner— and whatever underlying message went along with that—and that she'd called a second time and found a woman answering his phone.

Aida cut one dainty bite from the fish she had ordered and confronted him about just that. "The last time you were here you said you'd like to see me again. Then there's a woman living with you. I can only guess that you either work very fast or you were seeing her last time you saw me."

Well, shit. Jason was stunned. That was a lot more involved reasoning than he'd planned on. He'd braced himself for "why did a woman answer your phone?" not a series of possible ways he was a complete asshole. And why was he always the asshole? "Neither."

He took a bite of his sandwich, which looked a little pasty. As he chewed, burning time to make her wait, he realized it tasted a little pasty, too.

Aida blinked. And won.

He gritted his teeth and started talking. "I'm not the jackass you paint me to be."

"Well, you suggested you were interested in me. Then you don't follow up at all. If you don't like someone, just say 'thank you' at the end of the date. I thought we had a good time, you didn't. What I can't figure out is why you're here now."

"I—"

He didn't get out more than that lone syllable before she railroaded him.

"Oh, God. You want to grease the wheels so I'll pull information for you." She looked down at her plate.

And Jason looked up to heaven. *Lord, save me from women.*

"Would you be interested in the whole truth?" That's what Amara had told him: be honest. He figured he couldn't dig himself a deeper hole than the one he was already in.

She looked him square in the eyes. "That would be a refreshing change."

Damn her. "No, it wouldn't. I didn't lie to you and I—" he held his hand up to stop her, "didn't mislead you. Would you like to hear it?"

"Sure." She went back to cutting her fish, and he wasn't sure if she would listen or not.

"I meant to come back and see you again. But things happened at work." He didn't mention that he hadn't come back to Montgomery because of what he'd inadvertently stirred up, but he was pissed at her assessment of him and so he played the pity card. "We had a mountain fire and we lost two men. One of them right in front of me."

"Oh my God, Jason, I—"

"—and the woman in my apartment is my new roommate." He bit into his pasty sandwich again and figured he was stuck until Jernigan showed up. It was like being on a junior-high date and having to wait for his ride. He wasn't prepared for Aida's next question.

"Is she pretty?"

"What?" Like it mattered what his roommate looked like. He says two men died in his unit and she wants to know if his roommate is pretty? And the fact was she didn't have to worry. Amara wasn't his type at all. He liked women who dolled up. He liked blondes with long flowing locks. He particularly liked them with a decent rack. All things Amara didn't possess. And Aida did.

She spoke slowly, as though he had gone stupid. "Is . . . she . . . pretty?"

Well, hell, maybe he had.

"Sure."

"Then I'd rather we not continue seeing each other." She spoke the words as though she were talking about the weather. And after the conversation they'd just had, he agreed with her, but for entirely different reasons.

When he didn't say anything, she took another bite of her lunch and offered up, "I'll be glad to still help you locate anything on your brother, though. That's my job. . . It sounds like you found out a lot between last time and now."

Though Jason was grateful for the sudden shift in conversation, he wasn't quite sure how to wrap his head around it. So he decided to go with the flow. "I hit a brick wall, but J—" He stopped himself and re-assessed things. What if someone came looking for information about the boys? There was no reason to think they would, but no reason to think they wouldn't.

Putting his hand out suddenly, he stopped her arm and got her attention. "Look, I ran into some trouble. It's part of the reason I didn't come back when I thought I would." How to say this? He went back to Amara's idea that he should be honest, even if he couldn't tell Aida the whole thing. "I don't think it has anything to do with my brother, but if anyone comes and asks what you pulled for me, can you withhold that?"

She blinked and pulled back to peer at him, "I can't tell anyone what I pull. Unless they come with a subpoena. CPS information is confidential. I had to verify that you were Jason Mallory and that you were requesting records only on your own family before I could give you anything. You don't have to worry about me breaking the law."

He breathed a sigh of relief. "That's good to know. Then you likely won't get asked anything anyway. It was stupid."

She looked at him sideways again. "That's just weird, Jason. What have you gotten yourself into?"

He shook his head and checked his watch. Then he gave another sigh of relief, though he fought to hide this one. "My friend is expecting me out front in a few minutes. I'm sorry, I have to go. It was good to see you again."

She nodded at him.

Okay, maybe it hadn't been a stellar second date, but at least he'd figured out where he stood with her. He glanced back and saw she was still looking at him. Her expression suggested that he'd made up the whole "someone might ask you questions" thing so he could go back to his girlfriend in his apartment.

He almost laughed out loud at the thought but figured that wouldn't go over very well. So he went out the front door and stood at the side of the street with his fists shoved into his pockets while he waited for Clark to come back around. This sucked. He needed to be driving next time.

But as he slid into the passenger seat and the warmth of the car, Jernigan said, "Well, it was a good thing you weren't with me and that we weren't in your car."

"Why's that?"

"The number Smith called from is a pay phone." They already knew that. "About three blocks away from Montgomery fire house number four."

Well shit. The thought careened through his head and was immediately followed by the thought that "well, shit" and its equivalents had been in his head too much lately. "I don't suppose you got lucky enough to see some firefighter using the phone?"

Clark laughed. "No, no one in uniform was there. In fact, it was at a gas station and I watched for a while, pulled up my GPS on nearby things and then went by the fire house. I didn't see anything unusual. But it makes sense that whoever called you was from station house number four."

Then he switched topics. "Did you patch things up with the hot blonde?"

Hot blonde? Aida was pretty but he never would have used *hot* to describe her. "Nope. That ship has sailed."

"Did our link into the CPS archives sail with it?"

"Nope. I'm not that stupid." He turned to Jernigan. "Does everyone think I'm an idiot or a jackass?"

"What?" Jernigan looked at him sideways while still navigating through the unfamiliar streets.

"I didn't kill our link to CPS. It was all very polite and there had only been one spur-of-the-moment dinner before. Well, and one lunch. And a few phone calls. Maybe I am an idiot." He sighed.

"No worries. I didn't think you were an idiot, I just know sometimes people get vengeful over things they shouldn't. Anyway, we are off to Deason's house. Back to where we started. If we're lucky, he's home."

Jason nodded. They'd planned the day out, knowing they had to see what the scoop was on Deason then, if he seemed like a good bet, somewhat blindside him. That way he wouldn't have a chance to get in touch with anyone if he was dishonest. And if they were under-paranoid and someone *was* watching them, no one would have a chance to get to Deason first, because it wouldn't be an arranged meeting.

They pulled up to the small house and immediately noticed that the garage door—left open when the couple pulled out that morning—was now closed. It was as good a sign as any. Walking up the small sidewalk, Jason thought that if the Deasons weren't home they wouldn't be able to just walk back and sit in the car and wait. The neighbors would be really suspicious if they did that. They were likely to have the cops come bang on the car window while they watched. And that wouldn't do them any favors here.

Luckily, the door opened, and Mr. Deason looked them over before inviting them in. It was almost as stupid as leaving the garage door open when they left, but hopefully he was just honest and thought everyone else should be, too.

Deason looked like a clean-shaven Santa, and Jason didn't want to believe this man could be anything other than kind. But you never knew, and when they went in, Jason wondered if they'd be shot dead there on the shag carpeting in front of the square stone fireplace.

He relaxed a bit when Mrs. Deason came around and asked if they wanted drinks or anything to eat.

Clark did the talking, explaining that Jason had gotten a call from the couple's son. He told them how there was trouble with the case, and that they'd checked him out with the neighbors before coming back to interview him.

Jason thought that was an excessive overload of info. If Deason was Smith, or was in with Smith, then Clark had just sold the farm. But if Deason wasn't with Smith, maybe he needed to know what might come down the pipe. It was a crapshoot either way, and Clark seemed to be going for the more-flies-with-honey approach.

Then Clark pulled out a confidentiality agreement for Deason to sign, and the old man just asked his wife for a pen—no comment, just a big bold scrawl across the page and a weary, "Things weren't right then, and they still aren't."

He didn't know much. Only that he'd cried foul and had been shut down. His job had been subtly threatened, and the psychologist had stated Deason wouldn't be able to return to work if he didn't let go of his ideas.

The older man shook his head. "After a while, I started to believe them. I was only a few years on the job. I hadn't seen what they saw at the Pelias Apartments. I hadn't been in the upper floors of the building. But I had swept the two lower floors and I stood outside the fifth-floor window at the top of the ladder, looking in."

Jason looked at Clark. Though his frown was slight, it was clear that the two were thinking the same thing.

Clark sat back to encourage Deason to roll with it. And roll he did.

"I didn't realize I had been right until about seven years later when I was left to clean up another fire with an investigator. He looked at the building we were in and rapidly pointed out three things that made it pretty clear he was looking at arson. They all matched Pelias Street. I've seen other things since then: the way the smoke came out the windows. That the fire went horizontal before vertical. Pelias was an old building nearly thirty years ago and they didn't have the codes they do today. Uncontrolled fire goes up."

Clark pulled the conversation back around. He asked a handful of questions and, using his nice pen and legal pad, wrote diligent notes. For a moment Jason wondered why Clark didn't pull out his laptop, but a quick look around the house answered that. Not much here had been updated since the late seventies—so paper and pencil it was. His brain snapped back when Clark asked, "And what was the name of the psychologist you saw?"

Southfield Fire Station #2

SHIFT	A	
	O'CASEY	CAPTAIN
ENGINE 2	WANSTALL	LIEUTENANT
	MONDY	FF2 / EMT
ENGINE 5	STANDARD	ENGINEER
	WEST	FF2
	NAGY	FF1 / EMT
RESCUE 3	DONLAN	ENGINEER/PARAMEDIC
	GRIMSBY	FF1

Chapter 14

There was yet another new face in lineup. Brandon Nagy was up from Mobile FD. He was full of "y'all" and drawl and he made Donlan cringe each time he spoke. It was all Jason could do to keep from cracking a smile during line up and he had to admit that felt good.

The shift had been on eggshells since Bear Mountain. And most of the others had been hyperaware of what was said around Jason and Standard since they had watched as Bloomberg died. It was a senseless tragedy, and they were all trying to shake it off.

Adler introduced Nagy, told them he was on his way up to FF2 and should be there within the year. For the first time Chief instructed all the current FF2 and higher ranks to help. "I want each firefighter in this house ranked as high as he can be. I want each of you with higher ranks helping those not yet there to achieve more. I want this house to have the most knowledge and the best track record. And I'll find a way to pay you all for it."

All down the line eyebrows went up. No one commented that the "best track record" had to start from Bear Mountain. Bloomberg had been a freak accident, simply bad timing. But Connelly had made a mistake—which was how most firefighters died in fires.

If you followed all the rules and regulations, you were too slow to be effective. You didn't save what needed to be saved. But if you didn't follow all the rules, you ran risks. Connelly's risk hadn't paid off. None of them had thought anything when he and Railles had separated a bit to cut the line they were working on. They were within feet of each other, but further apart than regulations allowed. Because stray sparks could close the gap—

179

and they had. The wind had kicked; the flames had rushed the uncut ground between the two men, burning leaves and blowing embers, catching fire to the brush around Connelly. Railles had retreated. Connelly couldn't.

When they found him, he'd dug into the ground—just as he should—buried his face and hunkered down in hope the fire would run over him. Something had caught his tank, maybe a branch, probably pulled at his gear, and fire had rushed up his back, and he had baked alive. In spite of the face mask and filters he was wearing, the heat had seared his throat and lungs. In the end he'd just let go. But nothing made any of it better. The only thing that would help was time.

As Adler surveyed the house—alive again in a way it hadn't been for a while—he understood that though it would get better, it never got any easier. Each time was the worst for a different reason. And he wondered how many losses he could shoulder before he had to tap out. He wasn't ready to retire yet; there was still so much to do. He had to clean up Pelias, the mess he had left since the beginning of his otherwise unblemished career. Not that anyone else knew about Pelias, but for years he had left it buried, though it would come up and take a bite at him sometimes. There was no way to keep it buried now. Not with that boy here as a grown man who trusted him and followed his orders. They would all sleep better when this was finished.

He hit his office and tried to complete his paperwork just like any other weekday. But after a few hours of checking candidates and calling for interviews, Mondy came into the office, interrupting with an agenda. Probably more Pelias stuff. At least he didn't sit down.

"Hey Chief, who was the psychologist you saw after the Pelias fire? The one who wouldn't clear you if you continued to investigate."

Adler frowned. "He was the appointed one. Some guy."

"Do you remember his name?"

Probably not. But he sat back in his chair, closed his eyes and wracked his brain. "Williams."

"Ben Williams?"

Okay, that was disturbing. Mondy had already known before he asked? "Yes."

Jason nodded and sat his butt down in the guest chair. *Damn.*

"Jernigan and I talked to Jack Deason the Second yesterday. Back in '85, he protested the Pelias fire, too. Thought it was arson and got shut down. He was given the impression that he was the only one who thought that way."

Adler blinked as the information soaked in. "He saw the same psychologist and got the same instructions I did?"

"Sounds like."

That rattled around in his brain a bit and he tried to get it to stop. "This Ben Williams, what about him?"

Jason nodded. "I think the question is: how many of you were there? Each of you thinking you were the only one convinced that Pelias was arson and told you were wrong."

"Who knows. But, honestly? Two is enough."

Jason agreed. "Can I call Jernigan from here?" He wanted the privacy of the office. They were trying to involve as few people as possible, but he knew there was no way they'd keep this in their little group for long. Deason was already in, and the girl from the CPS office. Who knew who else?

The call was short; apparently Jernigan had been waiting for it. Jason clicked his phone off. "He's on it. And we're going to try tracing my birth mother. See if we can find employment records, old friends, that kind of thing. Anyone who might have known what was going on while she lived in the Pelias Apartments."

He didn't add "anything that might have gotten her murdered." He didn't need to.

Adler turned the conversation. "I assume you're here because chores are done?"

Jason nodded.

"We need to have training today." They'd missed it too many times to make their mark for the month. No one was going to fault a station with two deaths for not making the training numbers, but it was time to catch back up. They needed to be as good as possible. "Call everyone into the training room."

Jason headed out, gathering A-Shift as he went. Grimsby was running today's training as part of his EMT certification. At least that part was going right.

Adler only joined them half the time, but today he'd be there. He finished the forms he had been working on when Mondy had interrupted him and then headed to the back room. He stepped to the front near the whiteboard and, with a small glance, Grimsby stepped aside.

"I have news." Though he could see it on their faces, Adler appreciated that they all managed to hold in their groans.

"One: I don't think it will happen, but Gold Standard has appealed their loss of the EMS contract for the city of Southfield." He let that sink in for a moment, then continued. "If the appeal holds, we'll have to cut back to seven per shift. But I don't think it will. We had to hire to be ready for taking over EMS, and I'm not worried. I just didn't want you to hear it from anyone else."

"Thanks, Chief." It was Standard who said it. Adler remembered sitting on the other side of the table and how he'd never said much when announcements were made. He respected Standard all the more for knowing his chief was a human, too, and that a simple "thanks" went a long way. A few more voices echoed it.

Grimsby started to step back into place behind the lectern, but a small shake of the head kept him back.

"There's more and it's not good. No one's job is in jeopardy or anything, but . . ." He couldn't take it, standing there with all of them looking at him. Just thinking it broke his heart. He motioned to Grimsby, then to all of them. "Just gather up. I need to sit for this."

Once they were all pulled up in a huddle in the space that normally made a walkway between the desks, Adler sucked it up and started. "Some of you may have already heard some of this, but I'd appreciate if you hold comments until the end. The police had a BOLO out on Merriman, Tunstall, and Platt. They were found last night. Tunstall and Platt are Gold Standard EMTs. And Platt's an idiot—luckily he rolled on his friends."

There were looks of shock around the table. Well, maybe they hadn't known. Mondy knew Castor in the PD and there were more than a few friendships with officers. Hell, the fire station was nearly back-to-back with the local police. He was genuinely surprised they didn't know all of this well before he had.

"Apparently, Merriman talked them into lighting the campfire against the ordinance. Told them he could control it, that the ordinance was for people who didn't know what they were doing. Not surprisingly it caught the trees nearby, and—rather than put it out or call anyone—they took advantage of it."

He almost couldn't speak; his stomach rolled. And again he wondered how much more he would have to shoulder before he tapped out. "They gathered their things, used dry branches to light a few more spots—"

Eyebrows went up all around the room and more than one mouth dropped open.

"They decided that a big fire would use our resources and demonstrate how much their services were needed. They thought it would get Merriman's job back and keep Gold Standard employed."

It was Mondy who spoke up. "If they set it on purpose, then why leave their bag? Why not do a better job clearing out the evidence?"

"Platt said they were gathering it, but the fire jumped and they ran. Merriman convinced them that everything would burn."

Adler didn't like Merriman, but he loved him. It was like having a bad child. Before this he had simply been unruly, removed because he was a possible danger to others. How right that assessment had been. "The concern now is whether they'll be prosecuted for first- or second-degree murder."

Unable to continue, he turned the floor back over to Grimsby to go on with the afternoon's training. Then he stopped in the doorway, interrupting poor Grimsby one last time. "If I ever hear of any of you breaking ordinances, I will fire you. Even if you do actually know what you're doing. We lead this community by example."

A chorus of strong "Yes, sirs" made him feel better. He was halfway back to his office when the phone rang.

The bell followed shortly, and Engine 2 and Rescue 3 headed out to the onramp at the freeway to handle the overturned semi and subsequent fire.

∧   ∧   ∧   ∧   ∧

Amara walked in the front door of the fire station and immediately figured out that she had done it wrong. The front door was for random people wandering off the streets, not for those in the know. Two of the firefighters on shift looked her up and down, while one of the older ones came forward and quickly tried to insert himself between her and his shift mates. "Can I help you, ma'am?"

She put her hand out for a more formal introduction. "I'm Amara Bellamy. Nurse Practitioner with the State Forestry Service."

Nope. Nothing. No flicker of recognition at all. Lovely. "Is Chief Adler in?"

"Yes, ma'am. Is there a message I should give him?"

She held back the sigh, but only by sheer force of will. "He knows who I am." Then she bit her own tongue and tried again. "I've been invited to lead your trainings for the next several days."

"Oh." He led her down a short hall to a doorway. As an afterthought, he added, "I'm Jack Standard. Engineer."

Amara nodded. Though she knew the EMS rankings, she had no real clue what an engineer was. Making a mental note to learn more before she came back the next day, she entered the Chief's office with a smile and introduced herself all over again. At least she'd talked to him on the phone briefly this morning.

They worked out some logistics; she had to come teach the same class each afternoon for the next three days to cover all three shifts. Chief Adler made it clear to her that timing was an issue— there was no guarantee of start time, they could get interrupted at any time, and they might not even run training on a particularly busy day.

She laughed. "I'm writing my doctoral dissertation. I think that's why they asked me to do this. Plenty of adjustable time on my hands."

He laughed and asked if she wanted a tour.

"I've actually been here before as a visitor. I'm friends with Alex Weingarten—Leo is my cousin." Then she wondered if Adler knew about Alex and Leo, if maybe she had just mistakenly come perilously close to outing them at the station.

But Adler nodded. "Leo comes around to see Alex once in a while. But Alex isn't in today."

"No, but my new roommate is: Jason Mondy."

"Oh! You're replacing Kelly?" The words seemed to come out of his mouth like an errant child he couldn't control, and he was instantly embarrassed.

Amara couldn't help but laugh. "Only for the rent money."

"Thank you for understanding." Then he turned back to a real conversation. "You're welcome to check in the back, I'm pretty sure Jason is in."

"I will." She neglected to mention that her roommate wasn't speaking to her, and that she was pretty sure the last thing she'd said to him was that he was a jackass.

Wandering through the station house earned her a handful of odd looks and offers to "help you, ma'am?" Mostly she politely refused and said she was "fine." But as she got toward the back room she asked the young man lounging on the sofa if the room to her right was the training room.

"Yes, ma'am it is. Can I help you?"

Ah, yes, there it was again. Maybe she should finally say yes.

"Actually, you can." She walked into the room and surveyed the layout until he appeared behind her. There were a handful of desks scattered across the space and three long tables in the back. The wall behind her had a whiteboard and a series of markers scattered in the tray.

She turned to the firefighter and almost bumped into him, he was so close. He spoke first. "I'm Kellan West. What can I help with?"

Amara took a step back, then pointed. "Can we move the tables around?"

"Sure?" He looked confused.

"I'm sorry," She introduced herself yet again and explained that she'd be back the next day. That she'd have the usual CPR dolls and they would need to lay them out, both on tables and on the floor.

Kellan pointed out past arrangements they had used. "Will we be re-certified at the end of the training?"

She nodded. "They said the station houses were swamped and that they were bringing the training to you rather than making you go get it. Something about wanting to prove that everyone was up to date. I'll be at Station House One next week."

She was midway through various possible projector set-ups when Jason came in.

He stood with his arms crossed. "Hi, Amara."

It wasn't the friendly greeting she'd hoped for, but it was better than it could have been.

Kellan looked back and forth between them, clearly able to tell they knew each other. "I'm going to go back to the game." He made some random pointing gestures and left the room, causing Jason to roll his eyes.

"What are you doing here?" As though she'd showed up at his work just to pester him. *Good Lord.*

With a sigh, she explained one more time why she was in the station house, then she sucked it up and did what she should. "I'm sorry. I shouldn't have said what I did."

It felt odd talking to him here. She'd insulted him at home but apologized here—on what was definitely his turf. But she hadn't seen him at home. Not enough to get two words out.

He didn't look shocked, but he had definitely been unprepared for her to say she was sorry. His arms nearly fell out of where he'd locked them across his chest in a cross between a threat and self-protection. "No. You were right."

"What?" Great, now she was the one who was off-balance.

He sighed. "Don't make me say it again." His eyes rolled away.

She let at least part of it drop and turned the conversation a bit. "Did you see her? Make up with her?"

He laughed. "Yes and no." His face scrunched up and he scratched the back of his head as though that would unjumble what was obviously confusing him. "She seemed a little crazy. She said she didn't want to be involved with me since I was living with another woman and she didn't believe me that there were other things going on—that my not calling right back had nothing to do with her."

"How did she seem crazy?"

"She . . . thought there was something going on between us. She was upset that I hadn't called since last time I was there—which I apologized for! And she wouldn't accept my apology."

"That's her prerogative." Amara had to wonder how that apology had been given. There was every possibility that he'd shouted it at her. She doubted he had the skills necessary to smooth things over with a woman.

"I don't think she believed me about . . . about . . ."

"Your secret club?"

His eyes rolled again, as though he couldn't stop it. She made a conscious choice not to be offended.

"For lack of a better term, yes."

"Well, your secret boys' club is a little odd."

A movement in the corner of the room caught their attention. Rob Castor and Clark Jernigan had just come into the training room.

As Jason watched, Amara's gaze flicked back and forth between the two of them. She murmured under her breath, "Speak of the devil. Devils, actually."

Castor looked at Amara with a bit of a squint in his eye. "I didn't realize someone else would be in here."

"No worries. I'm done with the room for today. But I will need it for the next three days or longer if training gets interrupted." She headed out the door, figuring it was time to leave anyway. She needed to swing by the Red Cross center and gather the training kits they were donating, but she turned back at the last minute. "Is there a 'Members Only' sign to hang on the door?"

"Funny." Jason stood there. He didn't close the door, but the three of them were clearly waiting until she left. So she did.

Bart English came in next and Jason headed off to tell Adler they were all there. They got some funny looks as the two walked through the station house. But the Chief just reminded the rest of the shift that they weren't to answer any questions about Jason if anyone called, and that he was to be alerted if anyone did. It was Chief who closed the door to the training room.

"Let's hope we don't get a call during this . . . shindig." He pulled up a chair and waited for the younger men to tell him what they had.

Pulling out his black messenger bag, Jernigan started to arrange his supplies—something Jason had become used to. Though for a moment, Jason thought the reporter had grabbed *his* bag, then almost laughed to himself. Cleary, it was the bag of choice when hunting down a quarter-century-old arson.

Once all his materials were laid out, Jernigan asked, "Ready?"

According to the look on Adler's face, the answer was "five minutes ago."

But he started talking and redeemed himself. "Okay—we know both Adler here and Deason were evaluated and eventually cleared to return to work by the same psychologist after the Pelias fire. That therapist was Dr. Benjamin Williams—"

"Was?" English interrupted in the moment that Jason was trying to get his mouth open to ask the same thing.

"Yes. *Was*. Williams died in a car accident in the mid-nineties." Jernigan pulled out an article he'd printed and English, Castor and Mondy leaned over to glean what they could.

It was the Chief who asked, "Is that suspicious?"

He hated thinking that, but it was where his head was now. Well, for a second, until his thoughts turned to keeping Abby and the girls safe from this fallout.

Jernigan shrugged. "It was a car accident. I don't think we can rule anything out, but it didn't happen in the middle of the Pelias cover-up—the accident was a good ten years later. And it sure didn't happen because of anything we stirred up now. So I'm guessing it's not. But there's no way of knowing for certain. No way to tell if this is an ongoing cover-up that we stepped into now, or if it's been essentially closed since the fire and we're the ones who reopened it."

That took some of the weight off Adler's shoulders, but nowhere near all.

English came in again. "So we can cross Williams off the list to interview. To see if he was pressured or what."

"Yeah," Jernigan turned that paper over, "That one's not going to happen. And that's exactly why we have a lot of irons in the fire." He pulled out another sheet. "Jason and I went to Montgomery a few days ago."

Jason let the reporter update the others on the interesting-but-so-far-useless information about the pay phone location, Deason's corroboration of arson, and the papers Aida had given them about Daniel.

His heart clenched.

Why now? Why did it feel bad to tell everyone about this now? It was almost as if his mother had come in and was using the projector to show naked videos of him as a kid—uncomfortable and a bit embarrassing—though he couldn't figure out why.

"Daniel Mallory was admitted to Jackson Hospital Emergency Room in the early morning hours of July twenty-ninth of '85."

It seemed like such a clinical recitation, something even in Jernigan's tone made it feel rote, made it feel less like it was about his brother. But everything about Daniel felt off. He peered over at the notes on the pad of paper the reporter had been reading from. One of those specially lined papers Jason always passed by at the office store, it held a column with times, dates, the phone number and the name of the person along with the information he'd learned. He must need all of it to back up his stories should anyone ever question him.

The information was written in messy but decipherable handwriting, and Jason jogged his brain to see if any of it triggered some kind of memory. Had he called his little brother "Dan," "Danny?" Some other nickname that was locked in his head? Or was it simply gone forever?

He almost missed the reporter's next statement. "So I followed what Aida gave us and found out that Daniel Mallory was in the PICU—Pediatric ICU—for seven days, and he was then transferred to Greil Memorial Psychiatric Hospital."

"I'm sorry, what?" Jason sputtered.

Castor was frowning. "Psychiatric Hospital? Our boy was nutso?" Immediately contrite, Castor turned to Jason, "Sorry man. That's your brother."

Though it had been rude, Jason had hardly heard him and so he waved it away. He'd said worse at times himself, "Why was he in the psych ward?"

Jernigan shrugged. "No info on that yet. I do, however, have Alcia Mallory's high school transcript."

He held it up as though it was a thousand-dollar bill, and they all looked at him like now *he* belonged in the psych ward. When no one seemed to understand his pride, he gave in and spoke. "Look, the stuff on Daniel Mallory, that's for Jason. We have no idea if any of it will lead around to the arson or not. But the transcript tells us Alcia Mallory went to high school in Montgomery, at Carver. And that she graduated in seventy-five."

Again, no one got it. English even asked. "And that means what?"

"It means that there are possibly people still at that school who remember her. Maybe a teacher or a principal. Someone we can find." He tapped the spot on his notes where he'd jotted the info. "She lived on Pelias Street—all of fifteen blocks from where she graduated high school. That means she grew up in that same area—at least for high school. According to school districting, no more than seven miles from Pelias."

Castor caught on. "And that means there are people in the area who knew her. People who might know why she was at the center of an arson."

Holy shit. For the first time, it occurred to Jason that they were going to go dig up dirt on the woman who gave birth to him and raised him to age seven. Whatever she'd done had given her two children within the handful of years after she graduated high school and had likely gotten her killed. He didn't think he wanted to know more about it.

Jernigan seemed ready to pack up and head out to start the research right that moment. "Mondy and I will head back to Montgomery in the next day or two to see if we can find anyone who knew her and to check in at the hospital."

"You can't do it by yourself?" Jason hated feeling this way, like he was going to vomit. But he hated more feeling that way for a whole day in Montgomery. He'd avoid it if he could.

Jernigan shook his head. "As her kid—as the brother—you'll have access to things that I likely won't."

Well shit. And there it went again, his new mantra.

"Okay," English broke into Jason's sweat-fest of nausea. "Why aren't we pulling the city files on the arson? There *are* records. Someone signed off that it was accidental, and that person was lying. We need to know who signed those forms. The person who lied on the paperwork is likely our man. So why don't you just go pull the reports?"

Jernigan looked the ADA in the eyes. "Because those are on paper in boxes somewhere in the archives. When we pull them, we'll raise red flags. I don't think anyone is going to be paying attention to Alcia Mallory's old high school teachers, but if the arson is still important, someone will have eyes on those archives. They may even have the desk person call and notify them as soon as we make the request. And there's every possibility that person will come in while we are still pulling the files."

That stopped the nausea, replacing it with cold fear. And Jason hated that even more, because Jernigan was right again.

Shaking his head, Adler cut in. "We can send in the request. No one has to go there."

The quiet in Jernigan's voice was all the more concerning. "I guarantee you, if you send in that request, it will come back that the records were lost. We have to do it in person. So, before we pull those reports, we need a stockpile of information to fall back on. Hopefully, we'll already have a heads-up on who was behind the arson. Oh, and when we go, we'll all go together."

Castor asked the question they all wanted to know, "Safety in numbers?"

"Probably not. But definitely our best bet at it."

Chapter 15

Jason

"I don't want to eat oatmeal. It looks like baby mush." He was already falling asleep and he had to deal with this?

Amara shook her head at him. "You sit there with that huge fishbowl of cereal, and you complain that it gets soggy at the bottom. I'm just saying that you need a better method."

He woke up enough to protest, "Oatmeal is not the answer."

"Fine, then have eggs and toast." She ate another bite of that mush that she loved, sitting there at his butcher-block table in what he couldn't help but still think of as his kitchen and his apartment.

The fact of the matter was that he shouldn't think that. Not only did Amara now pay half the rent, but it had never been *his* kitchen or *his* apartment. It had been Kelly's. Jason was simply riding out the lease.

He took another big bite of cornflakes and forced himself not to make a face. They *were* mushy. "So what makes you the authority on all things breakfast?"

Her spoon stilled and she blinked at him several times like maybe he'd gone dumb. *Who knew?* Maybe he had.

"Um. . . nine years of school in human physiology including nutrition? A Nurse Practitioner's license? Most of a PhD?"

Not knowing how to respond to that, he took another bite of cornflakes and instantly regretted it. The bowl was huge and half-full of a mush that resembled her oatmeal more and more by the minute.

Realizing he shouldn't argue with a woman before he was fully awake, he stared into the bowl unable to find a bite he was willing to put into his mouth.

"But I like my cornflakes." *Wow.* He didn't think he'd whined like that since sixth grade and his father had made a comment about acting like a man.

His stomach grumbled.

Amara laughed at him. There she sat, enjoying mush, all bright-eyed and bushy-tailed. Or at least bushy-haired—it again defied gravity. "I'm not saying you should give up your cornflakes. But eat a regular-sized cereal bowl of them while you fix something else. Something that won't turn to mush on you, has better nutrition, and won't leave you hungry again for some hobbit-like second breakfast."

"Fine. You were right about Aida, too. You win." And she did. She had education, logic, and a J.R.R. Tolkien reference on her side. He had nothing but a bowl of mushy cornflakes and the need to make it into bed without a rumbling stomach.

Her eyebrows went up. "Does that mean you're going to try oatmeal?"

"If you insist." He sighed like he was put out. But if she fixed the cornflake problem, it would be worth it.

Before he even finished the sentence, she had a glob of it perched on the end of her spoon, which sat about three inches from his face. He ate it. And it wasn't so bad, which he said.

Her laugh startled him. "Of course it's not. It's full of sugar. I'm not a tofu lover or anything. I wouldn't eat anything that tasted bad. Give me a big plate of ribs any day."

"You eat ribs?"

She looked like a tofu-lover, with her hair wound up and her sweat pants and her face clean of makeup. Then again, she'd had on nice pants and had her hair all brushed into a real ponytail yesterday at the station.

"Love ribs." She polished off the oatmeal and rinsed her bowl in the sink before heading off to her room leaving that as her parting statement.

Jason had to ditch his cornflakes and run them through the garbage disposal. For some reason, almost every time he ran it, he thought about getting a dog. A dog would have loved the dead cornflakes. A dog would have looked at him like he was a god for

PHOENIX

giving it the leftovers. But a dog didn't survive long with a man who had a twenty-four-hour work shift.

He figured that once he got a wife, he could get a dog. But it was much harder getting a wife. And with his track record, he was going to find it harder than most. At the moment, it seemed a shame you couldn't just go down to the pound and pick one out.

He headed back into the bedroom and stripped out of the uniform he was still wearing. It hadn't seemed economical in any way to change into sweats just for breakfast, when all he was going to do was strip down and crawl into bed.

Knowing he wasn't going to sleep well, he had stayed in one of the recliners in the break room the night before. He'd been reading for most of the time, confident that sleeping likely wouldn't do him any favors. And each time he did nod off, he had jerked awake some time later—glad that he wasn't in a room with six other people who slept lightly and would have been woken by him popping up randomly. It would be even worse if he called out or screamed. And at this point, he honestly didn't know what he did while he was dreaming.

He'd been doing better for a while, but lately it seemed the more they dug up the worse his sleep patterns were getting. He had no idea if that was because he learned more about his brother or if that was because there was real concern about the arson and about someone wanting to stop their research.

Tomorrow he would head into Birmingham to pick up Clark and they would head down to Montgomery again. Though it was a bit out of the way to pick the other man up, Jason wanted to be the one driving this time.

And to do so, he needed to get some sleep. That his sleep schedule was out of whack was an accepted fact at this point. He was just concerned about getting enough hours to stay alert during work and to find out what he needed to about Daniel and about Pelias.

Though the blackout shades were pulled and the covers were around him and he was dog tired, nothing happened. He forced his eyes to stay closed. But sleep refused him.

For some reason his brain was wide awake. Right now, his body hated his brain with the fire of a thousand suns. His brain felt like it was turning over inside his skull—as though the thoughts were powering actual movement in there. But he didn't even think he could find the muscle power to hold his book and read.

Daniel.

There were so many things he didn't know about his brother. And he wasn't going to learn them lying here in bed. He was going to get started on it tomorrow and there was nothing he could right now do to move that forward.

And while he couldn't get any info sooner, he *could* put it off—which he would have to do if he didn't get any sleep today.

Still something about Daniel nagged at him.

So he made use of his refusing-to-sleep brain and went through everything he'd learned, everything he'd gotten from Aida, everything that Chief had told him about pulling the two boys out of the fire. Jason disregarded anything that was specifically about the arson and focused on what he knew about his brother.

Strobel had pulled Daniel out of the Pelias Apartment fire. Strobel had then died from those injuries. Daniel had gone in the ambulance to Jackson Hospital. He was in the PICU for seven days. Then he was transferred to Greil Psychiatric Hospital where they took further care of him.

Tomorrow Jason and Clark would go to Greil and see what records they could pull, probably talk to the staff and see if anyone remembered Daniel Mallory. Then they would get the next clue and the next and they would follow those until the trail ended. Until he had the paperwork in his hands, and knew everything he could find out about his brother. Then he could tell his mother that he'd found the boy. And he could lay the issue to rest.

After what seemed like hours of repeating this information to himself, he finally fell asleep.

∧ ∧ ∧ ∧ ∧

Clark lived in Birmingham in a building much like Jason's—nice exterior, parking garage underneath, clean neighborhood, no character.

After the other man settled in the passenger seat of the older model car, Jason asked, "You live here with your girlfriend?"

Jernigan didn't have a wedding ring, so "wife" was unlikely. Then again, maybe "boyfriend" was the answer coming.

"Just me."

"You must be doing well." The words slipped out before he could stop them. His brain was only half in the conversation even though he was curious.

Clark clicked his seatbelt in place as Jason pulled away from the curb and answered as though he didn't mind the question. "I have a two bedroom and I paid for a lake view. I like my gadgets. I get to work from home a lot, so I save on wardrobe and gas. And I don't go out a lot or have expensive habits or girlfriends. I save as much as I can. Carry over from a poor childhood probably."

Jason figured he didn't know much about it. He'd always thought his parents were plenty well off, but as he got older he realized how they'd shuffled things around and saved up for his senior trip and summer camps, things like that. So he didn't comment on what Clark had said.

In fact, he held his tongue until he got onto the freeway headed for Montgomery. "Are we going to straight to Greil?"

"No, we need to go to Carver High first. We need to get there about lunch hour when the teachers might be free to tell us about Alcia. Staff at the hospital will be there all day. We can't hit the high school late."

"Do we know how long Daniel was at Greil?" He found himself using his brother's name more and more.

"No. But we should be able to get a release date when we go today—you being family and all."

"Something's been bugging me." He swerved to avoid an older car trying to drift into his lane. He hated when drivers did that. He'd had to cut enough people out of their cars from someone else doing exactly that. And it seemed it was never the idiot who caused it who got hurt. Jason pulled his thoughts back into order, carefully dividing them between the road and the conversation. "If Daniel made it out of the PICU in seven days and was transferred to a psych hospital, that means he was relatively stable, right?"

"Sure. Physically."

It was like everything in his chest quit moving. "All this time I've been planning on finding a death certificate for my brother. But I'm not going to find it, am I?"

Clark's voice was steady, and the low tone indicated he understood what Jason wanted to know. "I don't think so."

"I'm going to find him alive, right? He's a few years younger than me. He may have a family. He may have been adopted, too. I don't know if he would even remember me." Jason forced himself to calm down so he didn't hyperventilate while driving.

This was what had been rolling over in his brain last night. It was the transfer to Greil Psychiatric that changed everything. A dying child wouldn't be transferred. Psychiatric patients had some physical problems, but not the kind that tended to lead to death certificates.

He stayed silent for a while. Clark must have sensed that it was a shift for Jason, so he waited and patiently watched the scenery for a while. But it didn't last the whole trip.

After some point that Clark must have decided was a reasonable wait, he asked Jason, "Do you mind if I interview you?"

"What? Why?"

"Because depending on how this plays out, I may write a book. Regardless of whether it's an article or a book, you'll be one of the key characters. The story of your brother—especially now that you know he's alive—is pretty big. It would be nice to have an interview from you before you find him."

He had to force his brain to stay on track so he could keep the car in his own lane. "You really think we're going to find him?"

"Yes."

Okay, he *was* going to start hyperventilating. But his job required that he be able to push emotions aside and focus. Jason used that skill now. "Why are you so confident?"

"Because I still have a job."

"What the fuck are you saying? Plain English, please." His own life was too difficult to follow these days. Anything less than perfectly spelled out terms were too difficult for him to grasp right now.

"I'm a reporter, still making good money and getting additional syndications while my whole industry is in upheaval. But I have a job. Because I can write pretty well and I can find *anything*." He pulled out that ever-present laptop and clicked it on.

For a moment, Jason wondered what it must be like to be that jacked in to his technology. He owned a laptop, but it pretty much stayed on his desk. He surfed, he researched things for work, stayed in touch with his mother and old friends. But he wasn't what anyone would call "linked in." His job wouldn't change much without his computer, but Clark seemed to practically have an IV drip from the thing. Soon he wouldn't have to type words at all. He and his laptop would be so in sync he'd just think them.

Actual spoken words from Clark broke into his thought pattern, and Jason had to focus on what he'd said.

"Sure. I guess you can interview me. It looks like you mean now."

"Why not? We're stuck in the car."

And stuck on the same freeway all the way into town. "All right."

"What was it like being adopted?"

Well, that was loaded. Rather than ask for clarification, Jason took a deep breath and told what he figured Clark wanted. "I remember a little bit about being with a foster family. I remember their faces, a nice older couple. The woman had big blue hair. And I remember my mother and father coming to take me home. They had a bike waiting for me, and my room was painted blue, and my father said he hoped I liked it and if I didn't we could repaint it together."

Clark typed furiously, then inserted another question. "You call them your 'mother' and 'father'. When did they become that?"

"Right away. My mom hugged me that night and said I was her best dream come true." He tried not to get choked up. She said that all the time, even sometimes still. "For a while—maybe a few weeks—they talked about how much my mother had wanted a child. I remember thinking that my father had gone along with her and that he didn't really have a stake in it. But then he started saying how glad he was that I had come. That he didn't want to pressure me at first, but what did I like to do? So he took me out to get a baseball glove. I remember always wanting to learn to throw a ball. And he taught me."

"So you remember wanting to know how to throw a ball from before you were adopted?"

"What do you mean?" He risked a sideways glance at Clark, but the reporter wasn't looking up from his screen.

It took Clark a moment to find the words he seemed to want. "You keep saying that you don't remember anything from before you were adopted. But that can't be right."

"Yeah it is."

"Really? You don't have any stray images? Any memories of

being loved? Or being lonely? Or happy? No odd pictures of an apartment that you can't place? No memories of being small?"

Jason shouldn't have done the interview, at least not in the car. Those questions made his teeth hurt from holding back how much he hated the truth there. He had to push himself to speak or Clark would think he was being a jackass, and he'd had enough of people thinking that about him. "I don't remember anything like that. I've tried. I don't remember my birth mother or the brother I'm looking for. I don't know what color eyes or hair they had. I don't have any stray memories of a baby or some other kid with me." He took a deep breath. "I remember almost everything after I was seven. After I moved in with my Mom and Dad it's all very clear. But it's just blank before that, and I don't know why."

Clark was typing again rather than speaking. And Jason couldn't tell if that was a good thing or a bad thing. He could see all this in some book in the future. People would read it and know things about him. When he'd thought before that it felt like selling his soul, it hadn't really hit him that he had.

Or really, he hadn't so much sold it as he'd given it away—traded it for a path to his missing brother. His *live* missing brother. But the trade was done, and Jernigan believed he could find the brother. Find *Daniel*. He didn't have any doubt.

"What if he died?" Jason just blurted it out.

"Your brother?"

"Yes." He looked only at the line on the road; there didn't seem to be much of a rush into Montgomery today, and they had most of I-65 to themselves.

"Well, if he were dead, I'd still find him."

It was a statement as though they were looking for a book in the library or a piece of evidence in a fire, not for a person.

Clark interrupted those thoughts, "But I'm sure he's not dead. It's highly unlikely. Very few American males make it past age four but die before thirty."

"What if he doesn't want to be found?" And why was Clark still typing? Jason was asking the questions now.

"That's a bridge we'll cross when we get to it." Then he changed topics. "I have a guess why you don't remember anything before you were adopted."

"Really?" That was news.

"You were in a fire. That's traumatic enough on a kid. But chances are your mother was murdered. I'm sure anyone would want to forget that if they could."

"Do you think maybe my brother forgot, too? Maybe he doesn't remember me either?" Somehow that would make things simpler. He wouldn't be at such a disadvantage. It would ease the burden of guilt that had become much heavier upon finding out that his brother had lived.

Logically, he would have thought that his brother being alive would lessen the load—it meant he would be able to meet the brother and explain how they'd been separated, apologize. But it did just the opposite. By simply being alive, his brother had carried it with him all these years. Unless he, too, had blessedly forgotten.

They were getting close to Montgomery, and Jason was grateful for the change in topic again. "Keep your eyes out for our exit."

Ten minutes later they stood in the parking lot of Carver High. An older building in an older area, it stood as a testament to the passing of the last half of a century. It was exactly what Jason wanted to see. This was where they stood the best chance to find out something. He turned to Clark, "Do you think we'll get what we need here?"

"Nope." He said it with simple conviction as he gathered his bag from the back seat. "But we'll get something that will lead us to what we need. It's probably at least two or three more steps down the road—if not more. But we have to start somewhere."

Given that underwhelming assessment, Jason figured he'd just tag along. He had no idea how to go about this. But he hadn't done so badly by himself—he had found Aida and gotten a decent amount of info from CPS. He had similar hopes for Carver High.

Clark led them into the building, and they were shepherded into the office right away by security. Just the industrial feel of the place was different from his small town high school in Madison. He had always wished he'd grown up in the city but was grateful now to his parents for making a different decision.

As they stood at the desk waiting for someone to find a minute for them, it hit Jason that—had the fire not happened, had he stayed with his birth mother—he would have likely attended this very school with its cold, regimented feeling. He looked around the place and his gaze settled on Clark who had flashed his credentials from the *Montgomery Advertiser* and was getting them led into an office in the back to meet Dr. Jefferson.

The principal was an older man; his salt and pepper hair was lighter than his deep skin. He looked happier than the industrial walls seemed they would allow.

Clark did most of the speaking, explaining only in vague terms about some story he was doing, and how Jason was Alcia's child.

Jefferson gave a small smile, "I remember her. Only a bit, she was my student one semester back when I started teaching. You'll do better with one of her other teachers maybe."

He called in the woman from the front desk and asked her to pull the old high school transcripts.

Jason just sat and listened, but Clark pushed, "Can you tell us what you do remember about her?"

"I was her literature teacher, before I got my masters and got into administration. She was smart, very smart." Then he hesitated and looked at Jason, "How much do you want to know?"

"Everything." Clark spoke in that same certain tone he had used earlier, the one that said he knew what he was doing and that he'd find out what he wanted, one way or another.

With a nod, Jefferson continued. "Well, she wasn't lazy, but she didn't want to do her school work. She wanted to be someone . . . special. And she was determined to be that."

"Did she want to be famous?"

Jefferson laughed a little. "I think that would have satisfied her, but it wasn't her goal. She wanted people to know who she was, and she wanted some power. Which is something a lot of the kids here don't have."

Clark scribbled on his pad, the laptop gone again. This time Jason suspected that maybe he just didn't want to flash the tech in the halls of this school with metal detectors and security at every door that wasn't chained.

The woman from the front desk came back with some papers. They were originally pink, but had yellowed over time. Obviously a back copy of bruise paper, there were four years of transcripts. Jefferson flipped through them. "Here, she had Mrs. Karnak three years in a row for math. You're in luck, Mrs. Karnak refuses to retire. Do you want to look through the file?" He held out the pages to the two men.

"Of course." Clark took them and handed half to Jason. There were grades of the kind he would never have been allowed to bring home. Between the four pages she started with a 3.7 GPA and dwindled to a 1.9 her senior year. There was a conversation going on in the background and Jason only caught snippets of it as Clark made plans. He was too busy soaking up information about the woman who had given birth to him and raised him for seven years. The last page was stiff and he jerked a bit at the sight of the four proof copies of her yearbook photos.

Her hair started clipped back in ninth grade and became more sophisticated as the years passed. Her makeup got heavier, and the senior version was almost unrecognizable as the girl who had walked into Carver High as a freshman.

Alcia had a straight nose, bright eyes, high cheekbones, and a smile that changed from fresh to sultry. And he didn't recognize any of it. She had his dark hair and blue eyes. But the shape was different. He saw some of his own features, but nothing jogged his memory of a woman he knew. Surely she had hugged him and picked him up when he asked. But all of that was gone.

Clark's voice came through and rattled his already disturbed thoughts. "We'll be back at one thirty then. And those copies would be wonderful."

It took Jason a moment to realize they wanted him to hand the papers back. But it sounded like they would come back later when there would be a full set of photocopies waiting and Mrs. Karnak would be on her planning period. Jefferson even set them up by having the front desk call Mrs. Karnak's room and let her know that she would be having visitors.

Since there wasn't enough time to visit Greil and get back to Carver if they hit on anything at the hospital, they grabbed a fast-food lunch. Jason was grateful that they ate in relative silence.

He wasn't an overly emotional man. Not by a long shot. The women he dated seemed to be attracted to him in the beginning because he was always on an even keel, then get pissed because he didn't open up. So this onslaught of information tipped him off his axis. Clark's questions played with his balance and seemed a little too personal. Though he knew the reporter was asking the questions that he would want the answers to if he were on the other side.

But it sucked to dig into his own psyche. And it sucked more to realize that when he did, he couldn't find anything. Not even something small—no flash of memory or sense. The pictures of the woman he knew was his birth mother triggered nothing.

He had gathered his stray thoughts by the time they came back to the school. The security guard led them to the office again, only this time they were each handed a large envelope with all of Alcia's information, which they each had to sign for and produce a driver's license. They were given visitor's badges and escorted through a series of halls to a room marked with a metal tag that stated "Mrs. Karnak—Math".

The woman seemed that she might shatter if touched, but she offered a handshake that was surprisingly strong and brought to mind Jefferson's comment that she refused to retire. She allowed a polite round of introductions then got right down to the point. "So you want to know about Alcia Mallory?"

Clark nodded. "Anything you remember about her."

"Grades?" She settled herself behind her desk, her movements slow but sure. At their nods, she continued. "She started ninth grade with an A, got low Cs in tenth and then spent her senior year repeating the required Math Eleven class."

"Do you know what caused that?"

"She quit doing the work. She was plenty smart enough, but math wasn't where her focus was."

Jason tilted his head; there was something about the way she said it. Though he couldn't articulate what he needed, Clark could. "You can tell us anything. Even if it's not complimentary to her, we need to know. Her overall GPA dropped the same way. Her yearbook pictures change radically. What do you think happened that changed her?"

"She discovered men."

"Boys?" Jason couldn't help the word that popped out of his mouth. All that for a high school crush? He remembered when he had realized the opposite sex wasn't just a thorn in his side, but his grades didn't drop—not like that. His life didn't change as radically as Alcia's seemed to have.

And Mrs. Karnak seemed to realize that he was off track. She almost laughed. "Not boys—men." She leaned back in the old wooden chair and started talking. "Alcia was smart, and when she came in as a ninth grader she was Harvard bound. Nearly straight As, volunteer work. She was padding her college applications. Sweet kid. She came from a rough neighborhood and she wanted out. She was willing to work for it."

"And 'men' happened?" Clark asked exactly what Jason

wanted to.

The woman nodded. "She got older. She started attracting the attention of some of the boys, and she just sloughed them off. But then she started changing and she started talking about some man who was taking her out, buying her things.

"Her teachers were worried. We had conversations about how to intervene. At her age, it seemed dangerous. We warned her, but she thought everything was fine. We spoke to her mother, but her mother didn't care. Alcia's attentions shifted. I think she saw the men as her ticket out for less work and faster reward. Her grades dropped and by the time she graduated—just barely—she was bragging that she was going to get married. She even had a ring that made some of the teachers jealous."

"But she never married." Clark supplied.

Mrs. Karnak shook her head. "I remember her from all the conversations the teachers had. Back then we called her an 'at risk' student. But I remember more because she died in that fire not all that long after."

It had been ten years later, but Jason didn't comment. Maybe a decade was "not all that long" in this woman's vocabulary.

Jernigan pressed, "Do you know anything about her home life?"

Another head shake. "I think she had a single mom—we only spoke to the woman once, and on the phone. Having a single mother was more concerning in those days. This area was never the nice section of town, but the sentiment at the time was still that single mothers were to be pitied, and jobs for women weren't what they are now. I don't think her mother was very educated, and from Alcia's clothes I would guess they didn't have much money.

"Do you think anything changed about that situation before she died?"

"No, I don't. Several of us teachers kept up on the gossip. We were curious, this eighteen-year-old girl had snagged some grown man with money then didn't get married. Over the years she had two kids and the rumor was that the boys had two different fathers. Again—that was more concerning in those days than it is now."

Clark thanked her and they left the school just as the bell rang and the halls flooded with teens heading out to different classes. Though it brought memories of his own high school days, his head reeled from the fact that Daniel might only be his half brother.

Before he started the car, Jason turned to Clark. "Do you think these 'men' may have had anything to do with her death?"

"I'd bet on it."

Chapter 16

Jason

Greil Memorial Psychiatric Hospital was thirteen minutes from Carver High—or it should have been. At three thirty in the afternoon cars and people began clogging the roads. Kids were getting out of school, crossing streets while cars waited and buses sat stopped at every corner. Jason navigated the streets as well as anyone not familiar with them could. The voice on his phone told him which way to go, but not how crowded it would be nor how many times they would have to wait through the same light.

On a pretty, tree-lined street, the hospital resembled a school in Jason's mind—even more than Carver High had. Greil was a sprawling single-story brick building, mildly protected by chain-link fencing and natural hills. But he pulled into the parking lot without facing security or even a barrier.

Unable to stop himself from comparing the two institutions, Jason noted that the security here was much less visible than at the high school, though he had no doubt that it was there. He and Clark were stopped at a front desk bordered by doors—there was no way to sneak by unless it was on your hands and knees, and even that didn't look like it would work with the bevy of staff hanging around.

Clark walked right up and motioned for Jason to come with him. This time he didn't pull out a badge from a local paper, just introduced himself by name to the man at the desk and started asking questions. "We're looking for information about a patient that was here years ago. How do we go about doing that?"

It took about five minutes to get past the restrictions. The hospital couldn't give out information except to family members.

Well, they had one of those. Proof of relation was required. They had that, too. Round and round until Jason wouldn't have been surprised by a cavity search, and finally they were sent to the records office in the far reaches of the building.

Not allowed to wander back by themselves, they were escorted by one of the orderlies or maybe he was just staff. He spoke occasionally, giving a small tour while they passed various places in the building.

On the one hand, it was much as Jason suspected. Nurses and other blue-scrubs-clad staff handed out the occasional medication or helped a patient. There was a large room with a TV and a small cluster of people watching it—though they didn't seem quite *right*. Jason had no idea if that was because he knew it was a psychiatric hospital and so he assumed something was wrong with the people, or if it was because something really was off. They passed a second room with another TV, this one playing cartoons. Younger people sat around this one. Most were older kids, but there were a few people who were big enough to be adults yet still laughing at stupid cartoon antics as though they were five.

Jason stopped and searched their faces wondering if he would see Daniel. But Daniel wouldn't be there, Daniel was now thirty. And possibly had been in the other room.

As his breathing sped up, Jason fought the urge to turn and run back. To call out his brother's name and see if anyone answered. He didn't even know what was wrong with Daniel, why he'd landed in here in the first place. But everything he didn't know yet seemed to pale in comparison to the fact that he might come face-to-face with his brother this afternoon.

Clark didn't seem as affected by the walk-through as Jason was. He asked a few questions about the hospital, recent changes, how the staff liked it. And the orderly answered him, but Jason couldn't hear much beyond the buzzing in his ears.

He had walked in, assuming this was another fact-finding mission. They would come here, learn something, and then—later—take the next step toward finding Daniel. It had not occurred to him until just now that Daniel might still be in residence. Hell, he was still adjusting to the fact that Daniel was likely alive.

Finding it harder and harder to breathe, Jason focused on the walls as they walked. They passed a hallway with dorm-like rooms sprouting off of it. He couldn't imagine living here. For almost thirty years. And he had left his brother here to rot.

Nearly forgetting that he had put it there, Jason shoved his hand into his pocket and his fingers closed around the bullet. It was a reminder that, though things looked like shit, he might just walk out of it okay. But it was only with supreme effort that his breathing finally slowed.

The orderly dropped them in a back-office room, said a polite good-bye, and disappeared. The room had two parts, the bulk was clearly for employees and a very tiny front section was for holding people like him and Clark, someone coming for information. It was obvious from the layout that they were not to walk around and open any of the myriad file cabinets that lined the walls, nor touch any of the archaic but functioning computers on the desks.

Coming out from behind a partial wall, a rotund woman plopped into the seat at the front-facing desk, smiled and asked, "How can I help you?"

Again, Clark explained their situation, and again Jason fought hyperventilation. They had to show birth certificates—both his and Daniel's, his driver's license, his face—which she scrutinized against the license before taking all of it to make photo copies. Apparently, the front desk had just been a practice run and this was the real deal. She was the warden of documents, and no one was to be told anything unless everything checked out.

But it did. Jason hadn't known for certain that he would pass muster, but he was "the brother," and if a brother couldn't get any information, then who could?

The woman looked him straight in the eye and said, "We usually only give information to children and parents."

Keeping his calm, lest this actually lead to a cavity search, he answered her the same way. "Of course, but our mother died years ago. Before my brother was admitted actually."

"Do you have any proof of that?" She had looked round and jolly and kind when she came out. Now she was squinty-eyed and distrustful, a brick wall they were having to fight their way around.

And crap, he wasn't sure what constituted proof of his birth mother's demise. He had the newspaper article and a copy of the obituary Clark had found—and no clue if either of those would suffice.

Internally, the clench in his gut loosened a bit at being thwarted. He wouldn't come face-to-face with Daniel today. He had been stopped through no fault of his own. And it would take almost a week to come back here. He had his paramedic class and work and it would be good to have time to adjust before he actually met his brother—his mentally damaged brother. They had waited nearly thirty years to meet; another week wouldn't hurt either of them.

"Yes." Clark's voice joined the conversation, taking Jason out of his relief. "I have proof." And he produced a death certificate.

Suddenly wide-eyed, Jason yanked it away and scanned it. He saw that her death was listed as accidental and due to smoke inhalation and burns. Then he got a hold of himself and handed it back to Clark, who was eyeing him.

The woman at the desk took the sheet and looked it up and down, then went back to the copier and made herself a Xerox of that as well. This time when she returned, she was Mary Sunshine again. She handed back the certificate, popped the copy into the blank folder she had started on Jason, and said, "What can I tell you?"

Jason considered himself a smart man, so he let Clark ask the questions.

"We know Daniel Mallory was admitted to this hospital at age four in early August of '85. What was his diagnosis?"

"Give me a minute." She went back and shuffled through older file drawers. Jason saw now that they didn't really need labels; you could simply pull dates by the vintage of the filing cabinet. She came back with a thick folder and invited the men to pull up the two chairs and look with her, though they were looking upside down. "Here."

She turned a paper around to face them and spoke at the same time. "Mutism is the official diagnosis. But there's a concern about Sudden Onset Mutism, Apraxia, or Motor Neurological Disorders."

"I'm sorry, what?" Jason asked it at the same moment Clark spoke up.

"Could you clarify that?"

He felt like an idiot. He had a EMT license, knew a good amount of medical lingo, even some psychiatric disorders—lord knew they saw enough of them on runs—but he hadn't understood a word she'd said.

She smiled a bit. "The mutism just means that he didn't speak." She pulled other papers. "Sudden Onset Mutism is a possibility listed. It says here—" she pointed "that the staff tried to get in contact with someone to see if Daniel was speaking before the fire. They couldn't find any family members, though they did find an old ER record for the boy. It didn't mention mutism at all, but all that means is that he didn't seem abnormal at the ER nearly two years before, and it doesn't tell anyone if he was speaking normally then or even when the mutism started."

Okay, so his brother didn't speak. "What else?"

"The apraxia and possible motor neurological disorders are things they tested for but didn't find evidence of. Doesn't mean they didn't exist though. 'Apraxia' refers to the brain's inability to get the mouth to speak, and the motor disorders would have to do with him not speaking because something in his mouth or vocal chords had failed to function." She pointed to another page. "There's a concern about a severe injury to the head, but no evidence existed of one. Not that the doctors here could find and not in the PICU records from Jackson." She turned a page and kept going. "There's a note of possible tissue damage from the combination of asthma and smoke inhalation. But he was brought here because the pediatricians at Jackson upgraded his lungs to functional. The doctors here were quite convinced that wasn't the cause as well. That was completely ruled out."

Jason was still absorbing that when Clark asked the next question.

"How long was he a patient here?" Jason saw that at some point a small pad of paper had come out. Clark had it perched on his knee and was jotting things down unobtrusively.

"Until May of '86."

"What?" *Good God.* He needed to get his brain on right. He was simply reacting to what was coming at him. In his own defense, things were coming way too fast. "He was here less than a year? Was he better when he left?"

The records keeper beamed at him, the earlier she-devil entirely gone. "Let's see."

As though they would release him if he weren't. Or maybe his health had declined and he'd been sent back to Jackson Hospital . . . where he had then died. Maybe Clark had been overeager in his belief that Daniel was alive. There were definitely things wrong with his brother. Maybe he hadn't made it.

Jason's stomach plummeted again with the possible loss of a brother he had never met and had been afraid to meet just minutes before. The roller coaster he was on today was going to kill him. He had to get home and get some sleep and then get back to work. He glanced at his watch.

"Here." She pointed out something meaningless to him. "He was released with the mutism diagnosis still in place. But he was much more communicative apparently. It seems he didn't want to communicate with anyone in any way when he came here, but by the time he left he had a whole arsenal of communication methods. Just none of them involved him actually speaking."

"Did he have any visitors while he was here?"

"I'd have to check the visitor's log and get back to you on that."

"That would be great, thank you. Is there an official request we need to fill out?"

Jason almost laughed at the way Clark rolled over her. He was polite about it, but it was clear he wanted those records. They went back and forth on that, until she had promised to mail any information including the guest logs from any guests Daniel might have had. And Clark dove straight for the next question.

"Who was he released to?"

They stayed and asked a few more questions, then waited while Clark had the entire record copied. Mary Sunshine's eyes had squinted at that, and she had started to turn into her demonic self when the girl at the back desk had popped up. She'd come in sometime while they had been speaking and had stayed silent until then.

"It's not like we're that busy." Then she smiled at the men. "It will take a little while, but if you're willing to wait, I'll do it now."

"Of course." Clark smiled back at her and she lit up, but she turned that attention to Jason.

She looked at his chest for a moment, then back to his face. "Are you with the fire department?"

"In Southfield, yes." *God save him from badge bunnies.* So he didn't say anything else, and after a moment of smiling at him, she snapped-to and said, "Well, I guess I'd better get these copied." And she hopped off.

When she was out of earshot and Mary Sunshine had walked away to take care of something else, Clark spoke under his breath.

"You know, I don't think you're that much better looking than me."

"I'm sure I'm not." He laughed for the first time all day.

But Clark shook his head. "It's the never-ending saga of the jocks and the nerds."

"I was a nerd in high school. But I did letter in baseball three years in a row."

"Shut up. I'm still clinging to the belief that when we all grow up, the nerds will win. It's the nerds who have the mansions on the hillsides and the trophy wives, right?"

Jason laughed again, this time drawing the attention and suspicion of Mary-Not-So-Sunshine. But it didn't stop him. "I'm sure you'll reign supreme in the end."

"I'm thirty. Shouldn't I be winning by now?"

For a moment, they seemed like friends. And Jason figured he could use another one in this mess that was becoming his life. But the moment passed, and they sat silently, no longer interacting, each fiddling with his phone and nearly ignoring the other.

It took the better part of twenty minutes for the girl to photocopy the full file, and when she was done she handed it back to Jason with another grin. Mary Sunshine, looking dour again, called an orderly to come escort them out and went through a quick and curt rundown of what needed to be signed when someone received a copy of a file.

The orderly came and took them away before the women were done, and Jason was relieved he didn't have to smile at the girl again.

It was easier going in reverse down the hall. This orderly said hello to various people as he passed—staff and patients alike. Jason had a good idea how far it was to the front door, he wasn't worried that his brother might be staring at the TV or shut away in one of the dorm rooms. Daniel had been released into the foster system. There was no telling where he was now or what he'd been through to get there. If he had been lucky, he went to a loving home and was adopted. Only more research would let them know.

Jason was so buried in his own thoughts that it was the orderly who realized they'd lost Clark for a moment.

He was several doors back and speaking to a nurse. When Jason finally realized that everyone had stopped, he turned and looked to find the orderly approaching Clark and the other staff member.

His brain was fried. He needed dinner. He needed to get home—an act that involved him driving for over an hour on a single monotonous highway. Highways put the best of drivers to sleep. But he shook off the thought and walked back to join the conversation that seemed to keep the other three in smiles.

His brain focused enough to hear the end of what Clark was saying.

"—the *Birmingham News* mostly. But I've posted a good handful of pieces in the *Montgomery Advertiser*, too. There's always a picture with the piece these days. And there's a picture on the online papers, too. I've done a few video podcasts on the web, though I wouldn't say I was very good at it yet."

The nurse's grin was genuine and she seemed happy enough to be here, but she gave a self-deprecating laugh at Clark's statement. "Oh, I'm sure I didn't see you on the web. I don't do much of that. My daughter got me on the email, but that's all I do with the Internet. But I read the papers, including the *Birmingham News.*"

The woman smiled and put her hand on his arm. It was covered with the large freckles that elderly people had, and as Jason looked he was surprised to see she was older than he had first thought. But that phrase, "the email," should have given it away.

Jason smiled, too, as the orderly turned to the woman. "See Betty, now you've met a real celebrity and your day is complete."

Her eyebrows went up. "My day *is* complete. I'm off in fifteen minutes." But she held her hand out to Clark, "So nice to meet you in person."

The orderly pulled them away and kept them going down the hall. Jason couldn't help but comment. "So you got recognized? Score one for the nerds."

Though that made Clark laugh out loud, he pointed out, "Yes, I was recognized by an old woman who still reads print papers— the one part of the job that I'm not making any real effort to get recognized in."

"Still, it brings the mansion on the hillside one step closer."

"If only."

They checked out at the front desk and were back at the car as the light started to fade. Jason hated the shorter days of winter, the sense of the light leaving and the dark closing in on you just a little more with every sunset. The dusk was the last thing he needed while he drove, so he told Clark to find them a burger joint with milkshakes, thinking the combination of cold and caffeine was his best shot at staying awake on the ride.

"I know just the spot. A bit out of the way and we'll have to wait, but I found this place when I was down here several years ago and the burgers will make you drool."

Jason shrugged. Maybe it would bring him around. "Then let's do it."

Once again, they were relatively silent as they ordered their food and then waited while it was being made. They were coworkers of a sort, not really friends, even if there had been a few moments.

It was awkward, Jason thought, to spend nearly a whole day with a co-worker and have these conversational dead spots. But he grabbed the already greasy bag and accepted the pot of ketchup the girl behind the counter offered him and balanced it all with the milkshake while getting the car unlocked.

It was another ten minutes of smelling the burgers before they were on the freeway. And though Clark was willing to unwrap his and dive in with a groan that he couldn't quite hide, Jason wasn't going to eat while he drove unfamiliar roads, smack in the middle of rush hour. That was what happened when you worked his job. Some guys became fatalistic and pushed every boundary. Jason had fallen to the cautious side.

As soon as he hit the freeway, he had Clark hand him the burger and he found he had to stifle his own groan. It had to be a thousand-calorie grease bomb, but it was about the best burger he'd ever eaten. He still had his mouth full when he said, "Okay, you win. This was worth it."

"The milkshake's made with real ice cream, too. I think the burger's so good partly because they use real cheese, but there's got to be more to it than that." Jernigan took another big bite and the conversation closed.

The burger was gone far too fast, and Jason was left with a fist full of plain white waxed paper. But he wadded it up, pushed it into the plastic grocery bag that was serving as his in-car trash, and went after the fries.

He was staring into the full dark that had descended while he ate. The lines on the road were the bright gold that came when headlights were the only light source and the blacktop appeared to absorb any illumination. The dashes passed by in a rhythm that threatened his dull brain and full belly. Taking another drink of the milkshake, he hoped it would keep him awake, if not as something to do, then maybe because of the shot of cold and the sugar. Though it was too late, he wondered if he shouldn't have gotten a Dr. Pepper, too.

Just when the car was too quiet, Clark broke the stillness. "Can I text Aida as if I were you?"

"What?"

"We need her to find Daniel Mallory in the foster system. We can tell her the exact date he went into the system and see if she can find out where he went next or if he aged out or what."

That was a good point. "I can just call her."

"It's dinner time. And I thought you two didn't leave things on the best of terms."

Another good point. "And texting makes that better?"

They needed Aida—or at least someone in the CPS office who could and would find them records. Each time he asked her for help, Jason thought it would be the last time he needed something from CPS, and each time he was wrong. Of course, he'd always been told, and sometimes at top decibel, that texting was *not* the way to talk to a woman. Still, here was Clark telling him the world was otherwise.

"It's not so much that texting is better. But I'm a writer, I'll make sure the tone is right. And then she can have some time to decide if she wants to call back from home or work or whatever. It puts her in more control, which is nice."

All of that made sense, but didn't change his doubts. In the end, he decided there wasn't much he could do to screw things up more and he was probably better off leaving things in Clark's hands. So he dug the phone out of his pocket and handed it over.

Within a minute Clark set the phone aside and declared he was done. Since it was his phone and the message had been sent as though it was from him, Jason had to ask, "Just what did you do?"

"I thanked her for all her help in the past and asked if she would call me back."

Jason was just starting to cringe at the open-ended feel of the message when Clark added. "I said we found out more information about Daniel and that we were hoping she'd be able to find the records now if she was willing to help."

Jason couldn't stop his head from nodding. That was good. It was far better than anything he would have said. It was short, sweet, opened with a "thank you" and was very clear that he wasn't texting about anything social.

"Ball's in her court now." Clark was saying just as the phone rang. He held it up. "Look at that. It's Aida. You have to answer it."

"Hit the button and hand it over?"

Clark did just that, and Jason found himself stuttering out a hello before he was quite ready.

"I saw your text. I'm more than happy to help find your brother. What's the new information you have now?" Her voice was sweet and calm and held none of the censure he'd detected the last time they had spoken.

He explained how they had the exact date Daniel had entered the foster care system and that he'd entered from being a patient at Greil Memorial.

"Is that the psychiatric hospital?"

"Yes."

"So he was deemed well enough to go into foster care?"

Jason heard a slight scratching sound in the background and assumed she was writing this down. "Yes."

Clark was already scrambling through the photocopied file and spoke in low tones. "Dr. James Leon signed him over to a social worker by the name of Leslie Windham."

Jason repeated that information to Aida word for word.

"Wow, that's great. I should be able to find him from there!" She made a few more shuffling noises, then spoke again. "Well, obviously, I'm not at work right now, and they won't let us have access to the system from home. So tomorrow morning is my first chance to look this up."

"Of course." At Clark's urging, and because the reporter could clearly hear the entire conversation, Jason added, "I really appreciate you doing this, it's—" he was watching Clark mouth the words, "an unbelievable help."

That earned him a thumbs-up from Clark and a smile in Aida's voice. "It's really not a problem. I just want you to be aware that first I have to take care of the people who come in. I can't put this in front of them, but I'll get to it as soon as I can."

"I figured as much. Thank you."

"You're welcome." Then she did the nicest thing he could think of and said she'd call him tomorrow with an update, and polished it off with "Good night."

He'd been afraid she'd want to talk about something else, then there would have been awkward moments where neither of them knew how to end the conversation. But she'd taken care of it. "Thank you again, good night." And he hit the "end call" button before anything else could happen.

Jason was handing the phone back to Clark as the reporter commented, "That looked painful."

"It was."

"Is talking on the phone always a trial for you? Or is it just talking with women in general?"

Yes, there were too many people out in the world these days thinking he was an idiot. And he'd been giving them too many reasons to believe it was true. "No, not always. And sometimes with women it's okay. But not with her. I don't know what to do with *her*."

"You have no idea how to relate to women as friends, do you?"

What was this? Dr. Freud investigates? He almost said so, but felt the need to defend himself. "That's not true. I get along just fine with Wanstall."

The Birmingham exit to Clark's apartment building presented itself and Jason was glad for the distraction. But it didn't distract the reporter at all. Maybe that's why he was good at what he did.

"You called her 'Wanstall'. I rest my case."

"She's a woman."

"Not to you. She's a firefighter who happens to be female. There's a difference." Clark put all the papers back into the folder and then pointed out a copy shop and directed Jason to turn into the parking lot. "I think each of us wants a copy of this to read tonight. So we definitely need another one."

Though he obediently turned into the lot, this time it was Jason who picked up the bone of the conversation and followed through. "I don't see the girls falling all over you. Weren't you the one complaining? So why should I listen to what you have to say about women?"

"Touché." Was quickly followed by a muttered, "Damn jocks." But then Clark volunteered to pay for the massive photocopying, saying he could write it off.

They walked out with the duplicated files and Jason took the copy of the copy, figuring Clark would be better at making heads or tails of things in it, and therefore should have the more legible version. He dropped the other man off at his apartment and headed home.

If it could be called *home*. It was just a building. And he was beyond ready to move out of it. Moving didn't bother him the way it did some people. Maybe that was because he didn't amass a lot of stuff—he sure didn't have half the things that Kelly had. Knick-knacks and gadgets, clothing and make-up, it took so many things to make up her life. Or maybe it was because he wasn't attached to the place. Amara had already found a corner coffee shop and tried out the pizza parlor down the street.

As he unlocked the door, Jason found himself wanting a place to call home, something that evoked the kind of cocooned feeling he'd had at his mom and dad's. Something of his own. When he pushed the door open he was enveloped by heat and the smell of food. "Oh, God, that's . . . wow."

Amara's hair bobbed where she sat on the couch; it twisted and turned until she got herself cranked around to look at him. "It's beef stew. I made enough for you to have some if you haven't already eaten."

What a horrid caveat. "And if I have already eaten?"

She laughed. "You can still have some."

He was walking into the kitchen, lured by the smell emanating from the crock pot, when it occurred to him that she didn't know what she'd gotten into. "How much did you make? I've seen the way you eat."

She laughed again and came into the kitchen behind him. Where he had been reluctant to even lift the lid and be tempted to eat all her food, she had no compunctions. She pulled down a bowl, grabbed him a spoon, and ladled a huge helping for him. "I made as much as I usually do, then added a serving for you, then I doubled all of it. I've seen they way *you* eat."

He took the already warm bowl in his hands and fought the urge to just stick his face down in it and inhale. Grabbing a napkin from the kitchen counter, he tried to be civilized. He seated himself at the butcher-block table and groaned out loud at the first bite. "If you tell me this is good for me, too, I may die and go to heaven."

"It is. But I won't tell you that." She turned and left him there, went back to the couch and the papers he hadn't seen when he came in. She was in eyeshot but not really there.

Still, the smell wafted around him. He had come in to find food waiting, and he was sitting at *his* table in *his* chair. And for a moment, it felt like a home.

Southfield Fire Station #2

Shift	A	
	O'Casey	Captain
Engine 2	Donlan	Engineer/Paramedic
	West	FF2
Engine 5	Wanstall	Lieutenant
	Mondy	FF2 / EMT
	Grimsby	FF1
Rescue 3	Standard	Engineer
	Nagy	FF1 / EMT

Chapter 17

They went on a run as soon as they clocked in. A small portion of C-Shift was still hanging around and, along with Standard and Nagy, helped both engines get out the door. As always with actual reported flames, Adler followed behind in the red pickup.

Missy hit the horn twice and rolled out of the station; all the gear she was wearing was welcome padding in the cooler temperatures. They left the bay doors up during the day all year long. It was a sign of goodwill to the community, a "doors open" policy that she loved the idea of but hated when she froze her ass off on duty. She wouldn't be getting cold where they were headed though.

The town wasn't big enough for a long drive, and Gold Standard had EMS on site before they arrived. That almost never happened. But this fire was a short distance from the EMS station, and they seemed to be making more of an effort to put a better face to the community since two of their own had started a fire that resulted in two deaths.

Though Missy was grateful the FD wasn't facing the same scrutiny, it was only because Merriman had gotten his ass fired before he did it—though he might not have started that fire if he'd stayed on shift. He might not have felt the need if he thought he had a chance at an appeal. Missy had heard from everyone on A-Shift that Merriman had called them each personally and asked for a recommendation for a chance to overturn his firing. No one had said yes, at least not that they admitted to. Missy thought Merriman was a moron for asking in general and for specifically asking her. He seemed to have no concept that she would think about all the times he had dismissed her as "just a girl" when he asked. But then again, she couldn't help but wonder if the world would have been safer if Merriman had remained buffered by A-Shift. He couldn't be such a fuckup if they had all kept trying the way they had before.

But she shrugged it off for the new burden she carried as soon as she put the rig into park.

The flames shot nearly fifteen feet in the sky, and the address of the fire had become unnecessary about five neighborhoods back. People huddled on the street—or what passed for it. A grid of graveled drives divided the trailer park into neat rectangular lots. Missy was impressed that even within the small cluster of mobile homes there was a nicer section and a poorer section. This was not the nicer section.

An older woman held what Missy assumed were two squirming dogs, one under each of her beefy arms. She didn't seem to notice the cold though she only wore a nylon nightgown and wrapper. Her hair was up and so was her voice.

"They was smokin' the weed! I knew this would happen. That stuff's illegal."

Missy fought the urge to tell the woman thank you for the update, but she had work to get to.

She and Mondy geared up nearly in sync: hoods, jackets, helmets, tanks. Donlan came around the corner of the truck, identically decked out, and held up three fingers. Chief was sending the three of them to flank the home and check for survivors—though they all knew there would be none. Trailers burned hot; they were metal containers of kindling just waiting for a spark and some air.

The fire blazed up on one side of the unit, as Missy did a quick look around. Jason was near the end that was actively burning, looking for a way to hack in, but that was its own problem. Though they needed to see if people were alive, you didn't just put holes into a vessel on fire—you could feed it oxygen and make things worse. And there was no way to go up top for proper ventilation, not with the whole structure in trouble like this one was.

She was able to open the trailer door and withstand the blast of heat and smoke that came at her. It was always a challenge to breathe when your eyes were telling you not to and your lungs were speeding up from the adrenaline that hit your system. Still, she kept herself regulated and made it far enough inside to see that the entire other end of the trailer was fully involved and that there were three corpses on the couch, the one closest to the flames having suffered actual burns.

For a moment she bent over and fought the urge to vomit, visions of Connelly flooding her mind to the point that she almost couldn't see where she was. The State Forestry nurse had given the word and all the crew had known that whatever they could do wouldn't be enough. Almost worse than the fact that they had quit believing they could save him was that the moment they shifted, she had gotten a view of him—some of his skin had burned and cracked into thin black sheets that revealed red, raw skin underneath. His face had boiled; with the mask in place it didn't burn, but nothing could save him from the heat.

The mental pictures were wreaking havoc on her control and she was sucking down air too fast. And though it was only a moment, she was wasting time. Turning, she exited the trailer to find the others in gear just beyond the reach of the flames, the hoses now running as they doused the trailers on either side of the one that was currently on fire.

It would not be salvaged, but the others might be. And more importantly, job one right now was to keep this fire from spreading. In these close quarters, the firefighters were the only thing that kept it from jumping from one of these mobile tinderboxes to the next and the next.

Donlan and Mondy checked in, and she gave the order that it was time for Donlan to head up and finally vent the sucker. A short ladder and an axe did the job. Smoke quickly gushed from the hole he had created at the roof vent, and the Bostonian made short work of getting off of there.

They directed the water into the trailer, aiming at the fire.

She found she was afraid of steam now. Images of Connelly's face haunted her. Steam was like a dose of pure heat, and it was so easily made with a slightly misdirected hose.

They all felt Connelly's loss—even though he hadn't been on their shift, even though they all worked very hard not to let it show. Frogurt had gone quickly. He literally had not known what hit him, but Connelly was the horror story of this job. That you might suffer terribly before you could let go was a fate worse than death. So they bottled it up, and after the first few days, talk of Connelly had ceased.

She was too close to the fire. Chief was motioning to her, and she could feel the heat coming off the trailer in one huge wall pushing back on her. Turning around, she found Mondy unrolling another hose from Engine 5, and Missy went to help him.

In relatively short order, they had the fire out. Not that these things were ever actually short. A good fire burned and smoldered for a long time, and it took hours to chase down every spark and hover over every smoking ember until it was dead.

Later, when they were confident they had it smothered, the three corpses were carried from the ruins and delivered into the hands of the waiting EMS team. Before the bodies were zipped up, Missy had another flashback to Connelly and the Bear Mountain fire, but she didn't think anyone else would see that she was suffering. They were all good at hiding it and Missy was no exception. With force, she pushed her focus back to what was in front of her.

She was no M.E., but it sure didn't look like the three smokers had struggled.

Donlan came out from the trailer doorway, now lacking the actual door, "Yes, my friends, that is one Class-A bong in there." He peeled the mask he had put back on and grinned. "Actually it has about five hoses, which makes it a hookah, right?"

"Like I would know." She found a grin for him. She'd never been one for drugs of any kind, but pot held about the least appeal for her. Stoned people were slow, life was fast. Fire was fast. Dying because she was too stupid to get out of the way was worse than going out like Connelly.

By the time they packed everything up and hauled it out of there, the woman next door was back in the lawn chair on her small gated porch and the dogs were running around like toddlers in a playpen, but yapping. She was telling everyone who passed that the potheads next door had gotten what was coming.

Jason climbed into Engine 5 beside her and muttered, "You'd think a little compassion would be in order. They're dead."

"Yeah." Missy waved at the woman, "You notice she's been saying all that with a cigarette firmly between her fingers?"

"Yeah, it's the fifth one since we let her back into her unit."

"You've been counting?"

A half-grin twisted his mouth. "I like to have a scale to rate hypocrisy. I think smoking while you bitch about people dying in a fire is way up there. Definitely a nine or ten."

They rode back to the station house in silence. Grimsby sat in the back and kept to himself, pretty much as he had since Bear Mountain. Jason and Missy exchanged a look, as if to ask if either knew anything about the junior firefighter. There was always the possibility that something like this would make him rethink the job. He'd either leave or become completely dedicated.

Jason wondered if he shouldn't say something to the Chief. But then he figured the Chief already knew about it, as he did about most things. There would be showers to take when they got back, paperwork to do, chores to complete; he didn't need to coddle Grimsby.

When they walked in, the six of them found that Standard and Nagy had made a quick run to an older person who was having breathing problems. They had also finished all the chores around the house.

Jason surveyed the way the bays shined. Then Standard and Nagy stepped in and started cleaning the two returning engines. He dove in to help, figuring he might as well clean the trucks while he was already dirty. Wanstall turned back from heading into the house to come add her own muscle, but Jason waved her away.

"You're the lieutenant now. You get to sign off on the paperwork. You do that. I'll clean."

She made a face at him, the paperwork was definitely the short straw. But he used the rag in his hands to get the mud out of the grooves in the bumper and hoped that Grimsby decided to stay with the job. The only thing that Jason truly worried about was that one day the Chief would retire and things would change. But for now, this was a good crew. The best.

Ten minutes later Donlan appeared. He'd showered because he was clearly clean, but his hair was too short to be wet. He nudged Jason aside and said only, "You smell."

Later, after he'd showered, and after a quick training session led by the Southfield FD Training Officer, Jason was left with nothing to do but lounge around the station. The day seemed pretty quiet, and the guys scattered throughout the various rooms to watch TV and read and later a few went on food runs. He was bordering on being bored to tears when a familiar face came into the room.

"Jernigan!" Jason's head snapped up. "What are you doing here?"

"New information." He pulled an envelope from his black messenger bag and waved it around. "Got a minute?"

"Sure." Jason stood up trying to think where they should talk, as it probably shouldn't be in the break room. But Clark was already headed the other way.

Jason found him with his head in Adler's office, explaining that he had something.

Adler motioned them in and gestured for Jason to close the door behind them. "Whatcha got?"

Clark turned to Jason first. "Did you hear from Aida?"

He shook his head. "But I've been here all day. I assume she'd call my cell, but she's called the home phone before. So it's hard to say for sure."

"Okay, what I have here, . . ." he slowly started sliding pages out of the envelope, "is the M.E.'s report on the autopsy of Alcia Mallory."

He spread them out on Adler's desk. His movements deliberate, he aimed all the pages toward the Chief, who looked them over while Jason only got glimpses. The Chief carefully read each one, but all Jason saw was type accompanied by several generic sketches of a female body with wording and arrows filling in information. One sketch was of the head in profile and front view.

"This is not good." The Chief's voice was solemn.

"What?" Frustrated, Jason held out his hand.

But Adler didn't hand over the pages, "This is the autopsy report on your mother. Are you sure you want to see it?"

Jason kept his hand out. "*My mother* is still alive."

Clark shot him a sharp look. But whether that was because he thought Jason was callous or because he expected him to lose it at the sight of the drawings, Jason wasn't sure.

With obvious reservation, the Chief handed the papers over and Jason thumbed through them. They were disturbing, but that was because they were an autopsy report. And because she should have been his mother. Still he couldn't find any of the things that he was looking for.

Clark nodded but didn't take the pages back. In fact, he didn't touch them again. "That's your copy." He pulled another envelope out for the Chief, "And one for you, too."

Adler looked another page over front and back. "It says cause of death was burns and smoke inhalation. But it doesn't mention an accelerant or the fact that she died of fire burns rather than heat or steam burns."

Jason leaned forward, the papers gathered in his hands. "So the M.E. was in on it?"

Shrugging, Clark gave his best guess. "The signature doesn't always belong to the person who performs the autopsy. You can see there's a second signature to some of the work on one of the pages."

Jason looked and, sure enough, Jernigan was right.

He kept talking. "What's missing is significant. If what Adler says is true, then, yes, someone got to the M.E. and had the autopsy altered or at the very least downgraded. The autopsy itself isn't suspicious at all."

Jason took a moment to look at Adler. "Are you sure what you saw, Chief?"

The older man frowned. "Seriously?"

Jason couldn't look at him. "Right now, it's you against them."

"Don't forget Deason." He growled.

"I'm not saying that, Chief. It's just that you're the only one who saw the body. Well, the only one still alive. Is there something you can point to that just makes it incredibly clear? In case this becomes public before we figure everything out?"

Adler growled again. He didn't like being questioned—although that alpha male part of his personality went with the territory, he figured. "There were active flames in the room. Parts of the kitchen were burning, and some of those flames were seven feet tall. I remember a can or two popped in one of the cabinets when we went in. But the couch was done. There was a person on it, burned to death, and the couch burnt. It was already a briquette even though the rest of the room was still roaring. That woman was burned and done—and the only thing that does that is accelerant."

Jason nodded. But Adler wasn't finished.

"It was so bizarre and so telling of arson—imagine, in a building that size, we thought we'd found the origin. The only reason we didn't get a picture was because you couldn't get a camera into that kind of heat in those days and because we heard . . . a . . . noise. That would be *you*. We saved *you* instead of running an arson investigation in the middle of a burning building that was starting to run cracks on some of the walls."

225

Jason pulled back.

Adler hadn't told him that before. He hadn't said anything that made him sound like more of a hero. Though that was not a revelation, Adler held back anything he could when it came to himself.

Clark looked between the two of them. "What? What am I missing?"

Adler leaned back and let Jason fill him in. "When there are cracks running along the walls, the building is in danger of collapsing. In general, it means you can't save anyone else and you get the hell out."

"Wow."

"I'm sorry, Chief." Jason looked him in the eye when he said it, but Adler didn't find any comfort in the apology.

Jernigan was no longer paying attention to the back and forth between the firefighters. He was pulling out his laptop and powering it on. Without looking up, he started talking, "Actually, that's exactly what I wanted to ask you, Chief."

"Hmm?" Funny that the reporter should start calling him "Chief" too, just like the other guys.

"I wanted to do a comprehensive interview with you about the Pelias fire."

"We already told you what happened." He frowned. This was not his idea of a good time.

"Yes, but I wasn't recording everything, and I really want just your side. I want all the details, what you had for breakfast that day, everything." He was nearly grinning.

Mondy gave the reporter a slap on the back and raised his eyebrows at Adler. "Jernigan here may write a book about us when this is all done."

"Shit." Adler leaned forward. "I don't want to be in a book."

Jernigan didn't look upset by that at all. "You already agreed to be in the story. You traded that info for my help with the research. I think I've proved a huge help here."

There was no arguing that fact. Adler tried to change the subject. "Speaking of that, how did you get the autopsy report on Alcia Mallory without raising flags?"

He grinned. "I know people in the M.E.s office. I had them pull me several batches of reports. I said it was for research. I just made sure that one of the batches had this one in it."

"Very smart."

"Thanks." But Jernigan's focus was back on his computer. He appeared to be starting up a document or such. "I had my friend pull it, too. That way there's no real record of it—no request form or anything like that. So, are you ready for that interview, Chief?"

Nope, the kid didn't miss a beat. "Only if I get final say on how it goes to print." He'd heard that somewhere in a movie. And he hoped it worked.

It didn't.

At least the kid shook his head as though he regretted that. "No can do, Chief. I'm the writer. But I'm building my reputation on telling things the way they are. I do promise not to sensationalize anything or write with any kind of bias."

Then he turned to Jason and said, "Do you mind leaving us alone for this? I want to record everything and avoid interruptions, that kind of thing."

Adler didn't know what kind of explanation that was, but Mondy didn't seem to mind. He stood and started to leave before Jernigan motioned to the autopsy papers that were still in several piles on his desk. "Those are yours. You should take them."

Mondy took them gingerly and pushed them back into the envelope before taking it with him out the office door. "You have fun, Chief."

Sure, right, Adler grumbled in his own head. The last thing he wanted to do was give an interview about one of the best and worst nights of his life—a night that had occurred over a quarter of a century ago. But as Jernigan had aptly pointed out, this was his pound of flesh for helping. He wanted a story and he was going to get it out of them; it would probably be best if they all just cooperated.

The pesky little pull-apart laptop was ready to go, as though it was just waiting for him. There was another small silver item on the table, looking like a tiny skyscraper. Adler could only guess that it was a recorder—digital, from the looks of it. *Our boy Jernigan wouldn't be so primitive as to use tape.* But that thought made him feel old and feel that this case was very old, and that in the end, they had very little chance of cracking it.

Jernigan apparently thought otherwise. He typed something then looked up. "If you could rank that day – the Pelias fire – against all your other days, how would you rank it?"

Perceptive little bugger, wasn't he? "Marrying Abby, the birth of my children, those are the only things that outrank it in that direction. Nothing out ranks it in the other."

Clark nodded, an absent gesture most of his firefighters gave when they were paying attention but also focused on something else. Adler waited.

"Before the call, what was that day like?"

"That's always the worst of it. Most days are good. And there's almost never a warning before hell breaks loose." He sighed and settled back into his chair. The least he could do was get comfortable, he'd likely be here a while.

"What rank were you then? How long had you been on the job?"

"Firefighter one. I was working at Burkeville just over a year, but that was as a volunteer. The ranking was new."

"Did you like your Captain? Your coworkers?"

Every time he felt he answered one question, two more came at him. *Shit.*

"I was afraid of him, we all were. He was a hulk of a man who was always right. It was much more military-like back then. Orders came down from the top, everyone followed. In those days, firefighters learned to think for themselves but keep their mouths shut. These days we *try* to train them to do that."

"When the call came in for the Pelias fire, did you know it would be rough?"

"Oh yeah. The fact that Montgomery was calling us for backup meant it was bad. Before we got there we knew it was only one of two options. Either everyone was already there and they still needed help—we were the little Podunk volunteer unit—or else it was so bad that the extra five minutes faster that we could get there than anyone else would have made a difference. Sadly, both seemed to be true."

"Talk me through it from the call."

Great. Adler did not like reliving this. But he told himself it wasn't just for Jernigan's story, it was in case anyone could see a thread, anything that might help. So he talked.

"I was at home, that's the only reason I got the call. We didn't even have pagers. We tried to hang out at the station and took shifts. But that call from Montgomery meant that we were all needed. I hopped in my pickup and headed the three blocks down to the Burkeville station. I was the last one into Engine 1. We pulled out as guys started parking and grabbing gear and filling Engine 2—they were probably three minutes behind us.

"I remember being excited and afraid. At that point I'd seen a handful of fires. But this was likely going to be the biggest and most dangerous.

"When we pulled up, our driver had to jockey to get close to the buildings. Other trucks were already mainlining into the hydrants. We could, but like a lot of rural stations we carried most of our water in the trucks. So we got set to dump that first."

Jernigan's fingers flew, and Adler figured he was typing everything verbatim. So he stopped to let the reporter catch up, but that only earned him a restless gesture to continue.

"We were put on an adjacent building, on the left from the street side. Our job was to douse it and save the residents of the apartments next door. You know how it is downtown, no room between the buildings, and in those days no fire walls. Steel framing but lots of wood used in everything else, flooring, walls, ceilings. So we just wet it down.

"Jake Strobel was my partner that night. You've seen we still go everywhere in twos. That's old code. He was older than me, worked in the Montgomery system, and volunteered on some of his days off. He was divorced, and I guess he filled his time that way. He trained me, at least a lot of what I knew then."

Jernigan already knew how Strobel came out, but it was interesting that Chief was more attached to him than just a one-time partner for a fire.

"So Strobel and I were sent on break and we made the mistake of standing in front of the Pelias Street Apartments to do so. The Montgomery Chief knew Jake and must have thought he was on duty, because he hauled us in for a search. The building was so big and they had to get the searches done before they could douse it—"

Jernigan interrupted. "Why? Don't you start trying to put it out right away?"

"No." Adler leaned forward and pointed. "You know you should talk to Mondy about this. He'll tell you all about the physics of fire and buildings. But you don't walk up and douse a fire. There are lots of problems there. Heat and water makes steam, and that'll burn you a lot faster than smoke, plus you can't see through it at all. You have to vent a building first, and Montgomery had guys that had monkey-climbed from the top of the ladder—which wasn't tall enough—up the fire escape and then boosted and hauled themselves onto the roof. They were chopping holes for ventilation. You change a fire with water or oxygen or anything and it gets unpredictable. You open doors or break windows and you can create flare-ups. So you don't just start dousing old, burning wood structures until they are properly vented and until all the live people are out, and it's okay if it collapses with the rest in it."

"Oh." But Jernigan's fingers never stopped moving. He'd been researching this for a while now, but he hadn't heard that before. Then again, even though he was really good at his job, he couldn't hope to learn someone else's entire profession in just a few weeks. Maybe he would ask Jason more about it later. "Go on."

"So they hoisted us up on the ladder—"

He pointed, "Like that one, out there?"

Adler bust out in a huge guffaw. "That's a million-dollar truck, son. It has stabilizers and hydraulic lifts and a basket. In those days the ladders went up manually. Montgomery was doing well, they had already upgraded from wooden ladders. We got hoisted up to a fifth floor window and searched from there."

"What did you find?"

"Fifth and sixth floors were empty. Those people and the floors below had gotten out. Seventh had a few bodies on it, near the stairwells. The stairs had been origin points and the eighth floor was pretty much sealed off by fire. That was another good indicator that it was arson. That the multiple start points were so clearly defined and so clearly at all the exits. No one was meant to get off the eighth floor.

"Luckily the building was old and a lot of the apartments didn't have anyone living in them. There was a body here or there. Typical inhalation deaths. Then there was 187—and the door was an origin and so was the couch. Strobel walked in first, he was the senior partner. He made a sign to me that it was bad."

Clark looked up, trying to think about all the ways things had been different. No audio communication built into the gear. Air tanks not as safe. And Chief's comments about some stations still having wooden ladders were actually disturbing more than anything else. But something bothered him. "So if all the stairwells and the door to 187 were origins, then how did you get in? Did you just hunker down and run through the fire?"

"On the stairwells, partly yes. The walls were burning, but the stairs were metal. We only made it through because we were in full gear—anyone else's shoes would have melted to the steps themselves—and because of the accelerant."

Clark frowned.

"The accelerant starts the fire, and anywhere it is burns hotter, faster. So it burns out faster, too. The door to 187 fell off on its hinges and was nearly charred ash by the time we got there. We were looking at the body when we heard the noises. Just high-pitched something. But it sounded like it might be human.

"We started running. Darting around that apartment. It wasn't big. Two small bedrooms, one bath. We split up, like we should never do, but if there was a person alive, that was our first priority. We looked under beds and in closets, because that's where people go, even though they shouldn't. But there was nothing. Strobel pulled me back out into the hall and we stopped and listened. We made some banging noises and got nothing. So Strobel took a deep breath, peeled his mask and yelled. Then he put the mask back on and did it again. Finally, we heard something. So we ducked into 188, where we thought we heard the noises and we started over. We were mid-search when this kid came barreling out of one of the bedrooms and rammed right into me. I think he was half-blind with the smoke."

"That was Jason, right?"

Adler nodded. "Didn't know that at the time. Hell, I didn't know that until just a few weeks ago. But, yes, that was him. I grabbed him up under my arm like we were taught to do with kids, and he fought me the whole time."

"Scared?"

"That's what I thought. We forced the air mask onto his face, and he tried to push it away. Most kids do. But I held on tight and we ran him back down the hallway. The fire was louder by then, bigger, the guys up top had been working on venting but they hadn't done enough yet. A window at the end of the hall popped and the air rushed and the fire followed."

That stopped Clark. He tried to imagine being in a hallway filled with fire, then all the air rushing in one window and the fire rushing along to meet it. But Adler started talking again and Clark's fingers started moving.

"So we hunched down and kept going. And that's when we saw the cracks really start to shoot down the walls."

"How?"

Chief motioned with his finger, a horizontal line running zig-zag. "They would run fast, like those pictures you see of earthquakes, and every now and then, it would split. So we picked up the pace and barreled down the stairs, protecting the kid from the fire there. Then went back out the fifth-story window with him. The three of us climbed down together, and we got about halfway before people saw that we had a kid with us and they started cheering. At that point, he was the only live save.

"That was amazing. I figured we were heroes. Strobel and I were there for Burkeville and had gotten commandeered by Montgomery and pulled out a kid. I was thinking *this is why I do this job.* But we set him down and he didn't stop fighting. When I pulled off my mask I could tell he was screaming and yelling. Most kids go into shock, but not that one—at least he didn't curl into a ball and stare out sightlessly like a lot do. He was hard to understand, his throat had inhalation damage. But then he broke and ran for the ladder. He tried to go back up, and that's when we realized there was likely more going on. So we listened. And it took a while, but we figured out that he was screaming about his brother.

"He kept trying to go back up the ladder. So Strobel grabbed him, shook him—which we know better than to do now, but we were crazy that night—and told Jason he was going back, but he needed to know exactly where his brother was. And Jason yelled it all, but gave us details, told us his brother was in the closet in the apartment we'd found him in. Told us which bedroom. Everything."

Adler looked at Jernigan. Though the little recorder still had the red light on, his fingers flew as though he was the only thing preserving this interview. Adler didn't get it. Maybe it would make a great story, but to him it was a wild and shitty night. "So Strobel and I start to go back in. Right then, the guys on the roof got the place vented, and that means the fire starts to move. There was a lot of cracking and popping, but we headed back up anyway—we knew there was another kid in there. Everything was crazy and no one watched Jason, everyone had turned to look at the building. Turns out he was on the ladder behind me, coming along to grab his brother."

"What?" Clark's head popped up from his laptop and his fingers stilled. "He tried to go back into the fire? To get the brother?"

"Yeah." Adler spoke as though it was obvious. "So I stayed behind with Jason, someone had to hold him back. Strobel came back out with the brother a little while later. He was badly burned, couldn't speak above a whisper. But he said the brother had been stashed in a closet. That there had been a hole at the back and that there were clothes pushed into every gap. They had relatively clean air. He figured they were still alive because the two of them had been in the closet most of the time. Jason probably left the brother and went to find help. You know the rest."

But maybe he didn't. "That's all kind of shocking. Mondy seems so indifferent to the brother—almost completely cold. Doesn't remember him, doesn't remember anything. He didn't go in the ambulance or follow the brother. I know you said he told you how to find the brother, but I didn't realize that he was trying to go back in."

"I think that's why he fought us. Everything he did once we picked him up makes perfect sense if you look at it as though he didn't want to leave the little brother behind and he was trying to get us to go back. Jason was relatively clean when we first saw him, not covered in soot or anything. So I think he must have come out of the closet to look. Maybe he heard us." Adler's face took on a bit of a far-away look. "He was just seven, but he was ready to run back into that building to save his little brother. I'm as surprised as you that he doesn't remember him."

Clark put that new bit of information aside and asked another question. "Strobel later died from the injuries he sustained that night. Were you surprised that going back in killed him?"

"No." It was plain that this was not the first time that Adler had thought about this. "Strobel was an experienced firefighter. I'd heard about cracks running down the walls, I'd read about the dangers of going into a building while it was being vented. But Strobel *knew*. He fully understood that he might not make it out with the kid at all. Remember, he'd lifted his mask and yelled the first time we were looking. So he already had some lung damage. It's the only thing that ever let me get over that: he signed his own death certificate going back in. It was a trade—him for the kid— and he knew it."

Chapter 18

Jason

Clark called the next day and asked about yet another trip to Montgomery. Jason turned him down, partly due to the rolling feeling in the pit of his stomach. He knew he needed to follow up on this, needed to go to Montgomery before someone else caught on, before someone blew it open wide. Though he had a legitimate reason not to go—he had class—he still simply didn't want to go. He wanted to let go of whatever waited in Montgomery and pretend it didn't exist for today. He wanted to study for his Paramedic class; he was already a bit behind, mostly because of all the research he was doing into his own genetic past.

Clark agreed to wait until after Jason's next shift, when he would have two whole days off with no shift and no class, then they would travel again.

Granted the short reprieve, he sat in his room at his transplanted desk and tried to study. But the desk was for his computer, not his books, and studying wasn't working here. Giving up, he carried everything in to the living area and settled in at the butcher-block table and found Amara holed up on the couch, papers spread everywhere, highlighter clenched between her teeth, laptop open.

Her head jerked up, "Did you want to watch TV?"

He laughed. "Sure, but what I *need* to do is study. I'm good here."

Amara grinned then turned back to her work, her focus absolute. Dressed in workout gear, mass of curls perched happily on her head, she seemed comfortable in spite of the position she was contorted into. Almost to the end of her doctorate, she was a professional studier. Jason figured he could learn a thing or two from her. But, aside from the comfortable clothing, which he had already figured out for himself, there was nothing he could put his finger on that made her better at it.

So he hunkered down and set himself to note-taking and trying to maintain his focus—which didn't work anywhere near as well as he wanted. Eventually, after wracking his brain over a particular concept too many times to count and not making any headway, he interrupted Amara's intense attention to highlighting.

"I'm sorry, but I'm about to give up on this one. Can you help?"

No gloating, nothing but a "Let me see." She padded over to the table on bare feet, toes tipped in an unexpected red polish. She asked before she turned the huge paper textbook her direction and read the page he was stuck on. "Oh."

"Yeah?"

"Yeah, this is a crappy explanation." She sat down in the other chair, turned the book back to him, and proceeded to explain why two seemingly contradictory medications would be given simultaneously in certain situations.

Relief sank in, and he nodded, finally understanding what he was supposed to do. "That actually makes sense. Thank you."

"Sure. Feel free to ask me anything else. I don't know all of it, but I'm glad to help where I can." She stretched and headed to the fridge for a bottle of water. "Really, anything that distracts me from that dissertation is welcome!"

"Seriously?" That was a shock. "You look so content over on the couch."

"Good God! I hate it. I hate studying."

Jason frowned at her. "So why did you choose to spend all that time in school?" That made no sense to him. Though he loved to learn, a life of studying and discussing things and being at the mercy of what various professors believed to be "the right way" —each of them different—was not for him. But Amara had seemed to have a Zen-like oneness with her papers.

"Eyes on the prize, baby." She laughed and headed back to the couch. "Once I get done with this, I can work almost anywhere I want. I can teach and run trainings. And get about half again the salary—which is really important. Though I'm not as bad off as some, student loans are still a bitch."

He hunkered back down over his own books and made it another hour before he interrupted her again. Again, she offered advice without any regard to the fact that he was using up her study time with his problems. So he went for the trifecta.

"Can I ask you to look at an autopsy report for me?"

She pulled back and blinked at him, clearly thrown for a loop.

"Sure. But what are you doing with an autopsy report?"

Wasn't that a good question? He explained just a little "Well, it's over twenty-five years old. And it's for my birth mother—"

"Wait—does that mean that you were adopted?"

He nodded, still filtering what to tell her and what to hold back. "I was in a fire that killed my birth mother when I was seven. I don't remember anything about her. Then I was adopted by my mom and dad."

"Whoa. If she had you until you were seven, she's hardly just your 'birth mother'."

He shrugged. None of it was straight-forward and that was one of the biggest problems. "But I don't remember her. At all." And he consciously shut down that part of the conversation. "Anyway, I recently came into possession of the autopsy report and wanted you to look it over for anything . . . hinky."

"Hinky? So you think there's something 'hinky' about your birth mother's death?"

"That's the question." He got up and headed into his room, both to get the paperwork and to stop her line of questioning. He didn't want to go through the whole sordid story again. He had enough of it with Clark calling and all the trips to Montgomery and the interviews. But he did like that she immediately started referring to Alcia as his "birth mother." She asked questions, but she took his answers at face value.

Maybe Clark was right. Maybe he didn't know how to relate to women as friends. He had certainly expected her to use the information or at least pick at it like a loose sweater thread, pull at it until she thought she had the whole thing unraveled. But she did neither.

Returning with the envelope Clark had given him the day before, Jason simply handed it over to Amara and waited. With a quick glance up at him she pulled out the papers and started reading.

He tried to give her space—tried to patiently stand by. And she was *reading*, every word on every page and occasionally flipping back to re-check something. Though it surprised him, he realized that's exactly what he wanted. He needed someone who knew what they were doing to nit-pick it and look for inconsistencies.

As he stood there biding his time, he decided to throw in the towel. He was done studying for now, so he gathered up his books and note papers and pens. His stomach grumbled making Amara look up at him. So he was hungry, sue him.

It took another minute before she put the papers down. "It looks like she died from catching on fire."

"Yeah, that's pretty much it."

"God, that's horrible."

He agreed with that, too. But there wasn't much anyone could do about it at this point, and as awful as he thought it was, he didn't have any emotions tied to it other than the usual sick-to-his-stomach feeling that he got when people did atrocious things to each other.

Amara went on. "It says she was found on the couch."

He nodded.

"But she was on fire."

Jason nodded his head again, even though he wasn't following.

Amara frowned. "I really don't see anything 'hinky' here except this one inconsistency. And you seem to really think she was murdered."

"I didn't say that." In fact, he'd been very careful to *not* say that.

"Well, there aren't many other 'hinky' things associated with deaths and with autopsy reports. And I'm very aware that you have some girl-free Scooby-gang thing going on with the ADA and the reporter. So I'm pretty confident you think she was murdered."

He sighed. This was the trade-off. Women like Kelly tended to simply take what he told them until faced with undeniable and blatant evidence to the contrary. Amara thought for herself. And maybe did it a little too well. Then again, maybe that was a good thing in a woman who was his friend.

"Okay," He tried the neither-deny-nor-confirm tactic. "What was hinky about her being on the couch?"

"See here?" She held up the report, pointing first to the drawing then to a spot in the writing. "The body is burned more on the front and less on the back."

He read from the report, "—consistent with being seated on the couch." Then he looked up at her. "She *was* on the couch. So I'm not sure what's off about that."

"Well, *why* was she on the couch?"

He reconsidered his earlier position, maybe "thinking women" were not a good thing. He did not get this. "Why are you sitting in that chair?"

"Because I'm not on fire."

"What? . . . Oh! Oh, Jesus Christ." His breath hitched, and his eyes went unfocused. His voice traced his thoughts though he didn't really mean for it to. "People on fire run around. They don't realize they can't get away from it and that running makes it worse. They don't just sit quietly on the couch and burn to death."

She nodded. "I don't think they even could if threatened. I mean, if someone had a gun on you and you're on fire."

He breathed in, the ideas coming in with the oxygen and settling badly. "You'd still run. They could shoot you, but that's of no consequence if you're on fire. Your nerves wouldn't function and if nothing else, you'd jerk around. Holy. Shit."

"Yeah." Amara handed the report back to him. "That's hinky. The only way I can think that someone burns to death sitting on a couch is if they were tied there. Still, there's no evidence in the report that she was tied. Nothing at all, except that she was sitting on the couch."

Absently, he took the papers and wandered into his room to file them back in his bag. He was coming back to thank her when he had a thought—something to get away from the macabre direction of his thoughts. "Can I buy you lunch? To say 'thank you for your help'?"

She thought about it for a minute. "I really should work on my dissertation."

Jason admired her ability to stick to it, but he wanted to get out and he didn't want to eat alone. He kept waiting for "Smith" to call again. For the apartment to get ransacked by someone looking for the papers. Papers that—according to Amara's new revelation—held indications of murder, despite the cover-up.

And he was suddenly concerned about Amara. She lived here with him. What if something went down and she was here alone, because he was literally out to lunch? He didn't think it would happen. Anyone who was watching them had to realize that he was watching *them*—i.e. too many of them. Trashing one apartment and finding papers wouldn't hide anything. Someone would have to steal all of Jernigan's stuff, *and* Chief's, and so on. But Jason still wasn't comfortable leaving Amara here.

If she didn't go, he wouldn't. And he wanted to go out for lunch. He was tired of sitting here staring at his own walls. So he played his trump card.

"Ribs."

∧　∧　∧　∧　∧

"Of course, come on up."

Clark was driving again, but Jason figured that alternating driving was the only way to make things work. He'd offered to foot the gas and everything, but Jernigan had said he would drive this time. The only thing left for Jason to do was either become pushy or give in. He opted for giving in: they needed Clark for the research and connections.

Besides, he'd already put this off, the only thing left to do was face it with some decency. He'd gone to class, answered questions with information he'd learned from Amara, and helped the teacher start warming to the firefighters in the class. Alex had given him a nudge in the ribs and a thumbs-up, though the last thing Jason wanted was to swing the other way and become the teacher's pet. But doing well was definitely the goal. He wasn't going to half-ass this and disappoint the Chief.

He'd had his day off and another shift. He'd managed to keep his mouth shut about what Amara had noticed in the autopsy report. And yesterday Aida had finally called with information about Daniel's foster care record.

Jason took a deep breath. Clark had been buzzed in and was coming up the elevator. They were going to trade what they had. Castor, English, and Chief would be brought up to speed at the next round-table, which they'd already called for Saturday, figuring they could take a table at Jenkin's, way in the back of the bar, in the middle of the day. Between the music and the lack of crowd at that time, no one would overhear or figure them out. Mostly, it was an excuse to get some beer involved, which Jason figured he needed.

Because Clark had the day planned, Jason had gotten up at his usual six thirty time. He was trying to stay quiet so Amara could sleep in, but the knock at the door had to wake her. Bolting to grab it before Clark knocked again, he berated himself for not having anticipated better. When he swung the door wide, he gave a hushed, "Hey."

Clark looked at him questioningly, until Jason put his finger to his lips. "My roommate is still asleep. We should stay quiet."

"Sorry, man. Didn't know."

"I'm sure it's fine." But the knocking had probably woken her. It was her front door, too. "Whatcha got for me?" He had things to share, too, but he wasn't quite ready to tell them.

Clark pulled out a folder of papers and held them up for Jason. Taking them, Jason settled in at the table and started thumbing through the pages. There were grids and signatures, dates and highlighted lines. But Jason shook his head as he looked through. It was only as his brain synthesized the highlights that he figured it out. "The name is 'John Smith'. You think this is someone visiting Daniel? It doesn't say who he's visiting. And Smith is the ultimate common name."

"No, it doesn't show that he's there for Daniel. But there's nothing about him before Daniel was admitted." He flipped the pages and showed the dates. "It's monthly, while he's a patient. And the visits stop when Daniel is discharged."

Jason shook his head. "It's coincidental, yes. But . . ."

"It's more than that. Look." Clark flipped the pages. "The early ones are hard to read. You can see that in the later ones someone else wrote out the name. In the early ones you can see he wrote 'John Smith.' But in the later ones, where a staff member signed him in . . . Look."

And there it was—the thing that made this visitor the same person who had called Jason to "check up"—the staff signed him in as "Captain John Smith." Repeatedly.

"Shit." Jason scrubbed his hand down his face. "This means he had a driver's license issued to that name, right?"

Clark shrugged. "I don't know. It seems their security was more lax back then. They repeatedly let this Smith guy in without logging who he was visiting. He's in and out within twenty minutes each time. So it looks like he's just checking up on the kid."

"We only know that because you figured it out. How did you even think to look for visitors?"

"It's what I do." He shrugged it off. "Daniel was a child whose only relative was a seven-year-old. Anyone who visited him would be significant."

Jason nodded, "But there's another issue. This means that it hasn't really stopped. I had hoped that no one was really checking up on this. I mean, I got that call from 'Smith' a while ago, and then nothing. So I was hoping it was a one-time thing."

Clark shook his head. "No. My guess is they're monitoring the records from the Pelias fire. Like I said, I think if we pull them, we'll send up flags. I also think they may be watching you. Or me."

"You?" *Why would they think to watch Jernigan?*

He laughed. "You're suddenly buds with a well-known investigative reporter and the two of you take trips to the home city of the Pelias fire at least once a week if not more often. And this whole pattern of activity is new. Anyone worth their salt has eyes on me, too."

Well. Crap. There it was again.

But Clark's expression turned solemn, "I did find one thing." He pulled out another page, another photocopied guest register from Greil Memorial, and slid it toward Jason. "In all his time there, Daniel Mallory only had one visitor who was listed as specifically coming to see him."

Jason looked at the highlight, this one in green rather than the yellow that marked each of 'Smith's visits. He even recognized the signature. *Fuck.*

William Mondy.

"My mother said my dad followed up."

"Really?" Clark looked at him. "They just decided not to take the brother?"

"They wanted him. Dad said he followed up on it. Mom said he told her that the only way they would get my brother was in a pine box, or something to that effect."

"Wow."

"So my dad went and saw him." He stood up. "There's more. Aida called me and emailed me a bunch of info she found now that we had the name and everything."

Jason headed for his room, grateful for the chance to have just a moment to himself. This was going to be another long day in the car and Clark had just shown him that his father had actually gone and seen the kid. The only consolation he could give himself was that Daniel was listed as being entirely uncommunicative. Jason dug through his bag and pulled out the pages he had printed from Aida's email.

With a deep breath, he stayed there one more moment. This whole thing was getting harder and harder.

No matter that he didn't remember his brother, he hadn't fought for him. He'd left him behind and his brother hadn't died . . . And God help him if he found Daniel and Daniel remembered him. Though his parents had tried to adopt Daniel, they hadn't tried hard enough. Aida's records showed that. And not only had Jason and his parents failed little Daniel, the system had, too. Instead of calling the people who had expressed interest in taking him, they had simply dumped the child into the system.

Jason was cowed that it was such a colossal waste of money if nothing else. No one cared that his mother wanted another child. No one remembered that his father had visited and been told the kid was likely to die. But he couldn't believe the state wouldn't make an effort to get a kid adopted out when there was someone who would take him—and his monthly foster care fees—off the state's hands. But it hadn't happened.

He had to go back or Clark would wonder what had happened to him. He pushed himself up to standing, feeling as though he were physically facing some foe, and headed out the bedroom door.

Amara stood in the middle of the living room, her back to him. Clearly, they'd woken her up. She was still in her boxers and T-shirt, her hair hanging in wild curls down past her shoulders, one hand buried in it, elbow up. "Jason?"

Clark turned around from the fridge. He gave a quick "sorry" and pointed behind her.

As Amara turned around, Jason got a better look. She still bore the imprint of a sheet or pillow on the side of her face, her hand came down out of her hair and she didn't look like she was all in there yet, but her voice was clear. "Secret boys' club meeting in the kitchen?"

He couldn't help but laugh. "Yes—"

She woke fully in an instant. "Please tell me before you invite four grown men. I just want to know so I'm dressed."

Clark joined what was passing for a conversation. "I like the way you're dressed." He held up the milk he had pulled out. "I made coffee. I hope you don't mind."

Amara was stalking off to her room. Though her body language was anything but, her voice was friendly. "If you made good coffee then it's fine."

Luckily she'd just woken up and wasn't at full speed. Jason was, and he intercepted her before she hit her bedroom door. "Hey, no one else is coming. Just Clark, and we were just trading info before we hit Montgomery in a bit."

He saw her shoulders relax. "Then I'll get a cup and head back to my room." She turned again, this time aiming for the kitchen, and her long legs got her halfway there before he could even start talking.

"I was going to tell Clark what you found in the autopsy. Why don't you tell him?"

Clark's gaze snapped to Jason from where it had been glued to Amara. Jason frowned. Clark had met her before, but maybe he just hadn't expected her in her boxers and a T-shirt with no bra. He hadn't realized it was that obvious until Clark was staring at her. But Jernigan was looking at him now, "What did she find in the autopsy?"

Amara looked at him, too. "Do I get to join your secret boys, club?"

At first Jason laughed, but then realized she was serious. "Of course. It's not really a boys, club."

She mumbled, "Coulda fooled me." But then she headed to her bedroom again, saying she was going to get dressed and be right out. At least she looked awake now.

This time he let her by and headed into the kitchen where Clark was giving him an odd look. Well, maybe he had made that decision on his own, but this whole thing had been his baby from the start and it *wasn't* a boys' club.

"She's hot." Clark's voice was lowered so it wouldn't carry to Amara's room. Even as Jason's eyes narrowed at the thought that Amara was anything other than . . . Amara, Clark spoke again. "I can see why Aida was concerned."

"Aida never met her."

"Yeah, but that voice. It's kinda low and really sexy."

"What?" Jason made himself a cup of coffee. If there was one thing he did know about women, it was that they took forever to 'get dressed'. Because that included putting on makeup and messing with their hair and god knew what else.

Clark already held a mug in his hand. He must have pulled it out of the woefully understocked cupboards. "Look, if you aren't interested in her, do you mind—?"

Jason nearly dropped the pot of coffee in an effort to cut the man off. "Do not." He didn't know why he was so vehement about it, but he was. "Look, if she's in, then you hitting on her is going to be a problem. No one hits on Amara. I have to live with her."

Clark nodded. "Fine. So she found something in the autopsy report?"

"Yeah." They seated themselves at the table, and Jason pulled out what he had from Aida. "Look at this first though."

Clark took the papers, his eyes changing focus as he scanned from one social work document to the next.

Jason pointed things out. "He was put into foster care. He was in six different places, all in or around Montgomery. One group home in his early teens, but the others were with families." He pointed to one spot, but almost couldn't say it. "He aged out of the system on his eighteenth birthday."

Clark read over the reports. "He started talking by the time he turned ten."

"Yeah." Then he pointed to the note that made him sick to his stomach. "There's a little checkbox at the bottom of each form. It says he's not available for adoption due to his diagnosis. It's like he was a puppy at the pound."

Amara was out by then, shocking Jason with her speed. She was fully dressed, socks, shoes, and everything. Her hair was pulled back into a bun. Though pieces of it escaped, she really looked quite well put together. "There are a lot of kids stuck in the foster care system who shouldn't be. Why was he listed that way?"

Jason looked up at her. "He didn't talk. Actually, when he was originally released from the hospital, he went to a mental institution, because he didn't want to communicate at all. But later he was released and put into the foster system."

She poured herself a cup of coffee and, seeing that both the chairs were taken, leaned against the counter. "They never have time to reassess the diagnoses. It could have saved him, huh?"

"Probably." There was nothing more he could say. And certainly nothing he could do at this late date. "I've done Internet searches for him."

Clark looked up.

"And I get nothing. I searched when we first learned his name, everything I could think of. Google, Ancestry, hospital and police records. After learning that he made it to eighteen and was still in Alabama, I tried again. I even had Castor pull his driver's license. There are two Daniel Mallorys in Alabama and they're both black. And that's it. This Daniel Mallory never had a driver's license in the state." He sighed. "It's like he disappeared."

Clark and Amara spoke at the same time. "Maybe he did."

Great. Jason looked back and forth between them.

Amara spoke first, "He might have gone to another state— just hightailed it out of town."

Jason followed that with, "Maybe he died. What does a foster kid do when they get kicked out of the system with a high school diploma or less?"

Amara took another sip of the coffee she was nursing. "Join the military? Head for New York or LA to make it big?"

Clark pushed all the papers back into one pile. "We'll find him."

"You're always so sure." Jason studied him.

"It's what I do. I could never do what you do, I could never be a singer or a pro-athlete. But I'm good at this."

Was he really? Jason figured they had found plenty, but "find Daniel" remained at the top of the list. He turned to Amara and changed the topic. "You want to tell Clark what you found on the autopsy?"

"Sure." And she went on to explain about the body being found on the couch.

"Holy shit." Clark's face went white, then his mouth dropped open.

Apparently, that Daniel had aged out of the system and disappeared was not a surprise. That Smith had visited Daniel at Greil wasn't a shock, or else he'd gotten over it before this morning. But Jason had never seen the reporter act this way.

Clark must have seen him staring, because he started to talk. Or he tried to. After a sputtered start, he actually made words. "This is evidence. It's real, admissible-in-court *evidence.* We haven't had any of that before."

"What?" Amara asked.

Clark stood up and dragged his hands down his face. "The call to Jason was from a pay phone. There's no evidence that Pelias was arson, only two older firefighters who were too new to be credible at the time. All the paperwork cleared the fire as accidental and even Alcia Mallory's death is ruled accidental. This is the first thing we can take before a judge and use. It's big."

Jason sat for a moment absorbing that. But Clark didn't. "Let's go. Let's hit Montgomery. Because there's a nurse on shift today who worked with Daniel. If we're lucky, maybe she can ID our Captain Smith."

"You think she'll remember a man who visited one patient almost thirty years ago?" That sounded far-fetched and not at all worth another several hour trip. "Maybe we should see if we can find Daniel's last foster family."

Clark shook his head, "There's not enough time for that. Not today."

Jason started to protest. The family could at least point him to where Daniel had gone when he left. But Clark started explaining.

"You can go back tomorrow or call them if you want. But it doesn't get us closer to cracking the arson. That's what has someone watching us. Besides, the nurse at Greil is on shift today. I checked. We need to go."

"Okay." Jason didn't like it, and he had work the next day. He didn't like being closer to Daniel than he ever had been and then putting the search on hold. But he did it.

Clark turned to Amara, "Are you coming?"

"What?" She jerked back and for a moment it looked like the coffee she had just refilled would slosh. "No, I don't think so."

"Well, it seems you're in the 'secret boys' club' now." Jernigan offered her a smile and Jason thought, *I told you not to hit on my roommate.*

She tipped her head. "My dissertation isn't going to write itself. . . which is a damn shame. You two have fun."

In less than a minute, they both had their bags over their shoulders and were heading out. He asked questions of Clark on the way, about how to find the family that Daniel was staying with when he graduated. About what to ask them, if calling was just as good or if he was better off visiting. He asked how Clark was going to find Daniel, what were the next steps? Should they consider looking for a death certificate?

Normally he was used to Clark peppering him with questions, things that made him want to squirm. At least today he was the one asking.

They made it to Montgomery in record time and Clark drove right to the entrance of Greil Memorial Hospital, without the circling they had done on their previous visit. They parked and threw out the fast-food wrappers in the trash can as they entered the building, and headed in through the front desk. This time they walked up, driver's licenses in hand. They signed in like pros, rather than the uncertain neophytes they'd been last time. Clark even had them call Betty Gaither to the front desk; they had an appointment.

It took a good ten minutes for nurse Gaither to extract herself from whatever treatment she was delivering. But when she appeared, she was the same nurse who had recognized Clark from his picture in the paper.

All smiles, she greeted them warmly. "Why, I was so surprised when you called and asked for my help! What can I do for you?"

Jason stood back while Clark turned on the charm. "Is there somewhere we can sit? Maybe with a table, where we aren't around anything distracting?"

Betty led them back to the employee break room, then to a table on the far side, near a wall that was entirely windows. A slightly overlarge playground sat atop a mulched-in section in the yard. To the right was a workout area, complete with chin-up bars, practice beams and exercise plaques. It didn't look like what Jason thought a mental hospital would. Then again, it probably didn't look like what it had looked like so many years ago. His mother had said they'd been counseled not to mention his brother, to just let him let go. But Jason wondered what the counselors would say today?

Then he pulled his attention fully back to Betty and Clark. After all, this was more important for today than finding out where Daniel went when he turned eighteen. Clark was explaining the situation. About Daniel, about a little boy, who didn't speak and was originally belligerent.

There was a clear moment when Betty's eyes lit up and the memory clicked into place. She remembered Daniel. "I'd been here about five years at that point. They said he'd been in a fire and lost his whole family, so no one knew if he spoke before that or if it was due to the fire."

She took a short breath, and when neither Clark nor Jason filled the space, she kept going. "Honestly, I think it was from the fire. The way he took care of himself, didn't whine, but knew how to do what he needed and when to turn his back on someone. That was a child that had been cared for, not a kid who had never communicated with people. I remember thinking that he communicated just fine. The psychiatrists simply didn't like what he had to say, which was basically that they could all go screw themselves. Oh, my God, I cannot believe I just said that!"

Jason laughed out loud. Well, Betty had some grit. He liked her better for her slip. "Don't worry about it."

Clark took the embarrassment that kept her silent for a moment as a chance to mention the visitor Daniel had every month. He even told her that it was "Captain John Smith." And again, they could both see the moment she remembered the man. She even said, "Yes, yes, I remember him. He came like clockwork once a month. Such a sweet man."

That made Clark's eyebrows pop up. Jason thought he hid his reaction better than that, but there was no telling. "Why do you say that?"

"Well, that little boy had no family, and Captain Smith was one of the firefighters who pulled him from the building, and he always came in and checked to see how Daniel was doing, every month."

Clark was thinking. "Did Daniel talk to him? Or enjoy his visits?"

"Oh, no. I think he gave Captain Smith the same message he gave all the personnel. The Captain never smiled. Just checked to make sure the boy was okay. Quit coming when Daniel went into the foster care system. I assume he kept up with him."

"Hmmm." Jason hadn't thought of that. Would it be possible for Smith to have tracked Daniel from home to home and visited? He would have to ask when he called the Morales family, the last Daniel had lived with.

"Do you remember what Captain Smith looked like?"

"Oh, yes." Betty smiled. And Clark reached into his bag. He had printed dozens of old photos from somewhere. But Jason recognized them. They were firefighter portraits, taken each year like school pictures, for I.D., newspaper articles, and the like. His own current photo had run beside the picture of him with the Thurlow boys under his arms.

While the hairstyles were military short, and the uniforms hadn't changed much over the years, Jason could still easily tell these were out of date. In fact they looked mid- to late eighties. He wanted to ask Clark where he'd gotten them but didn't want to question the reporter in front of Betty.

She was shaking her head as Clark laid out photo after photo. She did stop and squint at one, but then gave the same tiny shake of her head. So Clark kept bringing out more photos. He'd already passed twenty and appeared to have another ten to fifteen still in his hand when Betty smacked her finger down. "That's him. That's Captain Smith."

"Are you sure?" Clark said it in such a way that he was simply asking her for a measure of confidence.

Betty had it in spades. "That's him. A little gruff, but he had a great heart." She beamed.

Clark still asked her to go through the rest of the pictures and see if maybe she wanted to change her mind. Or if maybe she recognized someone else associated with Daniel.

She didn't.

Betty was as confident as a witness could be that the picture she chose was Captain Smith. She had bought Clark's measly explanation that they thought if they could find Captain Smith, he might lead them to Daniel. Clark had told it as a sob story no one with a heart could resist, unless she noticed the gaping holes in the plot. Betty didn't.

"I hope this helps you boys out."

"It does." Clark thanked her profusely, but she turned to Jason.

Clasping both of his hands in hers, she gushed, "I sure do hope you find your little brother. Ultimately he was a sweet kid with a bad deal. I wish you both the best of luck."

She walked them back up to the front desk, wishing them more of that good luck as she went.

Jason didn't say anything. He'd memorized the face in the picture before Clark had packed them back up. He could pick Smith out of a line-up now. But he waited until they were back in the car. Clark didn't say anything, just put the gear into reverse and casually exited the parking lot.

Surprising Jason, he pulled in at a strip mall three blocks away and yanked his bag into the front seat with him. Reaching in, he extracted only the picture Betty had identified. First he held the picture up to Jason, and when he turned it around, Jason realized that Clark had been reading the name off the back. "Jerry Brady."

Jason blinked. Something felt familiar about the picture. But instead he asked Clark. "How confident are you in Betty's assessment? How certain are you that this is Captain Smith?"

"Very."

He let that sink in for a minute—then scrambled when Clark got out of the car. They were at another office supply store; the stop hadn't been random. The reporter was at full speed. "We need a full photo-quality copy of this picture for each of the guys. And for Amara, too, I guess. She needs to be able to recognize him if he comes to the door."

He asked Jason to handle the photocopying, so he could take notes on their encounter with Betty Gaither. And he popped out his little laptop right there at the counter and started writing. Then he looked up. "Wait, wait."

Clark handed over a card for the store. "This will cover it. And we need copies of this, too." He grinned and searched in his bag until he pulled up another picture. It was the same man, but much later in his life.

Jason stared. "Where did you get this?"

"I have all the most up-to-date copies for these guys. So we can identify him now."

"Shit." Though that was important, he didn't like that this felt like quicksand. Which meant it was best not to struggle, so Jason took the two photos and made seven sets of copies, just to be safe.

They finally climbed back in the car and passed a place to get milkshakes on the way out of town. Jason needed it. These days in Montgomery were always a slam to his system. While they waited at the drive-through window, he asked if they might not go see the Morales family?

"I'm sorry, I don't have time." Clark turned to him. "But you should call them tonight or tomorrow. Take notes. Tell me what you find."

"Sure." He tried not to let himself be disappointed. But he was.

The milkshake helped a little, still the drive back seemed interminable. The silence in the car didn't help.

Finally he spoke. "There's no real doubt now that Alcia was murdered that night."

"No."

"And that Daniel and I were there."

"Yeah, you were."

Jason sighed. "I'll bet that's why I don't remember anything and why Daniel didn't speak. It's not just the trauma of a fire. I'll bet I watched my mother get tied up and burned to death on a couch."

Clark's voice was solemn. "I don't have any real doubt about that. You know what it means though, right?"

"No." Jason took a long pull on the milkshake, but when Clark spoke he wished he hadn't.

"You two are the only witnesses to the murder."

Chapter 19

Jason

He'd called the Morales family almost immediately after Clark dropped him off. There was plenty of the day left, even if the reporter was booked. At least he'd prepped Jason with a handful of questions to ask. More importantly, Jason found there were things he suddenly wanted to know about his brother.

He'd had to explain to Amara what he was doing, who he was calling, and why he was so damn nervous. He wiped his palms along his jeans, hoping the Morales family would tell him they'd stayed in touch with Daniel, but that was a best case scenario and he wasn't banking on it.

Amara was excited for him, or maybe taking pity, and volunteered to take notes if he wanted to put the phone on speaker, so he could just talk and not worry about recording the information he found. At first, he turned her down, wanting to keep the conversation to himself, but he quickly realized that her offer was smart.

He found the phone number easily enough through the Internet. Since the address matched the one where Daniel stayed over ten years ago, Jason hoped it was still occupied by the same family.

He needed to calm the buzzing in his system, but there was no way to do that except make the call. Grabbing the house phone and taking a deep breath—with a glance at Amara—he sat himself at the table.

She didn't say anything, just found a pad of paper and a pen—unlike Clark, she was relatively low tech. Pulling the chair over so she sat on his left, she settled in quickly and set her hand on his arm.

Jason had no idea if that was a sign that she was ready, or if she was just trying to calm him down.

He tried to soothe his nerves—a big breath, closed eyes, hands on the table—but none of it worked. In the end he gave up and just dialed.

"Hello?"

He'd practiced it in his head, and luckily the words came out as though he was a reasonable person. Thank God. "Hello, you don't know me, but my name is Jason Mondy—formerly Mallory—and I'm looking for my brother. Is this Nico Morales?"

"Yes, this is he. Let's see, Mallory . . ." There was a pause. "Yes. Who is it that you are looking for?"

"His name is Daniel Mallory, he's my brother, and we were separated when he was four and I was seven. I traced him to you. Your house is the last foster home he was in before he aged out of the system just over ten years ago."

"I remember Daniel." There was fondness in the man's voice, but also caution.

Unexpected pressure pushed at the back of Jason's eyes. "Can you help me find him?"

"I don't know." The caution came stronger into Nico Morales's tone. "We haven't seen or heard from Daniel since he left. I'm sorry, I don't know where he is now."

Amara had made a few notes, though there wasn't much to record.

Then another voice came onto the line. "Hello? Are you Daniel's brother?"

"Yes."

"This is Lisa Morales. If you find Daniel will you have him call us? We miss him."

Jason felt his heart fall. He'd hoped that they would be able to give him something more, even though he hadn't expected it.

"Of course. When I find him, I'll tell him that." Then he took a deep breath—he still had questions to ask.

Nico hopped off the line, tending to children Jason heard in the background. They must still have foster kids. But Lisa was more than happy to answer whatever he asked.

Daniel had left on his eighteenth birthday, had packed one bag, hugged everyone, and gone out the door on his ten-speed bike. They would have liked for him to stay, but they'd been assigned another foster child who was arriving that afternoon and needed the bed.

Jason squeezed his eyes shut, comparing that to his own eighteenth birthday. He'd slept in his own room that night. He'd been given a car—an old beater, to be sure—for his trip to college the next fall and he'd spent the day at the lake. But he pushed that formerly happy memory aside and asked for more.

Daniel had an August birthday, so he'd graduated high school before getting tossed out of the system.

For his own curiosity, Jason wanted to know about Daniel, and Lisa had satisfied that, talking like a proud mother. He had been good at math, Bs and As, but truly excelled in English and history. He'd done advanced classes in both and always posted As. He'd been on the yearbook committee. But no one knew his plans for after he left. Neither of the Moraleses' had been privy to that information. Daniel had played that close to the vest.

Amara wrote quickly, getting all the major points, and Jason breathed a sigh of relief that she had thought of it. He would have remembered every word, but it was nice to have a scribe.

He asked about friends—but Daniel didn't have many that the Moraleses had met. Jason wondered if that was about Daniel or just part of being a foster kid. It sounded like they had a full house, and these people were caretakers but not family. Though he'd been there for three years, Daniel might have been very adult even before he arrived. Jason figured you grew up fast in the foster system.

Then he asked Clark's question: did Daniel have any visitors? Adults who came to check on him?

Lisa thought on that one for a while. There was a man who came by, and Daniel seemed concerned about him. It had taken her a while to realize that the man had been checking up on Daniel, but she'd found Daniel one afternoon staring out the window, eyes locked on the man standing beside a car just beyond their tiny property. When she'd pressed her foster son, he'd only said he didn't like the man and to keep the other foster kids away from him.

Shit.

She confirmed that Daniel had never gotten a driver's license while he was with them.

Jason was winding up the conversation when Amara tapped his arm and pointed at the paper with her pen. On a separate sheet she'd written, *Pictures? What high school did he go to?*

He hadn't even thought of that, but he quickly asked Lisa to help him out just a bit more before hanging up. As usual, he felt he'd found only a portion of what he was looking for, and dug up some additional trouble when he already had enough.

Lisa had a few pictures with Daniel in them; she promised to make copies and mail them, but it would be a while. He'd attended Jefferson Davis High School during the three years he'd lived with the Moraleses, and he'd graduated from there.

They sat at the table in silence for a minute after Jason said "thank you" and hung up. Amara let him speak first, but his brilliant opening line was, "Can I keep that piece of paper?"

"Sure." She tore it off the pad and handed him the sheet of neat script. "You're working tomorrow, aren't you?"

He nodded.

"Hmm." She stood and went to the fridge where she pulled out a soda. Only it wasn't a soda—it was some organic juice with fizz thing. But she reached in again and handed him a Dr. Pepper. "I just thought you might be interested in heading back down to Montgomery and checking the Jefferson Davis Library."

"To interview teachers who knew him?" He popped the can, the fizz a small comfort that at least some things didn't change.

"You could. But I was thinking you could look through the yearbooks. They keep a copy of all the past yearbooks in most school libraries."

"Oh." He hadn't known that, though it made perfect sense. He could see a picture of Daniel, at least know what his brother looked like. At seventeen, Clark would have been old enough that Jason could recognize him now if he ran into him on the street—should he ever be so lucky. But he didn't want to go. "I feel like all I do is drive down there and learn interesting things but never get what I need. No one ever says, 'Of course, Daniel Mallory lives three doors down, with his wife and two kids.'"

Just the idea made him dizzy. He always thought of Daniel as a kid. They researched Daniel-as-a-kid. But he was a grown man of thirty now—if he was still alive—and he might very well have a wife and several kids. The Morales home was Daniel's last known address—from more than twelve years ago. That was a long time to track an adult who left behind no information or usable clues.

Amara grabbed Jason's arm and walked him to the couch without being obvious about it. But he waved her off and headed into his room where he filed the page into his bag of all things Mallory.

When he emerged, she was still in the same spot where she'd curled herself on the couch.

He had to ask. "Do you think I'll find him?"

"Yes." That was all. It was a confident response borne of simple conviction.

"Why do you think that?"

"Because I think Clark will be able to dig him up. I've been reading his work while avoiding my dissertation this week." She rolled her eyes. "He's *good*. He's straight forward, relatively unbiased, and he seems to be able to ferret out anything. He gets people to tell him things they don't tell anyone. Maybe he just asks the right questions."

Jason nodded and slumped down onto the couch. "Well, I hope it's soon."

"I don't think it will be."

Great. "Why?"

"Lisa Morales said that man visited Daniel at their home. And you and Clark said there was a visitor to Daniel at the psych hospital. If it's the same man, he'd been watching Daniel all that time. If Daniel is as smart as everyone says he is, and if he remembers his mother's murder, then there's probably a reason he disappeared at age eighteen. He probably made every effort to hide himself."

"Shit. Pardon." He hadn't thought that far ahead, but he didn't think he could string any coherent thoughts together right now. She was right, but he couldn't deal with it.

He lived a life with enough ups and downs. And in his job it was okay to just take things as they came, and better to let them roll off. No one got on his case that he didn't cry over Connelly and he didn't tell anyone about the hole in his gut over his friend. That some nights when he slept, Connelly looked him in the eyes and gasped for air his lungs couldn't use. And Jason didn't tell anyone about the raw burn that said he hadn't done right by his brother.

He turned to Amara. "You know, I think I'm going to turn in early."

"Oh no you don't." She grabbed his hand as he tried to walk off.

"What?"

"It's only seven and you haven't had anything to eat. You'll be back up at two a.m. hungry."

He pulled gently at his hand, but she didn't release it. "I promise not to wake you."

"Seriously? Please wake me up! I'd love a good excuse to sleep in and avoid the tail end of my dissertation. But I'm more worried that you'll go into work without enough food or rest."

"I'm fine."

"No, you're not. You just say you are as if that makes it so." She held up her hand when he tried to protest. "I'm a nurse, don't argue with me."

So he gave an uneasy laugh until she suggested a nice greasy burger that would put him into a coma. "No, no more burgers."

"Teppan? Where they cook Japanese food in front of you? My treat. I want to celebrate, I'm this close to finishing my first draft." She held up her fingers with a smidge of space between them.

"Aren't you supposed to celebrate when you finish?"

"Have you seen the amount of work that I put into that thing? I'll celebrate when I damn well feel like it."

Jason laughed for real, and he liked the feeling of it.

^   ^   ^   ^   ^

He had rolled home from shift on Saturday morning, napped and changed into jeans and a non-SFD T-shirt. He frowned into his closet, which still needed an upgrade from fire-fighter-all-the-time.

For the first time, he invited Amara to join an official Scooby Gang outing to Jenkins. But she declined, claiming to be within inches of finishing her thesis.

So it was only guys piled around the back table in the same arrangement they'd been in last time they'd been here—the first time they'd met to discuss the Pelias fire. Chief looked at Jernigan with a sigh. Clark, perceptive guy that he was, saw what they were all thinking. "I'm in Connelly's seat, aren't I?"

They all nodded.

"He's the one who suggested you bring me into this, right?"

Another nod went around the table, but Clark handled it by lifting his glass, "To Connelly, a good man . . ." He touched the rim to Chief's, and Adler caught on.

"Like a son to me . . ." He tipped to Castor who added "A fine firefighter."

Jason nearly choked at his turn, but managed, "A good, good friend."

English put in, "A smart man" and passed it back to Clark who ended with, "Who will be missed."

For a while there was silence as beer levels dropped. But the mood was broken by the waitress who missed all the signs, leaned in, and smiled, "Y'all need another round here?"

Jason, for one, was grateful for the break and said "yes" as Adler looked back and forth at them all, "Do you have anything new?"

Boy, did they.

They started with the autopsy and the evidence it had hidden. Jason credited Amara with the find, explaining that he'd given her entrée into their club, and that she'd turned down the beer today.

Castor was more concerned that Alcia Mallory had been dead when she burned, but Clark dispelled that idea right away. "The autopsy is clear that she died from burns. No evidence of anything else, like gunshots or . . . skull damage."

Next Jason shared Daniel's name and history, as well as the fact that he'd disappeared at age eighteen. He mentioned the call to Lisa Morales two nights before. That someone had visited Daniel at the foster home. And that it was probably the same man who had visited regularly at the hospital.

Jason smiled. "Amara also suggested that we get pictures of him. So Mrs. Morales is gathering photos. She's going to make copies and mail them."

Clark looked surprised, then asked. "Good thinking. When will we get them?"

"I can't imagine they'll get here any faster than a week."

Clark asked if anyone else had something to add. Jason was thinking that Jernigan was taking the brunt of the work but probably getting the most out of it in the end, when English spoke up.

"Well, I'll start with this: I am awesome. I felt useless, so I started fishing. And I landed a big one."

They waited while he grinned, "So, here's what I thought: Pelias burns to the ground, it's arson, apartment 187 is the focus, and it's covered up by the fire department. So what's the connection? Why is the fire department covering this up?

"So I pulled what I could. I can't subpoena things randomly, but I do have friends. I thought maybe Alcia worked at the station and saw or heard something she shouldn't. But there's no record of that. She was employed elsewhere—nothing there. So I called a friend at the phone service and asked for any calls between 451 Oracle Street and Pelias Street Apartments 187."

"Those are some old phone records." Clark frowned.

English grinned and took another hit off his beer. "My friend has been with AT&T since they were Bell South and she thinks I'm a sweet young man. She won't make copies or violate any laws, but she's more than happy to answer specific questions. And that one got a huge hit."

"What?" They all said it in unison.

"Starting in December of '84, the calls are heaviest, back and forth. After mid-April, they only go from Pelias to the fire station. Then in July there are a few calls before the building burns."

"Holy shit." Clark mirrored Jason's outburst, and the waitress turned to see all the men looking at English with their mouths open.

She came over and grinned again, foolish and out of place. "Is it time for another round, boys?"

Chief nodded. "Yeah, this one's on me."

She gave a saucy little grin, called the Chief "sugar" and sauntered off.

Jason realized she was exactly his type: stacked, flirty, and about as deep as a cereal bowl. Today it left a bad taste in his mouth.

Clark picked up the thread after the waitress was out of earshot, but Jason figured they could have the whole conversation right in front of her and she wouldn't have a clue.

"So Alcia was calling the fire station . . . repeatedly." He thought about that for a minute, then continued. "When Jason and I talked to the teacher at her high school, she said Alcia was really smart and on her way to college. Then she discovered men and figured she had another ticket out. We asked—the teacher did not mean 'boys,' she meant 'men.'"

Castor looked at Jason. "I know she was your mother, but do you think she was seeing a firefighter?"

Jason bit back the *'birth mother'* response that came naturally now. "That makes sense with all we know. Firefighters cheat—"

Chief interrupted, "Not all. I don't. You don't, that I know of."

Jason laughed. "They all walk out on me before I can. And no, we don't all, but you have to admit the numbers are high. And a love affair gone wrong is a good motive for murder."

Clark then gave his evidence: Betty Gaither's ID of Jerry Grady as the man who had been visiting Daniel at the hospital. He then started into information on Grady that was news to Jason.

"Jerry Grady still lives in Montgomery. He's had three addresses since '85, each one nicer than the next. He's past retirement at Oracle Street but still there for some reason."

Chief snorted at that. "The reason is that retirement sucks. The longer you wait and the higher you get, the better your payout. Plus, we tend to be active people."

Clark conceded. "Okay, so that's nothing out of the ordinary. By all accounts Grady is a family man. Same wife for forty-two years, three daughters, now ages thirty-five to forty. Seven grandkids."

English shook his head. "And that's our best choice for a murdering bastard?"

"We don't know that he did it. Only that he helped cover it up. It would be nice to figure out why. Here." Clark reached down into his bag and pulled out the pictures of Grady. He handed out copies of the current photo to each of them and followed up with the mid-eighties shot. Everyone looked at them for a minute, then Castor's mouth dropped open, just as the waitress approached.

Clark waved her away and luckily she got it. Winking, she turned and left them alone so Clark could ask Castor if he knew the man.

"No, I don't." He turned his attention, "Jason, have you seen this?"

"Yeah." Jason nodded, wondering what was going through his friend's head. "I was there when Nurse Betty ID'd him."

Castor looked from English to the Chief, "Does anyone else see what I see? Or am I fucking out of my head?"

English nodded. "I see it."

"Holy crap." Adler added.

Jason looked to Clark, who looked as confused as he felt. "What?"

Castor turned the picture around. "This is *you*, Mondy."

"No, it's—" And he saw what they were talking about. From the look on Clark's face, it was the first time he saw it, too. "Oh shit."

Castor nodded. "He's related to you. My guess is he's your dad."

"He is not my 'dad'." His heart was beating faster, his eyes racing around the table to each of his friends. "Do you really think he fathered me?"

It was Chief's voice that tried to be as gentle as possible. "I think there's a really good possibility of that, son."

∧   ∧   ∧   ∧   ∧

Jason pushed harder on the gas. His mother had promised him pork chops. Still it felt like he was fleeing rather than going for a visit.

He'd convinced Amara to come with him. Her first draft of her dissertation was finished and emailed, and he'd been a little pushy. He didn't want her staying there by herself.

So he'd told his mom he was bringing his roommate and asked her to fix up another room. He'd told Amara that it was the only way she was going to get any home cooking out of him. He didn't tell her that he was going to catch his mother up on what they'd learned so far—though he didn't think he could handle doing that until the next morning. Then he'd proceeded to bitch for the whole ride—about Grady and that if they had connected all the dots right, not only was his mother murdered, but she was murdered because of him.

"Jesus." He smacked the steering wheel. "My very existence is the best motive for my mother's incredibly violent murder. And probably the reason my little brother never talked. And . . ."

Amara took it all in.

She should be celebrating. She'd accomplished something major through a lot of hard work. It wasn't over yet. But she deserved a break, and here he was making her work even harder just to deal with him and his shit.

Still, she did it with grace. She asked questions. Even asked permission before she went digging in his bag to find the picture of Jerry Grady. She examined it in the fading light. "I didn't catch it on my own, but yeah, I think they're probably right. I'd be really surprised if you weren't at least related to him. Do you think he's Daniel's father, too?"

Jason had no answer for that and shrugged. At least one person thought Alcia had kids by two separate men. But both birth certificates listed the father as "unknown."

"Do you think he's been watching you the way he watched Daniel?"

Jason almost drove off the road the idea gave him such a bad case of disgust. "Okay, I can't arrive at my Mom's like this." He tried to make light of it. "She'll only ask questions and then I'll never get any pork chops. So, new topic: how was the dissertation?"

That was a stupid question.

But Amara ran with it. "Exhilarating and terrifying."

"Why terrifying?" He didn't know the first thing about getting a PhD.

"Because this is the first draft. I did a lot of work and it's likely they'll tell me it's complete crap and I have to re-do the whole thing."

"Oh. It's like waiting for an essay grade. Times a thousand."

She laughed. "Or a thousand thousand. Only there's no return date on when I get the grade back. And eventually, I'll have to present the whole thing before them and defend it while they try to tear it down. They may just call me in for a first round, rather than give me things to fix."

"Ouch."

"Yeah." She twirled a curl that had come loose absently around her finger. It was the singular outward sign that the topic made her nervous. "My only consolation is that it's a pain in the butt to get the three of my committee members in one room, so they probably won't do that until they've torn me a new one and made me completely re-write it five times. But there's no rule that says they can't."

Jason took the turn off the freeway and Amara looked around. There wasn't much to see as the sun had set a short while ago, but her dark eyes saw something.

"This is quaint. Real small-town America. You're lucky."

He was beginning to realize that. "Thank you. . . . for coming with me. My mother will gush over you, which is better than I've been doing. I'm sorry I'm such a mess."

She laughed. "Yeah, the next time you get your birth father ID'd by way of a picture of a supposed criminal . . . weren't you in a bar? So the next time that happens, I expect you to handle it better."

"Good God. I hope to hell it doesn't happen again. Medically speaking, it can't happen again, right?"

She laughed. "I only know the one way."

Before he realized it, he was pulling into his mother's driveway and it felt almost as good as being wrapped in a warm blanket. But he wondered what Amara thought of the older house. It didn't match the modern lines and sleek look of the apartment he hadn't helped pick, but where they both lived.

She settled his thoughts right away, "Oh, this reminds me of my house in South Carolina."

He wanted to ask about that, but his mother was coming down the steps, hand positioned at her brow to shade from the sun.

Amara called out. "Hi, Mrs. Mondy."

Merry Mondy was suddenly ecstatic. "You brought a girl home, Jason."

Here he went—at least it was a good distraction from everything else. "Mom, she's my roommate."

"You're living together and you didn't tell me?"

"Yes, because she's my *roommate*. She pays half the rent. And sometimes she cooks for me, so I'm using your culinary skills to pay her back." He grinned as his mother's attention was successfully pulled from berating him for bringing home a girlfriend she'd never heard of. "Amara just finished her thesis today. I told her your pork chops would be a good way to celebrate."

Merry put her arm around Amara, "Well, you come on in and tell me about you." Then she called back over her shoulder. "Jason, you bring the bags in."

He laughed at her since he'd already popped the trunk. "I'm ahead of you, Mom."

The two women were setting the table in tandem when he went by with the bags and announced, "I'm putting Amara's things into the sewing room."

His mother waved him by. "Whatever you want."

Jason looked at his roommate. "Don't worry, there's a bed."

He was answered with a smile and a deep breath. "It smells so good."

"It usually does around here."

In the short period of time it took him to drop the bags into the right rooms, everything had been put onto the table. He was grateful as he could almost feel his stomach invert from hunger and wondered if Amara felt the same. It had gotten late while they were driving, but she'd never complained. No, that had been him. He'd complained about everything but his hunger.

In moments, he was seated at the table, grace had been quickly requested, and he was shoveling food into his mouth, much to his relief.

His mother asked him how things were at work, and he brushed her off each time with something about Amara. "She came to the station and taught our training class two weeks ago." "She helps me with my Paramedic class when I get stuck."

Each time, his mother turned her attention to their guest. She also got some information that Jason had never thought to ask. Amara had grown up in South Carolina with a single mother who had died in a car accident at the end of high school. She'd gone to live with Leo and his parents. Then Leo had settled down with Alex, and they all took it upon themselves to look after her.

All of that was news to Jason. But his mother turned back to him. She wanted to ask him something but hesitated. Into that space, he threw more bait. "Amara's already a disaster relief nurse."

"So you understand what Jason does."

Amara laughed at that. "I don't think I'll ever understand what Jason does. I'm with most people, I run *out* of burning buildings."

Merry nodded. "But you know some of the tough things he deals with."

It was Jason who picked up the thread. "Amara was the lead on the team that tried to save Bruce Connelly."

He shouldn't have said it. But his mother reached out and squeezed his hand, just a small gesture that she understood what he felt, even if he didn't show it. Her voice was a little scratchy when she spoke. "That was a tragedy. But I'm grateful every day that it wasn't you."

Having declared that, she stood up from the table and asked if anyone wanted dessert. Jason said yes, and he and Amara ate huge bowls of premium chocolate ice cream while his mother hit the kitchen.

"Mom?" He called out between bites. "Aren't you having some?"

"No, apparently I'm having Tums. That barbecue sauce on the pork chops gave me heartburn and dairy won't help." She came back out a minute later and told them she was headed to bed.

"Thank you for dinner, Mrs. Mondy." Amara smiled from behind her spoonful. "We'll clean up."

"Oh, don't worry about it. Jason can get it."

Amara laughed and looked at him. "I like her."

Merry laughed, too, and pulled his roomie up for a hug. "I'm so glad you came."

"Me, too."

Jason got a hug, too, though he wondered if his wasn't just a little less enthusiastic than Amara's had been. Still, Amara helped with the dishes, and they both pled exhaustion and turned in. He had just crawled in when he heard a soft knock at the door. "Yes?"

It was his mother. She came in and sat on the edge of his bed where he propped himself up. "Why are you still up?"

"Heartburn. I couldn't lay down yet, so I was reading." Then she got down to brass tacks. "Why is that lovely girl in the other room? You're a grown man, I'm not going to impose the same rules as when you were a teenager."

He laughed. "That desperate for grandchildren, Mom?"

"Yes." She laughed too.

He tilted his head at her, genuinely sorry. "It's not like that, Mom. It's not what you think it is."

But she just laughed again. "I know what I see. And I think it's actually not what *you* think it is. Good night, baby boy."

The door was closing softly behind her while he still had an odd frown on his lips. She used that phrase sometimes for him. But he'd always found it strange that she called him "baby boy" when he'd never been her baby. He'd been Alcia Mallory's baby boy.

But he was too exhausted to let it keep him up, and before he knew it, he was awake, the sun's rays streaming through the window. There was a gentle noise coming from downstairs, so he crawled out of bed. In deference to Amara being there, he looked both ways before crossing the hallway in his boxers, quickly showered, and then did the same on the way out.

As he came downstairs, he saw that the women were again in the kitchen, working in tandem. His mother was old-fashioned that way. She liked keeping her house, being in her house, and having guests in her house. So they were making eggs, bacon, and toast.

Jason considered himself on time, since he showed up as things were getting slid onto plates. His mother's plate had only toast. "Mom?"

Her grin was rueful. "Toast and Tums."

"Still?"

She nodded at him, then turned to Amara. "As you can see by my waistline, I'm no stranger to eating my own cooking." But she shoved them into the dining room before Amara could make a return comment about his mother's weight.

They were halfway through breakfast when his mother came out with it. "Can you tell me what's on your mind with Amara here?"

He turned to his roommate, who was looking a little stunned. "I told you she was good."

"Hm." Amara swallowed her toast. "I thought you were hiding it much better than that." But she put her hands up in a sign of surrender, and Jason took over.

He told his mother about Jerry Grady first. That they were pretty certain the man was his birth father.

Merry took a deep breath at that and got up to get the bottle of Tums. She took another one and then slapped the bottle onto the table in front of her as though she were doing shots at a bar.

Jason put his hands into his pockets. He didn't know if he should tell her the rest or not. It was pretty disturbing—and might be more so to her. But amid the change in his pocket, he felt the smooth surface of the bullet. It served as a reminder that you could come out of a shitstorm okay.

And in that moment, Merry caught him in her stare. "I'm better now. You keep going. I can see there's more."

Amara sat quietly through the whole thing. As Jason spoke about Daniel, about finding the foster records, Merry Mondy became more and more pale. She was quiet and unmoving, except for one hand that came up to clasp the locket his father had given her.

Jason told her about his dad's signature in the guest log. That it looked like he'd come to check on Daniel and been refused the chance to adopt him. He didn't say that his parents should have fought harder. That they should have demanded Daniel be re-diagnosed. His mother's pale face was already too much for him.

And when her voice came through, it was reedy. "I wanted him."

"I know, Mom." There were tears at the edges of his eyes for her. She didn't have the second child she wanted. It was made all the worse by the knowledge that the child had been there all along.

She whispered the next line through her tears. "Where is he now?"

"I don't know. He disappeared after he turned eighteen."

"Oh . . . my . . . God." Her hand clutched harder at the locket, and she sniffed.

Amara launched into nurse mode. "Mrs. Mondy, why don't we get you over to the recliner?" She was already standing next to his mother and Jason flanked her on the other side.

But Merry waved them off and stood on her own. Then she clutched at the locket again, said "Oh, my God." And passed out cold.

Jason caught her, thinking he shouldn't have told her all this. Not all at once. But she would have been mad if he hadn't.

He was laying her on the floor as he realized something was very wrong.

"Jason!" Amara's voice cut through the haze in his brain. "Call 9-1-1."

Her fingers were already leaving Merry's wrist and feeling for a pulse at the side of her neck. She shook her head.

Then she spoke again, louder. "Jason, I've got this, call 9-1-1."

This time fear and adrenaline drove him to the phone. He dialed and waited for the operator to pick up. As he did, he watched Amara pace off the placement of her hands and begin CPR. He wanted to yell at her to go faster, but he'd only counted two rings of the phone, so Amara was doing it right.

He was concerned about her breaking his mother's ribs. The woman was just over seventy, and though healthy, there was nothing that made up for being older.

On the third ring the emergency operator picked up and he started talking. He gave his name and the address, said he had a seventy-one-year-old female having what he thought was an MI.

Amara spouted some concerning information to him, but he relayed it. "No breath sounds, bilateral. No pulse. For approximately twenty-five seconds. CPR has been initiated."

He pushed the speaker button and set the phone on the floor where he dropped to his hands and knees and did the things his frantic mind told him to.

He slapped his mother's face, as gently as he could. "Come on, Mom! Wake up!" He knew she wasn't asleep.

He felt her wrist for a pulse and shook his head when Amara looked at him. Then he tried her neck with the same result.

Amara worked for hours it seemed. But she wouldn't let Jason take over. She told him to hold his mother's hand and keep talking to her. The operator began conveying instructions: how to find the sternum, to then move two finger widths down. When she started explaining how to stack your hands for proper CPR, Jason yelled at her.

"I told you we already started CPR. Get that god-damned ambulance here."

The operator's voice was far too calm. "It's already en route, sir. I just wanted to be sure that you're doing CPR properly."

He yelled again. "She's a fucking nurse practitioner with a PhD. She's doing it right. Just get me a fucking ambulance!"

A long forever later, Amara said, "Time?" but didn't break stride.

Jason didn't know. He didn't even know what she wanted. But the operator did.

"You've been on the line for two minutes and forty-five seconds. Which puts your estimate at three plus minutes. The EMTs will be there in less than thirty seconds."

Amara sent Jason out the front door to flag them down.

Though he saw the sirens and the precarious way the vehicle tilted at the turn, they came too slowly. He directed them onto the grass at the front of the house, then right through the front door.

They flooded in, three of them. Moved Amara back and took over in a cold, precise manner. Then they loaded his mother onto a stretcher—the only thing that had happened fast—and put her into the back of the ambulance.

He watched it race down the driveway, stone-still in his shock.

Amara asked him for his keys and proceeded to unplug the toaster and check the stove knobs. Then she led him out the front door and locked it behind them. After shuffling him into the passenger seat of his own car, she put it in reverse and said, "They're taking her to Huntsville Memorial."

He nodded absently. "She didn't have a pulse."

"No."

"What are her chances?"

"Not very good."

Chapter 20

Jason

They had stayed at his mother's house for three days. Numb to the world, Jason let Amara do everything. She made sure he ate, medicated him to make him sleep, answered his cell phone, and called in to the Chief to explain what had happened.

Jason overheard part of that conversation, but mostly he remembered the Chief saying, "Oh, you have got to be shitting me." Which wasn't something the Chief usually said.

He looked at his mother's funeral only as the next in a short string of increasingly harder funerals to attend. And even Bloomberg's funeral, which was easy by comparison, had been a gutfuck.

People asked to speak to him. Amara even tried to have a conversation with him more than once. But he didn't speak to anyone. He'd uttered maybe ten words in three days.

Though Amara had known his mother for barely twelve hours, he'd let her handle everything. She asked what funeral home to call, and he'd shrugged. She'd presented two local places, and he'd chosen the one with the nicer looking façade—he'd chosen by pointing, then refused to participate in any of the other funeral decisions.

The next day, they got a call from his mother's lawyer. Amara had found a copy of his mother's will and funeral plan in a file drawer, carefully labeled, and easily identifiable to anyone looking. He hadn't even thought to look. It hadn't occurred to him that his mother had planned this out.

There had even been a letter to him, which Amara had handed over. He figured she'd read it, since it was simply stapled to the top of the stack, more like a cover sheet than anything else. But he'd sat in the old upholstered wing-back chair and stared sightlessly into the front yard with the paper dangling from his fingers. It wasn't until the letter slipped from his grasp and made a soft scratching noise as it hit the floor that he finally gave it his attention and read it.

His mother started by saying that if he had other plans for her, that would be fine, but that she had done this because she didn't think he would have the wherewithal to deal with funeral arrangements in the event of her death. She didn't want him to have to think about what to dress her in, or where to take her body, if he didn't want to.

She had composed a checklist for him, exactly where to go and who to ask for. A funeral home, a service, a plot, everything had been paid. All he had to do was show up and mourn.

Jason wasn't certain he was capable of either.

Amara found the lawyer and got him out to read the will. It was almost as simple as it could be. His mother had left a chunk of money to a charity that helped place foster children with adoptive families. It was clear from the accompanying letter that she and his father had given to this charity for years. And that was it. Though there were recommendations—she preferred any books he didn't want to go to the local library, her clothing to Goodwill—everything else went to Jason.

With the actual legal copy of the will was a sealed letter to Jason. He hadn't opened it yet. Wasn't sure when or if he'd be able to.

Though he didn't speak, and though he lost time staring out the windows, Amara still treated him like a person. He wondered why she wasn't grunting and pointing at him—communicating with the same lack of concern or caring that he did. But she spoke to him as she always did, asked him questions as though he would answer. It took him two days to wonder if it was a nursing technique.

Though it was casual, she found him every few hours, needing to talk to him. He was becoming convinced that she was checking in, that—purpose or no purpose—she would be there, starting a conversation with him every so often like clockwork.

"The funeral is this afternoon." She stood in front of him, but all that was in his unmoving vision were bare feet with bright pink toenails.

Then he smelled something and looked a little higher. She held a pan and a spatula. His brain registered that he should like the smell, but it got no further than fact, he felt nothing.

She spoke again as though he were part of the conversation. "It's time to sit down and eat." And her feet walked away.

Amara expected him to be at the table in a moment. He would have to overcome an incredible inertia to get out of the chair, but he would do it. For all that he was bigger than she was, all that he should be able to overpower her and stay where he was, refuse her insistence that he go about at least some of the daily tasks of living, he couldn't. She was an immovable force. It was simply easier to rise from the chair and sit at the table. So he did.

He had just seated himself when a plate appeared in front of him with a thick sandwich of pulled pork already heated and smothered in barbecue sauce. It was accompanied by green broccoli dripping with butter and two horse-pill-sized vitamins. Leave it to a nurse to serve him vitamins with his lunch.

At least, he assumed they were vitamins. The other option was Vicodin, but he was pretty sure Vicodin was white. These were coated and almost creamy in color. He would ask, but he had no voice, and his desire to know exactly what the pills were rated about a 0.1 on a scale of 10. So he took a swig of the ice water and downed the vitamins first. The near-freezing water chilled his esophagus and cramped his stomach. So he stayed very still for a moment and ignored it.

When Amara sat down and joined him, he noticed her sandwich wasn't smothered in sauce, and her broccoli was bare of butter. She was trying to put calories in him, he could tell. Or maybe trying to make it taste better so he would eat it. The problem wasn't that he needed it to taste better, he just needed it to *taste*. And nothing did.

He shoved the sandwich in his mouth and took a bite. Chewing was methodical and necessary; spitting it out was simply too much trouble.

"I have a dress for your mother's funeral." Amara's voice cut through the noise in his head.

He nodded. She hadn't packed it, certainly. Had she run home? Purchased a new one? But again his desire to know was far outweighed by the need to not break the cocoon he was in.

"I went out yesterday and got it." She ate her own sandwich without gusto, but with human motions that he lacked.

Jason took another bite. And another and another until he'd made it through half of his food and was unable to go any further. He wanted to thank her for the meal. He'd done nothing since returning home from the hospital. But he couldn't make his mouth work to say 'thank you.'

For a moment he sat there and wondered if this was how Daniel had felt—empty inside and having nothing to say. He couldn't help but think that Daniel had felt as alone as he did now, as though he'd been dropped into a foreign place. Jason couldn't imagine going through this at age four—how frightened his brother must have been, knowing things were wrong but not being old enough to fend for himself. Jason, at least, was not at the mercy of strangers. His mother's death had not been violent, though it had still been scary.

The lump that grew in his throat threatened to cut off his air, so he simply quit thinking about Daniel and turned his attention back to the gray void that had filled most of his time since he'd arrived at the hospital and been told his mother was already gone.

Fighting the extreme gravity that was keeping him in his seat, he stood and carried his plate into the kitchen. Going to the sink was new. Even yesterday, he'd sat at the table and stared at the food he had stopped eating until Amara had taken it away. Today, he cleared his place. But had no idea what to do with the leftovers.

He imagined he could look down and see a dog. A dog would love half a thick pork sandwich and maybe even the broccoli. A dog would love *him*.

He didn't realize that he was standing at the sink, crying, until he felt the hand on his back. He suspected that, even though she couldn't see his face, Amara knew exactly what he was doing. Luckily, when she spoke she didn't say anything about his tears.

"She was gone before we got her to the floor. No pain, no worries. And—despite what we had been talking about—she was happy. She told me earlier in the evening that she was glad you were looking for Daniel. And that she was glad you'd gotten rid of Kelly."

Just when he'd had enough and was holding himself back from turning around and knocking her arm away so she wouldn't touch him, Amara changed direction. "You need to get in the shower. Then we'll get dressed and head to the funeral home."

Without nodding, he turned and headed up the stairs. He showered by rote and hoped that when he was finished he was actually clean rather than just wet. He emerged to find a suit laid out on his bed. Upon closer inspection, it turned out to be his. Amara had gone home and retrieved it from his closet. There was a shirt, tie, dark socks, shoes. Again he wanted to find the voice to say "thank you," but it just wasn't there.

He rode in a chauffeured car to the funeral; it picked the two of them up at the front of the house and allowed him to not think at all. He stayed stoic through the drive, numb and empty.

It wasn't until he stood in the church and saw all of A-Shift and most of C begin to file in that he understood. He wasn't numb because he was empty. He was numb because the dam was necessary to hold everything back. Sitting in the front row of the church, listening to the minister speak of Merry's good works and kind soul, it threatened to break.

He squeezed Amara's hand tight enough to break bones and held back the apology he wanted to whisper, because who knew what would come out with it. His uncle Jenner sat beyond Amara with his wife but not their children. Jason had known Jenner since his folks had adopted him, but he'd never known the man well. Merry's brother had never been communicative, though Jason remembered his mother reaching out several times each year and keeping the lines open. But he was the only family that showed for the service.

When the funeral was over, people filed out, some hugged him and wanted him to say something soothing to them. Sometimes he managed a murmur, but it was Amara who supplied actual words.

But the hugs people forced on him required that he let go of his roommate. Without that contact, he was lost, a stick in class-five rapids. He blindly embraced people he didn't know. Nodded as they told him how much they loved his mother.

Clark Jernigan had come. So had Rob Castor, some wildly beautiful woman on his arm. English was there as well. They all told him they had his back and proceeded to exit through the large ornate doors at the back of the church. Without warning, Jason was pulled into a tight embrace by Chief Adler, who gruffly spoke near his ear. "You still have a big family. Remember that."

Alex said something much the same. Then, sensing the dark depths of his friend's mood, he turned, smiling, and pointed. "Look, Wanstall is a girl."

Sure enough, Missy was in a dress and heels, her long hair down around her shoulders and hanging nearly to her waist—a fact that seemed to surprise everyone. Though her hair had been up, they'd seen her in a dress twice in the past month, and Jason hated thinking about why.

One by one, each of his fellow firefighters hugged him or shook his hand and headed out the back of the church. Jason followed, needing air, needing the walls and the polished wood and Jesus to all stop reminding him why he was there. As he finally exited the building himself, he saw his co-workers pile into several cars and head back to Southfield.

It took thirty minutes to clear the church, to listen to platitudes and heartfelt comments alike. His uncle Jenner only shook his hand, though his aunt took him in a big hug and cried for him. But then they left and Jason knew he might never see them again.

They piled into the back of the rented car, and he stayed quiet on the way home. It was four p.m. by the time he changed back into jeans and a long-sleeved shirt and was headed out the door. But Amara caught him.

It was the first time he'd driven anywhere since his mother had died.

"Where are you headed?"

He shook his head, all he could do.

"Can I come?"

He looked her up and down. She'd changed into jeans and sneakers, too. She wore a nice sweater and her hair was still up, she still had on the makeup she'd worn. Her face looked like a portrait of herself—her skin too flawless, her mouth too well defined. But he nodded.

She didn't run back inside, didn't make him wait, just slid into the passenger side and never asked for the keys or asked to drive. She didn't ask where they were going, but when they pulled up in front of the Huntsville Animal Shelter, she put her hand on his arm. "Cat?"

He shook his head, though a cat would be a better idea. A cat would be okay for twenty-four hours without him. But he wanted a dog. He needed a dog.

Her hand stayed where it was and they stayed in the car, Amara looking at him, Jason looking straight ahead at the shelter. "It's a living creature. This shouldn't be decided at a time like this."

He shook his head. He'd been thinking about this for a long time. Besides, no one else loved him now that his mother was gone. He needed to take care of something, or else he might simply meld into the wingback chair that looked out over the street. "Okay. I'll be glad to take care of him while you're at work."

He turned to her. Jason had known she would. Amara would always step up, and she would fall in love with the dog, he knew that, too. It wouldn't be too much of a burden to be responsible for it one day out of three. He gave her a smile that was small, but as big as he could make it.

Surprisingly, she didn't smile back. "But that only works for three more weeks. After that, you'll have to find something else. At least you have a little while to come up with something."

Like a punch in the gut, it knocked the wind out of him, surprising him with its ferocity.

He'd forgotten.

The lease was up in three weeks. And Amara was moving out. So was he. He needed to find a new place, put down a deposit and go about the business of moving. Maybe Alex and Leo would dog-sit. He told himself it would be okay. So he pocketed the keys and climbed out of the car.

They were at door before Amara said, "You'll have to speak to them to get the dog."

∧ ∧ ∧ ∧ ∧

He let Amara drive his car back to Southfield while he held his dog on his lap. The shelter had named him Banner—after Dr. Banner, who was The Hulk. The dog had been found in a creek covered in green goo and very angry. Jason had *almost* laughed at the story and so he kept the name.

Banner was about four months old, still playful, but already housebroken. Jason didn't think he could in good conscience leave a small puppy and random floor puddles with Amara or the next caretaker. Plus, someone else would adopt the little puppies. Banner needed a home. And so did Jason.

Amara had graciously shopped with him and the puppy to get a proper collar, leash, food, bed, all the many things a dog needed. She hadn't commented that—though his words were few—he was speaking again.

To an extent it made him feel childish, but since he was still upright despite the gaping hole in him, he didn't care. And Banner loved him, which was exactly what he needed.

He'd gone to work the next day, reluctant to leave the dog behind, but knowing he had to get back to his usual life. Chief had called him into the front office as soon as he spotted Jason at the table at seven-thirty in the morning.

"You need to go home."

On the contrary. "I need to work."

Adler had sighed, a great big, sad sigh. "I know you do, but your head isn't in the game yet. And that's dangerous to the others . . . no matter how much you want, or *need*, to work, I can't let one person endanger another."

Jason had fought back the only way he knew how. He stood with his hands behind his back, legs slightly apart in a near-military stance. "I'm ready, sir."

"No, you're not."

Most of the time he liked that Adler didn't pull any punches but not right then.

In the end, he had convinced the Chief to give him a little rope, and he'd been commanded not to hang himself with it. Adler had told him he could stay for shift, but would only go on low-level runs, not on anything with actual flames or anything that could turn ugly. And Jason had relented; it was the best offer he was going to get. So he set about getting his head back in the game.

He'd done well until everyone started going to bed.

There was something in the air. He could tell they were trying to be normal around him, but none of them were good enough actors to nail it. While he was fairly certain they didn't know what Chief had told him, it appeared they felt the same way. To be fair, they were stuck, too. No one quite trusted him in a crisis, everyone wanted to say the right thing, and anything might set him off at any given minute.

So bit by bit the others wandered off to bed. Jason stayed up for the nightly romantic comedy, reading a thriller through most of it, barely noticing when Wanstall and Nagy wandered out halfway through.

Donlan and Grimsby, who were usually up the latest, were clearly at a loss for the right thing to say. Grimsby just mumbled that he was headed to bed and gave a curt wave as he walked out of the room. But Donlan tried.

"I'm sorry man. You've had a real short stick here lately."

Jason nodded. It would be foolish to deny what was patently true. But his lack of conversation didn't stop Donlan.

"I'm really sorry for your loss, man. Don't tell the others, but I'd be curled in a ball on the floor, sobbing like a baby if something happened to my mom." He reached out and laid a heavy hand on Jason's shoulder. "I know she wasn't even your real mother."

Jason bunched his hand into a fist and—in order to keep from socking Donlan and starting the first fistfight in the house in over five years—shoved it deep into his pocket. He encountered loose change for the soda machine and that stupid bullet. Shit was bad when Donlan was trying to be sensitive.

Though his jaw was clenched tight, Jason managed to force out a "Thank you, man."

Finally, it was just Jason and the TV, and the TV was more nuisance than comfort. The problem was, he was still afraid to go to sleep. The one place he had relied on—his mother's house—had become another memory that kept him awake. He didn't remember sleeping, but that didn't matter. When shift change was over he got to drive home and count his first day back.

He'd been planning to walk in the door, beeline for his bed, and pass out. But he heard Banner even before he had the lock undone, the low but menacing bark a clear indicator that someone was approaching. Jason wondered when he was going to get turned in to the super for having a dog. When he opened the door, he didn't care.

The dog was so excited to see him that he almost couldn't get into the apartment. Banner jumped. He wagged his tail. He licked. And Jason got down on his knees and let him.

"You two are cute." The voice came from over the back of the couch. Amara looked like her old self—yoga gear, curls perched precariously on top of her head, highlighter in hand. "He's been fed, and I walked him an hour ago."

Jason extracted himself from the field of dog enough to say, "You didn't have to. I would have done it."

"No worries." She slid back down into the deep couch while Jason hung up his jacket. He couldn't see her, but he didn't have to. She'd be there with papers stacked in her lap, working on whichever one was on top. There would be other piles around her on the couch and the floor, though with Banner now she wouldn't do that.

Her voice came again. "I just made some scrambled eggs, so I made extra for you. You'll have to nuke them and make your own toast though."

And somehow she had done what none of the guys at the station had been able to do. She had treated him as though he were normal. Even though he wasn't. He hadn't seen the right side of normal since he'd forced down two bites of the eggs his mother had made him, before telling her what he'd learned about Daniel. Though he'd spent twenty-four hours putting up his best front, he didn't do that with Amara. There was no point; he had nothing to prove to her. But she let him catch a whiff of the eggs and head into the kitchen to make his own toast. And it was clear that "making extra for him" was about the equivalent of tripling the batch she made for herself. But she didn't let it seem like a big deal.

Instead of hitting the table, he came and sat on the arm of the couch, the only place left now that the floor was no longer an option for papers. "Did you get any feedback from your committee?"

"Yeah." The word was a little drawn out and he waited. "It wasn't that I was brilliant and all I had to do was show up for my defense. That's for sure. But it wasn't scathing or horrible either. So, back to the drawing board."

"Did you miss any deadlines because of . . . last week?" It suddenly occurred to him that he didn't know if she'd even checked her email to see about the response from her team while they'd been in Madison, he'd been so far inside his own head.

But she laughed. A big, loud laugh. "There are no real deadlines here yet. I'm beyond ahead of schedule for most students. But I just don't want to draw it out any longer than I have to. Unlike a lot of other PhD students, I have a great pay grade waiting for me. I don't want to be a perpetual student. So, no, it's not possible for me to have missed anything last week. I'm good."

She smiled and picked up the highlighter again, then a pen, then the highlighter. His eggs were almost gone anyway, and he ate the last few bites while heading to the kitchen sink.

He stood there and looked down at Banner, waiting patiently for scraps—scraps that Jason had just eaten. He finally got a dog, and the first thing he did was eat everything on his plate. But the soft spot in his heart got the better of him, and he made another piece of toast and split it with Banner.

Then he headed into his room, telling Amara goodnight as he went. He brushed his teeth, stripped and changed out his old underwear for clean ones, pulled the blackout shades, and was ready to fall face-first, finally, into bed. But Banner whined.

"Here, boy." He spent five minutes coaxing the dog into his bed and wondering if dogs could sleep all day.

Jason curled up into the covers and was pulled under, lulled by the dark and the even breathing of the dog. But he didn't stay there for long.

He popped awake, thinking it was a few minutes later and was surprised to find out that his alarm clock thought it was noon. But he laid back into the pillows, lulled by sheer exhaustion and a desire to not wake the dog.

Later, he heard Amara open the bedroom door and whisper, "Come here, boy. Good boy." But as he was still halfway asleep, it took a moment to realize she was talking to the dog. By the time he opened his mouth to say thank you, the door was already closed again, the dog and girl gone, and he was once again mostly asleep.

He stayed that way, dozing in and out of a state that wasn't restful but wasn't anywhere near awake. His body felt like lead and occasionally he was reminded of reality. He relived Bloomberg asking him about cracking noises. He saw Connelly stare up at him, burned but speaking.

"Run." The voice wasn't Connelly's but a rough gravelly sound that barely resembled language. "Get out. Get out!"

Yelling clearly hurt the burned man, but in his mind Jason knew it was a dream, that Connelly was gone, and that—as bad as it had been—it hadn't been as horrible as this. With no warning, the scene changed and his mother hugged him, fed him dinner, and told him he'd find peace again. Even though he'd lost his friends, even though he was adrift with all the things he'd learned about Daniel, about Alcia Mallory, and the fire that had orphaned him, he would be okay. She smiled at him and in dulcet tones told him, "You will always have me."

But he didn't.

His cogent brain realized that she was gone, and so he fought to run after her, to hold on to this one last piece of her that he had. This last visit, where he could see her, smell her perfume and the food she had made for him. He could feel her hand on his face, and for the first time in his life it struck him that her hand was so soft because she was old. She'd turned seventy and then seventy-one, she'd become elderly and he hadn't even noticed.

Though she smiled and tried to feed him more, he couldn't ever reach her. Though he called out to her and she spoke in turn, she didn't communicate—as if they were each having their own side of two separate conversations.

"I don't think I'll be back, Jason Mallory. But you have Daniel now. Just eat your eggs and you'll be fine."

But he didn't have Daniel and didn't want to eat his eggs. He couldn't get a grasp on her, and as he fought his way through the dense haze that separated them he came closer and closer to a surface where the reality was that she no longer existed.

"Jason. You're going to be okay."

Her voice changed. It became deeper, huskier, soothing in a way that disturbed him all the more because he didn't want to be soothed, he just needed to hold on to the only anchor he'd ever had.

Making a desperate dive, he jumped for her, and got something—a brush of soft skin, a fistful of fabric—and nothing that he needed. Blind with fear, he leaped again, but water or haze held him back and though he touched her one last time, she disappeared as hands grabbed his arms and pulled him forcefully from sleep.

"Jason, stop. Stop."

His eyes pried themselves open in the dim light, even though doing so was an admission that all was not well. He stopped fighting as he realized there was nothing left to fight for. But the hands held him and moved him back and forth.

"Jason, look at me. Jason."

Amara wasn't big enough to shake him, but she seemed to be trying, and he would have laughed at her if he hadn't been so soulless and empty. Shoving clumsily at her hands, he pulled himself free of her grip and said, "I'm good." Only it came out whispered and slurred.

"No, you're not. You're not sleeping well. You're grieving, Jason."

Only as he began to process the words, did he feel himself trying to fall back asleep, as though he could exit this world so easily, just tap out and be released from life.

Amara wouldn't let him. "Look at me. You need some water, but I don't want you to fall back to sleep. You should wake up, try to get some distance from the nightmare." She laid one soft, cool hand against his cheek. "Stay here. Stay with me."

She was trying to force him to look at her.

"No."

"Jason."

He didn't want to fight her, didn't want to hurt her, but he also didn't want to lose the fight. Though she wasn't big enough to take him on any other day, today she would win.

"I'm going to get you a glass of water."

"No." This time his hand reached out and grasped her, his fingers reaching almost all the way around her upper arm. He whispered what he wished was true. "Banner loves me."

"Yes, he does." She quit trying to pull away.

"And no one else does."

"That's not true. You just don't know who yet. Or you do, but you won't let them love you because you're hurt. I've been there." She settled in beside him, ignoring the fact that he still held onto her as though she were the anchor he needed. "You feel alone, like you can't connect to anyone or anything."

He nodded, wondering how she could get it so right, when no one else did.

"You think you'll never have stability again. And maybe yours is worse than mine was because you've already been through it once before . . ."

She kept talking, but her words disappeared into the roar in his head. Memories burst clear in his skull. Arriving at the emergency foster home the night after the fire. The older couple he'd lived with for several weeks before his parents found him.

He had never forgotten the old memories, but they had faded with time, though they were now suddenly fresh. He remembered being small and petrified. Having no idea what each day would bring. Not knowing where he would go to school or even if he would. He remembered curling in a ball on the strange bed and crying every night. No one had come to hold him.

As an adult he could look back and wonder if the emergency relief foster family was simply too used to children crying every night to even make the effort to comfort them. That thought—that he had been lost before and had come full circle to the worst part of his life—was what finally cracked the dam.

Curling into a tight ball there on his bed, he broke.

^   ^   ^   ^   ^

He came awake to contradictions. The incessant pounding noise was discordant to the warmth and comfort he was curled into. He breathed deeply, trying to find a reason to pull himself out of the heaven he had found and heard the sigh his lungs issued.

Only it wasn't his.

The voice was soft and came with a warm breath at his neck. Gentle arms were wound round him and anchored him to the earth in exactly the way he had so needed.

The voice came again, "The door."

This time he recognized it as Amara's. With that understanding, the warmth and glow quickly receded to be replaced by another cold hole in him.

What had he done?

As he shifted in his attempt to wake, he felt his skin against hers and it became startlingly clear that they were naked. As he moved, he was flooded with memories of letting everything out last night. Of crying in a ball until he had a headache and a hoarse voice. Then, to his shame, he remembered kissing Amara.

And it had been he who had grabbed her. Searching for something good, he had kissed her. She had gently tried to extract herself from his grasp several times before giving in and giving over.

Now as Banner barked, he bolted from the bed, grabbing boxers and jeans from the closet even as he headed toward the front door where the pounding noises continued. He hopped into his clothing, yelling that he was coming and feeling supremely grateful to whoever was at the door for giving him an excuse to run from the soft, naked woman in his bed. She'd been coming awake alongside him; he had simply acted faster and run first.

Having just buttoned his jeans, he popped the locks on the door and pulled it open with no concern for who he might find on the other side.

It turned out Clark was his salvation.

"Hey, Jason," The reporter stepped into the apartment though Jason hadn't really invited him. "You had me worried. You weren't answering your phone."

Jason frowned and for the first time wondered what he must look like, if maybe Clark was more worried now that he'd laid eyes on him. "I'm a firefighter. I work odd hours and sometimes I sleep a whole day away."

Clark shook his head, "You haven't answered since mid-afternoon Thursday. I was getting worried. Chief said you left when shift ended yesterday."

Jason had to acknowledge that was concerning. "Yeah, well I'm here."

But Clark didn't take the hint and leave. His eyes searched the room. "I wanted to ask if you had gotten the pictures from the Morales family yet. It's been a while."

"No, they haven't come yet." He still stood in the entryway, but none of it seemed to sink in to Clark's brain.

"They came yesterday while you were asleep." Amara had appeared in the doorway to his bedroom. He noticed her yoga gear from yesterday morning, but any fool could recognize her mussed state and the fact that she had not come from her own bedroom but his.

Though he'd missed everything else, Clark caught this and sent Jason a look. Jason didn't change his expression at all, but inside he groaned. This was becoming a clusterfuck.

Clark smiled at Amara. "Did you look at them yet?"

She shook her head. "I thought Jason should first."

"Do you want to check them out now?" He looked a little overbright, and Jason didn't like the idea that Clark was excited about the development with Amara, for something that—in Jason's book—wasn't good.

He'd had enough. "It's not a good time. Maybe another day." He would be back at work tomorrow; hopefully he'd make it through without sleeping the day away, crying and fucking his roommate. *Shit.* "I'm sorry, I'm still not ready to deal with any of this. I have enough on my plate."

He'd meant dealing with his mother's death, and something must have shown on his face, because Clark read him correctly. "You should be glad you had her for as long as you did."

"What?" He was taken aback at the overly simplistic solution.

"You're lucky you had her." It was simple and forward, but in light of everything he was thinking about—the pictures, Daniel, Clark, and Amara standing behind him and what the hell he was going to say to her—it grated on his nerves that Clark felt he could or should say that.

"I *am* grateful for her. But you don't know anything about it."

"You didn't kill her, Jason. She was seventy-one. She was old. Heart attacks are common in women her age. It wasn't you."

By the time he got to the last part, Jason was in a full rage. How did Clark even know what had happened? He turned to Amara and glared at her for a moment. She had been the only other person there when his mother had died—had she been telling everyone exactly what had happened?

Breathing heavily, he turned back to Clark, his temper barely in check. "You have no idea what you're talking about—"

Clark pushed back, just as mad. "I know exactly what I'm talking about. You lost her, but she was old. You had her for a long time and you're acting like an ungrateful bastard. I would have given anything to have had her."

Jason would have pulled back and punched him, but Clark was stalking across the room, still ranting. He started shoving his way through the mail until he ripped at a manila envelope that he found.

As he turned, Jason saw that Clark's face was red with his own rage. "You're an idiot, Jason. You can't see what's right in front of you. All this time, I've been *right here!*"

He yanked at the papers in the envelope, throwing them at Jason one by one.

Mad again, Jason yelled. "What the fuck are you doing?"

Clark stalked right up to him, stepping over and on the pictures he'd thrown. He slapped the brown envelope against Jason's chest, his voice shaking, "You walked away from all of it. And you're one lucky bastard, you got everything. You never appreciated it and you can't see what's right in front of you. You're a fucking moron."

Then he walked out of the apartment, slamming the door behind him.

Shaken as much by his own rage as by the other man's, Jason's training took over and his eyes swept the scene to be sure that everyone was all right.

Amara stood stunned in the doorway to his bedroom, Banner tucked behind her legs as though he could hide there.

Determining they were okay, Jason lifted his hand to where he'd reflexively grabbed the envelope Clark had smacked him with. The neat script in the return address was torn, but clearly read "Mrs. Lisa Morales."

Frowning, Jason looked down at the floor. The pictures were of a blonde kid, some with other kids, some random shots around what must be the Morales house. But a five-by-seven that looked like a high school portrait caught his attention, and Jason reached down to pick it up.

Though the hair color was completely different, the photo was still instantly identifiable as Clark.

Southfield Fire Station #2

Shift	A	
	O'Casey	Captain
Engine 2	Wanstall	Lieutenant
	Grimsby	FF1 / EMT
Engine 5	Standard	Engineer
	West	FF2
	Nagy	FF1 / EMT
Rescue 3	Donlan	Engineer/Paramedic
	Mondy	FF2 / EMT

Chapter 21

Missy kept a wary eye on Jason. The others were still stepping lightly around him—though they were all going through a lot, Mondy had caught the worst of it. He had watched as Bloomberg died. In the same day, he'd lost his personal friend Connelly, and now his mother. The way Missy had heard it, the woman had collapsed practically in his arms and was gone before she hit the floor.

So Mondy had every reason to be on edge, which he had been last shift, but even so something was different today.

As far as she knew—and she'd asked everyone, including Chief—none of them had talked to Mondy since last shift. So no one had any real idea why he had changed from "partially-shut-down" to "paranoid." Missy was carrying on a raging internal debate about whether to leave him alone or just corner him in the back room and ask point blank what the hell was going on.

The big thing in favor of shaking him down was that if Jason had a legit reason to be paranoid, they all needed to know so they could stay safe, too. And if he didn't, then they all needed to know so they could stay safe from him.

But she'd asked Donlan how Mondy was after the EMS run they had done that morning. Donlan said he was alert, to the point and still not his usual self. But Donlan had brushed it off in that way that she'd found to be typically male. As though, since Jason had not spontaneously combusted on the run, everything must be fine.

Missy didn't think it was.

But no one agreed with her. Everyone was focused on the fact that today was the last day Gold Standard EMS operated in town.

There were two shiny new ambulances in each of the three fire stations. All of the firefighters had three new shirts that read "Southfield Emergency Services." The new patches depicted fire and rescue and EMS separately.

The EMT guys had just graduated their class. Advanced EMTs would be out in two days, and Mondy, Baxter, Railles and Weingarten would be Paramedic ranked by next week. Missy was deeply grateful that she hadn't had to change what she was doing to keep her job. She had nothing against EMS runs, but what she wanted to do was fight fires. Getting EMT training would have slowed down her track and she wasn't interested in that. She would have left Southfield FD if she'd been forced to do more, even though she knew other houses wouldn't be like this one. There weren't that many Adlers out there. But it hadn't happened. She could stay here and keep climbing the ladder she wanted to climb. The only thing bothering her about the job was Jason. And his connection with Chief and that odd "boys club" that occasionally met at the fire station.

She tried to let it go and focused on grilling a sandwich she had brought with her. Turning on the stove and starting to cook was considered a good way to start a fire. Like magic, using the stove in Fire Station #2 would create a fire on Woodland Street, which in turn would set off the bell before she could eat the sandwich. It was just a law of the universe.

Missy flipped the sandwich and waited for a call. She shook her head as Chief walked into the break room and gathered them all up; it figured. But it turned out not to be what she expected.

He rubbed his hands together. "Okay, just a reminder . . . Saturday."

Some of them held back groans, but Adler didn't let that stop him.

"Saturday is the barbecue. I want you all here at nine a.m. Please bring your families. Wear the new T-shirts. B-Shift will be in uniform but the rest of you should be in pants or jeans."

There were various reactions. They all knew the drill by now: play nice, make good with the community, let the kids play on the fire trucks. Don't let Gold Standard act as if they had been run out of town. Adler reiterated that. "I want you all to be prepared if there's any protesting."

"You heard anything, Chief?" Donlan piped up from where he stood against the wall.

"Nope. And if any of you do, I want you to tell me. We are now the only game in town and we need to be seen in the best light possible."

There were a few sighs at that, but that was about it, so Chief continued. "Do you want the good news?"

There were audible yeses from the crowd.

"Delta Cross and the city worked out the budget. Though it is small, everyone will get a pay bump—"

He had to stop and wait for the cheering to die down. As he scanned the room only Mondy didn't appear to be celebrating. He stayed still, a flat smile on his mouth the only concession to good news. Adler didn't comment on it.

"And those of you who increased your EMS or even your firefighting ranks will also see raises from those advances."

Another round of cheering went up. "The overall bump goes into effect tomorrow and any change of status will see that raise when it becomes official, so our new EMT, Grimsby, will be official as of today's shift. West will see his Advanced EMT bump on Sunday with the unit raise, and the Paramedics hit on Wednesday—provided you pass your certification." He pointed at Mondy.

But Jason only gave a slight nod.

There were a few questions and he answered them easily. But Mondy worried him. After everyone had wandered back to where they had been hanging out, he pulled Mondy into his office for a chat.

"You're still not quite in there. You're not worried about passing your Paramedic test, are you?"

Jason shook his head.

"Is this about your mother?" Normally he wouldn't have said anything so blunt, so lacking in nice words to buffer it. But any time one of his men could be a danger to the others he needed to know.

The firefighter didn't even look at him. "Nah. Some other shit fell into my life. I'm sorry if I'm not dealing with it better. I should be used to it by now."

Adler sat back, his eyes wide as that statement hit him. Though he was no shrink, he'd seen one several times as course of duty. Since he'd achieved the rank of captain, part of his training had covered how to talk to his men. He'd asked about the test wrong. The "you aren't, are you?" question put the person answering in a difficult spot to say "yes, actually I am."

But that didn't sound like the issue here; it was more that Jason sounded like he'd resigned himself to living in the shitstorm he'd been facing lately. Adler had no idea what to do about it, so he sent out the best feeler he could. "Do you want to talk about it?"

The "no" he got back wasn't a surprise. Mondy wasn't a talker. It had been surprising that he'd opened up about getting rescued from the Pelias fire; it wasn't surprising that it had taken him seven years to do it.

Adler had started to ask more when Jason put his palms down on his knees and pushed himself to standing. "I know it doesn't look like it, but my head's in the game, Chief—despite the fact that shit rolls downhill and I seem to have moved into the valley."

Adler didn't stop him from leaving. If he had, it would only have created a big stink. And if your Chief was questioning you, then so did everyone else on shift. Things were probably safer with Mondy walking out and pretending things were some facsimile of fine.

The phone rang then and he picked it up.

The last of the information coming in made him steel his own heart and pray that he'd made the right decision about Mondy when the bell went off.

∧ ∧ ∧ ∧ ∧

Donlan climbed down from Rescue 1 and cracked his back. Had this happened any day after today, they wouldn't have put the kids into the back of the white and orange Gold Standard ambulances. They would have popped the cherry on the new SFD ones at the back of the bay.

Tomorrow, when they handed off the house to B-Shift, they would change the parking pattern for the trucks. Chief had set Mondy on the redesign of the layout, and Mondy had polled them all on what had to be at the easiest access. When they came back Saturday, the extension ladder truck would be nearly stuck in the middle of the bay—it came out so infrequently in the small town that they often joked that rather than Ladder 6 it should be called Christmas 1.

But today, they had taken the two Rescues and an Engine and pulled thirty-eight screaming elementary school children from a bus that had gone over the edge of a road. Donlan shuddered. His kids were older, but they still rode the school bus. This one had gone through the guard rail as though it were made of paper. It had been several old growth trees that happened to be right in the path of the bus that had saved the children and the driver. Nothing manmade had done the trick. The road had failed— crumbling under the weight of the bus at the edge. The brakes on the bus simply hadn't been able to stop it. The guard-rail had been useless, and the bus had gone nose down over the edge.

So Donlan took a moment to thank his Maker for sturdy trees. And Nylon webbing.

As much as he hated the screaming kids and the need to lower each other through the emergency exit to pull the kids up, he'd gotten a rush from the whole thing. Add the adrenaline to the hours on site and the megamug of coffee he'd decided to down that morning and he had to pee like a racehorse.

Figuring that pissing down the drain in the bay was not okay in "Abalama" and that no one wanted to mop up after him anyway, he headed inside before taking care of the gear. It *was* taking care of the gear to *not* piss on it.

It wasn't until he came out that he saw the man sitting on the couch in the break room.

Donlan stopped cold, his back straightening and the adrenaline speeding again through his already wiped system. "Who are you?"

Then, before the other man could stand or even answer, Donlan added. "Why do I know you?"

At least he felt marginally better that maybe he had seen this person before. Besides, in the two seconds it had taken him to ask, he had made an assessment. The man was dressed in khakis and a button-down white shirt. It was open at the collar, no tie, but pressed and clean. He didn't look like a drug addict, and Donlan couldn't see a gun or even a place to hide one. Also, a man would have to be an idiot to break into a fire station for several reasons. Fire men were alphas; they would kick your drug-crazed ass into the ground and call themselves heroes while doing it. Also, if you wanted money you were pissing in the wind if you were trying to find it at a fire station.

"Um" was all that the other man offered, though he did look tentative and a little unsure what to do now that he'd been caught here.

Ryan Donlan crossed his arms. It was a show of confidence, an "I'm so very not afraid of you that I don't even need my hands free" bold move. But what did he have to fear from Button-Down? He wasn't afraid of men. He'd faced his own demons long ago—that his wife would have to get her own job if she wanted to live in the manner to which she wanted to become accustomed. Later, he'd learned to deal with the fact that she out-earned him. So the expensive shirt and slight shuffling of feet only made Donlan stand a little straighter, frown a little more.

"I'm Clark Jernigan. I'm . . ."

Donlan tipped his head to the other side and waited. It was as though Jernigan didn't know what he was. Maybe he *was* on drugs. "Go on."

"I'm here to see Jason Mondy."

Again he sounded unsure of himself. Something in his voice made Donlan think maybe he'd gone a little too far with the power stance. Jernigan sounded as though he expected to be beaten up just for being here.

Still, the entire shift was right outside and even Missy could take this guy. So Donlan gave out information he might not have otherwise. "He just came back with the truck. Should I tell him you're here?"

"Ummmm. Maybe I should just wait here."

Donlan gave a meaningful look around the room, one that said he was cataloging every item and if any were missing he would make the replacement from Jernigan's teeth. "Suit yourself."

He headed back out to the bay for cleanup and kept his mouth shut around Mondy. It wasn't hard to do. Mondy—who was usually middle-of-the-road for chatting—had apparently taken some vow of silence. He'd said maybe three words in the last two shifts.

They all headed in for showers later, and the group stopped dead as Jason saw the man still in the same position on the couch and growled, "What the fuck are you doing here?"

Jernigan stood, wiping his hands on his pants, clearly nervous. "I wanted to apologize."

A-Shift apparently hadn't been able to take in Jernigan's presence, stifle surprise at Jason's sudden anger and walk at the same time. They must have made noise as they all crashed into each other. Adler came in through the hallway, looking to see what was making the commotion. Though his men usually turned to him as he entered, treated him with the respect of his rank, no one moved. Everyone was too entranced by the beginnings of the whopper argument to do anything like pay attention to the Chief.

Adler stepped forward. "Jernigan? Did you learn something new?"

Mondy's eyes—still focused on the reporter—narrowed. No one probably realized it but they all swayed back just a touch at the menace in his eyes, Adler included. Only Jernigan stood his ground.

The stone coldness of Mondy's glare had everyone on edge. They expected that from Donlan, there were the occasional outbursts of temper from Grimbsy. Wanstall would simmer. But Mondy generally just said his piece and went back to business as usual. He hated the people who perpetrated the crimes they sometimes saw the after-effects of, but this icy throw down was new. Even his voice lacked any inflection or warmth, "Yes, *Jernigan* did."

There was something in the way he said the name, and the way the reporter colored and looked as though he'd been hit. Most of the shift looked worried now. There was an attack going on in the house; they were trained to deal with things outside the house, not inside.

Without his expression changing, Mondy's voice lightened. "Tell them, Chief. Tell them all what we've been working on. Tell them why Jernigan keeps coming around."

West's voice rose out of the group, thin and shaky. "Because of the change to EMS, because he's writing articles."

Mondy stared at the other man. "No. That's not it. Tell them, Chief. They have a right to know."

With a slight nod, Adler turned to the rest of the group. He had no idea why he was doing this, but with what they had learned about Grady and since they now had convincing evidence that Jason's birth mother had been murdered, the crew needed to know what was going on. So none of them would unknowingly open the door to the devil.

"I started as a firefighter about twenty-eight years ago. I was a volunteer down in Burkeville." He explained about getting trained, about how Montgomery firefighters often lived in Hope Hull and did off-hours work at Burkeville. He told them about Jake Strobel. Then about Pelias.

There were questions and the usual reminders that there were no GPS tags back then. That they often trailed rope and followed it out of the building when they couldn't see. He told them about the two little boys, and how Strobel went back for the little brother. And only then did he look at Jason.

Mondy hadn't moved through the telling of it. His jaw was clenched and his eyes almost glazed. When Adler raised his eyebrows, Jason gave just the slightest nod.

"About two months ago, Mondy and I were talking and it turns out that he's the boy—Jason Mallory—that I pulled out of that building in Montgomery."

There were gasps. Missy's jaw fell open. A handful of them turned to stare at Jason, who acted as though nothing had happened. And Adler had to admit that he still didn't know what was happening. They hadn't discussed bringing everyone into the loop. Jernigan had specifically said he wanted as few people to know as possible to keep the chance of leaks to a minimum. But he wasn't protesting now.

Just trying to hang on to what he knew, Adler told the rest of them that they "didn't know" any of this. He explained that Pelias was a murder/arson case and that it had been covered up. That Jason had gotten a phone call from someone following up when he first looked into it. So someone still alive and well wanted to keep Pelias quiet. And at least one person involved was capable of murder. Adler promised to show the shift the pictures they had of Grady, but he sure as hell didn't have them on him.

And that was it. He was out of information. Out of things to share, but Mondy hadn't changed expression. Only focal point.

Glaring at Jernigan, he ground out his next command. "Tell them how we looked for my brother. How we went to Montgomery so many times, interviewing people, following the trail. Tell the Chief why the trail goes dead when Daniel turned eighteen."

Clark Jernigan turned and faced Adler as though no one else was in the room. His shoulders sagged with the weight he felt on them. Jason was right, he owed this. "No one can find Daniel because that's the way he wanted it. He legally changed his name when he turned eighteen."

It was Jason that he had to get through to, so he turned back around. Stuck doing a 180 between the two men he needed to convince, his position was awkward both physically and emotionally. They might never forgive him. "He dyed his hair blonde during his teens, so that when he left he could go back to dark hair and become less recognizable."

Jason practically hissed at him. Clark had a mountain to climb to get back what he'd broken.

"Tell them what *he* changed *his* name to. Tell them." The low fury in his voice hit him like a pressure wave.

So he nodded. "Clark Jernigan."

Wide eyes turned to look at him, and Adler must have been taking a breath when it hit, because he started to cough. No one moved to help him. He didn't seem to need it. But Clark needed to keep talking. "I'm Daniel Mallory. I'm Jason's brother."

Adler nodded and cleared his throat. Thankfully he was acting more rational than Jason was, but he frowned. "So you knew the first time you came for an interview?"

Clark shook his head. It was all so tangled. Before he gave his answer to Adler, he turned to be sure Jason was still there and still listening. "No. When I turned eighteen, I was basically kicked out of my foster home. But I had been applying to colleges. I went to Duke on scholarship. I had to do a lot of paperwork with the name change, but it helped, and there was a woman in financial aid who got me grants and loans, and I learned to be a journalist. I needed to learn how to find what was missing."

He turned to Jason then. Though everyone in the house was riveted, he spoke only to his brother. "I moved back to Alabama and looked everywhere. I checked out every Jason of the right age. I couldn't find your birth date, but I had it narrowed down to a range. I started in Montgomery, went to Mobile, then found something in the CPS records that traced my brother to Madison County. So I looked there. I didn't know your last name."

Jason spoke again, still unmoving, his words still shot through with venom. "So you knew when you got here? When you saw me?"

"No! I thought you were a very good match for my brother. Everything was right, but I couldn't jump to conclusions. I'd already found two other Jasons who I thought were you but turned out not to be." He took a deep breath. "I didn't know until you told me about the fire."

And Jason broke. "That was *months* ago!" He yelled it, flung his arms out in a mad gesture that caused the crowd to take another step back.

Clark flinched but didn't move.

Jason wasn't done. Red-faced, he advanced, "You let me search for you. That nurse at Greil recognized you and you brushed it all off! Told her it was from your picture in the paper. No wonder you were so confident that we'd find 'Daniel'. And you had all of us sign away our rights to this story so you could deceive us and get famous off it."

"No!" Clark spun and shook his head at the same time. He met Adler's eyes and said it again. "No! I will let you all have final say on anything that gets written. That's not what this is."

Adler stood straight. "We can sue you for fraud, son."

At the same time Jason spoke. "Excellent. Don't write it."

Clark turned back to his brother, feeling like a racquetball in a particularly vicious game. "I won't write it at all if you don't want. That was never what this was about. I didn't say anything because . . . because . . ."

They all looked at him. Trained, battle-hardened warriors, every one. Even Wanstall—whom he'd hoped for a little sympathy from—stood with her arms crossed and her chin up.

He had not wanted to do this here, not like this. But he owed Jason, and he owed the Chief, too. So he steeled his back and, without looking at anyone, started speaking. "I just wanted to meet you. I wanted to know what kind of man you had become. You don't remember me or our mother, but I remember you. I remember a big brother who grabbed me from behind and carried me around with him . . . all the time. I remember you hiding me in the closet when Mom would get in a fight with one of the men who came over. I remember you breaking the hole in the back of the closet—making it larger—and crawling through next door to the babysitter's and that we scared the crap out of her the first time we showed up in her guest room."

He took another breath, because this was the hardest. "I remember the night of the fire, and that you pushed me into the closet and closed the door behind us. I remember it locked, I think now that they used the same door everywhere in the units, it was cheap construction. But I remember crawling through and hiding in the closet next door for forever. And then you *left me there*. You ran out to save yourself and you never came back for me. I screamed for you until I couldn't scream anymore. But you saved yourself and left me there to die."

He looked up and saw that Jason was as white as the dead. "No. That's not true."

This time it was Clark's turn to be mad. "How do you know!? You don't remember *any* of it. I was *four*. When they pulled me out, you stood there and watched them take me away. You didn't say anything. Didn't even tell them my name when they asked you. You didn't come to the hospital. You didn't find me. You were the only thing I had and you left me in the fire and then let them take me away."

"Oh shit."

The dam was cracking and his voice raised. "You got adopted and lived with a nice family while I was shuffled from one foster home to another. You didn't tell them to come get me. You didn't tell them you had a brother."

Jason staggered backward until his knees hit the recliner behind him and he practically fell into it. "I didn't know."

"How was I supposed to know that?" Clark pointed at his own chest. "So when I found you, I just wanted to see who you were. I just wanted to see how you lived with what you had done. I didn't have any plans after that. But you asked me to help find *me*! I didn't know if you were playing me or if you were as clueless as you seemed. So forgive me for not serving up my own head on a silver platter!"

A near silence settled over the entire house. Aside from Jason's ragged breathing where he sat in the recliner, his head in his hands, no one made a noise.

It was Adler who finally broke the silence and took the focus off the two brothers, Clark staring at Jason and Jason staring at the floor. "Why did you finally tell?"

"Jason got smart and asked my last foster family for pictures." He almost smiled, "But honestly, I've been trying to figure out how to say it since I interviewed you, Chief."

But Adler wasn't paying attention. He was thinking through what had happened. "So that's why you knew to check the visitor's logs."

Clark nodded. "I didn't know his name, but Grady came to visit me every month. From the moment I went into Greil, to every foster home I went to, he found me."

Adler absorbed that. "What did he say?"

Fighting the pressure behind his eyes, Clark shook his head. He hoped it looked like he was trying to clear his thoughts, but he was buying himself just a moment to keep from breaking down in front of these men who saw much worse and didn't break. "He never said anything. He never had to. I knew that he wanted me to stay quiet, so I did. But I got out and I got away as soon as I could."

It was the Chief who put his hand on Clark's shoulder. That touch started to seal the rift he felt between him and everyone else. It seemed narrower since he started this project with them, since he had found Jason and told himself that in a while he'd be able to move on with his life, start a new chapter, and have all the shit with Grady behind him. But that starting-to-heal wound had been torn wide open again when Jason had ordered him out of the apartment yesterday. When Clark had revealed himself as Daniel in the worst possible way. The simple weight of Adler's hand on his shoulder told him he didn't have "nothing." He was a long way from good, but no longer stuck at "nothing."

"Do you remember that night, then? Do you remember Grady murdering your mother? Is that what this is about?"

"I remember that night. There was someone in the apartment, and Mom was yelling. So Jason took me into our bedroom and we closed the door. But it wasn't Grady. It was a woman."

Chapter 22

Jason

Saved by the bell. The phone rang to punctuate his sentence to Amara. He'd just finished saying he was sorry and that he'd been wrong to take advantage of her as he had.

She had opened her mouth to speak, but he had railroaded her. On purpose. "I don't have time in my life for this right now."

Again, she had started to say something, but as she uttered the words, "Listen, I—" the phone had rung, drowning out whatever she was starting to say. Clearly frustrated, she had answered it with barely contained politeness then held the phone towards Jason. "It's for you."

He reached for it, grateful for an end to the conversation but grateful too soon.

Amara pulled the phone back as he reached for it and her eyes narrowed at him. "Don't go thinking you're such a prize. I felt sorry for you. But I don't have time in my life now for this either. Oh, wait. Ever."

She handed him the phone and sauntered off. Her bedroom door didn't even slam, it never did. And with his heart heavy and his shoulders weighted by the knowledge that he'd just acted like an ass, he spoke into the phone. "Hello? This is Jason."

"This is Jack Deason the Second."

Immediately Jason shed the dark thoughts. Maybe there was something here. "Oh, hello." There had to be something better to say than that, but he couldn't find anything.

Luckily, Deason supplied it. "I've been asking around in Montgomery. Subtle like."

Shit.

Anyone who said they were "subtle like" had probably been anything but. The flags were up and when whoever-was-keeping-tabs saw that, the shit was going to hit the fan—which meant sometime soon. But Jason didn't say anything; what could he do now? So he listened and hoped that what Deason offered would be worth a forced endgame.

"I talked to some of the guys who were here at the station house back then. And I found one who remembers Alcia Mallory. His name is Mike Estepp."

"Wow." Jason found a pen and notepad—right in the junk drawer where Amara stashed them. And he wrote down everything he could while he thanked Deason profusely.

He figured that was the thing to do. He had no clue whether this link Deason provided would turn out to be useful or not. This whole venture had been a series of dead ends, occasional revelations, and shit hitting fans at high speed. There was no reason for this lead to be anything new.

When he hung up, he stood still for a moment, wondering who to call next. He didn't want to call Clark, didn't want to speak to the man at all. Thinking—wrongly—that he'd been left behind was no excuse for Clark to turn them all into patsies so he could get his book written.

Jason didn't even want to contemplate what a best seller it would be: the reporter as the missing link. Surely people would think the worst of him and his friends. Adler and the fire station certainly didn't need that kind of publicity. Their only consolation was that it would take a while to write it and get it published.

He heard speaking from Amara's room and frowned until he realized she must be on her phone. He felt bad; he'd handled the whole thing poorly from start to finish.

Clark had been right, he had no idea how to be friends with a woman. As soon as his dick had entered into the equation, it had all gone to hell. He'd woken up warm and cozy and then he'd realized what he'd done and all he could think was that he didn't need another girlfriend. Apparently he didn't have time to do things right even when he did have time in his life—as evidenced by Kelly and all her predecessors. There was no way in hell he'd be able to do right by Amara now.

But clearly that hadn't even been an issue.

It became even less of one when she stepped out of her room with several packed bags slung across her shoulders.

Jason looked at her sideways. "You don't have to leave. We agree about what happened."

She gave him a look that said he had a brain size in approximation of a pebble. "That was Leo. He said Alex told him what's going on with you and your mother's murder. They want me to stay there. They think I'm not safe here."

Jason's mouth hung open.

She'd known about this investigation almost as long as he had. But she gave him no chance to protest.

"Do you *want* me to tell them that I knew all along? Apparently, unlike everyone else, I can keep a secret." She hiked one of the bags over her shoulder, "I'll be back in a week to move my stuff out. Alex and Leo will help."

He stood unmoving, not able to untangle the skein of emotion in him.

"Don't worry. You can keep the rent. I paid you through the end." And then she went out the door, before he could even offer to help carry something to her car. He didn't get to ask her if she had everything she needed or tell her she should keep her key and come back if she should think of anything.

Instead, he stood in his living room as he had just a few months ago.

The turmoil inside him ate at him like an ulcer, and there seemed to be nothing he could do about it. He had to get off this roller coaster. But that was the thing about roller coasters, no matter what happened—seizures, vomiting, heart attack—you had to ride to the end.

This latest twist had slammed him both ways. He had the paper still in his hand with the info Deason had given him about yet another person to talk to. He had to follow it through. Someone was watching him, so unless he moved and changed his name, he was in.

At the same time, Amara had zipped out the door before he had a chance to say . . . that she should stay. That he was sorry. That he was a jackass, but apparently he couldn't help it because that's just what he was.

Somehow the apartment was emptier now than it had been when Kelly had actually removed everything.

∧ ∧ ∧ ∧ ∧
.

Jason stood at the curb in front of his apartment waiting for Rob Castor to come. His hands were shoved into his jacket pockets, Banner's leash looped around his wrist along with a plastic bag containing another plastic bag of dog food and two dishes.

He hadn't called Clark; in fact he hadn't updated the reporter about any of it. He hadn't even updated his own thought process from "the reporter" to "his brother." And he had no intention of doing it any time soon.

Instead, Jason had called Bart English and Rob Castor to see if any of them were free to hit Montgomery today. He figured an attorney and a cop on his way to detective could interview people just as well as a reporter could. And they would do it without the ulterior motives.

With his nine-to-five gig, English had been office-locked today, but Castor was off shift and free. So Jason had left the station, and it had taken a good chunk of time to pick up Banner, shower, walk Banner, get dressed, and get Banner on the leash. To a certain extent it was like having a small child. But he found he enjoyed the day-to-day fuss of taking care of the dog. And the fact that Banner sat at the curb hunched against the cold wind just like him was comical enough to make him almost smile.

Castor pulled up in his low-slung sports car. Luckily it was older—he was after all living on a cop's salary—and he'd already said it was okay to bring Banner. He greeted the dog with a smile and a head rub as the stubby mutt bounded across the passenger seat and dove into the back. With a grunt and a lick of his paw, Banner made himself at home before Jason even said hello and got his seatbelt buckled.

Rob started to pull away from the curb, but Jason put out a hand, motioning for him to stay. Then he stared straight ahead and updated Rob on all the new cracks in the story.

"Shit, man!" The look on Rob's face was the same as if Jason had just slapped him. "Clark is Daniel?"

"Yes. And he's known it this whole time. And if you remember, the first thing he did was have us sign away the rights to the story, so now the whole thing is *his* story." Feeling just a small bit guilty, he added. "Clark did say he wouldn't write the book if we didn't want—that defrauding us wasn't his intention. But really . . ."

Rob was still slowly shaking his head. "All this time, Daniel was right in front of us. Dude, Clark seemed too perceptive. He always knew where to look and what to look for."

"Yeah. It's easy when you're the person everyone is looking for." It felt like a knife was going through his back. Again. Just the re-telling hurt. But he felt a little cleaner for doing it. Somehow telling it made his part in the whole debacle seem a little smaller, so he coughed up the rest. "And I slept with Amara, and she moved out."

Rob managed to resist the urge to taunt Jason about his manhood or his skills. Instead he looked over his shoulder and pulled out into the street, heading to Montgomery. "Man, seems like if life isn't fucking you over, you're doing it to yourself."

Jason had to acknowledge that lately that seemed very true.

Gaping holes had opened in his world. His mother's death had ripped tectonic cracks in his foundation. The search for Daniel, and the hope that he still had family, had been cruelly torn away. And Amara leaving—even rightfully so; he'd been an ass— had left him cold.

All that was left was the need for knowledge. To find out what had happened to his birth mother and stop whoever had brutally murdered her from coming after him. As far as he was concerned now, Clark was on his own.

But he didn't say that. In fact, he'd probably said enough for the whole week. So Jason stayed silent until Rob announced that he was suddenly starving.

They stopped at a pizza place along the way. The joint was old and shabby and looked like it was out of a seventies' movie about an axe murderer, and none of that kept it from being clearly the most popular place for miles around. They sat outside, jackets on against the wind, so that Banner could sit with them, his leash looped around the table leg. He even scored his own piece of some of the best pizza Jason had ever eaten.

A little too soon, the foray into normal life was over and they were back on the road to meet Mike Estepp. They were back on the trail of a murder and back into the only thing left in his life that made Jason move forward. His job was a take-it-as-it-comes situation now. His test was on Monday, but he was confident he was ready; after all, Amara had helped him study for a while. Aside from showing up for it, no forward momentum was required. The need to take care of Banner got him up in the morning. And he loved the dog. But one day was pretty much the same as the next.

Estepp would help them get closer to the end. According to Deason, Estepp was a contemporary. Only slightly younger, but he'd been at the house at the right times and most importantly, the man remembered Alcia.

Though he was looking forward to what he might find out, Jason was also dreading it. Who knew what the truth might be about the woman who had given birth to him? He already knew that the man who had probably sired him had stalked Daniel for years, never saying anything, but always threatening. Grady had been menacing to the point that Daniel had run away and changed his name. At least he hadn't been a murderer. Jason had hovered under that shadow for a while, not realizing how much it bothered him until he was relieved of it.

Now he treated this interview like they had when he and Clark had come to visit Deason the first time, so he didn't call ahead. They couldn't afford to alert the wrong people. And though they gained knowledge in leaps and bounds, they were only a small step closer to where they needed to be.

And they were screwed but good for evidence. Grady had never spoken to Daniel. Thus, though Clark could testify that the man came and visited every month, there would be no legal ramifications. Sadly, there were no laws against being creepy. And the fact that he managed to show up at every foster home Daniel was in didn't prove that he had access to child welfare records illegally. So that was of no use.

Most of what they learned had no real value as a case. They knew all about Daniel. They knew Alcia's history, or at least a decent part of it. And the hard evidence they had—that she had burned on the couch—was the only evidence on record that she had been murdered. It didn't point a finger at anyone in particular. All Clark remembered was that the murderer had been female. And he hadn't seen it happen. Couldn't swear that a man hadn't been there with them. And even if he could, he'd been four at the time and thus a crappy witness. He'd be a crappier one twenty-plus years later. Which pretty much left them up shit creek with only the hope of finding a paddle.

Jason prayed that Estepp knew something. Something of value. Or, at the very least, he could lead them to something of real worth rather than just merely being interesting.

An hour later, Rob pulled the sports car up in front of another small but well-kept house that clearly said "government employee." The grass was cut with military precision, and the flowers in the bed had been tended to near perfect symmetry. And when they knocked, the man who answered the door had a bearing that screamed firefighter, even though it also told of arthritis. His voice was crisp and modulated to lack any judgment or welcome. "Can I help you?"

Rob dove in before Jason could say anything, and Jason had to wonder if that was because Rob simply believed himself to be the better investigator or if he was worried about Jason's mood of late.

Rob gave the whole introduction of who they were and a brief statement that they were researching Alcia Mallory, who was Jason's birth mother. He played the lost brother card, completely withholding any mention that the lost brother was no longer lost and was in fact a fraud. Then he had Jason pull out an eight-by-ten photo they'd printed of Alcia. They had a whole folder full of glossies of all the key players, Clark had made them up to help people jog memories.

"Hmmm." From the look on Estepp's face, he remembered the woman in the picture. "Let's sit out on the porch."

The weather wasn't quite the sit-on-the-porch variety, but Jason couldn't fault the man. He was smart not to invite two well-built and obviously trained men into his home, especially when they showed up unannounced and wanted information about people in his past.

Estepp did offer them drinks, then ducked back into the house to get them while inviting the guys to make themselves comfortable. Jason figured the man was telling his wife to stay out of sight until he could assess the situation better.

The porch was lined with four wicker chairs, each bearing a cushion in the same shade as the over-tended flowers. Jason flipped the pillow over, revealing a cleaner side, then sat as Rob did the same. They chose chairs in the corner of the space and away from the front door, giving Estepp the clearest exit and not sandwiching him in between. He needed to be as relaxed and trusting as possible.

They both turned on the politeness as the older man came back balancing the three glasses of iced tea in his hands and put them on the wicker table which he pushed toward the middle of the group, also further confining them to their corner of the porch.

It took a minute for him to settle into his seat, tug at his slacks, get comfortable. He sipped his tea and gently set it back down before he finally spoke. "I remember that woman."

He looked Jason in the eyes. "You say she's your biological mother?"

Jason nodded, wondering where this was leading. Because from his tone it was clearly leading somewhere. Estepp didn't keep them waiting.

"I'll be glad to share what I remember, but you should know most all of it is uncomplimentary."

Rob spoke. "We understand that. Good or bad, we just want to know more about her."

But Estepp waited until Jason nodded in agreement before he started talking. "You want me to just tell you what I remember about her?"

Rob nodded but instantly contradicted himself by asking, "Do you remember the first time you saw her? Or at least a ballpark time? A year?"

Estepp thought for a moment. "I guess she was there from when I started."

"Did she have a job at the fire station? Did she volunteer?"

That made Estepp laugh, a low, rusty guffaw. "This is where it gets less than favorable."

Jason appreciated that the man was trying to be nice, using terms like *uncomplimentary* and *less than favorable*. But it didn't affect him, it wasn't as though she was actually his "mother"—he didn't remember the woman. "That's fine. Go on."

"She didn't have a job there of any kind. But she was around a lot." He took another drink of his tea. "She also hung out at Code 647, the local cop bar back then—"

He was interrupted by the sudden burst of laughter coming from Rob, and Jason looked sideways at him until he explained.

"You know some of the common scanner codes for murder and arson. Well, a 647 is a 'drunk and disorderly'." He chuckled again and Estepp tipped his tea in salute.

The older man took yet another sip and took up his story. "Code 647 was where all the cops and firefighters hung out in those days. It closed a long time ago. But Alcia Mallory was there a lot."

Jason didn't understand how the name of the bar where his birth mother had hung out had to do with the history he needed. But he had to find patience. Eventually Estepp would get to something he wanted. And they might also learn something else, if he could just stay still and listen. So he nodded his head and waited.

Estepp looked him in the eyes again. "This is the part I think you won't like. But I knew her name because everyone knew her name. Are you boys familiar with the term 'badge bunny'?"

"Yes." Jason answered as Rob nodded. But what he really wanted to do was say "*Oh, yes. We all know what badge bunnies are.*" It sounded as though the groupies for cops and firefighters were as old as either profession. There were women like that: they "collected." They even slept with military guys or anyone in a seriously macho profession. Navy SEALs and Army Rangers were prone to the bunnies, too. The higher the rank a girl bagged, the more "points" or street credit she seemed to accrue—though nothing else about the man mattered. He could be ugly or crude or a complete asshole. All that was needed was a badge and a completed sex act.

And wasn't that just lovely about his birth mother?

Estepp looked uncomfortable. "Well, we all knew her name because most everyone had slept with her at one point or other."

Oh. That was the unsavory part then. It was all Jason could do not to blurt out *"Did you? Sleep with her?"* But he fought to hold his tongue.

And was rewarded for it.

"I didn't. If that's what you're wondering." Estepp didn't look at him this time, though. "I know firefighters are thought of as a randy lot, and maybe we are, but we aren't all cheaters and alpha-male dicks."

The language was a little disconcerting coming out of the mouth of the polite-to-the-point-of-seeming-standoffish man. And Jason didn't exactly trust that last bit of info. But since he was relatively certain that a DNA test on Grady would turn up a match to himself, he didn't push it or worry over the possibility. He simply nodded at Estepp as though he was in complete agreement: clearly Estepp could not have slept with Alcia Mallory, because he said so.

Once that seemed to be established, the man continued. "So she was at the bar often. And I know a lot of the guys had been with her."

"Hold on." At that point, Rob started digging in the bag they had brought. He produced the folder of photos and pulled out the pictures of the firefighters in Montgomery Station #2 from the years around Alcia's death.

There was nowhere to spread them out, so Rob simply held them up one after the other and asked the firehouse veteran if he remembered the man, and if the man had slept with Alcia.

Estepp didn't agree right away and instead looked at Jason again. "You sure you want me to tell you this, son? It's not something I would want to know about my mother."

For the first time, Jason could actually smile. "She's just my birth mother. I was adopted and raised by a wonderful couple who are my real parents. So there's not anything you can tell me about her that will offend me. If you tell me anything about her genetics that I'll need to follow up with tests, I'll do that. But what she did or didn't do doesn't really affect me. I'm just trying to find my brother."

There. He had lied. His brother had already been found. *The lying prick.*

"Alright then." Estepp nodded and they started.

Rob showed pictures. Estepp remembered, then tried to find polite ways to describe the ways in which Alcia Mallory had serviced or been serviced by the man. And Jason took notes on a legal pad he rested on his lap.

By the time they got through the photos they had, Estepp had painted a pretty compelling image that the only men Alcia hadn't screwed were the ones who scraped her off when she tried to latch on to them. She was attractive and young, and Estepp said she was bright and fun. So it was a pretty small number of firefighters who had said no.

"She was looking for something." Estepp shook his head. "Maybe a husband, who knows? But whatever it was, she was going about it all wrong. Men don't want to marry a woman like that. And she didn't seem to expect anything from them except sex, so I never saw her tell anyone they couldn't take her home, and a lot of the time it was she who initiated things.

"She was a go-getter, that one. If she'd put that energy into something else, she could have really gotten somewhere." The thought clearly made him uncomfortable, and while Rob re-filed the photos, Estepp took another generous drink of his tea.

"She seemed to put all her effort into landing a man. And when she got pregnant out of wedlock, it put a damper on things for her."

That term, *out of wedlock* pointed out not only Mike Estepp's age, but also the era in which Alcia Mallory had been a single mother. Life and the conservative state of Alabama had probably not been kind about it.

Jason stepped in. "Was that her first or second child?"

"That was the first. Is that you? Or are you the second?"

"I was the first."

Rob stepped in then. "That makes the year 1978. Does that sound right?"

"It's spot on, son." Estepp continued, "She lost her job, and wound up working phones for something at night. I don't know. I only know we didn't see her much for a while. That was when all the new research was coming out about pregnancy and drinking. A pregnant woman would get herself thrown out of a bar then."

And today, Jason thought to himself. Instead of saying it, he asked a question. "Do you know or have an idea who the father of her child was?"

"I can't say for sure. But a handful of years later, it sure looked like Jerry Grady was the father of one of those boys."

"You met her sons?" It felt surreal to ask this man if he'd met "Alcia's sons." It meant Jason had met this man before. With Daniel. With *Clark.*

"Yes, I did. I guess that was you."

Jason nodded. "I don't remember it. I was adopted at age seven after she died. But I don't remember anything before that."

Dipping his head to the side, Estepp gave a small nod. "That may be for the best. The way she died was quite a nasty business. No one would want to remember that."

Rob put his hand up. "I want to stop for a second. We want to hear about that, but we've skipped a lot in between. Can you go back to after the first son was born? What happened then?"

Estepp shrugged. "After the baby was born, the first one, she started hanging around the bar again. I don't know what she did with the boy when she was out. She seemed to go back to her old ways. Honestly, nothing I saw indicated she was a fit mother, but a lot of people commented about how good she was with the baby. So she must have had a sitter for you."

It was odd to hear himself referred to that way. Odder still to hear that his mother had left him with someone else while she went out and picked up men in a bar.

"For a while it was like she didn't even have a kid. She'd show up at Code 647 or at the station house some nights when it was quiet. She'd latch on to one guy for a while. She'd done that with Jerry Grady more than once."

Rob asked a question they already knew the answer to. "Was Grady married?"

Estepp laughed. "In the biblical sense? No. That man always had a woman on the side, and a good portion of the time it was Alcia. If you're asking did he have a wife? Then yes, he did. She was a good woman, if a little meek. They had a nice house and three beautiful daughters. And I don't think she had a clue about what her husband was doing with those other women. Even though I remember more than one instance over the years where she came in the front door of the station house in her prim dress, sometimes with one of their girls by the hand, and Alcia Mallory, in her short skirt and tight shirt, would head right out the back."

He shook his head. "How that woman didn't smell the girlfriends on her husband remains a mystery to me."

Well, Jason was getting a much clearer picture of his birth mother and her activities. He wouldn't have put too much stock into Estepp's stories, except that they matched exactly to what everyone else said about Alcia. She was either a complete slut, or she wasn't but she was working hard to make sure the world thought she was.

With two sons born three years apart, in the seventies and early eighties, to two different men, Jason was definitely leaning to the former.

"Alcia even hung out once or twice and said hello to Mrs. Grady. That pissed Jerry off, but there wasn't much he could do in front of his wife without giving away what he was doing with his mistress. And it wasn't long after that Alcia started bringing the little boy to the station. She paraded him in front of the men; they were all nice to the kid, but she and Jerry started getting into some yelling matches."

"What about?" Rob leaned in, so intent in the answer that he nearly knocked over his untouched glass of tea.

Jason took the opportunity to take a sip. It was so sweet it made his teeth cringe, but he didn't want to seem ungrateful, so he steeled himself and took a big swallow.

Estepp looked at him. "Good, isn't it?"

"Oh, yes." He lied. Again. He was becoming proficient at it.

Then the older firefighter turned back to Rob. "I have no idea what they were fighting about. They would yell, but it was always in phrases that didn't spell out the whole story. At least the parts we heard. There would be silent patches in the fights, where I guess they were whispering important things, even though they were upset. At least Jerry was. He went around mad as a hornet for a good few months.

"He even grabbed Alcia by the arm and hauled her out of the station one day. Locked the front door right behind her. Which was stupid—even then we kept the bays open. But he made his point.

"And she made hers. She came back about a few hours later with steel in her eyes and her little boy in tow." Estepp sighed. "They fought for a bit, then settled something, because she quit coming around for a while after that."

"Define *a while*?" Jason asked the man.

"A year or two?" He shrugged. "I mean, I still saw her out at Code 647 fairly often. But she didn't come back to the station house. She hit up some cops, but that wasn't anything new. She wasn't really an issue again until after the second boy was born."

"What happened then?"

"That's when the shit hit the fan."

Chapter 23

Jason

Estepp leaned back in his wicker chair. He stalled by taking another swallow of his tea and drained the glass. So he excused himself for a refill and headed back inside.

Banner, who had remained quiet in the back of the car with the window down this whole time, finally took the opportunity to pop up. Jason smiled and waved at his dog with a promise to be there soon and take him for a nice long walk before they headed back home. There was no way he was getting up after that last pronouncement.

Rob leaned over and whispered, "Do you think he's just getting tea? Or is he conferring with someone about what to say?"

Jason had to laugh. "That's a pretty heavy conspiracy theory, man."

"There's a murder that's still getting covered up after a quarter of a century. A conspiracy is not out of the realm of reality."

Not wanting to believe anything like that, he put the spin he wanted on it. "He's probably just chatting with his wife. Telling her that he's okay and that the tea needs more sugar."

Just then, they saw Mike Estepp through the sheers on the big front window. He was emerging from his kitchen with his tall glass brimming with the colored sugar water.

Jason smiled. "See? Too fast for a real conspiracy."

At least he hoped so.

Estepp came out the front door with a smile on his face. "There we go, boys. Just let me know if you need more."

He took longer than Jason wanted to settle back into the chair, adjust his position and finally get started again. "The thing is, I don't really know what hit the fan."

"What do you mean? You *said* 'the shit hit the fan.'" Rob leaned forward.

"Well, things blew up. Alcia came back with her two little boys in tow, and though things had been quiet for a couple of years, they heated up again."

Jason asked "How old was the younger boy at this time?" just as Rob asked, "Was there anyone in particular that she was arguing with?"

Estepp took it in stride, answering Jason first. "The younger one was two, maybe three?" He put a question at the end of it, but since Daniel had only been four when the fire had hit, that helped narrow down the window a lot.

Then Estepp turned to Rob. "She was arguing with Grady again." Then he sighed and looked pained for the first time in the interview. "Look, I don't like saying this because I worked with the man a long time. Jerry Grady was a great firefighter. He always had your back. He trained hard and worked well with the other guys. But morally he was a black hole. He cheated on his wife, his taxes, any bet he made, and I'm pretty sure he cheated at Uno the few times we played it. And he didn't think there was anything wrong with what he did.

"But he knew his wife would think so, and so he lied to her and didn't seem to think anything was wrong with that either. And here's the problem: I have no real idea what Grady and Alcia were fighting about. I never overheard anything that gave me details or anything clear. There's nothing I can say for certain other than that Grady was calm and clear-headed for a few years when Alcia wasn't coming around. And when she did show back up, he got mean and irritated and short-tempered.

"There were rumors, and that's all I know."

No, Jason thought. *That can't be all you know.* "What were the rumors?"

Another sigh. As though it was difficult to tell. As though it was more difficult to speak it than for Jason to have to hear it. But then he seemed to get his thoughts together and started to talk. "First, it was that she got Grady back into bed. Then when things blew up it was rumored that she said the boys were his. And the worst rumor was that she was blackmailing him. So that she would stay silent and not tell the Chief or his wife."

Jason frowned. "What would telling the fire chief do?" He couldn't imagine Adler doing anything other than rubbing the bridge of his nose and saying something like, 'You got yourself into this mess. Deal with it outside the fire house.'

Estepp frowned. "He could have lost his job. No one wants a firefighter who's not a good man."

Jason opened his mouth to speak, to say that firefighters had the highest rate of cheating on spouses of any profession. If that was a legitimate criterion for dismissal, cities would burn straight to the ground. But he didn't say it. Clearly, Estepp thought the threat of telling the firehouse was bad. "So, she didn't tell anyone outright who the boys' father was?"

"Not that I ever knew of." Another swallow of the tea. "It was a shame how she died. Bad accident that. And you boys being shipped off like you were. But it sounds like you were adopted by a good family."

Jason just nodded and offered a closed-lipped smile. That simple gesture was much easier than saying what had actually happened. Or letting it out that, even though he remembered nothing of the fire or his life before it, he fully remembered the three months in foster homes before he was adopted and the scared, lost feeling that came with having no stable family. He didn't add that Daniel had felt that for twelve years.

Finally standing, the two of them thanked Estepp profusely. But as Rob stepped forward for a handshake he asked one more question. "Could you do us a favor and alert us if anyone else wants to talk about this, or asks you questions?"

"What?" Estepp raised one eyebrows, looking truly suspicious for the first time. "Why?"

"This is about Jason's mother. He's just now finding out some of it himself, and we think someone else is following up on the blackmail issue." Rob lied as seamlessly as an actor. "We have no idea who it is, but Jason here has received a few threats."

Another lie. Jason frowned and nodded agreement as though it was all very disturbing. At least the sentiment, if not the facts, was real.

But Rob kept going. "We can't stop you from talking to anyone else, but it would be nice to know for a change who's checking up on him."

Estepp looked between the two of them. "You mean you don't know who's threatening you?"

Jason shook his head, wondering how far in Rob was going to dig this hole and if he was going to tangle himself in the lie before he got them out of it.

But from all appearances, Estepp was taking them at face value. He nodded and took the card Rob held out with his phone number.

Jason was about to hand out his cell number, too, but a slight movement from Rob looked like a cue to hold back, so he did.

The older man wished them luck, then picked up the tea glasses and headed back inside his house. Jason heard the lock click as they went down the front porch steps.

They climbed into the car in a symmetric motion, and Jason announced that he needed to take Banner for a walk. They agreed to find a nearby park—dutifully coughed up by the GPS that was much sleeker than the car—and walk Banner while they catalogued what they had learned.

As they pulled out, though, Rob turned to him and said, "Blackmail's a pretty good motive for murder."

There was no good way not to agree with that. "So, the way it seems now, Alcia gets herself pregnant—with me, I guess—from Jerry Grady. Grady has a family and only wants Alcia on the side. She sets something up with him and all is well for a few years. Then she has another kid—either by Grady or someone else, we don't know—and she goes back to Grady and demands that he pay for the kids or something. Next thing we know, she's murdered."

Castor pulled up to a well-groomed park of a few acres, and Banner anxiously hopped to the ground. Jason let his friend take the leash while he found a flat spot and set out one of the dishes and filled it with food. Then he took the second and went in search of a water source. He found a drinking fountain at the far end of the park and stood in one position for what seemed like forever while it filled.

He returned to find that Castor had let Banner off leash.

"Isn't that illegal?"

Rob shrugged. "I'm a cop."

Banner didn't do anything wrong, didn't run after the people jogging on the sidewalk or the moms with strollers sitting at the picnic tables nearby. He just romped after a squirrel here or there. But Jason kept an eye out. "There's one huge hole in my theory."

"What's that?" Rob stuffed his hands in his pockets against the wind that had just kicked up.

"Clark said he remembered the night our mother was murdered. And that we went and hid in the bedroom because she was having a fight. He thought maybe we had gone in there when there was a knock at the door. He remembered her looking through the peephole, and he didn't remember who came over. But just before the fire he heard them yelling, and it was Alcia's voice and another woman."

"A *woman*?"

"Yeah." Jason nodded. It threw a whole monkey wrench into the deal. With what they learned today, the whole thing wrapped up neat with Grady. Except for the woman's voice.

Rob must have been thinking the same thing. "We can practically arrest Grady with what we have. I mean, if we can match your DNA to his, then call in witnesses who believe he was being blackmailed by Alcia. We have solid evidence she *was* murdered." He sighed. "But the idea that the last person that saw her alive was a woman just kills the whole neat story."

"Yeah." Jason gave up and stuck his own hands into his pockets. Banner had discovered the food and was gulping it down as though he hadn't been fed just before they left the apartment and then given a whole slice of pizza. Jason figured that was an after-effect of having been on his own. He was just a puppy—full-sized, but still in his early years—and being abandoned must have had a bigger effect on him than if he'd been a dog with a family for most of his life.

Jason turned his attention back to Rob. For several years now, he'd been studying arson as part of his goal to become a fire inspector, and he'd learned a lot about who set fires and why. And since learning about Alcia, he'd been looking up arson as a murder weapon. "It's highly unusual for a woman to set fires. Females are only five to ten percent of all arsonists. And they usually commit arson for revenge, rather than insurance money or just to 'see the pretty fire'."

Rob smiled. "Aren't *you* the encyclopedia."

"Yeah. I am." He laughed. "This is what I study and now it's coming back to bite me in the ass."

Rob tilted his head. At first he looked like he was listening to the slobbery noises that Banner was making as he cleaned out his dishes, but when he turned to Jason, it was with a different topic all together. "Do you think you got into this because of your history as a kid?"

Jason shrugged. But it didn't match his words. "I don't see how it could be anything else."

He waited a second, watching as Banner gave up on the food and went after a squirrel. But then he started talking again. "I was always told how I was the only one saved from a fire. How the firemen carried me down the ladder. My mother must have read the articles, but she never showed them to me or I would have known all along that I had a brother."

He shrugged again. "I always wanted to be a firefighter, and I guess that part's pretty obvious. But the investigator part could very well be due to something that I saw that I don't remember. Maybe some buried desire to bring justice to my first mother."

"I just think it's strange that you don't remember anything before you were adopted."

"Actually, I don't remember anything before the fire. There's a three-month difference of foster homes and being shuffled around. But what's your earliest memory?"

Rob thought for a minute. "Picking out a teddy bear for my soon-to-be-born baby brother."

"How old were you?"

Again it took a moment as Rob did a little math. "Five or six."

"See? It's not all that different."

"I guess not." He then pointed to the dog who was doing some business in the bushes. "Are we about ready to go?"

"Yup." Jason crouched down on his heels, calling, "Banner!" And the dog came right up to him. They clipped the leash, dumped out the last of the water, and loaded both dog and stuff into the back seat. Jason then turned to his friend. "Home?"

"Actually. I was thinking we would go to the records hall."

"For?"

"The fire report. I want to see if it really says the Pelias Street fire was accidental. And if so, I want to see who signed off on it." Rob grinned.

"I thought we weren't going to go until later." Then Jason conceded. "But Clark was going to be in charge of that, wasn't he? And he's out of the picture now."

317

Rob tipped his head as he plugged the address for Montgomery City Hall into his GPS. "Do you think you'll ever forgive him?"

At that, Jason let out a bark of a laugh, and Banner let out an actual bark in return. "He came to me, knowing I was likely his brother, and didn't tell me. Then I told him things about my past that made it clear that not only was I actually the brother he was looking for, but that I was looking for him, too. And he still didn't tell me who he was. I don't know if he would have said anything at all if Amara hadn't thought to have the Morales family send pictures of "Daniel." So, no. I don't see that happening."

Rob nodded. "Then let's go to City Hall."

Jason took a deep breath. This was what they had held out on. It was going to alert someone of importance; that was almost certain. But the fact was that Deason was running around talking to people about Pelias and Alcia already—even if he was being "subtle like." And they had just told a good portion of the story to Mike Estepp. There was no telling who would ask him something next or what he would tell them when they did. There was also every possibility that, while they had taken Banner to the park, Estepp had gone back in his house and told his wife everything they'd talked about and she'd called all the other firefighters' wives from the old station house, and it was possibly already all over Montgomery.

So "now" had become prime time to go pull the old records.

But, just for good measure, Jason pulled out his phone and called Adler at the station house. The call went right through to voicemail, so he left a message with the things they'd talked to Estepp about. He was halfway through the rumors of blackmail when he was cut off.

Rob laughed at him as he re-dialed and started up again, repeating enough to hopefully make sense. He ended the message with "We're headed to City Hall to pull the fire report for Pelias. We'll see if it matches what you were told."

There was every possibility that the paperwork said "Arson" and Adler was simply told to let it go. That maybe whoever was involved listed the cause of the Pelias fire correctly but then didn't pursue the investigation for whatever reason.

They parked at a meter, not expecting to be in for too long, and cracked the window for Banner. The weather was chilly enough that he would be good in the car for a while.

Inside the old gray building, the security measures were better than at the Southfield City Hall, but Jason had been here before and wasn't surprised by the security wand and walk-through metal detector. They walked in separate lines, Rob going through the side passage for police and security personnel in order to keep his gun on him. His badge was thoroughly inspected and recorded while Jason waited. Then they were sent on their way as though they just knew which direction the records archive was in.

They found it quick enough and were greeted by a young woman in slacks and a blouse—standard business-casual dress, except for the blue streaks in her hair and the five or six silver bars that pierced her face in various places. Contrary to her rebellious looks, she was the nicest person they'd met all day.

She recorded the reason for their visit as well as Rob's badge number, then led them into the back. "I'll pull the box for you that has the stuff you want. In the meantime you can go onto our system here—" she pointed to a bank of old computers hard-wired together, "and search some keywords or dates. The system will prompt you."

They sat down to get started, but she wasn't finished. "There was a tornado in '96 that damaged a lot of the records here. We had started scanning to computer, but the administrators back then started with the main document or documents from each case, then would scan all the additional material later. So rather than having all of some cases, we have the main docs of all the old cases but not all the additional paperwork. You can find the main documents and anything else that was scanned from the computer system.

"I'm going to pull the box that has any papers or microfiche from that time period or linked to that case. I'm warning you there's a good likelihood that some or all of it is damaged. But we kept it anyway." She finally took a breath. "Is there anything else I can get you before I pull those records?"

With a smile, Rob shook his head. "I think we're good here."

The two of them settled in to search. Jason put in the date and pulled up a slew of arrests from the twenty-eighth of July that year. After sorting through some arrests for flashing, a restraining order, a domestic dispute and a stalker, he found the report on Pelias just as Rob blurted out, "Got it."

Jason leaned over. Rob had searched the keywords *Pelias+apartment*, which meant that he had not only the initial call, as Jason did, but also a copy of the final report and a follow-up where two different firefighters had been cleared to go back to work after psychiatric follow-up on the Pelias fire. One of them was Jerry Grady.

"Holy shit." Jason didn't realize he'd said it out loud until he heard the noise behind him and turned to see that the records clerk had shown up just in time to hear him swear. "I'm sorry, ma'am."

She laughed. "Nothing I haven't said, and no one calls me 'ma'am'." She lifted the box a bit to show she had it. "I'll just put this on the table here. It's a combination of paper and fiche, and the microfiche machines are right there." She asked if they knew how to use them.

Jason and Rob both nodded yes, though he guessed Rob was doing what he was and saying he knew because he'd done it once a long time ago. Good to know the State of Alabama was running on paper copies and old film.

As he thought that, he heard a whirring noise and realized that Rob had already hit the button to print out a copy of the main report on Pelias. Make that two copies. He walked the five feet to the printer at the other end of the room and handed one to Jason.

For a moment, all was silent as they read the report, word for word.

Rob spoke first. "Adler was right. It's definitely listed as an accidental fire."

"Look." Jason turned his copy outward and pointed to the middle. "The 'accidental' ruling is based on the reports of two firefighters—Jerry Grady and a Jeff Beales—and the inspection by the police chief."

Jason recognized Beales's name from the list of firefighters Clark had rounded up from Montgomery Station House #2 in the mid-eighties.

Rob asked what he was thinking. "Beales hasn't been on our radar before this. Do we know anything about him?"

"Not yet we don't." But Jason pulled out his cell and ran a search. It took two minutes while Rob started digging through the box of Pelias Street fire records, but Jason finally got something. "Beales died in a fire five years ago. He was about to become captain of his unit, too."

He was thinking that it sucked that they wouldn't be able to interview the man, when Rob spoke.

"Well, then, since we're sitting here in the middle of the records hall, and we haven't been bombed yet, let's make use."

Jason didn't understand. "Why? What does this have to do with anything other than that we can't go back and talk to Beales?"

"You really think the two aren't linked?" Rob stared at Jason like his friend had lost his mind.

Jason almost laughed. "Wait, are you actually suggesting that you think Beales was knocked off because of some old Pelias Street paperwork?"

"Dude was about to become captain, we know he wrote a false report that covered up a murder, and he dies in a fire?"

Oh dear God. Jason always considered that *he* was just cooking up conspiracy theories where Pelias was concerned, but Rob was making him look like a naïve Pollyanna. "Rob. It was years later, and the fire he died in had nothing to do with Pelias. He was going to a new station house. The fact that a liar died while doing a dangerous job is a coincidence."

Rob still stared at him like he was an idiot. "I used to believe in coincidence. Then I became a cop."

Jason shook his head. Rob was going off the deep end as he approached his promotion. He'd already passed his exam. "How close are you to becoming detective?"

"Damn close. Close enough to remember you saying that deaths on the job were very rare, especially after the advances in technology starting in the late eighties, that death-by-fire had declined to almost nothing. So you want to tell me again what a coincidence it is that one of two men who signed off on Pelias died *in a fire* just before he's promoted out of the house with the man who was being blackmailed? I'm pulling the records. We're right here, it costs us nothing, and it can't hurt." He went off in search of the clerk and came back three minutes later with a grin. "Records are on their way."

"Fine." Jason was sorting through the papers Rob had pulled from the Pelias box. "Most of this is damaged. It looks like pieces of the reports are missing or water damaged. But I think I found Grady's signature on an initial paper."

He held up the document. Half the signature was blurred but it was still pretty clearly Grady's. The document itself was a water-stained mess with only a few words surviving intact in the lower right-hand corner. Jason examined it. "It lists the kitchen as the origin of the fire—"

"Not true, according to Adler." Rob threw in, not looking up from the microfiche he was examining through the overhead-projector-like machine. "This is a mess of water damage, too. I guess the records hall flooded with the tornado?"

Jason shrugged. "Broken water pipes are a huge problem after structural damage of any kind."

"I didn't think of that." He sighed and went back to trying to find a legible page.

Jason pulled out his cell again and snapped a picture of the report Grady had written. His phone made a small *chucking* noise indicating that the picture was ready for text or email just as the clerk walked into the room.

Trying to look casual, Jason slipped the phone into his pocket. The records were public, but he was unsure what the laws were about photographing and emailing copies. She seemed to not notice.

This time the clerk just had a USB in her hand. "Here, I pulled and copied all the records you wanted to this drive. Since this was a much more recent report, it's all on electronic storage. In fact, if you want, you can just do a search on the computers." She pointed back to the ones she had originally sent them to, then once again smiled and said she'd help them with anything else they needed, just let her know.

As soon as she was out of the room, Jason sent the picture of the main report to Adler, who replied quickly that it was completely false and he would testify in court.

Sitting down next to Rob and the microfiche, Jason started cataloguing what they had. "We have evidence in the autopsy report on Alcia. We have Chief, who will testify. We have Deason, who will also testify that he suspected arson and was shut down. And we have this paper, which is falsified."

That was all he could come up with.

Rob printed a few pages from microfiche but commented that he wasn't sure there was anything of use there. Then he moved himself back to the computer while Jason kept going through the papers in the Pelias box. Some were still stuck together, indicating that no one had come down here and messed with them or—God forbid—tried to read them since the water had come.

He was carefully peeling two pages apart when Rob said, "Bingo! I told you there was no such thing as coincidence."

Jason came right over. "What?"

"Guess who was the last person to see Jeff Beales alive?"

Surprised, Jason did exactly that and took a guess. "Grady?"

"You got it." Then Rob clicked his way through some other forms and pulled up something he'd searched. "Also, guess who was stuck in counseling again after Beales's death?"

"Grady." But this time it wasn't a guess. "So why is he killing people then feeling bad about it?"

"Receiving counseling doesn't mean he 'feels bad' does it?"

It took a deep breath and a moment to marshal his words, but Jason tried to explain that it kind of did. "I was almost sent to counseling after saving the Thurlow boys. Because I was having nightmares. And it wasn't from something that often sends firefighters into counseling. But there's going to be a record in Burkeville that Adler got counseling after Pelias, because he fought the fire report. If Grady got counseling and it got recorded then, yes, he was failing to do his job in some way. So chances were, yes, he was affected by what happened."

Rob frowned. "Is it that uncommon?"

"I don't know, but Standard and I were there when Frogurt died. And then Connelly died the same day. Almost the whole shift saw that, and we all checked out right away. No one needed 'counseling'—not on record at least."

Still frowning, Rob muddled that over. "And I don't believe in coincidence. Okay. Let's copy everything we can. Take pictures to your cell. Email those to Adler. There's a decent possibility that someone knows we're here. Susie the clerk was on her phone when I came out. No idea what that means, but . . ." He sighed. "Given all of it, let's just go straight to the horse. I think it's time to go visit Grady."

^ ^ ^ ^ ^

The drive home was somehow longer than the one out. Jason's bag was stuffed full of copied documents. They had more evidence and probably were in possession of other facts that they simply hadn't sorted out yet. But neither of the men was in a good mood.

They headed over to Grady's house. Just as Clark had said, he was in a nice neighborhood, in a nice house. Clark's description had been that the Grady family had moved three times—each place nicer than the next. It wasn't blatant, but it was clearly more than a firefighter could afford, unless . . . Unless he also ran a booming Internet business. Unless he was also independently wealthy. Unless his wife made a ton of money.

All things Jason would have to check out before he passed judgment.

The Grady family didn't seem to have any such reservations about passing judgment.

Rob and Jason had taken Banner on leash and walked right up to the front door. Jerry Grady had not anticipated this move, because he had not been on lookout—as evidenced by the fact that he hadn't answered the door himself.

A woman in her thirties had. She was brunette and golden-eyed . . . and distracted. She'd politely not quite looked at the men on her porch and was midway through a rote recitation of "hello, what can I help you with?" when her mouth flew open and she gasped.

"You!" she pointed at Jason like she knew him.

That had been unexpected. At a loss for words, he shook his head, trying to indicate that he had no idea what she was talking about. Rob had moved slowly to the side and seemed to be waiting to see how this unfolded.

The woman finally pushed her mouth back together and looked at Jason like an odd specimen. But then she said, "You look just like my father. Holy shit. Like one of the pictures of him from when us girls were little."

Jason was dumbstruck.

Though he had suspected Jerry Grady was his birth father, he hadn't expected to encounter this. The woman wasn't hostile, just fascinated in a clinical sense. She even yelled into the house without turning her head, "Marcy, you have to come see this!"

Another woman, around the same age and clearly a sister, came out wiping her hands on towel. Her own matching golden eyes were narrowed at the first woman. Her dark hair was curly and coming out from a haphazard clip at the back of her head.

Jason was unable to speak as she uttered in sharp tones, "I'm in the middle of making dinner."

But the first sister, who looked a bit younger than Marcy, was still awestruck and missed the rudeness in her sister's voice. "Look at him. Who does he look like?"

Marcy's finally looked at him, her gaze sweeping over, up and down. "He looks just like Dad did." Then she met his eyes. "You must be one of his illegitimate children. Is that why you're here?"

Jason shook his head.

Except that was almost a lie. He hadn't come because he wanted to meet his 'father'. Nor did he want anything from any of them. But the reason he was here—all the things that led to him standing on this porch talking to his biological father's daughters—was because he was Jerry Grady's illegitimate child.

At last he opened his mouth to say something only to be beaten to the punch by the first sister. She spoke not to him but to her sister. "You knew Daddy had other children?"

"Amber, don't be a fool. I love Daddy, but he's a whore. I don't think he's been faithful to Mom ever."

As Jason watched, Amber absorbed what was clearly a harsh blow, and though he hadn't dealt it, he had brought it about by showing up. "I just wanted to speak to him. I don't want anything but a few answers."

He didn't even get the end of the sentence out, he was drowned out by a loud hiss.

The sound came from an older version of the two women standing in front of him. "You! Get off my property!" Her voice screeched like nails on chalkboard. "I know who you are. You're the son of that two-bit station house tramp, and I won't have you here!"

If Jason was surprised then it was no match for the expressions on Amber and Marcy's faces. Amber even started to cut in. "Mom—"

But her mother shoved her away with something akin to brutality as she advanced on Jason.

He wasn't really scared. He was bigger than this one woman was. The other two weren't turning on him; they were still more fascinated by the scene in front of him than they were angry about anything. And in the corner of his eye he saw that Rob had been observing until the older woman had charged, and then his gun had come slowly out of the holster. At his side, Banner let out a low growl.

Mrs. Grady saw none of this. She only had eyes on Jason. "Your mother was a whore and you're a whore's son. She tried to pass you off as my husband's, but it was a *lie*. And now you will get off my property or I'll call the police!"

Behind her in the hallway, he saw two small children. No one else seemed to notice them, not even the man they were with . . . Jerry Grady.

Grady's eyes met Jason's, and Jason gave a slight nod as though to say "check". But then he turned, ignoring the older woman who was still yelling and facing the two younger ones. Regardless of what these people might do, he would not do anything to upset the children. "Marcy, Amber, nice to have met you."

And with that he turned and headed down the steps.

One of the daughters called out, "What's your name?" only to be screeched over by her mother's shrill voice saying he didn't have a name, he was just the bastard child of a whore.

It was Rob, still standing on the porch as Jason and Banner walked away who said, "His name is Jason Mondy and he's with the Southfield Fire Department."

There was a surprised, "He's a firefighter?" but Jason only thought he heard it.

The venom of the mother was turned on Rob. "Get your black ass off my property or I'll call the police."

A surprised, female shout of "Mother!" was closely followed by Rob's modulated tones. Jason could hear the smile in the words. "Ma'am, I *am* the police. Now you have a nice day."

By the time they had the car doors closed, the house had been sealed up tight, all the stragglers cleared from the porch and the door shut on the scene. Though the curtains in the front window fluttered, the two men pulled away without a wave or any other provocation. Jason could hear screaming from inside the house.

But as they rounded the corner, Rob commented, "I think you just met your half-sisters."

Struck dumb a second time by that thought—he hadn't made the connection himself—Jason stayed quiet and tense the whole way home.

He'd said a simple thank you to Rob at the curb of his apartment and realized it was one of the last times he'd get dropped off there. He had found another place, an eight-unit, four-story building. His new apartment was smaller in square footage, only one bedroom, and older construction in a poorer section of town. But he was a big guy and he managed to get a ground floor unit, so Banner would have a small yard. And, most importantly, the rent was less than half of this place, even with the dog.

Man and dog took the elevator up to their floor, worn from the day, body and soul. But when he turned the key in the lock Jason was hit with a sense of relief. He hung up his jacket on the hook and turned to see Amara, full bag slung over her shoulder, standing at the bookshelf that held the phone.

For a moment, she was just writing and didn't seem to notice him. Jason, on the other hand, noticed that it wasn't the apartment that made him feel the relief. It was some sense that she was there—even before he saw her.

Then she turned and offered half a smile. "I came by to grab some stuff. I listened to the messages just in case any were for me, and I was writing you a note."

Taking the small, green slip of paper covered in her neat writing, he held her gaze. He'd screwed up with her. Badly. And he had no idea how to say so.

With an ease he didn't possess around her, Amara began telling him what she'd been writing. "You have several messages on your machine. One from Chief Adler, reminding you about the barbecue tomorrow. Another from Clark. I saved them both for you, but you have to push the button, it's not blinking anymore."

"Thanks."

"But, when I first got here, about five hours ago, the phone rang. So I answered it. It was for you. A man said he was Captain Smith with the Montgomery Fire Department and he wanted to talk to you about your mother."

Cold fear swept through him.

It must have been Grady. And he'd spoken to Amara—which meant he now knew there was a woman in the house.

Without thinking, he grabbed her by the arms and looked into her eyes. "Leave. Get out of town. Now."

He'd faced Grady today, and the man was clearly pissed. This was the man who had murdered a woman. Or been party to it. He'd also appeared to have murdered another firefighter. He knew where Jason lived and now he knew Amara was here. "You have to get out."

Angrily she shrugged out of his grip. "Oh, don't worry. I'm leaving."

Fuck. Fuck. Fuck. But wasn't that what had gotten him in trouble in the first place? So he tried again.

"No, Amara." *Not like that.* "This guy, he's dangerous."

But she was already out the door.

Southfield Fire Station #2

SHIFT	A	
	O'CASEY	CAPTAIN
ENGINE 5	STANDARD	ENGINEER
	GRIMSBY	FF1 / EMT
	NAGY	FF1 / EMT
RESCUE 1	WANSTALL	LIEUTENANT
	MONDY	FF2 / EMT
AMBULANCE 7	DONLAN	ENGINEER/PARMEDIC
	WEST	FF2 / ADV EMT

Chapter 24

Clark walked into the station house without knocking or announcing himself. It was the only way Jason was going to speak to him. Because the fact of the matter was that he'd screwed up big time. And he knew it.

In holding on to the belief that he'd been left for dead, he'd shut out the only family he had. For twenty-six years, he'd lived to find Jason. As a child, he'd first held onto hope that his brother had been looking for him and would want him back. Then as a teen he'd been motivated by revenge for being left behind. As he'd matured, he'd told himself he just wanted to see the man who could do what Jason had done to him—the boy who could be the brother he'd had, then turn around and leave a near infant to a certain death.

In Clark's wishes, Jason slept every night haunted by the brother he'd left to die.

No such thing had happened.

And no such thing should have happened.

He'd been wrong.

Though his facts had been correct—Jason *had* pushed him into the back of the closet and closed him in while he ran to safety—Clark's interpretation had been all wrong. It was worse that the knowledge of seven-year-old Jason's motives had come, not from Jason, but from those who had pulled the boys from the fire.

Truthfully, Clark might not have believed Jason if he'd yelled or been mad—if he'd defended himself and his actions that night. He'd done none of it. He honestly didn't remember. But others did. The hospital records at Baptist showed that he'd been treated

later for having destroyed his vocal chords between the smoke
he'd inhaled when he ran into the fire to find help and the
screaming at the near-deaf firemen once he'd found that help.

As an adult, Clark now knew that being locked in the closet
was the best thing for him though he'd been petrified at the time.
Jason had shoved clothing around the bottom of the door and into
the hole they had climbed through from their own apartment.
They probably had the cleanest air of anyone in the building, at
least until Jason had run.

It felt odd and unsettling, the loss of his anger.

Clark hadn't realized he'd carried it like a physical weight
until he felt it lift.

Unfortunately, the lightness of being had been short-lived.
Quickly, Jason's anger had settled into the vacancy, and rightly so.

Clark had stayed away for a few days. Hoping—in a fit of
sheer stupidity—that if he left Jason alone, his brother would have
an epiphany and see things from Clark's view and forget about
being mad.

It hadn't happened.

He'd called and left a message.

His call had not been returned.

And here he was, probably about to get his head bitten off by
either his brother or one of the angry tigers surrounding him.
Clark suspected there was a family here in this station house. That
they might not always play nice, but if they all agreed that Clark
had fucked over one of their own—and he admitted that he *had*
done that—then they were likely to take turns tossing him like
sharks with a seal.

He stepped around the corner into the front area. He was
ready.

At the wide front desk, two of them sat, shooting the breeze.
They looked up as he came in. There were no polite greetings, no
"can I help you?" of the kind issued to the few random people
who walked in off the street. All he got were flat glares. They
knew what he had done.

For a moment, he stood there and didn't say anything. He'd
seen one of the trucks was gone from the bay, and he wanted to
ask if Jason was in, but the looks on their faces made him think
twice. Instead, he asked, "Do you mind if I go back?"

One of them shrugged. The other just kept staring. So he gave
a truncated nod and headed deeper into the station house.

He almost stopped short at the sight of Jason sitting in one of the recliners, reading a paperback. His brother looked up as soon as Clark entered the space, as though he could feel him.

With no hello to greet him, just another blank expression, Clark opened with the best he had. "I'm sorry. I should have told you sooner."

Jason nodded a simple agreement and put his head back into his book.

A sigh of frustration was not appropriate. He needed to patch things, not make them worse, so he struggled but held it in. While he waited to be acknowledged again, Clark let his gaze wander around the room. It was the same as it always was—neat, clean, and just a little worn looking. The wall behind the long table now held taped-up newspaper pages from the *Southfield Press*. Huge color pictures of the barbecue held on Saturday were surrounded by columns of print on various related topics. The room wasn't big; he could read the headlines from where he stood—there was a farewell to Gold Standard. A follow-up on Merriman, Tunstall, and Platt and the case that was being built against them for the Bear Mountain Fire. One was more general—what the new Southfield Fire and Rescue Department does: bold type headlined paragraphs about Fire Suppression, Education, First Response, Rescue, General Disaster and Accident Relief, Hazmat, and now EMS Services.

He saw all this from where he stood waiting for Jason to concede to his presence again. When he finished reading what he could on the wall, he gave up. "Look, I have more information if you want it."

"You can give it to Chief." Jason didn't look at him, just spoke the words into his book.

So Clark complied and went to get Adler. He waited while the other man filled out some paperwork; he wasn't in any hurry here. And if patience got him a little further with his brother, then he'd wait. When the Chief indicated that he was finished, Clark spoke for the first time. "I have more information about the investigation. I thought everyone should know."

Adler nodded slowly and crossed his arms. But no words came out. He just gave the same blank stare as all the others.

It hit him then: though Jason was his brother, and the one he'd been worried about, he'd screwed over the Chief, too. Along with everyone in the group and some of the firefighters, too. They had each invested time searching for Daniel, and he'd been right there, quiet all along. He was opening his mouth to apologize—something he figured he had a lot more of coming—but Adler beat him to it.

"Do you want a chance to explain yourself?" The arms stayed crossed, the expression flat, as though he was waiting for Clark to hang himself before he passed his own judgment.

"That would be nice. But I'm not sure I have a great excuse."

Adler still waited. Realizing it was now or never, Clark started talking. "I was never mad at *you*. I understand—in fact I've known for a long time—that Jake Strobel lost his life saving me. I visit his grave, every year. I don't know if that means anything to you, but I'm not a horrible person, and I work every day to make sure that if he had known who he was saving he would do the same thing again, that he would think it was worth it."

Nothing.

"I didn't tell you because I didn't know what kind of man my brother was—"

This time he got interrupted.

"You didn't give him a chance. Sounds like you had him tried and convicted before you walked in the door."

"I did." He could own up to his mistakes. "I was a kid when everything happened. And I didn't get any other perspective on it. I had no reason to doubt my memories. But I should have."

At that, Adler gave . . . just a little. "It's not that you should have told us earlier. I actually understand that. It's that you ran us like rats on a wheel. You had us go out and search information we didn't need to. You sent us on goose chases."

"No. No." He shook his head. "I didn't." *How the hell was he going to explain this?* So he just tried. He reminded himself that he was a writer and that he'd better pull out his best skills here. "I sent you directly to the source any time I could. I short cut every chance I had, every place you might have spent extra time, I put you in the right direction."

"Like it was a game?" Adler's face grew darker as he spoke. "That doesn't make up for the fact that you sent us out to find Grady and into Montgomery to follow up on things that didn't need to be followed up on. You sent us to find out things you already *knew*."

"No. I didn't. I didn't know who Grady was. I didn't even know that was the name of the man who visited me. I didn't know if the nurse at Greil remembered him, and we needed real research if we were going to prove anything. The only things I would have been able to stop was Jason looking into CPS—but he did a lot of that before I was involved. And I could have stopped him from checking with the foster families. But I was mad at him. I didn't want that kind of man to be my brother."

From the unchanging expression the Chief wore, he'd gained no ground.

Shit.

"The thing is, son, even if all that is forgiven, you had us sign away our legal rights to a story you plan to publish. We signed away things we didn't understand, but you did." The older man was leaning forward onto his desk. Not a good sign. And definitely a rough accusation.

"There's nothing I can show you or that I can do at this point. I *did* have you sign the paperwork for that. And my intention was to have a way to throw Jason under the bus for what I thought he did to me. Though I never intended to cause harm to the rest of you, I don't know how to tell you how much I hated him."

He took a breath then and as Adler waited, still flat faced, Clark put words to a history he'd never told before. "I grew up in the foster system. I was passed from house to house, though I wasn't a trouble-maker. I was mostly a paycheck. I was fed and clothed just well enough to be legal. I was put to work or ignored. At one home we were hit or locked into a closet—"

A whispered "*Jesus*" interrupted him.

"Don't. That's probably about the worst thing anyone could have done to me, but no one bothered about my background and very few bothered about my presence. There was one home I was in that was wonderful. I thought they loved me and hoped they were going to adopt me—which was stupid, because they had tons of other foster kids and they didn't adopt any of them. But I was shocked that as soon as the system suggested I be moved out, they sent me on to a group home with no compunction.

"And everywhere I went, this strange, frightening man followed me and every month made sure I knew to stay quiet. I'd seen him argue with Mom. And I saw him the night of the fire. He helped the EMTs load me into the ambulance, and the look he gave me scared the shit out of me. If I could have talked, if I had known to try, I would have had police security at the hospital.

Instead, I was tied to my bed by tubes and practically shitting my pants that I was about to be murdered."

Clark paused for a moment, but held up his hand to stop Adler from what he was about to say. "I'm not playing the sympathy card. I'm *not*. I just want you to understand why I hated Jason so much. I was convinced that he saved himself and never came looking for me. Other possibilities just didn't occur to me. Because he was older, I never really understood that he was just a child, too. So I didn't tell anyone when I suspected I had finally found the right Jason. And I didn't tell when I finally confirmed it. I should have. But I didn't know what I know now."

He shrugged. That was it. He'd played all his cards and he could only hope that Adler could find some sympathy.

"That's a harsh story, son."

"It is."

"The problem is, it's not me you have to convince."

"Thank you, sir." So he finally got to the business he came for, well, the excuse he gave himself. "I have some new information. I've been calling Jason but he isn't returning my calls. Maybe we could all sit down out in the main room?"

Just as he said it, the phone rang.

"Shit." Adler picked it up and listened, then put it down just as the bell started clanging. Without acknowledging Clark, he strode out into the main room where all the firefighters were gathering.

The Chief started pointing. "Donlan, West, you're out in the ambulance. Older woman with chest pain. The son called it in. He's with her, but a bit panicky."

Clearly used to the routine, the rest of them turned back to whatever they were doing. The emergency was handled.

Clark had followed the Chief out into the big space and decided to take advantage of the fact that he had Adler and Jason in the same room. The others here knew the story already, so it didn't really matter if they heard anything. And it *did* matter if he managed to get his brother to speak to him again.

Without taking the time to gather them into a cohesive group, Clark just started speaking. He aimed himself as though he and Jason were having the conversation. "Rob sent me the fire report that the two of you pulled from Pelias. I told him I thought it looked shoddy."

That, at least, turned Adler's head. "What do you mean?"

"The report was poorly filled out. There wasn't much actual information in it. Only names of some people who said that the Pelias fire was accidental. There was no description of the evidence or why they thought it was accidental."

Adler nearly frowned looking at him. So did Jason.

But it was the Chief that spoke. "Rob thought that was because it was old."

Clark shook his head. "No. I pulled a bunch of old reports to compare. The information then was of a different type. The autopsies have no DNA evidence, and there are no tests in the fire reports for trace accelerants, because the tests weren't developed yet. But to a certain extent, sometimes the reports were better—more thorough—maybe because they couldn't rely on testing."

He took a breath but got nervous when no one spoke to fill the void. So he did. "The report was often used as evidence in a court case. So they catalogued as much as they could. There should have been something in there about the origination points. Some kind of speculation about what started it. It's not there. Just a list of a few people who declared it an accident."

There was a pause again. Jason frowned at him, and Clark took it to mean that he'd said his piece and he should go now. But he wasn't done.

"I've been digging up what I can on Grady. And I asked Rob to help."

Even with that opening, Jason still didn't ask him anything—just sat in that stupid recliner and didn't forgive a damn thing. His brother was a hard man. And Clark had been stupid enough to build the brick wall he was butting up against. So he sucked it up and shared what he'd found, even if they didn't ask.

"Grady has received no inheritance that's on record. His wife appears to be a genealogy buff, so I pulled them up pretty easily on Ancestry.com. From there, I checked all the relatives I could find. No one in that family has enough money to support themselves *and* send more to the Gradys. Mrs. Grady has never held a job under her social security number. She attended college and married Jerry about one month after graduation. So the income isn't from her. And the mortgage on that house would be too big for his paycheck. Except that it's been paid down. The re-fi they hold on it is for less than a third the value of the house and they've only been living there for seven years. But the deed is in their names. So that wasn't helpful."

Again, nothing came, and he filled the space. "So, the Gradys are definitely living beyond their means. There's no source for the income to support it, obvious or not."

"So you think he's getting some kind of payoff?"

Adler again. Not Jason.

"That's my guess." Clark shrugged.

Then to his surprise, Jason volunteered something. "When Rob and I were out, Grady called the apartment. Amara talked to him."

Adler looked confused. "We knew that."

Well. Clark *hadn't.* No one had bothered to tell him that Grady had made contact again. "Did he say he was Captain Smith?"

Jason nodded. "But I was so worried about Amara, that I didn't make the connection – The thing is he called the apartment *before* Rob and I went to see him."

"Shit." Adler drew the word out, as though the saying of it bothered him.

Clark felt his lips press together and his eyes narrow. Another thing no one had bothered to tell him. "You went to *visit* him? *In person*? You didn't go to his house, did you?"

"Yup, that's exactly what we did. Rob is a police officer and he was armed." He was starting to put his nose back into his book when Clark exploded.

"And you didn't think to ask the rest of us before you did this? Or did you just confer with everyone but me? You know Grady harassed me all my life. You didn't think it was at least important that I know you did this?"

Jason stayed calm in the face of his ire. "It seems to me that changing your name and your look was quite effective. Grady hasn't harassed you since. He's moved on to me, and now to Amara. So, no, I didn't see the need to alert you."

And with that he put his nose back in his book. But it would have been impossible to miss that Clark stormed out of the station house.

Jason guessed that was the end of that conversation. There was maybe more to say between him and the Chief. But he stayed quiet. And stayed where he was in the recliner, book clutched tightly. It was the only way he knew to keep from looking like he was actively fighting the shaking in his hands. It was less that he didn't want the other guys to see it, and more that he wanted to ignore it.

So he sat there, with the book in front of him as though he were reading it. Fifteen minutes later he started to feel the crick in his neck and realized he hadn't turned a single page.

^ ^ ^ ^ ^

The call came at 2:30 that afternoon.

They all heard the phone from up in the Chief's office; they were tuned in to the ring that came just before the bell rang. Though they all went on alert for the bell, they snapped back at the string of swear words the man uttered.

For a moment everyone on duty all stood and looked back and forth as though one of them would offer a solution or at least a reason.

Because they were already startled, when the bell rang, they jumped.

Adler stalked out into the main room, his face pinched and his head shaking. He pointed and barked orders, just like last time. "Wanstall, Mondy. Kitchen fire."

Trying to be agreeable, they nodded, still wondering why he'd been swearing. And as they turned to gear up, he told them.

"I don't like this. This whole day smells bad. None of the runs this morning have panned out. There wasn't even anyone there when Donlan and West went on that last run. The first fire this morning looked like it had been set *after* the call came in. That's why Engine 5 didn't call for backup. They shut it down quickly and easily because it was fresh."

He rubbed his face. They all knew that the longer they talked, the longer their response time was. And they were measured by their response time. But Adler wasn't finished. "I also found out, just now, that Tunstall was released on bail two days ago. And this new 911 call came in on a cell phone."

That wasn't unusual. People often called from cells; they got out of the house then called in their emergency. It was often much safer than staying inside. But it did mean that the tracking system didn't work, and the emergency workers had to rely on the address given. Sometimes, you couldn't even trace the phone to the owner. The 911 operators always asked for name and information, but again with cell phones they were at the mercy of the honesty of the callers.

"Shit." Missy heard the word come out of her own mouth.

"Fuck." Was what came out of Jason's.

At a brisk run, she headed back into the locker room before meeting Jason out in the bay at Rescue 1. Popping up into driver's seat, she shifted a little to get her back comfortable and then made sure he was strapped in before they rolled out.

About three blocks away, she took a left through a red light while Jason worked the horn. Then—when they were safely past the intersection and he'd quieted them to just the sirens—she asked, "Do you think it's Tunstall?"

Jason shook his head then changed his mind and nodded. "It could be. He could keep us running all day. He already killed two of our guys with Bear Mountain. And then he had no cause to be mad at us."

"Sure he did. In his head, it all makes perfect sense." She went another mile before she murmured, "I don't like this."

Clearly neither did he.

They were approaching the address in question but could find nothing obviously wrong at first look.

There was no one standing on the lawn. Normally when people left a fire and called 911, they hung out nearby and waited for the trucks to show. But no one came out to greet them; no one even said hello.

There was no smoke coming from the property. Nothing leaked from the windows; no black plume headed skyward over the house.

Jason and Missy looked at each other and she did her job, calling all that info in.

Chief swore on the other end of the line, but then signed off.

They hopped down from the rig, not even donning their gear for this initial assessment. Doing a full visual inspection, Missy hoped to notice something that would explain why this was so odd, but she didn't find anything that made her feel better.

In fact, as she sniffed at the air she didn't like what she smelled. A vague chemical odor clung near the house, not at all like a kitchen fire. There was no telltale scorch of food and grease and appliances, no fluffy gray smoke that indicated wood and structural elements were on fire. But the chemical smell was reminiscent of . . . she couldn't place it.

Jason was sniffing the air, too, his eyes darting back and forth. The growing concern she felt had to show clearly on her face. The tight braids she wore didn't give her a place to hide her expression and she was no good at bluffing. Just as she opened her mouth to ask what he thought was happening, the walkie buzzed.

Chief's voice came through. "Are you in yet?"

"No, sir. We're at initial survey, sir. We don't see anything obvious." Her tone conveyed more than her words could.

Even as she spoke they began walking the property. They weren't ready to go inside, nor in this situation were they willing to take the usually trusting route and split up.

Adler's voice came through the scratch of distance. "Stay together. I mean it."

"Oh, we're already on that, sir."

Jason smiled at that. They were stuck like glue; the only thing they weren't doing was holding hands.

"Tell Mondy to put his walkie on. We're gonna keep the lines open for this one. Keep talking to me."

She didn't have to say anything; they were close enough that Jason heard and reached up to flick the switch on his walkie, already pinned to his suspenders. "Sir." He spoke just to make vocal contact.

They both had their tags hanging just inside the back of their gear pants, but they were out of range for Chief to follow their progress. Though Missy didn't like wearing strong electronic signals on her person—she was a big believer that the increase in brain cancer was due to cell phones—she still would have liked to have a long-range signal on her right now.

Adler didn't respond to Jason's voice, just gave a "Tell me what you see."

Missy, as lieutenant and highest rank, spoke, cataloguing their progress. "Outside of the house appears clear. There's an odd smell in the air. I can't place it."

She looked to Jason who motioned that he agreed with her.

The words came through with a bit of static. "Accelerant?"

"No sir." Missy was calm and polite, though she wanted to say, *no, of course it wasn't accelerant or I would have said so.* But she knew Chief needed to ask. And she knew her desire to snap back at him was a good indicator that she was stressed about the situation.

When she was weirded out, she was usually right to be so. The guys called it feminine intuition, but they didn't balk at her and usually paid attention. Still, there was nothing to say now.

Everyone was on their A-game. And Missy knew she wasn't the only one concerned about the feel of this run.

They were back around the small building just as the Chief's voice came again. "Listen guys. The call that Donlan and West went on—the possible MI? —it was at an abandoned property. Fairly recent, so it didn't look like a vagrant spot. But the house had been foreclosed."

Missy frowned, stopping at the front steps.

They had to go up and check things out. It was their job; they couldn't stay out here on the off chance that someone was inside, hurt or stuck. But their own safety was legally at the top of their to-do list. In fact, the majority of on-scene deaths, Connelly's included, were because firefighters neglected their own safety in favor of getting the job done. This time, the two of them held back.

Missy asked her question. "Wouldn't there be notices on the door?"

"Must have been removed." They could hear the warning in Adler's tone.

"Okay, sir. We're heading up the steps."

She knocked loudly on the front door and called out for anyone inside to come talk to them.

Nothing happened, and while Jason watched the door and tried to peer into the windows for signs of movement, she did a sweep of the neighborhood again. Several people had come out on their front steps. One in a bathrobe, looking at the truck oddly and pretending to drink some tea on her tiny front stoop. The other openly ogled the scene. Nothing unusual there.

When they tried the knob, they found it unlocked and pushed the door open only to be greeted by a slow rolling cloud of yellow-gray smoke.

Missy hollered out again while Jason updated the Chief on what they saw.

When there was no answer from inside, they turned back to the truck to get into their gear.

They lost contact through the walkies as they put the masks on. And though Jason and Missy could communicate through the comms in the face masks, they could no longer talk to the station. Missy signed them off from Chief, but before she disconnected, she heard him say he was heading over in the truck. He didn't like the yellow quality to the smoke. And he reminded them again to be smart.

Jason's eyebrows went up, confirming that he, too, had heard one last "Fuck this day" as the Chief set down the headset. Smiling to herself, she did a check on everything. Adler had some throwback tendencies. One was that—though his phone in the office was wireless—he hung it up by putting it back in the cradle. Which meant if he said something between signing off and setting the phone down, the other party often heard it. Missy had no clue if the man knew that. But that last swearing made her smile, if just a little.

Then she and Jason turned to each other and lumbered back up the steps. The front door stayed open, the cloud of smoke rolling slowly out and down the steps.

Pointing to it, she saw that Jason understood. But all he said was, "Yeah, that's not good."

She'd been hoping that he'd have more insight than that, with all his fire-inspection training. Her recent lieutenant exam prepared her for a lot. But what she knew was that smoke went up. Fire made smoke, and fire pushed that smoke along the air currents. With this much smoke some should have been headed upward before they opened the door. And opening the door should have at least started a plume up into the sky. Instead it crawled along the porch and faded out over the grass like a sinister gray-green fog.

She didn't like the color change either.

"Do you know why it's green over there and yellower at the door?"

They were standing on the porch, almost entirely enveloped in the clingy fog.

"I have no idea. This is fucked up." Jason's voice came through clear even though his image became more and more distorted as the smoke slithered between them.

Still, a job was a job. There might be someone inside. She couldn't discount the Chief's warning that the department was it for Southfield right now: EMS, Fire, Rescue, you name it. They needed the trust of the town. And that meant they walked in— even when it all looked hinky.

She put out one gloved hand and motioned for Jason to follow her.

Five feet in, they were reduced to just feeling their way around, nearly blind.

A grunt escaped her as she ran into what she was pretty sure was a low wall. Impressions of shapes made her think it separated the living space from the dining area.

She said so, grateful that they had a strong audio signal. Jason's voice was the only thing clear.

"I got nothing, Mondy. You?"

The words had just exited her mouth when she heard the crack.

"Fuck!" Mondy's voice reverberated in her head as she scrambled.

Grabbing his gear jacket, she threw herself over the low wall she had just run into, pulling his huge bulk along with her as best she could.

Jason was forced to follow, landing on top of her in their blindness. Another crack sounded through the thick air as they rapidly untangled themselves. Getting her back against the wall was her top priority, and she felt Jason making the same movements beside her. In fact, they were pressed together, side to side in spite of the thick gear. It was the only way she knew where he was. He was so close, even his breathing was obvious in its rapid rise and fall.

Jason's voice came through the fight for air they were both suffering, as they sucked their air tanks too heavily in the adrenaline rush. "Was that—?"

She nodded though she knew he couldn't see. Her eyes scanned the thick yellow-gray cloud in front of her, but nothing emerged. "Gunfire."

Chapter 25

Jason

The thought ricocheted through his head as Jason pressed his back into the wall as best he could. They had walked into a shitstorm. The thick gear was a hindrance, and though it was protection against fires and many chemicals, it did next to nothing to stop bullets.

Frantically, Jason scanned the area even as he tried to forcibly slow his breathing. When his eyes proved to be as useless as they had before, he pulled the thermal sensor from its place at his waist and turned it on. In a moment the small screen came to life and he pointed it in various directions around the small house—all of which yielded nothing.

No source of heat meant there was no fire, and his concerns about smoke bombs and well-laid traps graduated to full-blown confidence. He tucked the thermal imager away since it was apparently of no use here. He couldn't even find the person who had shot at them.

Assessing their situation, Jason decided that at best they were pinned down and would need their air while they waited for the Chief to arrive. Even in that good scenario they would have to wait through negotiations that could run long.

At worst, they were about two seconds from a bullet that would sever an artery or go right through the skull—at which point how much air was left wouldn't matter at all.

The fact that he thought through all these scenarios so rapidly indicated he wasn't lowering his adrenaline and therefore wasn't actually reducing his breathing rate at all. But there might not be anything he could do about that. He was tense, angry, and as close to scared as he was capable of getting about his own safety.

He knew his job was dangerous. Knew he could die while doing what he was supposed to. But he also knew that was unlikely if he did his job well. And he wanted his work to be about saving someone else—not his own sorry ass. If he'd gone while pulling the Thurlow boys out, he would have considered that okay. But going out like this? By gunfire in a house full of chemically created smoke? Not okay.

That's what Jason was convinced this situation was.

It had to be smoke bombs of some kind. There was no heat, no evidence of fire, no person who had called it in.

Nothing emerged from the haze.

Nothing except the sound of another crack. Another shot. This one coming long after the first two. At least by his count.

Without vision to help him—he had only the simultaneous hope and fear that something would emerge in front of him—Jason tried to listen. He couldn't smell anything that would give him useful intel, but maybe he could detect footsteps through the floor boards.

Beside him, Missy squirmed, obliterating the ability to detect anything around him by feel. Putting his hand flat against her, he tried to still her movements and wound up wondering what in the hell she was doing.

She was as well trained as he was, actually better. They were taught to use senses other than sight when stuck without it, so why was she wriggling like that?

His hand didn't stop her movements. Missy struggled against him, intent on whatever she was doing.

With no other options, Jason moved his hand to the wall next to him in a vain attempt to feel movements in the house. Nothing came through the gloves, so he risked taking one off.

There was every possibility that he was exposing himself to some chemical that would burn or seep into his system through the skin. But he felt he had to do it. No more shots came. Which to him said that someone was waiting.

Someone waiting just beyond the reach of the thermal imaging detector. Waiting with a gun and likely a gas mask and possibly some way of seeing them when they couldn't see him.

This was definitely a setup.

His only consolation was that Tunstall and Platt seemed as much like idiots as Merriman did. There was every possibility they had shot off a few rounds and then run out. But he and Missy couldn't base any movements on that.

So with his glove off, he placed his bare hand to the floor and the first thing he noticed was the cool feel. The lack of heat wasn't definitive, but was another good indicator that this wasn't a fire. And the skin on his hand didn't burn or tingle. This was possibly just a garden-variety smoke bomb. Well, a cheap smoke bomb with an armed assassin or idiot in the middle of it.

Aside from his hand tracking along the floor and up the half-wall they were tucked behind, Jason didn't move at all.

Missy, beside him, finally sat still after what had felt like forever but had probably only been a moment. He was surprised to feel her fingers running along his arm until they found his hand, then she took it in her own and directed it.

First he noticed her gloves were off, too. Some of that movement must have been her removing her gloves and tucking them away, just like he had. But a half moment later he was shocked at what his hand touched.

A gun.

Missy held what must have been a Glock or something similar. It was semi-automatic and slick from what he could tell by feel. With his brain filling in the view he couldn't see, shapes emerged, and he could make out Missy, one hand gripping the gun and ready to fire, the other returning his hand to his own care now that they had communicated.

He whispered, "Glock?"

"Mm-hm."

Low voices shouldn't travel beyond the masks they wore, and the two of them would not take those off voluntarily. The gear and the linked air tanks kept them breathing cleanly and not writhing on the floor while their eyes or lungs burned.

Jason pressed back into the wall and closed his eyes. His brain was working too hard to see. And he had to leave the reins to Missy now. Again he spoke as low as he could, "Full clip?"

"Yes." He felt her scanning the area as he had tried to.

She needed to be able to see. Chances were that she would shoot at the next sound that she heard. And they would both have to pray that she hit their shooter and not someone else.

Another crack rang out from the other side of the room. But it didn't seem to be headed their direction from the sounds and feelings. The walls didn't splinter near them; Jason didn't feel the impact of the bullet at all. Now he had both gloves stashed, one hand pressed flat on the floor and the other against the wall, hoping to be able to relay something of value to Missy.

He felt her move.

It started slow—in his adrenaline-flooded mind, at least— then as she rolled forward around the low wall, Missy gained speed until she was flying past him. And, even though he expected it, he jerked at the sound of her gun firing.

A handful of shots lit the muzzle as she tried to pepper the area the original shots had come from. After she fired, she scrambled back against the wall beside him, as though she hadn't just given away their position or shot blindly into space.

But he would have done the same thing.

His ears rang from the series of close-range blasts she'd fired. Still, he pushed her to the right. It was a gamble, but the wall was on his left; it was the only way to go.

Missy pushed back, shoving him further into the corner and herself closer against him.

Again, he let her make the decision. He thought they should get out of the spot they were in since she had just given away their position. But as his brain cleared, he conceded that she'd bolted forward before she shot, then scrambled backward after. Hopefully that was enough to keep this idiot from coming right up to where they were and laying into them.

The reverb in his ears kept him from hearing if the perp was coming toward them or moving at all. Quickly he pressed his hands back to the floor and wall and felt movement. His best guess was that he detected footsteps.

For a moment, he prayed.

Another round of shots came off, this time to his left. And not from Missy.

Jason sucked in a huge breath, slowly. Or at least he tried to do it slowly. His body was braced stiff enough to shatter if touched, but he didn't feel bullets slam into him.

He did feel bullets hit the wall nearby. He thought he might have seen some movement about five to seven feet to the right that could have been bullets hitting drywall or furniture and splintering something. He prayed that's what it was.

Missy moved her elbow, nudging him. Only as she moved again did he understand that it had been a signal. Not knowing what she wanted, he did nothing yet. He couldn't tell if she was signaling for backup from him or if she wanted him to stay put. So he sat—immobile—because he couldn't process anything else to do.

Except wonder what the fuck she was doing with a loaded gun on a fire run.

She popped upright, feet braced, and stepped square on the fingers of his right hand as she did it. Though pain shot up his arm, he could tell she had no clue she was standing on him, and he didn't move. She needed to be steady to set her shots.

With a randomness he could barely see, she swung first left, then right, then back left, peppering the room, high and low, with shots.

Jason imagined he could see her face, the fierce concentration he knew she would wear. But he couldn't. He could see her right boot; almost two feet away it was blurry and clouded at the edges due to the thick smoke. Her left foot, still perched on his hand, he could see with relative clarity, but more importantly, he could feel the reverberation of every shot she fired.

And Missy fired shot after shot after shot.

Eventually she was rewarded with a grunt.

At least Jason thought that's what he heard.

He discounted it when the wall behind him jumped and reached out and smacked him in the back of the head. Missy jumped, too, and he took the opportunity to yank his hand out from under her foot.

He was flexing his fingers to test them when his brain put the pieces together and he realized the wall had not smacked him.

Several things happened all at once.

Jason realized the wall "jumping" had actually been a bullet striking very close to him. It was the shards of exploding sheet rock that punched at the back of his head.

And the recoil from Missy firing was replaced with her body bracing and nothing happening. In the next moment, she slid down the wall and in his head he heard her swearing. "Shit, shit, shit, shit, I'm out. Shit."

Then the footsteps walked up to them.

He couldn't see anything, but the other person—he hoped to God there was only one of them—was no longer trying to hide himself. In fact, Jason heard a voice as the man approached.

The sound was partially muffled, obscuring the tone and timbre. He couldn't recognize the voice through what he assumed was a gas mask. But he easily made out the words, and the laugh that followed.

"You're out."

Next to him Missy stiffened.

Though he expected feet to appear in his vision at any moment, they didn't. The steps wandered, the shooter unable to find the two of them in the dirty fog he'd created. They weren't quiet as Missy dropped the clip out of the gun as though ammunition might magically appear, or if she would find a jammed bullet and be able to rescue it. But the other man probably couldn't hear much better than they could, the protective gear muffled everything.

What they could hear clearly was each other. The comm system built into the gear was sharp, and if they kept their voices low, what they said should be limited to the sound systems they wore. They should be able to communicate without anyone being able to overhear them.

"It's a man." Jason whispered. It was important that they had the same description for the report, and for the police later. And just in case one of them didn't make it out of this house. That way, whoever *did* make it out would have all the info.

"He's big. The footsteps are heavy. Doesn't sound like stomping."

Jason nodded his agreement, then realized his moment of stupidity and spoke it. "Yes."

"Holy shit!" *That* he said too loudly.

Next to him, Missy jerked as the sound reverberated through her gear and apparently farther. From across the room the footsteps stopped.

Frantically, Jason dug beneath his gear and down to his uniform pants. Straightening himself out, he pushed his fingers into the front pocket. His frantic heartbeat slowed as he touched the smooth surface of the stupid bullet he'd been carrying around with him for good luck. Or maybe as a reminder that sometimes you could walk away from the worst shit.

He sat back into the corner, once again pressed into the wall and Missy. Reaching over, he pushed the lone bullet into her palm and prayed that it was the right size.

At the touch, her voice came through his gear, "Where the hell did—never mind."

He heard the small scraping noises as she pushed the bullet into the clip and snapped it back into the gun. Jason sent up a small prayer of thanks for the prevalence of 9-millimeter guns.

Whoever was out there heard the noises, too. The footsteps resumed a softer tracking around the room while Missy fiddled with the bullet. Then they stopped again for just a moment before coming directly toward the spot where the two of them crouched.

One bullet wasn't anywhere near enough. Not in the blind land they were in. "We have to run."

"Yup." Missy's agreement came almost before he finished speaking, and her next words came as he was opening his mouth to say the same thing. "Over the wall and to the door."

As firefighters, they trained for blind situations. You didn't last long in a fire with walls collapsing if you didn't have either an innate sense for where the door was or at least a good working system for always remembering it.

He had that innate sense. Missy did, too. Either of them could walk straight out of here regardless of the smoke bomb. It was the maniac and the bullets that would be a problem. "Stay low. Zig-zag. Stick together."

Her voice again overrode the end of his sentence, and even as he heard the words the footsteps slowly came closer. "In three. Two. Go."

While she counted, they made sure they had a good wrist lock on each other, then Jason launched himself over the wall and at the floor below, dragging Missy behind him.

As they went, he thought he heard a grunt, but he *knew* he heard the crack of another bullet and the nearly simultaneous splintering of the wall they had been leaning against.

Missy pushed him as she got her feet under her, and they headed to the right, hands locked together, backs hunched over, trying to present as small a target as possible for two running people in huge gear.

Another crack sounded behind them and, somehow of one mind, they switched directions and headed on a leftward diagonal.

Time moved like glaciers. The door was close in the small house, but through the lens of danger it seemed much farther away. At a slight signal from Missy, they changed direction again.

Jason calculated about two more zig-zags before they should be out the front door. Only no light was coming in.

They'd left the door open, like they always did, and even with the thick smoke they should be close enough now to see something . . . some light, some vague beckoning halo from the outside.

The thought that the shooter must have closed it was still tracing through his thoughts as he heard the third crack and felt Missy take the bullet. She took another step and stumbled, her leg trying to go out from under her.

To her credit, other than the irregularity of her footsteps and the one single small grunt she'd had forced out of her as the bullet went into her, she made no other noise. Even hit, she did her best not to give away her position.

But then she twisted and headed toward the floor.

It took Jason a minute to figure out what she was doing as she extracted her hand from his grip and replaced her fingers with the warm metal of the gun.

Missy was down.

There was one shot left.

And it was his.

Turning, Jason planted his feet, having some weird thought—which suddenly seemed perfectly reasonable—that if Missy could take a bullet then so could he.

Unsure if he was seeing what he thought he was, he braced his feet as the smoke moved and shadowed into what he wanted to believe was a man.

If he was right, the shadow was raising his own gun . . . but Jason wasn't willing to spend his last bullet on an elusive form that he wasn't sure of.

But then a flash of orange-red confirmed the shadow. The crack of the bullet leaving the chamber seemed to come later, sometime after the wind moved past his hands—the only part of him that was bare to feel it. He braced for the impact but it never came. The bullet must have missed.

With that thought came resolve. Quickly, already set, he aimed and pulled the trigger.

The gun recoiled up his arms, nearly forcing him to take a step back. The yell from across the room either confirmed his hit or that he'd simply angered his opponent. It seemed an eon later before the thud of a body hitting the ground made him think he'd maybe actually gotten the man.

Reaching down, he grabbed the shoulder of Missy's gear jacket and pulled. Unwilling to let go of the gun even though it was empty, he hauled his partner one-handed and backward.

No noises came from across the room that he could discern through the heavy gear, but he backed toward the front door still braced for a hit.

When he got there, he discovered the door was not only closed but locked. The bastard had shut them in as an attempt to keep them stuck and make them easier targets. Though he would have thought it impossible, Jason got even angrier. But he kept his head and ran his hand along the seam where door met wall until he found the locks and reversed them. It took two tries to open the damn thing.

The outside light blinded him, and some deep noise filled his head with static. He blinked against the pain, but he didn't loosen his fist from Missy's gear until he felt the hand on his arm. At first he pushed at it, a fresh wash of fear shooting through him. But as he blinked, Chief came into view and the roaring noise cleared as he realized Chief was yelling instructions to him.

Jason shook his head; he couldn't understand a word. He pointed to his ears, trying to indicate that his head was still ringing from the gunshots, but as he did he realized that he still held the gun in his free hand and had nearly aimed it at his own head.

For a second he was struck by the feeling of all his strength draining from him like liquid, and, forcing a deep breath, he fought to stay upright and read the Chief's lips.

Before he could make anything out, he saw the gun the Chief held. Similar to Missy's, it appeared loaded and Adler looked ready to use it. Jason shook his head and yelled over the noise, "I think he's down!"

Missy began to move, and it wasn't until he looked down at her that he realized Chief had gotten her into a proper hold and was starting down the steps, away from the smoke that was following them out the front door, and that Missy was using one leg to help him.

It took another small eternity for his adrenaline-infused brain to realize that he, too, needed to get his ass off the porch. What if the psycho inside wasn't fully down? What if he got back up and still had bullets?

Jason didn't want to be in range.

His legs felt like lead but made it down the four cement steps without giving out. Keeping his mask on—he saw that the Chief had his on, too—he headed out beyond the rolls of green-tinged smoke, the movement far too calm in execution for having just walked away from a trap.

Loud noise rang in his ears, leaving him as good as deaf. So he scanned the area and saw the Chief setting Missy on the ground behind the truck. It was then that Jason processed that the odd shirt Adler was wearing wasn't a shirt at all, but a bullet proof vest. That startled him and added gravity to the situation. They all had the vests, but he couldn't remember the last time he'd worn it that didn't involve a training drill. They hadn't even gotten them on at the shoot-out.

The Chief was waving at him, and Jason figured his brain must have worked so fast inside that it was unable to work well now. His processing capability was much too slow. Chief wanted him to come over. And clearly to get down behind the truck.

Through the haze that was still in his brain if not in the air around him, he realized that Adler was operating as though there might still be danger from the direction of the house. Jason thought he'd have taken a bullet by now if whoever was in there was going to keep at them. But then again, his sense of time was poor at best right now. And he thought he was making rational decisions, but hadn't he seen a thousand drunk people thinking the same thing?

He walked slowly toward the truck, his focus on Missy who was talking to the Chief. Jason then found the noise in his head was in part the remaining loud wail from the gunfire, but also it contained voices. Missy and Adler were coming through on the comm.

Chief refused to take off the masks. Missy refused to concede to any serious damage from getting shot.

She looked up at Jason as he made his way into the shelter of the truck. Chief grabbed his gear jacket and yanked him down into the safe zone. Jason stumbled, unprepared for the movement. But Missy just looked at him and gave a thumbs-up.

Through his comm came her voice, clear and focused in a way that he hadn't yet achieved. She gave her best British accent. "It's just a flesh wound."

For the first time since they had left the house, he smiled. Missy grinned back as the pain in his head peaked. It was only the light flashing red in his peripheries that made his brain finally stitch the last pieces together.

Ambulance 8 had pulled up. And instantly it all made sense. The noise in his ears had not been ringing from the guns. It had been the approaching sirens, a sound he now couldn't separate from the flashing lights.

He stood and walked up to Donlan, who was stepping down as Rescue 3 parked behind the first vehicle, and Jason spoke through the mask. "I think I'm in shock."

His Boston accent getting thicker, Donlan barked instructions, taking over. He ran to check on Missy and took Grimsby with him, pushing Jason into the care of the newly minted Advanced EMT West.

Jason let West hover, followed instructions, and soon found himself stripped out of his gear jacket as he watched Donlan talk to the Chief. Jason hadn't really heard the words, though they'd all come through his comm, but apparently they were searching him for bullet holes.

And they found one, too.

He had a graze on the outer corner of his right shoulder. Surprised by it, he said he'd felt a bullet go by, but thought he'd just felt the air move. Apparently, the bullet had moved the outer layer of his flesh, too.

West checked Jason's gear pants and found no other holes, then commented to Donlan that none of the wounds seemed affected by exposure to the smoke. Jason then mentioned that he and Missy had their gloves off almost the whole time they were in, leading to a thorough inspection of his hands, which showed no damage that anyone could find.

One by one A-Shift began taking the masks off. Only the few who approached the house continued to wear them.

Blinking against the light and huddling under the thin thermal blanket he'd been given, Jason sat with his right shoulder bared as West applied the necessary first aid. He was still fuzzy when Rob walked up beside him and asked how he was doing and what the fuck he'd gotten himself into.

Only after answering did Jason question his friend's appearance. It was then he processed the uniform blues, the lights and that the number of people on scene had more than doubled.

Cops—including Rob—pulled on masks and stood at the doors as firefighters joined them, positioning the big fans from the back of the truck to blow the smoke out of the house. No one went in.

It took a good fifteen minutes for the house to clear. During that time, Missy was loaded onto a gurney and sent to the hospital in the back of Ambulance 8. Donlan must have given her something to kill the pain because Missy was almost chatty, commenting how she was getting to try out the new EMS service from the inside.

West had tried to send Jason along with them but conceded the first time Jason refused. Jason took that as a good sign. Though EMTs weren't allowed to offer up diagnoses—and West would never presume to do so—had the injury been truly bad or really needed stitches, West would have pushed. The fact that he completely backed down and proceeded to cover the wound with some gauze and tape told Jason that it was about as minor as it could be.

West finished up with, "You'll probably have a scar. But, hey, chicks dig scars, right?"

Jason just grinned. But he wanted to say, 'What chicks?'

He'd run them all off. Even Amara. And she'd fled faster than most. After one day as something more than just his friend, she'd been out the door. Piece by piece her things had vanished from her room. And he'd heard from Alex that she'd moved away already. The only evidence that she'd even been there was the finally useful junk drawer, his Paramedic license and the gaping hole in him that he couldn't seem to do anything about.

He tried. He tried to tell himself it was about Daniel. About Clark. About the loss of his mother. But the fact was those were entirely separate holes, and he felt them all distinctly.

And here was West, commenting on chicks when Jason felt like Swiss cheese. He almost wished the bullet had gone through so he'd have a physical hole to match the ones he felt.

Instead, he was handed an energy bar and told to eat it.

He did. Sitting on the bumper of the rescue truck and chewing methodically, he watched the completely un-action-movie-like standoff between the cops and the house.

Thanks to the fans and opened or shattered windows, the sickly looking smoke now poured from every orifice. But it still looked sinister in the fact that it seemed to bear weight and sank to the ground rather than disappearing heavenward.

As he watched the smoke move, it occurred to him that he'd likely killed someone. He didn't want to process that. Didn't want to believe it.

He was still struggling with the fact that he'd done something in complete opposition to what he'd dedicated his adult life to, when one of the officers on the porch called the all-clear and the police went into the house.

Again, it was completely unlike TV. In fact, there was little to no action. The door was already open, the house was mostly clear of smoke except for the small layer that clung to the floor and now slowly dripped down the steps. The police officers didn't holler out that they were there. Just called out, "hello?" at slightly above average volume.

Jason waited.

Slowly, the officers moved in, guns out and at the ready. There were no shouts, no wild declarations, just Castor, coming down the steps a few minutes later and peeling his mask.

He looked at Adler, glanced at Jason, and then gave his report to his own commanding officer.

"One person. Deceased. Male. Wearing a gas mask. Hudson nearly tripped on him. Looks like he died from bullet wounds. They're bringing him out."

In fact, they were bringing him out even as Rob said the words.

Three officers executed a textbook carry down the front steps and into the center of the lawn where Rob, the police chief and Adler all met them. Jason trailed behind tugging his torn shirt back on over the gauze and feeling the bullet wound tug for the first time.

With a nod from the police chief, one of the blues bent down and peeled the gas mask from the dead man. Shrugs were passed around as officers crouched to get a better look at his face. His shirt was bloody in two places—the dead center of his chest and lower near his kidney or something. Copious amounts of blood had soaked into his clothes. He'd died from bleeding more than from bullets taking out something vital.

But even as he thought this, Jason exchanged a look with Adler and Castor.

The three of them waited until the police chief straightened and looked to Adler.

Jason turned away and peered out at the sunset. It seemed he'd left the house in the middle of the afternoon, and that the sun had simply sunk as soon as the man was brought out. It had been plenty bright before then.

So he didn't see the Chief's face. But he heard the words.

"I've got an ID. He's a firefighter out of Montgomery. His name's Jerry Grady."

Chapter 26

Jason

He'd been put on psychiatric leave. There was no way around it. Jason had shot a man and killed him.

Missy was on leave, too. Though she was also seeing the shrink, she was technically on "medical" leave because of her leg. It was enough to make Jason wish he'd gotten just a little closer to that one bullet.

The shrink was having a field day with him, too. Jason became concerned that the doctor simply liked the case too much to ever declare Jason mentally sound and send him back to work.

While Jason believed he was actually taking the whole incident pretty well, the shrink seemed to be mining for psychiatric gold and Jason was just getting pissed. He didn't need to talk about his birth mother and the fact that he didn't remember her. He tried to be clear that he couldn't talk about Pelias, because all he knew about it was what he'd been told. The shrink tried to find veins of gold in Bloomberg's death, Merriman's betrayal, the dreams of Connelly and, of course, in the fact that Jason had shot and helped kill his own father.

To which Jason repeatedly replied, "He's not my father. My father is Bill Mondy."

Anxious to get back to work, Jason was going to see the shrink as often as he could get an appointment. At the fourth visit in the week and a half since the incident, Jason had stormed out half way through his session.

He'd yelled, "Jerry Grady provided sperm to a woman I don't remember and then he helped kill her. He's *not* my father. I've told you that more times than I can count."

The doctor had sat patiently in his chair, smug look on his face, and said "But he *is* your father."

Jason had held back his anger, sighing. "Your limited vocabulary makes you entirely unqualified for this position. I'm firing you on the grounds that you have absolutely no interest in clearing me for work or determining my safety as a firefighter. You have no desire for me to be mentally sound. In fact, you're actively trying to push me the other way."

"You sound very intelligent. I'm trying to find out what's in there, so it doesn't pop up later and interfere with your work." He motioned Jason to sit back down.

Jason didn't.

"No you're not. You've found an interesting case, and you want to pull it apart thread by thread." He held his hands out at his side in a mockery of regret, "Sorry, but the story's already been sold to the media."

Still the man sat there. "I'm only interested in your health. I'm the only one who can help you, Jason. Please sit." He'd gestured, open handed, to the couch.

"Please fuck off."

Jason had walked out with another twenty-seven minutes on the clock. He wasn't even to his car before he called Chief and left a message about what he'd done. Trying to make his case as clearly as possible, he added that he wasn't against seeing a shrink; he knew he needed to be cleared to return to work. He was simply requesting another doctor. He did not include that he'd told this doc to "fuck off."

Jason was trying to use his leave time as best he could.

He'd taken care of Banner full time, not having to leave him with Alex and Leo at all. They'd gone to an off-leash park nearly daily. Over the course of three days, he'd moved into his new apartment. The older building was just that—older, slowly falling down, in need of repairs. But the owner had told him if he fixed things himself he could take the supplies and a small hourly rate off his rent. The informal nature suited Jason, and the small yard suited Banner.

He moved most of his things himself, one carload at a time. He'd re-used boxes and even garbage bags, thinking that Kelly would have died of mortification at the thought of moving her belongings in garbage bags.

It had kept him busy, the slow process of pushing one apartment into another. He'd dumped each kitchen drawer into a plastic bag, labeled it, and realized his mistake only when he stood in the new kitchen looking at all the bags across the counter. There weren't as many drawers here, and the organization of the old place didn't make sense in the new.

As he stood there in his new-old kitchen, he had a small epiphany. He'd been trying to keep the organization of his old life in the new one. And it didn't fit any better than the drawers had.

His old life had his mother, a steady girlfriend, a regular-ish schedule. It had TV or a visit to Jenkins with friends on nights he was off work. It had the occasional event that said girlfriend would dress him up for.

The girlfriends had been interchangeable—he saw that now. Each time, he'd picked the next one in reaction to what had gone wrong with the one before, and still he'd consistently missed the point.

Though he'd started to make some progress in finding something different with Aida, she hadn't been right for him. And when he'd found something he should have held onto, he had kept the organization of his old life and ruined the new. But there was nothing he could do about that now.

Jason had called Rob to help with the furniture, the things he couldn't move by himself. Rob had beautifully pointed out that Jason was paying rent on two places while he slowly moved across town. And hadn't the whole point of moving been to save money?

They'd had pizza—on Jason—and haphazardly filled both cars with the remainder of small items from the old unit. He'd handed the keys to the front desk and not looked back.

So he'd found himself with a pile of things on his floor, while he rearranged the furniture twice in an attempt to see what fit the space and what fit him. He'd gone to the new shrink on schedule and was glad that it felt like this man was really just assessing him for fitness for duty. Surprisingly, that made it much easier to finally say how much Clark's betrayal had felt like a knife in the back.

He'd taken Rob to see Missy. They'd offered to bring her a pizza, but she'd balked, saying she'd eaten enough delivery to last a lifetime. In a small town like Southfield, that meant she'd subsisted on pizza and Chinese. So they'd taken her out to a nice lunch.

She'd worn jeans, girl shoes, some fuzzy sweater and her hair down. She looked like a normal woman, but drank a beer, talked about the bullet being a through-and-through and practically moaned her way through her steak.

With her cane hooked over the back of her chair, she became just Missy for lunch. But she lamented the injury and drew attention to it, "Because it's my right leg, I can't drive." She'd sighed. "But I'm going to start. I'll figure it out and drive with my left somehow. This steak has made it clear that I have to start eating better."

"I'll drive you. You shouldn't announce to a cop that you intend to hit the road injured."

Jason had just been about to volunteer; it wasn't like he had anything better to do anyway than help a friend out. But Rob's voice had uttered the words instead. Maybe "uttered" wasn't the right idea—the forward tone of the statements made Jason look at his friend with open eyes.

In his head, he muttered, *holy shit*, then spoke out loud, "I'll get you out of the house when this one isn't available." He hooked a thumb in Rob's direction, Missy's smile making it clear that she was both grateful for the rides and as interested in Rob as he was in her.

Jason got an earful on the ride back. He'd never heard Rob so keyed up about a woman, but Jason hardly thought of Missy that way. She was a co-worker. Just like he didn't think of Nagy or Donlan the same way he would if he'd met them out at some bar or through a friend. But Rob had no such distinction: though he'd met Missy before, he'd probably only seen her as one of the guys on A-Shift. Which was exactly what she'd worked hard to be. Well, that had changed.

"She eats beef. She shoots people. And she's already passed her psych eval, too."

That last one was like a jab in his side. "Yeah, well, it wasn't her birth father she shot."

The new shrink had at least understood Jason's argument on that one: that he'd been shooting, blindly, at a person shooting at him. He didn't know who it was. So the idea that he'd had some personal inner struggle whether to pull the trigger and end the life of the man who'd given him life never entered the picture—as the last shrink had tried to make it out to be.

"Speaking of . . ." Rob's voice pulled him back to the present. "Mrs. Grady is refusing to let her husband be genetically tested against you."

Jason sighed in response. "No surprise there." He wasn't even sure that he wanted it proven.

Rob seemed to understand that, and he got out of the car and followed Jason into the new apartment, greeting Banner with a head rub, rather than getting into his own car. "I know there's no love lost with Grady, but the advantage to having it done is that you don't wonder about anyone else, no matter what we find in the investigation or in the future. And it's just good to know your medical history. It could save your life."

"What does it matter? Mrs. Grady refused." Jason shrugged and plopped down on the couch, full from lunch and wondering what the hell to do with the rest of his day.

"Yeah, but the daughters volunteered. Seems they don't agree with their mother that daddy was a saint wrongfully accused by the whore Alcia."

"Oh." It hit him like a sudden wind. Opened his eyes and made him consider it.

Rob was perched on the arm of the couch, not quite committing to staying but not yet leaving either. "It's a swab to the cheek, bud. You can follow me down to the station. We'll hook up the girls. I have to tell you, I talked to the oldest and she seems real level-headed. Really wants you to do the test."

"Why? She just lost her father. In a bad way." He was silent for just a part of a second before he felt compelled to add, "*I* shot him."

Rob shrugged. "I believe her. She's Academy Award-worthy if she's faking it." Then he stood and dug in his pocket and produced a slip of paper. "Why don't you call her? Then you decide."

With that, he headed off to catch his 3pm shift and Jason was left awash in envy. He needed a job to go to. A week and a half was way too long to be off. And he had no re-entry date at this point. Just more shrink appointments and more wait and see.

He checked the weather and took Banner to the park before the rain hit. He promised himself he'd call the oldest daughter when he got back. So he and Banner stayed until they were drenched, and he was forced to do what he'd told himself he would. But he still postponed it, first with a shower, then a beer.

At four, he was convinced she wouldn't be home. So he manned up and dialed Marcy. He could picture her face. All three faces had seared into his brain—they'd meant nothing until he'd been headed down the brick walkway from the front door and Rob had told him he'd just met his sisters.

Marcy—damn her—answered on the first ring.

There were small voices in the background, and she said she needed five minutes to get somewhere so she could talk freely, then she'd call him back.

He was contemplating that she didn't want to make this call any more than he did, and then imagining that the small voices were nieces and nephews—which blew his mind—when the phone rang.

He hit the button. "Hi, Marcy."

"Sorry about that. My kids are small and love their grandfather. I don't know when I'll tell them about him. I counted on them being older before that conversation happened."

"What do you mean? They don't 'know about him?' They know who he is, right?" Jason was confused.

"Yeah, he's a wonderful grandfather—brings gifts, plays games. But I want them to understand when I explain that the kind of father and grandfather he is isn't the same kind of *man* he is." She sighed, and in the sound Jason heard her pain. She was rational (or one hell of an actress), just like Rob had said, but she wasn't indifferent. "I'm the oldest. I knew he cheated on my mom. All the time."

"Really?" That was fascinating to him. His own parents had been a stable, single, cohesive unit. It had rocked his world when his father died, partly because his mother still lived. He had no way to measure her as her own person while his Dad had been alive. That Marcy knew there was division between her parents and lived with it as a kid was beyond his comprehension.

"Yeah. I heard him sometimes on his phone with them. I caught him sneaking in after being out with some girlfriend. I remember commenting that he was wearing perfume that wasn't Mom's, even when I was little. As a kid, I was convinced it was all his fault. But as I got older, I realized my mother didn't care and didn't want to know. As long as she had her house and her pretty daughters and no one knew, she wasn't going to raise a stink."

"Wow." It slipped out and he immediately apologized for it.

When she asked, he explained about his mother and father. And he could almost hear her nodding as she said, "Good. Good. I'm glad you had a good life."

"Clark didn't."

"Yeah. I know." There was a pause. "As much as I wish that were different, there's nothing either of us could have done about it. We were kids. Neither of us even knew he existed."

A little of the weight lifted off of him, just at the thought that someone shared his burden. Marcy hadn't lived with Clark. But she felt the pain of not rescuing him, too.

Her voice pulled him back to the call.

"Sometimes I wonder if we shouldn't troll the state and look for others. You and Clark probably aren't the only ones. Daddy was a cheater. It wasn't just with your mother. I remember incidents long after she was gone."

Well, that was another rock in his shoe. One he didn't want to contemplate. But again, Marcy set him at ease.

"But I try not to worry, because I can't figure out a single feasible way to do it. I mean, do we genetically test every foster kid? They probably aren't in the system anyway, they probably have mothers. We can go through his things and look for names and addresses, but I'm not up for calling all his old girlfriends and upsetting their lives by asking if I have siblings."

"Me either."

And so they finally got around to what he'd called about. Marcy, who'd initially struck him as wary, motherly, and a bit stiff, was surprisingly easy to talk to. He found he was now anxious to go to the police station and get tested.

When he hung up, he was more afraid she would turn out to *not* be his sister.

She said Amber had already called Clark, and that Clark had said he'd come to Montgomery PD in an effort to keep the samples all together and reduce the likelihood of a mix-up. Jason agreed, saying he'd be there tomorrow. It wasn't as if he had anything like a job to do.

But he missed the house and the guys, and as he thought about it, he didn't want to eventually get back to work and find things had changed while he was gone. So he gathered Banner and headed to the station.

Partway there he called Missy and turned around to go get her. She was amazed to get out of her house twice in one day and just as glad as he was to see the guys.

She hugged the Chief when she saw him, though Jason opted for a handshake. They brought some food with them and sat at the table, talking to the guys. They answered questions about the call that had caused such trouble, the smoke bombs, and what the hell they'd been doing with guns and bullets in a fire.

Missy explained that she'd started bringing it to work after Jason and Clark had explained what was going on. Then she'd taken it that day when all the calls had been wrong. She'd never taken it out of the station house before that run. And she hadn't even brought it up to the house on the initial assessment, but once they had decided they thought it was a smoke bomb, she'd tucked the gun in the back of her waistband as she put on the rest of her gear.

Missy, at least, had been logical and thoughtful about her decisions. Jason had to confess that he'd simply left the bullet in his pocket after the shootout. He'd thought of it as a good-luck charm, run it through the washer, and basically ignored it. And, yes, the Chief had chewed him out—several times—for carrying a live round into fires, repeatedly. His only defense had been that he'd simply put it in his pocket and forgotten about it. It was pretty stupid. But he was pretty grateful right now. Who knows what would have happened if he hadn't had it?

Even Chief and the guys agreed, though the Chief had pointed out the possibility of blowing his own 'nads off with it. It had been Missy who countered with the extremely low likelihood of a single bullet exploding without a firing pin—even in very high heat. She'd laughed. "I'm more than willing to bank Jason's 'nads against my life."

"Thanks, Miss." He'd barely been heard above the gales of laughter around the table.

The Chief had been red in the face in an attempt to keep his own chuckles held in, when he excused himself. He stated before he left the room that he did not condone his firefighters carrying live rounds and that he certainly did *not* see any dog in his station house. Banner looked like maybe he smiled.

∧ ∧ ∧ ∧ ∧

Jason had come back to the station for at least one meal almost every day. He often picked up Missy, who was finally limping along without the cane. He got to know the guys on the other shifts better, and they all got to know Banner, whom the Chief repeatedly swore he could not see. Jason usually stayed until the bell rang and the house cleared out. With no one there, it was just bricks and mortar.

Adler noticed his repeated presence and asked how things were progressing.

"The shrink says I'm doing well and that he hasn't come across anything that would keep me from working, I just have an unusually long list of things he has to check me out on."

"Don't look at me." Adler held his hands up. "The psych eval form—which I *have* to fill out with this kind of death—specifically asks if you have had deaths in the family, or unusual family changes. All of it. It was just a series of check boxes."

"Figures." He hadn't blamed Adler. But it seemed he was never going to get out of psych, even though the new shrink was actually trying to be helpful.

Jason was on paid leave while he was being evaluated. So was Missy, for her medical leave. But the city was also paying overtime to the others who were filling in their missing shifts for several weeks. It was a drain on a department that never made it to anything near solvent. He was surprised by the Chief's suggestion that he come back the next day and start putting his fire inspector training to work.

"Doing what?"

"We need to do inspections of every public building in town. Frank has to rank priorities and do the walk-throughs. You can help pull records, determine need and maybe even go along and learn how to do the actual inspections. You keep hovering here, might as well have something to do."

Jason had blinked. Shadowing Frank, who'd been fire inspector for years, would be a huge benefit. He'd learn a lot. Frank worked Monday through Friday, regular hours. Jason could do part of his work here at the station house, with Banner in tow, and get some interning done, too.

"I'm in."

"Me, too, Chief." Missy's voice came through from the table. "I can do some of the record checking. Anything I can do at a desk to help out."

Adler smiled and nodded. "I'll let Frank know to expect you."

With that one exchange, Jason was suddenly useful again. From the look on Missy's face, she felt much the same. And that was how he found himself in the station, sitting at the front desk using the computer to pull local building code records, when Clark came walking in, a stunned look on his face.

Jason just stared at him. Didn't say hello like he did to anyone else who walked in off the street. For a moment, he contemplated offering up a greeting, just so he could tell the shrink he'd done it, but he didn't.

He was distracted by the dark suit and tie, the shiny shoes and very unshiny expression. Clark still hadn't said anything either. He looked like he was trying to form words, but just couldn't.

It was Adler who started the conversation. He'd stepped out of his office when Clark walked in, probably having seen him from his office window. "Are you all right, son?"

Clark shook his head no. But he did it like the Chief had asked if he "wanted fries with that?"

Jason looked at him again, but a little more closely this time. Something was wrong.

Clark looked a little rumpled, his keys dangled from his fingertips, and though he wasn't turning blue or falling over, he looked like he was thinking but not really breathing.

Adler took that in, too. "Why don't you sit down for a moment?"

He took one of the waiting chairs and pushed it to the center of the front lobby, right next to where Clark stood. But again the reporter shook his head as though a chair just wasn't quite what he wanted.

Since he didn't fall over, Chief and Jason glanced at each other and waited.

Someone else had come up into the doorway, Jason saw by the blue of uniform, but he didn't take his eyes off Clark to check who it was. Whoever it was waited at the periphery.

A moment later, another person appeared at the other side of the large open doorway to the hall back into the department. Still Clark hadn't spoken.

Then his keys slipped from his fingertips and made a small jingle against the floor. He jerked just the tiniest amount at the sound but didn't reach for them. "I went to the funeral."

Clark and Jason knew what he was talking about. But a voice came from the doorway, "Whose?" and identified one of the standers as Nagy.

"Grady's."

That explained the suit, if not the look on his face or the dazed way he carried himself.

"I left early and drove straight here."

The wrinkles in the nice fabric made more sense. He'd been down in Montgomery, where the Gradys lived and where they'd have the man buried. He'd seen their sisters.

"I heard the voice." Clark still didn't make eye contact with any of them. "I don't think I told you what was said the night Mom was killed. But I remember it. At least some of it." He rambled in a manner that wasn't normal, but he was saying something important, so they all just let him talk and didn't interfere, even though maybe they should have. "They had been talking, but not regular talking, it was loud and tense. Then I remember Mom yelled, 'I just want what's mine.' And the voice responded, '*No*, you want what's *mine*!'"

Jason was starting to put it together. He stood up behind the desk, as though being on his feet made it better. It didn't, but it afforded him a small illusion of control.

Clark had heard a woman in the house that night. There was every possibility that a woman had murdered Alcia. Why Grady was involved—aside from providing some genetic material—was a mystery. But Clark heard the voice again.

Jason finally entered the conversation. "You heard the voice at the funeral?"

Clark nodded.

He had a good idea who it was. It would make all the pieces fit together. But he didn't want to say it. He wanted Clark to say it first. "Who was it?"

"Mrs. Grady. Patricia Grady. She killed Mom."

After getting it out, Clark looked around and spotted the chair, finally lowering himself into it, as though he'd had just enough energy to say that, then he was done.

Adler pulled out his cell and called someone. From the sound of his side of the call, he was leaving a message for Rob Castor. He dialed a second time and got Bart English on the phone.

Then he started asking Clark questions, seemingly prompted from the ADA. "Was she still at the funeral when you left?"

Clark nodded.

Adler relayed that to Bart, then asked, "Does she know you know?"

This time a head shake in the negative. "I don't see how. I snuck away relatively quietly. It was a funeral after all. I didn't want to upset my sisters. But it doesn't matter."

His brother gave a sad grin that niggled at Jason's thoughts.

Adler relayed a few more questions. Where was the funeral held? Then he sent Nagy out with Clark's keys to get the funeral program from where he thought he'd dropped it on the passenger's seat. Was there a reception after? Clark shrugged and said he thought they were headed to the family home. He wasn't sure.

English already had the address from their previous research and he seemed to have signed off.

When Chief pushed his cell phone off, he looked up at Jason, then Clark, "They'll be sending the cops to her home to arrest her."

Clark's eyebrows went up. "They don't have any real evidence that I know of. And I think I would know of it if it existed."

But Adler shook his head and seemed to be repeating what he'd gotten from the ADA. "He said they have enough circumstantial evidence to hold her, and enough that points to her that they're hoping for a confession."

He looked like he was about to say something when his phone buzzed in his hand. Answering it, he gave only brief, single-word statements then signed off. When he raised his head, he looked Jason then Clark in the eyes. "English said he contacted Montgomery PD about it and that they are en route to pick her up. He also said one of the sisters had picked up the genetic results earlier today."

Jason was surprised, but Clark nodded.

"I know. Amber called me on the way home. She said she'd looked up my picture online and that she'd spotted me at the service. The funeral must have been over, but she said she'd seen me leave and wanted to know if it was because I'd found out."

He took a breath but kept going, still not quite paying attention to anyone around him, just seemingly needing to get it all out. "I've never met any of them. So I thought I could go to the funeral and no one would recognize me. I'd at least get a look at my sisters. I never had sisters."

There was a small pause before he added. "I still don't."

"What?" Jason couldn't make sense of that.

But Clark did. "She told me the results of the tests. You and I are genetically related. We are both Alcia's children. But you have three half-sisters and I don't."

Southfield Fire Station #2

SHIFT	A	
	O'CASEY	CAPTAIN
ENGINE 5	DONLAN	ENGINEER/PARAMEDIC
	WEINGARTEN	FF2 / PARAMEDIC
	GRIMSBY	FF1 / EMT
RESCUE 1	STANDARD	ENGINEER
	WEST	FF2 / ADV EMT
AMBULANCE 7	BAXTER	FF2 / PARAMEDIC
	NAGY	FF1 / EMT

Chapter 27

Clark looked at the board in the bay.

The shifts were all out of whack. Wanstall was still out with the injury that he originally had thought had been inflicted by his own father. Unlike Jason, Clark didn't have a "real" father to fall back on. When he had learned to ride his bike, no one had run alongside shouting encouragements and no one had picked him up when he fell; he'd learned from sheer determination and tended his cuts and bruises by himself. So when it appeared that Jerry Grady had sired Alcia's boys, Clark had automatically thought of him as his father.

Further solidifying that concept were memories he had of Grady from when he was a kid—just a few, just some flashes. But he remembered his mom bringing them to the station house, and Grady taking them across the street to the Dairy Queen that had been there back then. As an adult, he realized he'd probably sublimely enjoyed the treat while his mother pasted on a pretty smile and blackmailed the man they were with.

He remembered Jason from those outings, too. Telling him to get the ice cream off his chin, wiping his face for him. Kid things.

No one saw him standing here in the bay with his memories. The shiny trucks were the only ones that bore testament to his presence right now, and it seemed right that there were no other people here. He needed a minute to figure out what to do.

So he sat down in one of the rocking chairs that had been put in the bay for nice days and maybe as a place to wait out a shift change. It seemed like such a Southern thing to have a pair of white rockers in the station house. And maybe someone would come out and find him sitting here and force his hand. Even though it was a sunny and sharply cold mid-afternoon, the station house seemed unusually quiet for the moment.

His brain balked at that thought; he'd been here enough to know that they didn't like anyone saying things were "quiet." That word seemed to have a voodoo power that would set off the bell. And he wondered if just thinking it was bad enough.

If the bell rang in the next minute or two, he would have to apologize to the guys as they came out to get into the trucks.

But he still wasn't ready to go inside. At best, he was hollow—which was saying a lot, because he'd always felt hollow. He'd always remembered the family he'd had. It was small and with the knowledge of hindsight he could tell it was dysfunctional. But it had been a hell of a lot better than what he'd been left with after the Gradys had come through it.

He rocked in the chair for a moment, just waiting to be discovered. It didn't happen.

For the first time, he admitted that Alcia had brought her death upon herself. Though she'd been his mother, and a good one as he remembered, she'd played with people and probably believed she was owed for the choices she had made. As best he could tell from this perspective, she had dated married men and expected them to pay her to stay quiet later.

If nothing else, he could walk away with the sobering lesson that the world owes us nothing. We alone stand with our choices and we can do it with dignity or go down fighting the inevitable. He just wasn't sure where he stood on his own choices.

Clark remembered dying his hair as a teenager—deliberately leading the visitor to think his hair was lighter. He'd even figured out the man's schedule, and made sure he didn't have roots in his hair when Grady would show up. He'd used more golden shades of real blonde and not the white bleach that would lead someone to think he was just a teenager with a bottle of peroxide. He'd done anything he could to break away and not be followed when he left.

He remembered all of it—all of his choices—except the one when he'd begun this crazy quest to find "Jason."

There had been no decision. No point where he'd stopped and evaluated what he was doing. The search for his older brother was simply an integral part of who he was. The search had changed through the years—from the need for family to revenge to knowledge—but it had always been in him and he had never questioned it.

Even when he'd gotten close, when he'd found someone he thought might be Jason, he had never contemplated the end.

Yet here it was.

He'd found "Jason." And he'd found the real Jason. And the two were not the same.

The world he constructed from real memories wasn't real at all. He'd never considered another side to it, another point of view. Jason was not the cold, cruel man he had expected.

But neither had he welcomed Clark with open arms.

And that was his own fault, Clark knew. The world did not owe him a brother. And he had to live with the choices he had made.

He'd always believed that whatever fate he suffered, Jason would suffer it, too.

Clark was on the fast track to being estranged from the only family he had. But Jason was not. Jason didn't even need Clark, had no reason to come back. He had sisters now. Sisters who were reaching out to him, pulling him into the fold of the very family that had destroyed them.

Somehow, those girls had been raised to understand that they were not responsible for their parents' mistakes . . . and neither were he and Jason. But Jason was their brother. And Clark was out on his own, due to his own mistakes.

He rocked a little more, not yet gathering the courage to go inside and face what he needed to do.

He had come by the station house a few times over the last week. Jason had been at the desk, just as he had when Clark had wandered into the lobby to tell them he'd heard the voice of Alcia's killer. Jason was on leave until he was cleared fit for duty. So he was often here during the day, apparently helping with inspections, or he was off at the shrink's getting whatever counseling they deemed he needed.

Clark was given no such provision. Of course, *he* hadn't shot his own father. But aside from unpaid leave—which he wasn't taking—his own job offered nothing in the way of improving his psychological health. There was no shrink to console him because his brother was only his half brother. No one comforted him because—while Clark had been the one searching for years—Jason now had all his answers and Clark had only one.

Though he'd come by the house several times under the auspices of sharing information, he hadn't shared much. He'd been here mostly to see Jason, to try to make headway at forming some kind of bond with his brother.

He didn't share a lot with Jason, but it didn't mean he hadn't learned a lot. While Jason had been getting "shrunk," Clark had been taking care of himself—as usual—the only way he knew how. He was researching. The more he found out, the better he felt. So he found whatever loose threads he could and started pulling.

Mrs. Grady had mostly confessed to the murder, admitting that she'd tied the woman up and left her on the couch on the night of the fire. She also admitted that she'd left Alcia stuck there when she knew the place was burning. But her admission was given in a fit of rage after being taunted by the investigators. That was a trick as old as investigations and still very useful for getting confessions. Unfortunately, 1,001 police procedural shows had made people more aware of how it was done and that the cops didn't have to tell the full truth in the interrogation room.

Patricia Grady had caught on once she got herself under control and never admitted to setting the fires. But it was clear from the testimonies of Adler, Deason and others that Pelias had been arson. And arson on the eighth floor.

Though her prosecution was just starting, the police were considering the case closed. All of them except Clark and Castor.

Clark had pushed the officer to look further. Though he was certain nothing they found would change the course Patricia Grady was on, there were loose threads that no one seemed to notice. Clark had pointed to the police report on Pelias.

The final analysis of "accidental fire" had been handed down by Jerry Grady—who had obvious reasons to lie about it. Also, Beale had been in on it, but he was now dead and of no further help. But the police chief had signed off on the report—the report that wasn't a report; it was a shoddy facsimile of one. So why had the chief signed it?

It had taken a good bit of digging, mostly because he was doing it all on his own, but Clark had finally pulled out a name for the man who had been chief of police in Montgomery at that time. Then he'd matched the signature to be sure the one on the Pelias report hadn't been forged—which had been his first thought when he found out the name of the chief.

In '85, Jay Satterly had held that office and it *was* his signature on the report. Jay Satterly hadn't been police chief for long after that. There for just six years, he'd been one of the youngest police chiefs ever in the state of Alabama.

It had been only three months after Pelias that Satterly had gotten himself elected as mayor of Montgomery and left police work behind. He'd achieved it easily, becoming the youngest mayor in the state of Alabama.

Castor had looked at him askance when Clark pointed out the very short time frame between Alcia's death and Satterly's run for mayor. Castor had accused him of seeing conspiracies everywhere and suggesting that because the man had signed one poor paper didn't mean he had staged, suggested or had anything to do with Pelias other than shoddy paperwork.

But Clark pointed out that Castor didn't believe in coincidence either. And even the small possibility that Pelias paperwork had been an oversight had gone out the window after learning about the arson and his mother's murder. He would treat everyone who'd been there that night and everyone who had any contact with her as suspects until he was sufficiently convinced otherwise.

He was not convinced otherwise where Jay Satterly was concerned. And eventually Clark had convinced Castor, too.

Clark pulled Satterly's other reports from his tenure as Police Chief. None of them was as sparse or shoddy as the Pelias fire paper. The fact that it was an aberration was significant. Just because he was one thorough son of a bitch, Clark pulled reports by the men who had also signed off on Pelias. None of them had offered up such shoddy work on any other report he had found. It was not *just* an aberration; it was one for *all* the people involved. If that didn't scream "red flag" he didn't know what did.

Though he had convinced Castor to dig deeper and keep digging, Clark also pointed out that Satterly had not held another single position for as long as he'd been chief of police in Montgomery. The man climbed the ladder as fast as he possibly could. He ditched the mayor's office after just three years the first time a council seat had opened up. He'd moved county wide, and though he was in a less public position, he'd controlled more. He'd been state comptroller, secretary, representative, and finally governor. Now Senator Satterly had been climbing the ranks of DC government at breakneck speed. He'd never stayed in one spot for long—except for when he appeared to have gotten stuck at "Chief of Police."

And the Pelias fire was damn coincidental with his getting unstuck.

So Clark had dug.

He'd gone back to Deason and Estepp. Both said that yes, relations between police and fire had been good at the time. Satterly had often been at the bar Code 647 during those years.

And then Castor pulled Grady's phone records. He'd been in contact with Satterly at a personal number in recent months—since Jason had triggered "Captain Smith's" phone call. Then Clark had gone back through Alcia's old phone records. The last time he'd looked at them, he'd only been looking for calls to Grady, and he'd discarded the other numbers as non-interesting. But this time he pestered his friend with access for several old numbers that came up repeatedly.

Two had turned out to be old friends and had not panned out—though Clark had current names and addresses and would go to them if he needed more information—but one was a home number for Jay Satterly.

So why had Alcia been calling Jay Satterly? Chief of Police Jay Satterly . . . future governor and Senator Jay Satterly. Often the calls to Satterly came either right before or right after a call to Grady.

Had his mother just been going down her blackmail list? Had there been others? And if so, how?

She'd been blackmailing Grady over Jason. His existence was the reason she was pushing the firefighter for payouts. So Clark's brain had followed the logic to the one place it seemed to lead: he put together the fact that he was *not* Jerry Grady's son with the fact that there had been *another* man in a prominent position that Alcia had been calling on the same schedule.

He'd followed that logic all the way back to Montgomery, where he had done some on-foot research. He walked into the police stations and focused on the officers in the right age range, then he approached them and asked if they had worked with Satterly.

A handful had. The two who were willing to talk did not like the man. One of the officers openly questioned Satterly's integrity, stating that there had been musings at the time about how Satterly had come to get the appointment as chief. Clark had clarified that, no, the man had not been an obvious wunderkind and that a good number of other, better-qualified candidates had been passed over to give the gold stars of chief to the now senator.

The bitter man may have been one of those passed over; his thoughts on Satterly might just be sour grapes. Clark knew that. The same could apply to the other man who spoke of the former chief poorly. He'd stated that Satterly was more concerned with the media than with actual police work. Then he'd added that he'd known Satterly as an officer and found him much the same in that role—that the younger Satterly had not gone into the job to serve and protect but to establish himself in a position of authority. This man had not questioned the senator's integrity, but his moral compass.

What made Clark think he had something was that both the men he'd found who would speak of Satterly spoke negatively of him. There was no one who would say something positive to counteract these reports. Several men said they knew the senator, but refused to speak of him—which didn't sound positive. Why not speak about someone you admired or thought well of? But these three men said "no" and walked away as fast as they could.

But the final piece—the piece that pushed him to continue to dig—was that both the men who spoke to him recognized the picture of Alcia. Both said the word around the station at the time was that she was Satterly's piece on the side. Clark didn't mention that he was her child.

At 3 pm that same day—after walking through three local police stations looking for anyone who remembered working with Satterly—he headed over to the senator's local office and got lucky: Jay Satterly was in.

Clark spoke to his secretary—obviously the keeper of entry through the large double oak doors. He was greeted with the standard, "I'm sorry, sir, but you need an appointment."

She didn't seem to recognize him as a reporter, which was probably a good thing. Though he did some articles for the Montgomery area and a few things online, he was mostly out of Birmingham, a point in his favor right now. So he simply smiled and said, "Just tell him I'm Alcia Mallory's son."

He motioned for her to pick up the phone and ring the man behind the doors. Though wary, she did. And the look on her face—for just a moment—was priceless. She gathered herself, pasted on a big smile and said, "Go right on in."

That had been another brick in the wall.

With nothing to go on but his suspicions, Clark had played all his cards and bluffed some. Satterly asked him what he was doing, told him he was a fool and not to play outside his league. He refused to take a DNA test.

Smiling sweetly, Clark continued standing before the man's desk. "That, in and of itself, is telling. You understand that, don't you?"

Satterly had blustered, "I don't have to take a test for every fool who comes in here claiming to be my illegitimate child!"

But Clark had stayed calm. "A lot of us, are there? It probably wouldn't happen if you hadn't lived a life that indicated you would father illegitimate children."

The senator had simply turned red.

So Clark jumped into the space. "You understand that I'm a well known reporter from Birmingham, right? I can make this public. Fast. Like, within thirty minutes of leaving here I can have it all over the state that you refused to take the test."

"You're bluffing."

Forced to give the man points for standing his ground, Clark stood his, too. He was backed by proof, not bluff, on this one. "Log in." He motioned to the laptop open on the senator's desk. "Go to the site for the *Birmingham News*. Search for me." Then he added a calculated laugh. "Oh, wait. You don't have to *search* for me; my picture is posted as one of the main reporters featured across the top of the site on the homepage."

He waited.

"This is a secure system. It's not connected to the Internet."

"Hmmm. Use your phone. Or just find out in a short while that I'm not bluffing." He paused and added, "Oh, and I have old phone records showing calls both to and from your home and work to Alcia Mallory's home."

Satterly had gone white, and Clark had sworn the whole way home to Birmingham.

Whatever the truth was, Satterly believed it was possible his DNA matched Clark's. And so Clark believed it, too.

As he sat in the rocking chair, avoiding what he'd come for and wondering at the quiet in the station, he asked again, "Mom, what did you get yourself into?"

He'd been in turmoil for weeks now. Maybe that's why sitting and rocking and watching the few people go by outside held such appeal right now.

He'd found Jason; he'd lost Jason. He'd blamed the Gradys, he'd been welcomed by the daughters, and he'd lost them as family in as short a time as it had taken to comprehend that they could be his sisters. And now . . . now he couldn't even blame the Gradys.

Alcia had been his one constant through the years. The mother he remembered fondly. He'd known she was imperfect, but she was all he'd had. As he learned more and more about her, he realized she'd been good to her boys but bad to others. She may have even set up her blackmail scheme with the idea that it was good for her sons, but losing their mother at such a young age was not. Growing up to find out that she'd traded herself to married men for whatever it was she got in exchange was another loss. Finding that she was as much to blame for her death as anyone else involved was the loss of someone to hate. The loss of a place to lay all the blame. Much of it lay at Alcia's own feet. And Clark did not want to be mad at the only family he still had.

But he didn't still have Alcia, and he didn't have Jason. But maybe he could.

So, finding strength from the need to fix things, he pushed himself out of the rocker and went at last in search of his brother. He just had to convince the man that they *were* brothers, and that they should act like it, too.

He walked through the hallway, passing the Chief's closed door. When Jason wasn't at the front desk, Clark headed back into the main room, unsure of the reception he would get. He didn't want to have this conversation with Jason in front of everyone . . . again.

But Jason wasn't there.

Slowly, they all stopped what they were doing and looked at him, but no said anything. So Clark was forced to. "Do you know where I can find Jason?"

He expected blank stares and strict no's. Instead he was given directions to the building Jason was inspecting with Frank Rivera.

And that was it. Three minutes of time to find Jason. After he'd sat in that rocking chair staring blankly into the street, getting ready for the big confrontation that hadn't happened yet still might.

On the other side of town, he pulled up and recognized the warehouse he'd seen on the news and read about in the paper. Though he lived in Birmingham, as a reporter, he kept his eye on things in the surrounding towns. As a brother, he kept his finger on anything having to do with Southfield, and particularly with fire.

The warehouse sat at the edge of town. An old freshwater fish cannery that had been defunct for twenty years, it had gone up in a blaze three days ago. No one had reported it for hours as fire hollowed out what was left to burn. The fire crews had come and stopped it from spreading—but not Jason. It was on the other end of town from Station House #2, and even though each unit had sent a truck to help, his brother was still on leave from Grady's shooting. Word was that he would be back at work soon. Clark had been listening carefully to the talk around the station . . . since Jason wasn't speaking to him.

The word around town and in the papers was "insurance fraud" and that was likely what the Southfield Fire and Rescue Department was checking out today.

Through the busted windows, Clark could see the two men— Jason, dark-haired like him, and an older man who must be Rivera. They each held clipboards, but mostly Rivera pointed and spoke while his brother took notes and nodded, clearly the student in this situation. When Jason pointed, it seemed to be accompanied by a question.

This was what his brother wanted to do, Clark knew. Though Jason would willingly move to another town to become fire inspector, what he really wanted was Frank's job. From the looks of things, he had just enough time to finish his training before Frank handed it to him. There was no one else in Southfield who was vocal about getting that position. And Clark wanted it for him, because his brother wanted it.

For the second time that day, he steeled himself for the confrontation to come. Climbing from the car and closing the door without thought to the silence at the edge of town, he saw them both look over at the noise. There was nothing else out here— probably how the fire had burned unnoticed for so long. And as they both looked at him, he jumped to speak before Jason could say anything.

"Can I come up?"

"Sure!" It was Frank Rivera who responded.

The fire inspector worked out of Station House #1 mostly—he was possibly unaware of Jason and Clark's story. Or maybe he just didn't recognize Clark on sight and know that the automatic answer these days should be no.

So Clark didn't wait, just made purposeful strides toward the building. The doors stood open, or at least as open as a mostly missing set of doors could. The metal was now twisted and partially off its hinges. The scrape marks made it look like the firefighters did the damage, though the inside planes of both doors were charred and black, the dull gray paint sooty and flaking.

His face curled at the foul smell of old water, fire and burnt . . . maybe something had been alive in here? Or there had remained some cans of fish that had never been sold? He didn't know. The floor plan was open by design and by fire. Large vats that had once held liquid and possibly pond water from the fish hatcheries showed the fire damage, too. Shards of aged and smoked glass covered everything; some of the edges looked fresh, but many were old. Though most everything was missing—much of the cannery had been gutted and sold off when it closed years ago—it was clear that the assembly line had been on the ground floor and the offices suspended overhead where the managers could watch the line.

A metal staircase led up to the rooms, and Clark began climbing it, tentatively at first but becoming more sure as the steps continued to hold him. The place was a hull of it its former self, but it was impossible for his untrained eyes to tell what had been lost to sale, to time or to fire. The only thing he could see for certain was that the flames seemed to have touched everything.

He had another flight to go—this one shorter, from the lowest level of offices to the next row up where he'd seen Jason and Frank Rivera through the window. He could hear them now, talking about burn tracks and the marks on the building that were giving them a clearer picture of what had happened. The older man told Jason to watch for stress fractures in the metal, but Clark wasn't paying attention to what they were saying. He was using the sound to tell how close he was getting.

As he came into sight, Jason looked at him briefly then asked Rivera for a moment. He walked up as Clark cleared the top of the steps, his face stone cold.

"What do you want?"

"I have a lot of news for you. But what I *want* is to fix things between us." He sounded like a broken girlfriend. But he didn't care.

"What's the news?" Still cold, though the question itself was a concession.

They stood in what had once been an office, probably for the head of operations. The metal desk was mostly dead now. The walls were blackened and partly missing, and the floor-to-ceiling windows were blown out; only a few jagged pieces of glass still stuck there as testament to the way the office had once looked.

As Clark wandered over to look down into the vats, Jason barked out, "Don't get too close to the edge!"

"I'm not afraid of heights." Clark smiled and pointed at his feet. "I'm more afraid of these floors."

Jason waved him away. "Metal joist system." And with those three words that, to him at least, explained everything, he walked into the next office making notes. Clearly he expected Clark to follow.

So he did. And he talked. He spoke about pulling all the reports from the people who signed off on Pelias. He added how he followed the police chief's signature to Jay Satterly.

That got Jason's attention. Turning with raised eyebrows he asked, "Do you think he was in on it?"

Clark shrugged. "I think Patricia Grady acted alone to kill her." He didn't clarify who "her" was, didn't need to. "But I think both Jerry Grady and Jay Satterly had reason to help cover it up."

He explained about the phone records, his visit, and his threat. He watched as Jason forgot about the building he was inspecting and let his mouth drop open.

"You think *Satterly* is your father?"

"Yeah." A wan half-smile could say it all. "I told you, I can find anything." He'd found Jason, hadn't he? And he'd done it with only a name, a general age, and the memories of a traumatized four-year-old.

Jason scratched his head as he turned away. "Fuck, yeah. I guess you can." Then he turned back. "It's a shame he won't take a DNA test."

"Well, he will. He just didn't consent to it."

"Good God, are you suggesting running a test on one of our state senators without his permission!? And where the fuck would you get his DNA if he's not cooperating?"

"I already got it. I showed him copies of the phone records from our apartment." Though they'd always talked about 'Alcia's phone records', Clark had only been able to think of the beige phone that had hung on the wall, far above his small reach, when they'd all lived together. "I photocopied them and didn't touch the stack, just clipped the pages together." He smiled. He'd been smart on this one. He'd planned ahead. "So, the senator did exactly what I thought he'd do. I hadn't yet told him I wanted a DNA test, so he had no reason to be suspicious. Freshly photocopied stacks of paper stick together. And people still lick their fingers to turn them. I noted the page and circled the spot when I left."

"Are you serious? I grant you, that's brilliant. But he still didn't consent."

Clark couldn't help but smile again. Jason probably thought he was patting himself on the back for a job well done, but he was more just happy that he was finally having a conversation with his brother. They were speaking like men and not like enemies.

"His name isn't anywhere on the testing. I put my info down and am testing it against 'anonymous sample'."

"They'll do that?"

Clark nodded. "It's not admissible in court or anything. But I'll know."

And Jason did what Clark had hoped for; he finally asked about *Clark*. "Do you want it to be positive?"

Walking over to the window, he looked down on the parking lot, restless in this conversation, wanting things that may not happen. So he didn't correct Jason's assumption that DNA came back 'positive' or 'negative'. A shrug was all he could offer as a straight answer. "I'll be glad to know. I'd like it better if my father turned out to be someone interested in knowing me, someone I'd be interested in counting as family."

Jason scoffed at that and Clark's chest tensed at the implication. But his brother's words soothed him.

"Good luck with that. Alcia's taste in men did not run toward anyone you'd want to count as a father."

"That's true. If it's not Satterly, I'll just wind up searching until I find another asshole who's a genetic match. He probably won't be any better." He'd paced to the other side of the office, staying clear of the gaping holes in the wall that used to be windows and would land him in the old fish vats full of glass if he went too far or lost his balance.

Jason nodded. "If it matches, are you going to tell him?"

"No. I wouldn't blackmail him. I don't want him to come after me. He may not be a killer, but he's clearly more than willing to protect—"

He didn't finish the sentence because the floor had dropped out from under him.

His right shoulder jerked, sending a ripping pain shooting down his side and up his arm. He was pretty sure it had come out of the socket. And he was pretty sure he'd screamed.

All Clark could see was his feet, and beyond them—far beyond them—the tall metal edges of the vat below and the sharp spikes of glass everywhere.

Fighting the pain in his arm, he followed the noise above him and looked up.

Jason was flat on the floor above him, half his torso hanging into the space where the metal joists had given out, one arm reaching down to hang onto him. Clark saw more than felt the death grip his brother had on his wrist. Though he tried to grab Jason and strengthen the hold, he couldn't make his hand work.

The noise seemed to be a combination of pounding and something coming from Jason's mouth. It took Clark a second to realize that his brother was yelling actual words, and that they were directed at someone else.

The pounding was Frank Rivera, running through the burned-out offices from the other side of the building, and what Jason said stopped him cold.

"The floor is unstable, *don't* run! If you come in, walk *very* carefully."

Clark tried not to look down. He knew better, but did it anyway. With no control over the arm he was being held by, his body twisted slightly, his feet turning one way, then the other.

The metal edge of the vat mocked him. If he hit it, his best hope was to break his back. And who knew how sharp the edge might be? He could sever something, hit his head, lose a limb. There was no telling which way he would fall: maybe feet-first? Head-first? Tumbling through the air and hitting whatever part of him rotated to the right place and time?

And when he hit it the vat would win the fight. He'd once toured a working facility like this in high school for an article he was doing as a junior journalist. He'd asked why the thin metal didn't collapse from the weight of the water, and had been given a lesson in pressure and the strength of cylinders. No, the metal would not fold under him. And anything it didn't take from him, the glass below would.

He heard Rivera and his brother talking above him and almost smiled as he wondered if he should ask if there was anything he could do to help or if he should simply leave his rescue to the professionals.

He listened, waiting for a good break in the conversation, but there was none. They were arguing.

Rivera wanted to go down another floor and help Clark in, but Jason was concerned about the whole floor—and the stairs were on the other side from where Rivera now stood. He would have to walk across the entire office to get to the steps.

Only able to hear and guess where the inspector stood, Clark listened.

"I have to go. We all have to go down. I've been finding tiny stress fractures all over the place. It wasn't obvious at first, but this whole building is not as stable as we thought it was. We shouldn't have come in without backup."

His voice sounded regretful, and Clark found that funny since he was the one dangling over a very painful death and not even able to grab onto Jason's wrist and help support himself.

"Clark! Clark!"

He looked up at his brother's voice. "Yes?" *How could he be so calm?*

"Rivera is going down one floor. You'll see him in the office and he'll grab your . . ."

Legs. Clark was pretty sure his brother had said legs. But the words had been drowned out by a groan. A groan that he was pretty sure had been made by metal and not man. He didn't see Rivera yet.

Another groan came, this time telling him exactly where Rivera was moving. Then another came from above them.

"Shit!" Jason yelled it. "These offices are cantilevered. The whole thing is shifting on this side."

Rivera's reply came from further away as he made it to the steps. "I'm coming as fast as I can."

"This is my *brother*!" Jason yelled it right at the same moment the floor shifted and Clark felt them lower another few inches.

His toes were only about a foot above the floor of the office below now. But he was right over the window ledge. There was no guarantee he could get into the office and stay balanced enough to not fall right back out.

But those words had made him smile. He wasn't just someone to save. He was a brother.

Rivera wasn't coming any too fast. And when the floor shifted again, just a few more inches, he started to wonder if the firefighter would get there in time. Somewhere in the distance something heavy fell to the floor below.

Looking up, he spoke to Jason. "I'm glad it was you. I'm glad I found you and that you turned out to really be my brother."

He tried to smile, but Jason didn't return the favor. "Don't talk like that. We're getting out."

Rivera called out to him. "The floor is weaker down here than I thought. We didn't test it all the way out. Shit." His footsteps slowed as he made his way through the chain of offices.

Jason kept his eyes on Clark, even as he felt his brother's grip tighten, even as his skin started to slip in the sweat Jason generated from the strain of holding on to him. And they were only as good as the section of floor his brother had spread his weight on—the floor that had already proved itself unreliable.

Jason's voice came down to him. "We're getting out. We both get second chances here. I've screwed up so much. With myself, with Amara, mostly with you. I'm sorry. But we're getting out, so just hang on, little brother."

Clark fought the urge to laugh. If there was one thing he couldn't do it was hang on. His hand didn't work, but in his current situation that wasn't as big a worry as it might have been. For a moment he closed his eyes and decided he was okay.

He'd found his brother. And made his peace. He'd figured out what happened to his mother, and accepted the truth there, too. And if he got out of here—

Another groan from the building drowned out what he thought were instructions from Rivera. He felt hands grasping at his pants legs and slowly swinging him in toward the office below.

Rivera and Jason talked as they maneuvered, but Clark didn't listen. He thought about the fact that he was now perfectly poised to go head first onto the floor several stories below if they dropped him. He just hoped he died if he did.

Hands grabbed at his legs as another heavy item dropped and hit the floor above them.

Now that he was pulled under the floor, he could no longer see Jason's face, only the arm that still held onto his wrist.

Rivera yelled up, "You okay?"

It took a moment for Jason to answer "yes" and Clark was pretty sure he was lying.

Arms wrapped around Clark's knees and Rivera counted "One, two, three" as at the same time he jerked himself and Clark into the office and Jason let go.

The two of them smacked the floor—Clark felt it in more places than he could count. But before he could take inventory, Rivera rolled them into the back recesses of the office. With no grace, they hit the back wall, eliciting another groan from the building, followed by a thud on the floor above them and Jason's voice swearing.

"You okay?" Rivera yelled up again.

But Jason only answered, "You got him?"

The following "yes" that both he and Rivera yelled in response was lost as the floor above them gave way, and they watched as Jason rolled off.

Luckily, the lost piece of the floor above positioned him over still-existing flooring in the office they were now in, rather than over the open space below. Jason hung on, his torso in the office, legs dangling over the vats below, blood seeping out where glass shards had likely punctured him as he grabbed for purchase.

His right arm limp at his side, Clark rushed forward even as Rivera grabbed him to hold him back.

Some part of his brain made sense of that—there was no use running over unstable floor. But it was Jason who was searching for handholds in what was left of burnt industrial carpet. Jason, whose blood was quickly leaking out and probably dripping to the concrete below.

Clark leaped forward anyway, and as he did Jason looked up. Just then, the floor gave way and his brother dropped out of sight.

Chapter 28

Clark

Clark sat stock-still; the room was quiet but his thoughts were not.

He wanted to close his eyes and rest, but each time he did he was assaulted by images of Jason, grasping at the edge of the floor, hanging over the gutted assembly line, just as Clark had feared would happen and Jason had assured him couldn't.

When he did sleep, he dreamed that Jason held him dangling above the cement and metal workings of the factory, then repeated "Second chances, little brother" and let him fall. Those times Clark jerked awake, the horror of the dream becoming the still silence of the room.

Looking around, he saw that nothing had changed.

His arm was still in the industrial black sling that held it just so against his torso. Sometimes when he twisted the wrong way, pain shot to his fingertips. But he was told that was just a remnant of the surgery and a good sign that his nerves hadn't been damaged when his shoulder had jerked out of the socket.

They said he'd been lucky.

Jason had not.

With the building still groaning around them, Clark and Frank Rivera had bolted down the steps to the warehouse floor. Rivera had done the sensible thing and called Station House #1—the closest to where they were. Clark had done the brotherly thing and damned all logic and his useless right arm.

He'd begun lifting what he could and shouting for his brother.

Rivera had immediately caught him at it and tried to stop him. He tried logic—Clark hurting himself only took effort away from Jason when the crews arrived. Levering things off of Jason might hurt him more than leaving them. Rivera hadn't added the 'if he was still alive' that could practically be heard hanging at the end of each statement. He'd probably seen the crazy in Clark's eyes and knew better than to say anything like that.

So Clark had nodded his fake acquiescence and kept rummaging. He continued yelling, alternating near screams with moments of silence while he prayed for something in return.

But nothing came.

Just as the sirens made their way into his consciousness, he saw a foot. A booted foot.

He wanted to thank the powers that be—but the foot didn't move.

He was grateful that Jason was not inside one of the metal vats. That had been his fear. How would they find him? And how would they get him out? But that was off the table now that he had found something. He refused to think he might have a body.

Carefully and with just one hand, he lifted the smaller pieces of rubble away. And he found another foot.

His stomach turned and his brain refused to make the proper connections. But this foot was turned the opposite direction from the first. For a moment, he wondered about the two booted men beneath the wreckage, then he faced the fact that there was only one, and that both feet could not properly be attached to one body.

"JASON! JASON!"

The firefighters swarmed in as he yelled at the inert form under the broken joists and charred flooring. They climbed over fallen pieces, posted someone to keep watch on the offices above, and swarmed like army ants. With a hive mind they lifted the heavy pieces off his brother, never speaking.

Clark was pushed out of the way as a backboard appeared at the edge of the cluster. One man crouched down next to the exposed body and put his fingers to Jason's neck.

At that moment, time seemed stationary.

No one moved.

Jason's body was in a position he shouldn't survive, Clark even saw a bone protruding from one leg. But his stomach didn't turn this time. Not when they were all waiting.

The man kneeling next to his brother yelled. "Faint, but there! Load him up!"

And the clock started ticking again.

Clark's instinct was to call for an ambulance, but then he remembered they were the EMS now, two of their red trucks were parked outside, lights swirling, waiting for his brother.

Putting Jason on the backboard had been a trial. As they stabilized his neck and collected what seemed like spare limbs, he didn't move. Clark couldn't even see his chest rising and falling. Blood continued to seep, and the firefighters packed it with gauze and applied pressure. They called ahead to the hospital and demanded the best surgeons.

Clark rode in the crowded ambulance, refusing to let go of his brother's hand.

One of the firefighters had tried to examine his shoulder, but Clark had brushed him off. At the hospital, they had swarmed again, completely taking over the admitting office. People he recognized from Station House #2 showed up, one by one adding to the growing mob.

When Jason was wheeled away, they turned on him and tried to convince him to get treated. He'd caved when he realized Jason was gone and the waiting was killing him. Then he'd fought his own surgery, only consenting once it was pointed out that if he waited until Jason was out of his procedure he might miss when his brother woke up.

So he spent part of the first night out cold from a general anesthetic while surgeons picked through his own torn flesh and put his arm back together.

He wanted to say he was glad he had made that choice, that he'd been sitting there, waiting, when Jason opened his eyes. But he mostly didn't give a rat's ass about his arm. He would, later, he knew, but he didn't *feel* any better about it.

And he could have waited until Jason's surgery was finished. In the end it had made no difference.

It had been three days.

The number of firefighters had dropped to an average of just one at a time, dropping by periodically to check on any progress. There was none.

They didn't send flowers, but their wives did. Missy had come in and set a 9-millimeter bullet on the table by the bed. She said it was for luck. Jason didn't hear her and Clark didn't ask what the fuck she was talking about.

Leaving someone a single bullet usually indicated you thought they should kill themselves, but he was pretty sure Missy actually meant it was for luck. Besides there were no guns around.

So he sat here with no book, no magazines, no TV—the way he had since they'd arrived. He stared blankly into space and took the well-wishes of those who stopped by. But Jason had done nothing.

He hadn't woken up. Hadn't made any noise. Hadn't even moved in his sleep. But he hadn't deteriorated either.

The surgeon had explained to Clark—as Jason's "family"—that they had put everything back together. And that his brother had been lucky. He'd hit his side, breaking ribs but not his back—his neck and spine were still in full working order. His leg was broken in several places, but he hadn't nicked any arteries or ripped anything that medicine didn't know how to put back together.

The physician clearly thought highly of himself, stating that Jason had been "fixed" with metal rods, screws, and staples.

Needing to find something positive, Clark asked if his brother would be able to go back to his job. The surgeon had practically laughed, suggesting that the new leg would be close to bionic.

So Clark had nodded politely then asked the same thing of Adler, who gave him a straight answer. They talked about the surgeon's proclamation, and the Chief remained hopeful.

But that had been two days ago.

That same evening, the sisters had shown up. The Grady girls came right into the room, led by Marcy who told the nurse in no uncertain terms about Clark and Jason's blood relationship by Alcia, and the women's same relationship to Jason Mondy by way of Jerry Grady.

Though it was clear by the math that they had no relation to Clark, the same Marcy who steamrollered the nurse then marched up to him and embraced him in a hug the likes of which he hadn't gotten since he was four.

Clark was nearly in tears when she handed him off to Amber, who hugged him just as hard, then passed him to Leigh. The youngest, but still a good seven years older than him, she hugged him fast, looked him up and down, and marched out of the room.

Twenty minutes later she reappeared with a cooler, which she unpacked to produce lasagna, green beans, salad and bread.

He looked at her like she was mad. "What is this?"

She smiled. "Dinner. I have a good friend in town. They had just sat down to eat. And they shared."

"What?" He couldn't say more than that.

"I won't let you eat any more hospital food. But you have to eat."

"I . . ." His protest was futile.

They won.

Jason lay still on the bed, in the same position he'd been in for over twenty-four hours at that point. His head was only slightly elevated, wires and tubes were attached to everything, producing the monotone beeping that assured Clark his brother still lived. But suddenly he had become the patient.

The mobile tray was stolen from Jason's bedside, gently cleared and set up for the four-course dinner. Marcy disappeared for a moment then returned with a cup of ice filled with a coke.

She'd smiled at him, her southern accent sounding sweet but brooking no argument. "Caffeine and sugar. You need it."

They waited while he ate. Watched to make sure he consumed all of it, talked to him as though he was *their* brother, then cleaned up after he finished. Though he carried on his side of the conversation during his meal, he was unable to continue with the ruse after he finished.

"Why are you being so nice to me? Jason's your brother. Not me."

It was Amber who laughed at him. "He's our brother, you're his brother. Same difference."

Shaking his head, he dredged up everything he could think of. "But it's not. And I don't want you to realize later that *I* set all this in motion. *I'm* the one who started the things that led to your father being shot. *I* found the evidence they'll use to convict your mother. You can't just sit here and be *nice* to me."

Then he paused. "The lasagna was poisoned, wasn't it?"

Marcy sighed at him. Seemingly always level-headed, she was also clearly the one with kids. She took his left hand in both of hers. "No. Dinner was not poisoned. But as a general rule, don't let Leigh cook for you."

Leigh frowned at her sister.

Marcy ignored it.

Clark watched the interplay, amazed in the way that they interacted—they got angry at each other, spoke their minds, and got in each other's way. But then they would all align in formation and no one could get through them.

Marcy spoke directly to him. "We don't blame you. Do you admit that your mother had a hand in her own death? She slept with men she knew were married, and she blackmailed them."

He nodded. "There's no way to do that and not think it won't come back to haunt you. None of it was right."

"Exactly. *None* of it was right. Not what my Dad did—she was much younger than him and he took advantage. And not what my mom did—she married my father, and if I could see he was a philanderer when I was six years old, then she knew, too. In her heart she knew. And she chose to hurt your mother rather than leave the man who cheated on her."

She sighed. Then she started crying.

At least she wasn't as cold and logical as Clark had wondered.

"I miss them both. I don't know how to tell my girls that Grandma is in jail. And I know I have to tell them about Granddad before they hear it from some kid or read it somewhere. Mom and Dad were really good to my kids. And they were good parents to us. But they were never good to each other. There have been other women over the years. And other threats. This is just the one that came through." She shrugged through her tears. "But we found you and Jason, and you are no more at fault than we are."

He barely found his voice, "Thank you."

They stayed for several hours before Marcy and Amber headed off to the hotel room they had gotten. Leigh stayed behind to keep him company, and they watched the eleven p.m. rerun of Jeopardy together. Clark had harbored hopes that Jason would come around and jump in with a correct answer. But he didn't.

The next day, Leigh looked a little worse for the wear, but Marcy and Amber brought breakfast, which they all ate in the room before Amber stayed and Marcy and Leigh went to get the youngest sister fresh clothes and a shower.

When Amber left for a cafeteria run, Clark took advantage of the privacy. He pulled his chair up next to Jason's bed and started talking to him.

"You have to come out of this. Everyone needs you awake." He told about the sisters' and about Marcy's kids. He repeated what he'd learned about each of them. And what he'd shared about Jason earlier, though it was stupid. If Jason could hear, then he'd heard it the first time. "You have me and you have three sisters waiting here for you."

"You have three sisters, too." Amber stood in the doorway, holding a plastic brown tray with fries and two sodas. "Please accept that. We want you to come for Christmas and Thanksgiving. Oh crap—we need to know your birthdays!" She was rummaging in her purse, assumedly for paper and pen, when another voice entered the conversation.

"Oh, dear God." The tenor and weakness of it revealed her surprise. And concern.

Amara stood just behind him, her face drained of color as she looked Jason over. She shook her head and worked her mouth but no sound emerged.

"Amara." Clark turned and hugged her.

Then went about introducing her to Amber, though he had no idea what to call her. Was she 'Jason's old roommate' or 'his ex-girlfriend'? Clark wasn't sure what status, if any, they'd assigned to what they had. So he said, "Amara Bellamy, meet Amber Grady Hopkins, Jason's half sister."

Amber hugged her like an old friend. "Clark uses 'half' but us Grady girls just prefer 'sister'."

Amara now looked confused on top of shocked. She turned to Clark. "As in 'Jerry Grady'?"

He nodded. "It's a long story."

But Marcy and Leigh were coming back in the room just then, so he started over with the introductions. And that's how the day nurse found them.

She glared at Clark. "Family only."

Marcy jumped in. "She *is* family."

The nurse stayed focused on Clark. "I thought you were his only relative."

He sighed. "I was. But we just found out that he had half sisters and they're here for him."

"And her?" The nurse pointed at Amara, who drained another shade from her skin tone.

Marcy stepped in. "She's another sister."

"She's African American." Disbelief dripped from the nurse's every pore. And rightly so.

"Half." Marcy stood her ground. And was met only by raised eyebrows. So she went for the knockdown. "Look, my father liked beautiful women. Beyond that, he didn't care. With his recent death, we discovered more than we . . . expected." She waited a beat before she threw her best card. "His name is Jerry Grady—look him up."

Clark couldn't believe she'd played on her father's death. But she had. And the nurse walked away.

Amara didn't seem to realize what had gone down; she simply stared at Jason.

"I'm sorry." Clark whispered to her as she stood at the end of the bed. "He was saving me."

She shook her head. "He was always saving someone." It sounded regretful.

Seating herself in the lone empty chair, she stared at Jason and didn't move.

^ ^ ^ ^ ^

"My brother is a tough son of a bitch." Maybe if he repeated it enough the man in the bed would believe it.

"Don't I know it." Amara's voice was weary. She'd lost weight in the three days she'd been camped here beside him. On the fifth day, Marcy had gone home to see her kids and her husband and Amber had gone home, too. Both had promised to return and Clark believed them.

Leigh tried to get him to leave to sleep in the hotel room; finally he consented to getting a change of clothes and shower, but he'd done the whole trip in under an hour. When he returned, nothing had changed.

The doctors were getting concerned. They had hoped Jason would wake by now. But there was no playbook for cases like this. Patients woke when they woke . . . or they didn't.

Clark's arm had been checked several times by the nurses. They'd given up on getting the visitors out and wheeled a second bed into the room. Uncomfortable as it was, it was better than the chair though he and Amara only slept in spurts, always waking when the nurses or doctors came in to take vitals every few hours.

That was why Clark was surprised to wake up and see a horizontal shot of a nurse in blue scrubs bending over Jason. It took a second to shake the sleep that had hit him like a bag of rocks and realize that he'd practically passed out on the gurney and that's why the nurse had appeared sideways.

He sat up too fast, dizzied by both his rapid change and the creak of a voice that said, "Where am I?"

He nearly tripped jumping down from the gurney, the floor was further away than he expected and he ignored the impact in his ankles.

Shaking Amara too hard, he got the job done, and she blinked up at him, roused from a deep sleep. "He's awake!" It was barely a whisper and he prayed he wasn't dreaming.

Jason turned slowly to look at him, eyes blinking, the bruises underneath doing him no favors. "Clark."

He smiled. "Yeah, I'm here. I'm right here."

Then he turned and looked confused again.

But the nurse caught Clark's attention. "I'm going to let the doctor know he's awake. Keep an eye on him."

Though Clark nodded, his attention turned back to Jason, who asked, "Why is Amara here?"

Well, crap. That was not the reaction he'd expected from his brother. "She's here because I called her. I told her you were in love with her."

And now was probably not the time to drop that bomb.

Amara saw it, too—that the line had been a ploy of Clark's and not something Jason had actually said. Her voice shook, and that was no surprise: the whole ordeal had taken a lot out of her. Though she'd said nothing of her own feelings for Jason, she'd come the moment Clark called her and she'd stayed without comforts at his side for days. "It's okay. I'm glad you're awake. I'll just go."

"No." It was the first thing Jason had said in full voice, and even lying there in bed, bruises covering more of him than not, bandages and wires everywhere, his tone carried enough authority to make her stop. And he held out his hand to her.

His arm shook; he was taped to an IV line and suspending his arm was hurting him, but he kept the hand there until she took it, white clip on his finger and all. He gripped her fingers tightly enough to make Clark wonder if it hurt. Amara didn't say anything.

Jason did. "He's right. I screwed up with you. Stay. Let me fix it."

Amara looked him dead in the eyes, and Clark knew he was privy to something that should have been private, but he'd have to push past them to give them the space they needed. So he just stayed quiet.

She spoke clearly, not swayed by Jason's request. "Are you going to fix *you*, too?"

He nodded at her. "If you'll stay and help me."

"Nope."

"What?" Jason's grip tightened.

"You have to fix the things you need to, whether or not I'm there. You have to do it for you, not me."

He nodded again; the effort of simultaneously moving his head and keeping her from slipping his grasp was clearly overwhelming. "You're right. But stay."

Clark stepped in then. "Amara's not going anywhere. She's been here for four days waiting for you to wake up. You've been out for almost six. You rest. You two can fix things later."

Amara agreed, and when Jason wouldn't let go of her hand she just pulled the chair closer and sat back down.

Clark smiled. "I have to call Leigh."

"Leigh?" Jason asked.

"Grady. Your sister. . . our sister. She's in town. She's been here all along, waiting for you to wake up." He was stumbling over his words trying to get them all out. "Marcy and Amber were here for several days, too. They'll want to know you're up. All three of them will be here within the hour. I promise."

Jason looked confused.

But Clark knew what he needed, "Yes, they really want to be our sisters." He turned away to call Leigh, who screamed her glee in his ear, yelled that she had to call the others, and promptly hung up on him.

Laughing, he looked back to find Jason had pulled Amara closer and had somehow cajoled her into a deep kiss. In the doorway stood a disbelieving day nurse with her arms crossed.

"Family, huh?" She drawled.

Clark tried to explain. "I— . . . We— . . . You see— "

The nurse just laughed at him. "I won't protect you, but I won't turn you in. Hell, it's Alabama, and I work in a hospital. I've seen far weirder families than this."

As she turned and walked away, Clark settled into his skin. His brother was kissing his new girlfriend and probably had a long road to recovery. Clark hadn't checked in with work in over a week and might not even have a job anymore. But right now, none of that mattered.

He was finally sure of himself, unafraid, confident . . . part of a family for the first time in over twenty-five years . . . and happy.

Look for other novels by A.J. Scudiere:

Resonance

Vengeance

God's Eye

Available at Amazon, bookstores, and
www.AJScudiere.com.

About the Author

A.J. Scudiere lives in Nashville, TN and holds a Bachelor's Degree from New College and a Master's Degree from UCLA. A seasoned educator, A.J. has taught math, science and writing at every level from junior high through graduate level. These days A.J. is mostly found in front of the computer at work on the next novel.

Readers can visit AJScudiere.com

CPSIA information can be obtained at www.ICGtesting.com
Printed in the USA
LVOW050821070812

293209LV00001B/7/P